Luke frowned. have to tell ever that you're not

'But don't you *see*? I need a stand-in fiancé in order to be able to break up with him. I'll find someone for myself one day. But I have to get through the ball first. Please, please, *please* do this for me, Luke,' Abby begged. 'Just for a couple of hours.'

He released a long sigh. 'All right—you win. I'll take you for two hours. But you have to accept this is a one-off occasion and it will *not* be repeated.'

Abby had to stop herself from flinging herself into his arms. Or kissing him, which was even more tempting than she wanted to admit. 'I promise.'

'Oh, and one other thing,' he warned. 'I might be standing in for someone who doesn't exist, but that's as far as your little fantasy goes. Understood?'

'I hope you're not thinking I'd want you to actually *marry* me, because that's just utterly ridiculous!'

'Good to know,' he said enigmatically. 'See you tomorrow, Cinderella.'

Melanie Milburne read her first Mills & Boon novel at the age of seventeen, in between studying for her final exams. After completing a master's degree in education, she decided to write a novel, and thus her career as a romance author was born. Melanie is an ambassador for the Australian Childhood Foundation and a keen dog lover and trainer. She enjoys long walks in the Tasmanian bush. In 2015 Melanie won the Holt Medallion—a prestigious award honouring outstanding literary talent.

Books by Melanie Milburne

Mills & Boon Modern Romance

The Tycoon's Marriage Deal
The Temporary Mrs Marchetti
Unwrapping His Convenient Fiancée
His Mistress for a Week
At No Man's Command

One Night With Consequences

A Ring for the Greek's Baby

Wedlocked!

Wedding Night with Her Enemy

The Ravensdale Scandals

Ravensdale's Defiant Captive
Awakening the Ravensdale Heiress
Engaged to Her Ravensdale Enemy
The Most Scandalous Ravensdale

The Playboys of Argentina

The Valquez Bride
The Valquez Seduction

Visit the Author Profile page
at millsandboon.co.uk for more titles.

A VIRGIN
FOR A VOW

BY
MELANIE MILBURNE

First Published in Great Britain 2017
By Mills & Boon, an imprint of HarperCollins*Publishers*
1 London Bridge Street, London, SE1 9GF

© 2017 Melanie Milburne

ISBN: 978-0-263-93516-5

Our policy is to use papers that are natural, renewable and recyclable
products and made from wood grown in sustainable forests. The logging
and manufacturing processes conform to the legal environmental
regulations of the country of origin.

Printed and bound in Spain
by CPI, Barcelona

A VIRGIN
FOR A VOW

To my previous editor, Flo Nicoll.

It was wonderful working with you on
so many books. You encouraged me, supported me
and challenged me to constantly lift my writing.

I will never forget meeting you in person in Sydney.
Nor will I forget all the funny conversations
we've had over thirty-plus books.

Bless you for being wonderful you. xxxx

CHAPTER ONE

ABBY HAD ONE day left to respond to the invitation to the ball. One day. Twenty-four hours. Fourteen hundred and forty minutes. Eighty-six thousand and four hundred seconds. And if she didn't come up with a 'fiancé' by then she was toast.

Burned and charred and utterly useless toast.

She sat at her desk and stared at the gold and black vellum invitation with its fancy copperplate writing.

Miss Abby Hart and Fiancé

Panic knocked on her heart like a boxer's fist, threatening to punch it right out the back of her chest. She couldn't show up at *Top Goss and Gloss's* prestigious Spring Charity Ball alone. It was the biggest event on her career calendar. There was a three-to four-year waiting list for tickets. There were more senior people on staff than her who had never received an invitation. Receiving a personalised invitation from the head honcho as 'guest of honour' was a big deal. A seriously big deal. Declining the invitation was out of the question. Her boss insisted it was time for Abby's adoring fans to finally meet her fiancé. If she showed up at the ball alone she might as well take her resignation with her instead.

Everyone thought Abby was engaged to her childhood sweetheart. Everyone at work. Everyone online. Everyone on the flipping planet thought she was engaged. But she didn't have a childhood sweetheart. She hadn't even had a proper childhood. Not unless you could call being shunted in and out of foster homes since you were five years old a childhood.

'Abby, have you got time for a—? Hey, haven't you sent your RSVP for the ball yet? Wasn't the deadline like a week ago?' Sabina from Fashion asked with a frown.

Abby posted an *everything's cool* smile on her face. 'I know but I'm still waiting to hear back from my fiancé about it. He…he is super-busy with work stuff just now and—'

'But surely he's taking you to the ball?' Sabina said. 'I mean, that's what a fiancé does, right? This is the night everyone finally gets to meet your mysterious Mr Perfect. That's why the ball has been such a massive sell-out. I think it's so cool how you always call him that in your column and blog. You've created such a mystery about his identity. It's like it's London's best-kept secret.'

Abby had only been able to keep his identity a secret because Mr Perfect had no identity. He didn't exist other than in her imagination. Her weekly blog and column was all about relationships. Dating advice. About finding and keeping true love. Helping people find their own happy-ever-after. She had hundreds of thousands of readers and millions of followers on Twitter who wrote in for her advice.

Gulp.

Yes, millions.

Who all thought she was happily engaged to her own perfect man. She even wore an engagement ring to prove it. Not a bona fide diamond but a zirconia, which was so darn realistic no one had noticed it wasn't the real deal and she'd been wearing it for the last two and a half years.

'Oh, no, he would never let me down.' It sometimes scared her how good she was at lying.

'I wish I'd been invited to the ball,' Sabina said with a sigh that Cinderella would have been proud of. 'I'm absolutely dying to meet him. I'm sure that's why you got the invitation to sit at the boss's table. Everyone wants to meet this amazingly romantic guy who puts every other man out there to shame.'

Abby kept her smile in place but her stomach was churning so fast she could have provided enough butter for a shortbread factory. Two factories. Possibly the whole of Scotland. She had to come up with a plan. She had to come up with a man.

But who?

Just then a text message pinged in on her phone from her best friend, Ella Shelverton.

Her best friend who had an older brother.

Of course! It was a brilliant solution. But would Luke want to go with her? She hadn't seen him since that night six months ago when he'd been acting a little out of character, to put it mildly. She had never been that physically close to him before. He was always a little standoffish and gruff—understandable since he was still getting over the tragic death of his girlfriend, who had been killed five years ago. But that night when Abby had called in to collect something Ella had left behind the day before, Luke had been so out of it his head had rested on her shoulder and he'd slurred his words so much she'd had to help him into his bed. Once she'd got him into bed, his hand had taken hers and for a moment she'd thought he was going to pull her down to join him, but instead he'd touched her face as if he was touching a fragile orchid and then he'd closed his eyes and promptly fallen asleep. But she could still feel the tingles in her flesh if she allowed herself to think about it.

Which she absolutely never did.

Well…only occasionally.

'Is that your fiancé texting you?' Sabina asked, leaning forward. 'What did he say? Is he coming with you?'

Abby covered the screen of her phone with her hand. 'One of Abby's rules is don't share your lover's texts with your friends. They're private.'

Sabina gave a heartfelt sigh. 'I wish I had a lover's text to share. I wish I had what you have, Abby. But then, everyone wants what you have.'

What exactly do I have?

Abby kept her expression in caring colleague

mode. 'I hate to sound like an agony aunt but that's what I am so here goes. You're a gorgeous person who deserves to be happy just like anyone else. You can't let one bad experience with a two-timing jerk—'

'Three-timing. Possibly four but I'm not sure if he was boasting about the redhead.'

'Right, yes, I forgot—three-or four-timing jerk discourage you from finding the amazing and loving and commitment-friendly man who is out there just waiting to find a wonderful girl like you,' Abby said.

Sabina smiled. 'No wonder you're London's top relationships columnist. You always have the perfect answer.'

Abby had thought long and hard but eventually decided against calling Luke before she turned up at his house in Bloomsbury. She didn't want to give him the opportunity to fob her off using the excuse of being too busy with work. He was always working on one of his medical engineering projects for which he'd become globally recognised. She'd made Ella promise not to say anything to him about her plan until she had spoken to him in person. Ella was surprisingly keen on the idea of Luke taking her to the ball Abby had told her about it. Although, maybe it wasn't so surprising given Ella made no secret of the fact she longed for her big brother to get some sort of social life happening again.

Not that Luke was likely to answer a call from Abby even if he did have his phone on. He kept his distance from most people, but especially from her, which made his up close and personal behaviour that night all the more unusual. But the kind of conversation she had in mind would be much better done face to face.

And because she knew he was a sucker for a bit of home baking, turning up on his swanky doorstep with a box of chocolate chip and macadamia nut cookies still warm from the oven would hopefully work a treat.

Well, it would if he would jolly well answer his door.

Abby balanced the cookies under one arm and huddled under her umbrella, trying to ignore the icy spring rain spiking and splashing her ankles. She pressed the brass button for the fifth time and left it there. She knew he was home because there were lights on in his office and another one in the sitting room.

Maybe he has someone with him...

No.

She dismissed the thought out of hand. Luke hadn't had anyone with him since his girlfriend Kimberley's death five years ago. Not that he had been much of a party animal before that, but after Kimberley was killed in a car crash he became even more of a loner. He was the epitome of the locked down workaholic. It was sad because she couldn't help thinking he might be quite a fun person to be around if he let himself go a bit.

Abby finally heard the tread of firm footsteps and

took her finger off the bell just as the door opened. His frowning expression wasn't what you could even loosely call welcoming. 'Oh, it's you...' he said.

'Nice to see you too, Luke,' Abby said. 'Can I come in? It's kind of wet and cold out here.'

'Sure,' he said while his expression clearly said an emphatic no.

Abby blithely ignored that, stepping over the threshold and folding her umbrella, which unfortunately sent a spray of water droplets on to the plush carpet runner that was threatening to swallow her up to her knees. Maybe even up to her neck. 'Have I called at a bad time?'

'I'm working on something—'

'There are more things in life than work, you know,' Abby said, hunting around for somewhere to place her umbrella.

'Here.' He held out his hand with a long-suffering look. 'I'll take that before you take out a window.'

Abby gave him the squinty eye. 'I *am* house-trained. It's just your house is always so darn perfect it makes me feel like I'm walking into a *Vogue Living* set.'

He took the umbrella and placed it on a stand near the door, somehow without allowing a single droplet of water to fall. Amazing. 'Isn't Ella with you?'

'She's got a parent teacher meeting at school this evening,' Abby said. 'I thought I'd drop in by myself. To...erm...see how you are.'

'I'm fine—as you can see.'

There was a pregnant silence. A triplets or even quads pregnant silence.

Abby wondered if he was thinking about That Night. Did he ever think about it? Did he even remember it? Did he remember touching her so gently? Resting his head on her shoulder and then cradling her cheek in his hand like he was going to kiss her?

His eyes moved between each of hers in a studying way, like an academic trying to make sense of a complicated article. He was the only one who looked at her like that. In that quiet, assessing way that made her nerves start to jangle. As if he was searching for the frightened, abandoned child she had hidden deep inside herself so many years ago.

The child no one ever saw.

No one.

'Abby.' His voice contained a note of censure. 'I'm really busy right now so—'

Abby shoved the box of cookies towards him. 'Here—I made these for you.'

He took the box like he was taking a detonating device. 'What's this for?'

'They're your favourite cookies. I made them before I came over.'

He gave a God-give-me-strength sigh and put the box down on the polished walnut hall table. He led the way to the sitting room, offering her the sofa with the wave of a hand, but he remained standing as if he had set himself a time limit on her visit. 'What do you want?'

'That's a bit rude, don't you think? Just because I call on you with your favourite cookies you immediately assume I want something in return,' Abby said, folding her arms and affecting a wounded expression that wouldn't have looked out of place on a three-year-old.

Luke's gaze went to her pouting lower lip, lingered there for a beat before coming back to mesh with hers. When those dark blue eyes locked on hers something wearing feather slippers shuffled across the floor of her belly. He cleared his throat and scraped his hand over his jaw. 'Scraped' being the operative word because the amount of stubble he had going on there was a telling reminder of the potent male hormones surging through his body. He was normally so clinically clean-shaven it was a shock to see him so ungroomed. Not a nasty shock. A pleasant I-would-like-to-see-more-of-this-side-to-him shock.

Which was kind of shocking in itself because Abby had taught herself *not* to notice Luke Shelverton. He was her best friend's older brother. It was a boundary she had sworn never to cross. But for some reason her eyes were getting a little too happy about resting on Luke's staggeringly handsome features. His sapphire-blue eyes were framed and fringed by jet-black eyebrows and lashes, but his hair was a rich dark brown and was currently ruffled as if he'd been combing it with his fingers. Broad-shouldered and lean-hipped, with an abdomen you could crack walnuts on, he was the stuff of female fantasies. He had the sort of facial and body structure that would have made Michelangelo rush off to stock up on chisels and marble.

'Look, about that night...' he said.

'I'm not here about *that* night,' Abby said. 'I'm here about another night. The most important night of my life.' She took a quick breath and let it out in a rush. 'I need you to do me a favour. I need a fiancé for one night.' There. She'd said it. She'd put it out there.

Everything on his face stilled. His entire body seemed to be snap frozen as if every muscle and ligament and corpuscle of blood had turned to stone.

Even the air seemed to be sucked right out of the room.

But then he let out a breath and walked over to a drinks cabinet. 'I'm going to pretend I didn't hear that. Would you like a drink before you go?'

Abby sat on the sofa and crossed one leg over the other as if she was settling in for the evening. No way was she leaving until she had this nailed. 'I'll have a red wine.' White wine wasn't going to cut it this time. And she certainly wasn't in the mood for champagne.

Not until she convinced Luke to help her.

Luke came over with the wine and handed it to her. Abby tried to avoid his fingers in the exchange but somehow they both let go of the glass at the same time and it landed with a blood-like splash over the front of her brand-new baby blue cotton and cashmere blend sweater. Well, it wasn't brand new—she'd bought it at a second-hand shop for a ridiculously cheap price—but it was cashmere.

'Oops!' She leapt off the sofa, almost knocking him over in her scramble to get up. But her leap sent more drops of wine splashing over the cream carpet and the sofa. 'Oh, no…'

He steadied her with two strong hands on her upper arms; the sensation of his fingers pressing into her skin even through the layers of her clothing was nothing short of electrifying. He dropped his hold as if he'd felt the same voltage, and took a clean white handkerchief from his pocket. For a moment she thought he was going to mop her breasts for her but then he seemed to collect himself and handed it to her instead. 'Don't worry about the carpet and the sofa. They've been treated with a stain resistant.' His voice was so husky it sounded like he'd been snacking on gravel.

Abby dabbed at her breasts and tried not to notice how close he was. She could smell the subtle lime notes of his aftershave and a base note of something else, something woodsy and arrantly masculine. She could even see the individual pinpoints of his re-growth on his chin, the way it was liberally sprinkled around his well sculptured mouth, making her want to press her fingertips to it to see if it felt as prickly as it looked.

She balled the soiled handkerchief into one hand while the other pulled her soaked sweater away from her breasts. 'Do you have something I could wear while I take this off and rinse it?'

'Can't you just put your coat over it or something?'

Abby blew out a breath. 'This sweater cost me a week's wages.' No way was she going to admit it was second-hand. 'And don't get me started about my bra.' Which wasn't second-hand and had cost a packet because no way was she going to wear someone else's underwear. She had done that for most of her childhood.

His frown made his forehead wrinkle like isobars on a weather map. 'Unbelievable.'

'What? Why do you say that?' Abby asked. 'I work at a fashion magazine. I have to wear the latest fashion. I can't be seen out and about in last season's threads.'

'Don't they give you freebies or a discount?'

Abby moved her gaze to the left of his. 'I'm not a fashion editor. I just write a weekly relationships column.'

'Come with me,' he said and led the way out of the room to the downstairs bathroom. 'Wait here. I'll bring you something from upstairs.'

Abby closed the bathroom door and took off the sweater. She grimaced at the state of her bra. Why had she worn the virginal white one when she could have worn the red?

Because you're a virgin?

Don't remind me.

Which made her wonder…when was the last time Luke had sex? Had he had sex with anyone since Kimberley's death? Five years was a long time to be celibate if you'd had a regular sex life before. Which Abby was pretty certain he'd had. Men as sexy as Luke Shelverton did not have to work too hard to find lovers. One look from him and women came out of the woodwork like termites.

There was a knock at the bathroom door and Abby held a hand towel across her breasts and opened the door. Luke handed her a finely woven sweater the colour of his eyes. 'I know it's too big but I don't have anything your size.'

Abby took the sweater from him and held it against her chest along with the towel. She could smell the clean scent of wool wash on the soft fibres and even a faint trace of him. 'Ella told me she thought you still had some of Kimberley's clothes.'

His eyes hardened to chips of blue ice. 'Is this scheme of stand-in fiancé something you and Ella have cooked up together?'

Abby held the sweater against her chest like armour. 'No. It was my idea but she thought it was a good plan. She said it was high time you went to something other than a boring engineering function. And since you and Ella are the only people in my life who know I'm not really engaged, in a way you're the only one who can help me.'

'What about your family? Don't they know?'

Family. That was another thing Abby had done some considerable embellishing over. She hadn't even told Ella the truth about her background. Abby didn't have a family. She didn't want her friends, much less her adoring public, to know she had grown up in numerous foster homes with a bunch of other needy kids and overworked, overwrought, overbearing at times foster parents. The last family she'd stayed with had been the most functional, but even they hadn't kept in touch with her once she'd left the foster system.

Even Abby's surname was a stage name because she had more skeletons in her closet than she had clothes. She didn't want anyone putting her real surname in a search engine and linking her to a now deceased drug-addicted prostitute and a man currently in jail for assault with a deadly weapon. She couldn't bear reliving the shame all over again. Being reminded she had never been loved as a child should be loved, never protected as a child should be protected.

Never wanted.

There were some things you just had to keep private.

Abby couldn't quite meet Luke's gaze. 'Of course they know. But it's not like they can do anything. You're the only one I can ask to do this.'

'I'm sorry, Abby. You'll have to find someone else.'

Abby forgot about covering her wine-splashed bra and handed him back his sweater. 'Look, Luke, I know the last five years have been tough on you, really tough, but don't you ever want to just go out and have a night on the town like normal people do?'

His eyes flicked to her bra-covered breasts and then returned to hold her gaze in a steely blue trap.

'What's normal about pretending to millions of people you're in a relationship that doesn't even exist?'

Abby grabbed her sweater from the marble basin console and pulled it back over her head, thrusting her arms through the sleeves with such force she nearly tore a hole in one of them. 'I'll tell you what's normal,' she said, popping her head out of the collar to glare at him, not caring that her wavy hair was as ruffled and wild as her temper. 'It's normal to help friends out when they're in a pickle. But you keep pushing all your friends away since Kimberley died, which is so sad because your friends and family are who you need to get you through this. You're needed, Luke. Ella and your mum need you and I do too.'

His mouth was so tightly set a postage stamp couldn't have been pushed between his lips. 'I think you've said enough.'

No way had Abby said enough. She wasn't going to be put off her plan. She had to get him to agree to it.

She *had* to.

'My entire career is at stake here. I can't go to the ball without a partner. I'm supposed to be half of one of London's most influential couples. I'll be fired on the spot if they find out I've made him up. I want so much to raise funds for this charity. It's my way to really make a difference in the world. There'll be sponsors there who are going to pay hundreds, possibly thousands of pounds to see me there with my fiancé. You have to help me, Luke. You have to go with me. You have to!'

He slowly shook his head at her as if she were a child having a tantrum, his arms folded across his chest, his feet firmly planted like centuries-old tree trunks. 'No.'

Desperation was climbing up Abby's spine like hundreds of faceless creatures with hooked claws. So many people would be at that ball. Important people. Stars, celebrities, movers and shakers and even minor royalty. Possibly major royalty. Maybe the Queen would be there—she'd turned up at the Olympics, so why not the Spring Ball?

People were expecting to see Abby there with her fiancé. It was unthinkable for her to be there on her own. Her chance to do her bit for disadvantaged kids like her would be ruined if she didn't show up on the arm of her soulmate. The thought of those poor little kids missing out on the things she had missed out on because her fundraising attempt had blown up in her face was heartbreaking.

Why couldn't Luke do this one small thing for her?

Abby stalked past him out of the bathroom and went back to the sitting room, where she had left her bag and phone. 'Right, well, then. I thought you were a friend but clearly I'm mistaken about that.'

His expression showed no trace of emotion. 'Your sweater is on back to front.'

Abby looked down at her sweater and suppressed a groan. Why was she always so clumsy and gauche around him? It hardly helped her cause to be acting like a clown in a farce. She put her phone down and drew her arms out of the sleeves while still wearing the sweater and turned it around so it was facing the right way before poking her arms back through the sleeves. 'There. Happy now, Mr Perfect?'

Mr Perfect?

His eyes dropped to her mouth but then just as quickly jerked back to her eyes as if he was fighting some inner demon and only just winning the battle. 'Why didn't you say anything to Ella about that night?'

'How do you know I didn't tell her?'

'She would've mentioned it by now if you had.'

Abby let out a long breath. 'I didn't want her to know you were drowning your sorrows in booze. She worries about you enough as it is.'

He looked taken aback. 'I wasn't drunk...' He paused for a beat. 'I had a migraine.'

'A migraine?' Abby frowned. 'But there was an empty wine glass on—'

'I'd had one drink after work but it triggered a migraine. I get them occasionally.'

Did his sister and mother know about his migraines? Did anybody know? Abby couldn't stop her gaze from darting to his mouth and back again. Had it been wishful thinking on her part to think he had almost kissed her? Had she *wanted* him to kiss her?

Damn right she had.

'Do you remember anything about that night?' Abby said. 'Anything at all?'

'Not much.' His tone had an edge of something

she couldn't quite identify. 'I didn't…do or say any-thing to you that I shouldn't have, did I?'

She couldn't control the impulse to send her tongue over lips that suddenly felt drier than the car-pet she was standing on. His gaze followed every millimetre of the journey, leaving a trail of blistering, tingling heat along the entire surface of her lips as if his mouth and not his eyes had rested there. 'You mean like make a pass at me?'

A flicker of worry flashed over his face. 'Please tell me I didn't.'

'Maybe if you kissed me again you'd remember if you did or not.'

Are you completely and utterly crazy?

Abby had no idea why she'd issued such a daring challenge but it popped out of her mouth and was now hovering in the air between them like an in-toxicating vapour.

Or maybe she did know why she'd said it—be-cause she wanted him to kiss her. Had wanted it ever since that night.

A real kiss.

Not an almost one.

She couldn't pull her gaze away from his mouth, or pull her mind away from the thought of his firm disapproving lips pressing down on hers. Won-dering how his mouth would feel—hard or soft or somewhere deliciously in between. How he would taste—salty with a hint of coffee or mint or maybe even a lick of top-shelf brandy. She was getting tipsy on the images her mind was spinning—images of him taking her by the shoulders and pulling her against his broad chest and plundering her mouth with his.

Yes, plundering, like one of those swashbuckling heroes in the period dramas she loved to watch on rainy Sunday afternoons.

Luke stepped closer and placed his hand beneath her chin, his fingers warm and firm against her skin. She couldn't remember him ever touching her before, apart from That Night, but the same thing happened now. Nerves she didn't know she possessed leapt and danced and all but fainted at his touch. The space between their bodies pulsated with magnetic energy—energy that rippled in the air like an invisible current.

His eyes held hers in a searing tether that made something in her core quiver and a shiver rolled down her spine like a runaway firecracker. This close she could see every thick lash fringing his mesmerising lapis lazuli eyes, the way his pupils were black and wide like bottomless pools of ink. She could see the detailed sculpture of his mouth, the deep philtrum ridge and the well-defined vermillion borders, and wondered again what it would feel like to have those lips clamped to hers.

'Read my lips.' His voice was so firm it sounded as if it was underlined. In bold and italics for good measure. 'I am not going to the ball. Got it?'

Abby was more than reading his lips. She was studying them as if she was swotting for a final exam. Had she ever seen a more gorgeous mouth? Not that it was a mouth that ever smiled. She couldn't remember the last time she'd seen him crack a grin. But then, his air of brooding gravitas had always secretly fascinated her.

Abby had to get him to change his mind about the ball. She had to. Had to. Had to. Her career depended on it. Her reputation. The children at risk charity she was raising funds for would not reach its target if she didn't show up with a fiancé in tow.

She blew out a breath and cast him a shamefaced glance from beneath her lashes. 'Okay, so I might have misled you a bit about that night. You didn't kiss me. You didn't even try but—'

'Then why did you let me think I had?' Luke dropped his hand from her face and frowned as if he was doing it for *The Guinness Book of Records*.

Abby's cheeks were feeling so hot she thought she might end up with a world record herself. 'I don't know...'

'You don't know?' His voice had a razor-sharp edge to it that nicked at her nerves.

She bit down on her lip. 'I guess I was a bit shocked when I found you so out of it that night. I stupidly jumped to conclusions and assumed you were drunk.'

'But why mislead me to believe I made a pass at you if I didn't even touch you?'

'Actually, you did touch me.'

His eyes flared as if her words shocked him to the core. 'Where did I...?' He left the question hanging in the air.

'You put your arm around my waist when I helped

you into bed,' Abby said. 'And you rested your head on my shoulder and looked at me kind of like you were thinking about kissing me.' She couldn't bring herself to mention the way he'd stroked her face.

'There's a big difference between thinking and doing.'

Abby looked up into his frowning gaze and blinked back the sting of tears. She'd taught herself not to cry over the years but she was scarily close to breaking point. 'Please, Luke, don't make me beg. I'm really sorry about my little white lie. I shouldn't have made you think you'd almost kissed me. But I have a lot riding on this ball. It's just one night and then it will be over and I won't ask you to do another thing for me ever again. I promise.'

'Why's the ball such a big deal? Isn't it just another one of your show pony parties?'

Show pony parties? Was that how he saw her? As some shallow little party hopper with nothing better to do than have a spray tan and get a manicure? Which reminded her—she had to get a spray tan and a manicure. 'I know my career must seem ridiculously vacuous to a nerdy engineer like you, but I happen to love working at a gossip magazine and tomorrow night is the biggest fundraising event of the year,' Abby said. 'There's a silent auction as well as a live auction and amazing lucky door prizes worth thousands of pounds and a dinner cooked by celebrity chefs to raise funds for a children at risk charity. The ball has a three-to four-year waiting list for tickets. I can't not go because my boss will fire me when she finds out I've been pretending to be engaged all along. And I especially can't show up without my other half since we were nominated as one of this year's most popular and influential couples.'

His frown was a deep trench between his night sky eyes. 'You're going to have to tell everyone eventually you aren't in a relationship.'

Abby knew she would have to announce some sort of breakup eventually, but how much easier would that be if Luke stood in as her fiancé at the ball? She could even blog and tweet breakup tips once the ball was out of the way. The thought of telling everyone that she, the relationships expert, was single and still a virgin was not something she wanted to do in a hurry—if ever. 'But don't you see? I need a stand-in fiancé in order to break up with him. I'll find someone for myself eventually. Maybe I'll try one of those dating apps. But I have to get through the ball first.'

He did an I-can't-believe-you're-for-real eye-roll and made a move to the sitting room door, holding it open in a pointed manner. 'If you'll excuse me, I have some work to get back to.'

Abby knew this was her last chance to get him to change his mind. 'Please, please, *please* do this for me, Luke. Just for a couple of hours. You can leave early—no one will suspect anything. Think of all those poor little disadvantaged kids you'll be helping. You will literally be changing their lives by pretending to be my fiancé for two hours.'

He kept looking at her without speaking for so

long she began to mentally dictate her resignation letter. But then he released a long and weighted sigh. 'All right—you win. I'll take you for two hours, tops. But you have to accept this is a one-off occasion and it will *not* be repeated.'

Abby was flooded with such a tide of relief she had to stop from flinging herself into his arms and hugging him. Or kissing him, which was even more tempting than she wanted to admit. 'Okay. Okay. Of course. I only need you for one night. I promise.'

They briefly discussed arrangements about Luke picking her up and what to wear and then he walked her to the front door of his house. 'One other thing,' he said.

Abby glanced up at him. 'Yes?'

He seemed to be having some trouble keeping his gaze away from her mouth. It kept tracking back to it as if programmed to do so. 'I might be standing in for someone who doesn't actually exist but that's as far as your little fantasy goes. Understood?'

Abby wondered what he meant by such a comment. 'I hope you're not thinking I'd want you to actually marry me because that's just utterly ridiculous.'

'Good to know,' he said. 'See you tomorrow, Cinderella.'

CHAPTER TWO

LUKE CLOSED THE door after Abby left and let out a curse so blue he was mildly surprised to find the walls of his hallway were still white. Damn that girl. How had she got him to say yes? Had she cast some sort of spell on him? Why had he agreed to such a charade? He didn't do balls. He didn't do parties. He didn't even do dinners unless work required it of him.

And he definitely didn't date.

Since Kimberley's death he'd had no motivation to date. He felt the urge now and again but he just as quickly squashed it. He was a bad bet when it came to relationships. He had tried with Kimberley. And tried damn hard because with his father playing musical partners like some sort of born-again playboy, Luke had wanted to prove to himself he wasn't cut from the same cloth. But, for all his efforts to be a good partner, his relationship with Kimberley had floundered and he'd called time on it. He hadn't felt ready to take their relationship to the next level. Kimberley had stayed overnight several times a week and had even left some clothes and toiletries at his house, but he hadn't been willing for her to move in with him permanently. It had seemed *too* much of a commitment. Back then he hadn't been against marriage, he'd seen it as something he might do one day with the right person, yet over time it had become obvious Kimberley wasn't the right person.

But within hours of him ending their relationship Kimberley was dead.

The thought of a new relationship made him feel claustrophobic. Like someone was wrapping him in steel cords, pulling them tighter and tighter and tighter until he couldn't breathe. He couldn't think of the word commitment without his chest seizing.

But helping Abby with her little problem… Well, it had been rather nice of her to make sure he was okay that night six months ago, and he was grateful she hadn't sent his mother and sister into a fit of panic over him 'drinking' by telling them about it. Abby had come on her own to pick up something Ella had left behind the day before. He wished he could remember more about that night, but Kimberley's birthday was always hard and it always triggered a migraine. Always. He'd come home from Kimberley's parents' house, where they'd had a cake complete with candles. Even presents she'd never open.

They always invited him and he always went out of respect. Out of duty.

Out of guilt.

There was a part of him that wished he hadn't opened the door to Abby that night. He'd only been home half an hour and he'd had half a glass of wine—*foolish, he knew*—to try and ease the tension behind his eyes, but then the migraine had hit him like a sledgehammer and wiped out his motherboard, so to speak.

But he could remember Abby arriving on his doorstep with a sunny smile and those amazingly bright and clear toffee-brown eyes looking up at him like a cute spaniel.

And her mouth.

He had no trouble remembering her mouth. He could be in an induced coma for a century and still be aware of it. Dear God, what was it about her mouth? It never failed to pull his gaze to its plump fullness. It never failed to make him fantasise about how those luscious lips would feel under his. Damn it. It made him think of sex. With her.

Which was downright wrong given she was his kid sister's best friend.

That was a line he wasn't going to cross. There were some things you didn't do, and that was definitely one of them. That was, if he was actually interested in having a relationship with anyone, which he wasn't.

Not again.

He didn't want the responsibility of someone else's emotional upkeep. How could he ever relax in a relationship after being blindsided by Kimberley's tragic end? Even though he hadn't loved her, it didn't mean he didn't deeply regret her passing. Every day since he'd thought of all the things she was missing out on, the things her family were missing out on. Nothing he could say or do would ever make up for their loss.

He couldn't do that to another person, to another family. He was better out of the dating game so there was no possibility of anyone getting hurt.

But what was he going to do about Abby?

One of the little flashes of memory Luke had of that night was Abby's chestnut hair tickling his face when he leaned his pounding head against her shoulder. Her hair smelt of spring flowers. Her touch… He couldn't remember if she'd touched him first or if he'd touched her…

But no matter. The crucial thing was he remembered how it felt. It was the same feeling he had when he'd touched her face earlier. Her skin was as soft as the petal of a magnolia bloom. Her nose had a cute dusting of tiny freckles over the bridge that reminded him of chocolate sprinkled on the top of a cappuccino.

He might not have kissed her that night but he'd sure as hell wanted to. He remembered all too clearly. How could he forget a mouth like that, migraine or not? He'd thought about that mouth for the last six months. Thought and fantasised about holding Abby in his arms, touching her, kissing her.

And, yes, God strike him down, making love to her.

Luke wasn't sure why he'd finally agreed to be her stand-in fiancé. Well, maybe he did know. Seeing Abby's tears had triggered something in him. Worry that she would do something. Something silly and reckless that would destroy…

He pulled away from the thought. No, Abby wasn't like Kimberley. Abby was pragmatic and resourceful and resilient in a way Kimberley hadn't been. Abby's tears were understandable given the ball was a big deal for her. It was two hours of his time and he surely owed her that since her Florence Nightingale act six months ago.

Two hours pretending to be Abby's Mr Perfect.

How hard could it be?

Abby was trying to pull up her zip at the back of her ball gown when she heard Luke arrive at her flat the night of the ball. She gathered the back of her dress in one hand and shuffled out of her bedroom to answer the front door. She hadn't seen Luke in black tie before. Even in casual clothes he was traffic-stopping gorgeous. But in formal attire he would have stopped air traffic. Possibly even a space shuttle. At take-off.

He was certainly stopping her breath. She had to swallow a couple of times to get her voice to work. 'H…hi. I'm having some trouble with this zip. Do you think you could give me a hand?'

'Sure.' He stepped inside and closed the door. 'Turn around.'

Abby held her breath as his fingers drew the zip up her back, the gentle brush of his knuckles on her bare skin sending a shiver shimmying down her spine and straight into her lady land. Secretly fizzing and smouldering there like an ignited wick. She could feel the tall frame of his body within half a step of hers, triggering her hormones like they had never been triggered before. It was as if her body recognised something in his—something deeply primal and elemental. Her senses were singing like a mezzo-soprano in the Royal Albert Hall. If she so much as leaned back she could be flush against his chest and hips and…other things.

Male things.

But the zip would only go to a certain point.

'There's a bit of fabric caught up in the mechanism,' Luke said and continued working on it, bending over so his warm breath as well as his fingers brushed over her skin.

She suppressed a shiver and breathed in so he could gain better access, at the same time breathing in his aftershave, this time lemon and lime and a faint trace of bergamot with an understory of country leather. She couldn't stop thinking of his hands going lower, dipping down to the curve of her bottom, caressing her, shaping her, slipping his fingers between her legs…

Finally the zip moved all the way up and Luke stepped back. 'That's done it.'

That's done it all right. Abby hadn't felt so turned on in her life. She turned around and hoped her wicked thoughts were not painted bright red on her face. But it certainly felt like it. If she didn't stop blushing soon she'd be able to turn the heating down. Or off. 'Erm… I have something else for you to do… I'll just get it from my bedroom.'

Abby came back out with the fake diamond pendant she wanted to wear and handed it to him. It was a very good fake. You could hardly tell the difference. Hardly. 'The catch is so tiny I can never do it up by myself.'

Luke trailed the fine chain over his fingers, his narrowed gaze examining the 'diamond.' 'Who bought you this?'

'You did.'

His brows came together. 'When did I ever—?'

'Not you as in *you*,' Abby said. 'You as in Mr Perfect. My fiancé.'

His expression seemed to suggest he thought a white van and a straitjacket might be handy right about now. 'Are you serious? You actually buy stuff and pretend it's from someone who doesn't exist, other than in your imagination?'

'So? It's all for a good cause,' Abby said. 'I help people. It's what I do. I help them have better love lives.'

'While presumably having no love life of your own.' There was a dry edge to his tone.

'Like you can talk.' Abby turned around rather than face his piercing gaze. She had her hair in an up-do that gave him free access to her neck but even so every fine hair reacted to the presence of his fingers with tingles and shivers that went straight to her core.

'How do you know I don't have a love life?' she said, turning back around once the necklace was in place. 'I might have dozens of secret lovers stashed away.'

'None of whom you've managed to convince to take you to the ball.' He shrugged at her beady look. 'Just saying.'

Abby wasn't going to go into the details of why she'd got to the age of twenty-three without having dated regularly or had sex with anyone. Even Ella didn't know the full story. How could she tell her best friend her mother was a heroin-addicted prostitute? And that hearing her mother service her clients in the next room—and in the same room when she had been under three—had seriously messed with Abby's sexual development? She had only been kissed a couple of times and had called a halt before anyone could get any closer. She even wondered if she was frigid.

'I would have dated someone well before this but I got the job at the magazine, which, quite frankly, I didn't expect in a million squillion years to get,' Abby said. 'I was the least qualified candidate but somehow they chose me. I wrote my first couple of columns about my childhood sweetheart and somehow the readers assumed he actually existed. And then because they loved hearing about him so much I had to keep running with it.'

'How long have you worked at the magazine?'

'Two and a half years.'

His frown hadn't left his forehead but was now even deeper. 'You've been pretending for two and a half years that you're—?'

'I know it sounds crazy. It probably *is* crazy but

I wanted that job so much and I was prepared to do anything to get it.'

'Anything?'

Abby did a little lip chew. 'Well, maybe not anything, but pretending to be engaged to a guy who ticks all the boxes wasn't that hard. I mean, guys like that must exist, right? People do get married and live happily-ever-after.'

'Just as many end up in the divorce courts.'

'Just because your parents went through a hideous divorce when you were a teenager doesn't mean—'

'If we don't get going soon your two hours will be up before we even get to the ball,' Luke said, tinkling his car keys, his look more forbidding than a Keep Out sign on an army-training minefield.

Abby picked up her wrap from the back of the sofa where she'd left it earlier. She wrapped it around her shoulders, refusing to be daunted by the boxed up set to his features. 'If Kimberley hadn't died would you two have got married?'

'Abby.' His voice was like a stop sign.

'I'm sorry. Am I being pushy? I just wondered how long you dated.'

His lips were pressed almost flat. 'Three years.'

'Did you ever discuss it? Marriage, I mean?'

A muscle flickered near his mouth like a faulty switch during a power surge. 'Look, do you want me to take you to this damn ball or not?'

Abby hadn't worked in journalism for nothing. She had been known to get blood out of stones before. Whole litres of it. It was a trick of hers to get people talking about themselves so she didn't have to share anything about herself. 'Were you in love with her?'

He opened the front door and jerked his head towards the exit. 'Out.' His eyes were dark and brooding with bottled-up anger. Anger or something else…

Abby shifted her lips from side to side in a musing manner. 'Are you angry with me or at life in general? Grief can do that to—'

'Don't play the amateur psychologist with me,' he said. 'Save it for those foolish enough to fall for it.'

'I'm sensing a little resistance from you on the subject of your relationship with—'

'I wasn't in love with her, okay?' He took a deep breath as if to calm himself, one of his hands rubbing over his face like he wanted to erase something. 'And no, I wasn't going to marry her.'

'But you still miss her.'

He gave a movement of his lips that was closer to a grimace than anything near a smile. 'She was a nice young woman. She didn't deserve to have her life cut short.'

Abby touched his arm. 'I'm sure she wouldn't mind if you moved on with your life. You don't have to grieve for her for ever.'

The way he looked at her made her insides suddenly quiver. 'Are you offering yourself as a replacement?'

Abby dropped her hand from his arm as if it had been scorched. 'Of course not. You're not my type.'

'Not perfect enough for you?' There was a hint of cynicism in his tone.

'There is nothing wrong with wanting the best for yourself,' Abby said. 'Especially when you're a woman. Women often settle for second best or good enough instead of perfect. Why shouldn't we have what we want? Why should we have to compromise over something so important as a life partner?'

'So far the only perfect partner you've found is the one inside your head.'

'So far,' Abby gave a small nod. 'But I haven't given up hope yet.'

'Good luck with that.'

Luke helped Abby into his car but he was having trouble keeping his eyes away from her cleavage. The emerald-green ball gown was as sleek as a glove on her, showcasing her assets in a way that made his hormones honk and howl and do a happy dance. She wasn't super-slim but all her curves were in the right places—places he was getting hard just thinking about. The imitation diamond pendant—he knew it was an imitation because he could spot a fake a mile off—swung just above the shadowed cleft between her bra-less breasts, making him want to place his lips and tongue in that scented hollow, to taste the creamy flesh, to graze his teeth over the nipples he could see pressing against the silky fabric. The dress skimmed her waist and hips and fanned out behind her in part mermaid tail and part train. Her hair was in one of those up styles that looked like it took no time at all to do but still managed to look elegant at the same time. And it framed her face, highlighting the slope of her porcelain-smooth cheeks. Her smoky eye make-up made her brown eyes pop, but it was her mouth that kept pulling his gaze. Glistening with a shimmering lip-gloss, her Cupid's bow tortured his self-control like a yo-yo dieter at an all-you-can-eat banquet.

He had to stop drooling over her mouth.

Luke got in the driver's side of his car and curled his fingers around the steering wheel before he was tempted to reach across the console and place his hand on her silk-clad thigh. Was she even wearing knickers under that dress? The thought triggered a flare of lust so powerful it snatched his breath as if someone had grabbed him by the throat and squeezed.

Abby glanced at him. 'Are you okay?'

Luke opened and closed his fingers on the steering wheel. 'Yep.'

'You made a funny sound…kind of like you were in pain. You're not getting one of your migraines, are you?'

Now why didn't I think of that as an excuse? Not that he was the type of guy to renege on a commitment. When he made a decision he followed through on it. Two hours of his time was not a huge commitment. Thank God. 'No. Just not looking forward to making small talk. It's not my forte.'

'Don't worry, the music will be so loud you won't be able to hear yourself think.'

Which could be a very good thing given the things Luke was thinking. Things he had no business thinking. Things like how she would look without that green dress. How her gorgeous breasts would feel in his hands, in his mouth. How those sexy legs would wrap around his hips. How she would feel around him when he—

He slammed the brakes on his thoughts. He wasn't in the market for a relationship. Any sort of relationship. And Abby Hart with her happy-ever-after mission was the last person he should be thinking about. She was after the feel-good fairy tale. He still couldn't get over the fact she'd been pretending to all her readers and followers she was engaged to someone who didn't exist. Who *did* that? It took perfectionism to a whole new level. There wasn't a man on the planet who could fulfil her checklist. And he was the last man on the planet who would even try.

He wasn't going to try because he'd already been down that road and it had only ended in tragedy.

Abby began fiddling with the catch on her evening purse. 'Luke?'

'Yes?'

'There are a few things you need to know about our relationship...you know, stuff I've told my readers about you.'

Luke flicked her a glance. 'Like what?'

She nibbled at her lower lip for a moment. 'Like how you proposed.'

Shoot me now. He could just imagine what her

wacky imagination had cooked up. 'How did I—?' He couldn't even bring himself to say the word.

'You took me to Paris for the weekend and checked us into the penthouse suite of a ridiculously expensive hotel where you had organised fresh rose petals to be scattered all over the bed and flowers all over the suite,' she said. 'And you had champagne on ice and chocolate-dipped strawberries in a crystal bowl by the bed.'

'And?' Luke suspected he wasn't going to get off that lightly. Paris and champagne and strawberries and rose petals were within reason. But nothing he knew about Abby was within the realms of reason.

'We—ell…' The way she drew out the word made the back of his neck start to prickle. 'You got down on bended knee and told me I was the only one in the world for you, that you loved me more than life itself. You took out a ring box and asked me to marry you.'

Luke couldn't imagine ever saying something like that to anyone, but still.

'You had tears in your eyes,' she said. 'Lots of them. In fact, you cried. We both did because we were so happy to be—'

'Oh, for God's sake.' He made a choked-off sound. 'I can't remember the last time I cried.'

'I know some men find expressing emotion really difficult, but what about when you lost Kimberley? Didn't you cry then?'

'No.'

She gave a concerned frown. 'Oh…'

Luke had been so guilt-ridden he couldn't access

any other emotion. When he'd been told the news of Kimberley's accident he had felt completely numb. It didn't seem possible that the woman who had been in his house only a couple of hours earlier was no longer alive. He'd put the phone down after that ghastly phone call from her parents and picked up a glass where Kimberley's lipstick was still visible on the rim. How could she be dead? For the sake of her shattered family he had swung into action, helping to organise the funeral and dealing with the distressing task of informing people outside the family of her death. He had done it in an almost robotic fashion. He'd said all the right things, done all the right things, but he'd felt like there was a thick glass wall between him and the rest of the world.

It was still there.

'Her family was having enough trouble dealing with her death without me adding to their distress,' Luke said. 'I had to hold it together for them.'

He felt Abby's gaze resting on him as if she was trying to solve a Mensa puzzle. 'But what about when you were on your own? Didn't you cry then?'

'Not every person cries when sad stuff happens,' Luke said through gritted teeth. 'There are other ways to express sadness.'

'But it's really healing to have a good howl,' Abby said. 'It releases hormones and stuff. And you shouldn't be ashamed of crying just because you're a man. That's a ridiculous myth that harms men rather than helps them. Everyone should be able to cry regardless of their gender.'

Luke pulled up behind the queue of cars waiting to be parked by the valet team at the entrance of the premier hotel where the ball was being held. 'Okay, Cinderella. Anything else I should know about myself before we make an entrance?'

Her cheeks went a faint shade of pink. 'Erm… There is one other thing…'

The prickle moved from his neck to his spine. 'Go on.'

The tip of her tongue swept over her lips, making his groin tighten. 'You tell me you love me all the time. In public.'

Luke couldn't remember the last time he'd told his mother and sister he loved them, let alone anyone else. He wasn't a wordy guy. He *did* rather than *said*. His father was the opposite—lots of words and empty promises and nothing to back them up. 'O-kay.'

'And you use a lot of terms of endearment. Like honey, and baby, and sweetheart.'

That was another thing he wasn't big on, dropping cutesy endearments into every conversation. But a man had to do what a man had to do. 'Got it.'

'And we kiss. A lot.'

Luke's groin was asking for more room. Urgently. Just looking at her mouth made his blood pound and head south of the border. What would it do to him to actually kiss her? 'I'm not big on public displays of affection.'

'You are now.'

Freaking hell. What had he got himself into?

'Will you be okay with me kissing you?' Luke asked, frowning.

Her gaze kept flicking back and forth from his mouth to his eyes. 'Maybe we should have practised a bit first, you know, so we don't look stilted or awkward together.'

Now *he* couldn't stop looking at *her* mouth. Imagining how it would feel against his. 'Where do you suggest we practise? Here in the car?'

'We have time before the valet guy gets to us,' Abby said, glancing at the line of cars waiting to be parked. 'The queue is long enough.'

But was Luke's self-control strong enough? He hadn't kissed a woman in five years. Not unless he counted his mother and sister but clearly a peck on the cheek wasn't going to make the grade here. 'You really think this is necessary?'

She was already over his side of the car, her face so close to his he could feel her breath on his lips. 'Kiss me, Luke.'

Luke slid his hand along the curve of her cheek, his blood pumping so hard he could feel his erection pressing against his zip. He brought his mouth down to hers in a soft touch. *Just brush her lips and get the hell out of there.* He lifted off but her lips clung to his and something inside him gave way like tectonic plates shifting during an earthquake. He went back down again, breathing in the scent of her, relishing the fresh fruity taste of her. Her lips were soft and pillowy and tasted of strawberries or was it cherries? She made a little whimpering sound and opened to the stroke of his tongue, her tongue dancing with his, making his blood throb all the harder.

He didn't want the kiss to end. He could have kissed her all night. The feel of her lips against his, the flirty little flicker of her tongue made desire roar through his system like a rabid dog suddenly snapping its chain.

He crushed her mouth beneath his, cupping the nape of her neck so he could deepen the kiss even further. Her hands came up to link around his neck, her soft sounds of approval making everything that was male in him vibrate with fierce longing. He hadn't felt so turned on by a kiss in years. Possibly ever. Her soft mouth moulded itself to his, moving with and against his in a sexy rhythm that echoed the pulse and pound of his blood. Her perfume dazzled his senses, the luscious curves of her breasts pressed against his chest, sending a knockout blow to his self-control.

The sound of people cat-calling outside the car was the only thing that pulled Luke out of the moment. That and the flash of paparazzi cameras that were as bright and blinding as summer lightning.

Abby pulled back from him and gave a tremulous smile, her mouth slightly swollen, her cheeks flushed. 'Wow. Who would've thought?'

Right back at you, sweetheart. 'Please tell me there isn't going to be a picture of us kissing in tomorrow's tabloids,' Luke said.

She did that cute little lip chew thing again and grimaced. 'Sorry.'

CHAPTER THREE

ABBY WAS STILL trying to get her senses back under control when Luke helped her out of the car. Her mouth was tingling and so were her girly bits. Not just tingling, but aching and throbbing. She'd been kissed in the past but nothing like that. Luke's mouth had set fire to hers, making her lose all sense of time and place. But even more surprising...there hadn't been any awkwardness between them. They had kissed as if they'd been doing it for years. As if their mouths instinctively knew what the other liked.

The press surged closer and Luke put a protective arm around Abby's waist. She smiled up at him, her heart almost coming to a standstill when he smiled back. His smile made his eyes come alive in a way she had never seen before. It made him look younger, more carefree, less serious and forbidding. 'Ready?'

'Ready.' *I think.* 'Welcome to the limelight.'

The cameras were clicking so much it sounded like a round of military gunfire. And a journalist surged forward to thrust a recording device near

Abby. 'Everyone is dying to know who your Mr Perfect is. Will you introduce him to us?'

Abby smiled at the journalist. 'Sure—this is my fiancé Luke—'

'Hey—aren't you Luke Shelverton? From Shelverton Robotics?' another male journalist asked. 'You're the guy who designed that amazing technology that's revolutionised complex neurosurgery all around the world.'

Luke accepted the accolade with an on-off smile that didn't show his teeth. 'That's correct.'

'When are you two planning to get married?' the female journalist asked. 'Will we be hearing wedding bells this summer?'

Abby was still trying to think of something to say when Luke got in first. 'We're keeping the date a secret for privacy reasons,' he said.

'Do you have any dating advice from a man's perspective?' the male journalist asked.

'Just be yourself,' Luke said and began to lead Abby towards the entrance of the hotel.

But the first female journalist wasn't finished. 'What about some romance tips from London's most romantic man?'

Luke's fingers tightened on Abby's hand in an I'll-get-you-for-this-later gesture but he looked the female journalist straight in the eye. 'Look into her eyes when she's talking to you. Listen to her.'

'I'm going to use that in my next column,' Abby said when they finally got away from the press. 'Everyone is so busy on their phones these days no one ever looks at you when they're talking to you.'

'You owe me, young lady,' Luke said in an undertone.

Abby gave him a lopsided smile. 'Sorry about that. But hey, I thought you did a brilliant job. You seriously could have your own column.'

He gave her the side eye. 'Don't even think about it.'

Abby was thinking about lots of stuff. Like how warm and strong his arm felt around her waist. How the slightest movement of his fingers against hers sent an erotic charge right through her body and straight to her core. How when his eyes held hers something unravelled deep in her belly, like a ball of string let loose down a steep staircase.

And that kiss.

She hadn't stopped thinking about it. Her lips hadn't stopped tingling from it. How could a mouth that never smiled pack such a passionate punch? Her mouth would never be the same. It was permanently branded with the heat of Luke's kiss. Searing heat. Blistering heat. Heat that made her body shudder with excitement. She looked at his mouth and noticed a tiny smear from her shimmery lip-gloss was next to his top lip. She stepped up on tiptoe and lifted her hand and wiped it away. 'Oops, lip-gloss. All gone now.'

His eyes were as dark as sapphires, holding hers in a sensual lock as if he were mentally replaying every pulse-racing second of their kiss. His gaze went to her mouth, resting there for a thrumming beat before returning to her eyes. 'Did I tell you how beautiful you look tonight?'

'No, but—'

'You look dazzlingly beautiful,' Luke said. 'There isn't a man here who isn't wishing he could swap places with me right now.'

Abby knew he was only saying that because of the other guests close by. Of course, as her fiancé he would be expected to say nice things. Wonderful things. Things no one had ever told her before. He was acting a role and doing a damn fine job of it. But oh, how fabulous it would be if he really *did* mean them. When had anyone ever called her beautiful? She hadn't even been called pretty or becoming. She hadn't even been given the girl-next-door tag. She was bland. Unnoticeable. But how cool if he really thought her the most beautiful woman at the ball, just like Cinderella.

You are seriously out of your mind.

I know, I know. But he sounded so genuine.

'Thank you.' Abby smiled. 'But I'm not sure if I'll be able to eat anything while wearing this dress. My zip might not be able to take it.'

'Abby!' Felicity Kirby, her chief editor, came over in a cloud of exotic perfume and proceeded to air kiss Abby's cheeks. 'I'm literally gagging to meet your gorgeous Mr Perfect.' She beamed up at Luke and thrust out her hand. 'We would love to do an interview with you as soon as it can be arranged. Your work is absolutely amazing. I have a friend of a friend whose life was saved because of the tiny robotic surgical arm you designed for her brain surgery. I'll get one of my staff to contact you. Abby will give me your details and we'll—'

'I don't give interviews,' Luke said.

Felicity looked at him as if he'd just said he didn't breathe oxygen. 'But you must give an interview. Everyone wants to know about your romance with Abby. Like how on earth you kept your identity a secret for all this time. That in itself is worthy of a two-page spread. Now that we know who you are, we need to hear your side. You can do a guest blog with dating tips for the man about town. It'll be fabulous.'

'I'm sorry—I'm not interested.'

Felicity was undaunted and swung her gaze to Abby. 'Talk him into it, sweetie. He's a reader magnet. And so hot!' She fanned her face with her hand. 'No wonder you've been hiding him away for all this time. I wouldn't want to share him with anyone either.'

'I'll see what I can do.' Abby stretched her mouth into a smile.

Once Felicity had moved on, Luke pressed a firm warm hand in Abby's lower back, his low deep voice containing a thread of steel wrapped around every word. 'Do I have to say it again?'

'No. I heard you loud and clear.' Abby gave a little eye roll. 'No interviews.'

He let out a gusty sigh. 'I need a drink.'

She grabbed his hand and led him towards a drinks waiter carrying a tray. 'So do I.'

* * *

Luke stood with Abby a few minutes later with a glass of champagne in hand while she chatted to the other guests before the ballroom was opened for the main event. He put in a few words occasionally but he figured the less said the soonest mended. It was like being in a play but having read only half the script. Abby had told her readers things about 'him' that made him cringe. What sort of expert was he on romance? He had unwittingly sabotaged every relationship he'd ever been in and he had no intention of repeating those hard-learned mistakes.

And as for giving interviews. *Sheesh*. Were these people for real? If they wanted to interview him about his work then fine. But his private life was off limits. He could talk about work at a stretch, but he usually left it to his staff to handle media interviews. He liked working in the background and getting on with the research and design that led to the breakthroughs in medical robotic engineering that had changed lives all over the world. That was what he was an expert at doing. Not swanning around a gala ball making banal conversation with people he had nothing in common with and never would.

But it had to be said, Abby was looking smoking-hot tonight and he was quite enjoying the envious looks he was getting from the other men. He was also enjoying the way her body kept brushing up against his in the crowded foyer outside the ballroom. He kept his arm around her waist, and every now and again she would glance up and smile at him and something tightly closed in his chest would flick open.

He could still taste her.

The fruity sweet softness of her lips made him hungry for more. And, just like every other man present, he was having trouble keeping his eyes off her cleavage. Not that there wasn't lots of cleavage on show from the other women at the ball, but somehow it was Abby's that drew his eyes like a bee to highly prized pollen.

'Let's have a look at the silent auction while we wait,' Abby said, leading him to a display where various items were on show. 'You might find something you like.'

The only thing Luke liked so far was the way Abby looked in that dress. He was all for a bit of fundraising and it was an excellent cause, but none of the items in the silent auction particularly interested him, although there were a couple of original artworks that caught his eye. He had more than enough wealth to buy whatever he wanted when he wanted it. He was happy to make a donation without collecting any of the goods.

Abby seemed rather taken with one of the lucky door prizes that were also on show. She stood in front of the display of a week for two on a privately owned island in the Mediterranean with a wistful look on her face.

'Gosh, wouldn't this be great to win?' she said, pointing to the photo of a white sandy beach and the luxury villa that overlooked it. 'I'd love a week sunning myself on a private beach. Imagine being rich enough to own your own island!'

Luke had often thought about buying an island—somewhere to escape to and leave all the worries and pressures of life behind. Somewhere where the guilt that plagued him wouldn't follow. He'd even gone as far as looking at some online and taking a virtual tour. The thought of sand and surf and solitude was seriously tempting.

Almost as tempting as Abby.

'Great place for a honeymoon, eh, Abby?' one of the women from the magazine said on her way past.

Abby smiled at the woman and then turned back to Luke. 'You can win just by being here. How cool is that? There are stickers with numbers on them underneath all the chairs in the ballroom. The winning number will be announced at midnight.'

'Who would you take with you if you won?' Luke wasn't sure why he asked but she was looking so longingly at the display he couldn't stop himself in time.

She gave a self-deprecating laugh. 'I won't win. I've never won anything in my entire life.'

The doors to the ballroom were finally opened and Abby gasped when the stunning decorations came into view. She clutched Luke's hand in an excited can-you-believe-this? manner, reminding him of a small child at her first visit to a sweet shop. He had to admit the ballroom was nothing short of amazing. Garlands of fresh spring flowers adorned the room and taller arrangements were positioned either side of the stage, where a live band was playing the welcome theme. The tables were laid with crystal glasses and silver cutlery and there were even more flowers as centrepieces as well as colourful helium balloon trees.

The formal dinner began, and after Luke had exhausted his limited dinner party conversation repertoire he was relieved when the band started playing just as the dessert course was being cleared away. He took Abby's hand and stood. 'Would you like to dance?'

Her smile was like a ray of sunshine on a bleak winter's day. 'I'd love to.' She rose from her chair and leaned close to his ear and whispered, 'By the way, I told everyone you're an absolutely brilliant dancer.'

Of course you did. Luke mentally rolled his eyes. 'Let's hope I don't disappoint.'

Abby stepped on to the dance floor with Luke and his arms brought her in close to his body. One of his hands rested on her bare skin where the back of her dress was scooped out low on her spine. Her skin tingled and tightened and her breath all but stopped when his pelvis came into contact with hers, the unmistakable stirring of his body making her heart race as if she'd been running upstairs. Hundreds and hundreds of stairs.

She had been right about him being a brilliant dancer. His body moved in perfect sequence with hers as if they had been training for a dancing competition. Even the train on her dress wasn't an impediment as he moved her around the dance floor without once stepping on it or allowing anyone else to either.

It had been so long since Abby had danced with anyone. Ever since she'd pretended to be in a relationship she hadn't been able to attend parties without finding a reasonable excuse for why her fiancé wasn't with her. It had been far easier not to go. She hadn't even been out to dinner for the last couple of years unless it was with a girlfriend. Her social life—meagre as it was—had ground to a halt. She'd been trying so hard to fit in, to appear normal, and just ended up feeling abnormal and missing out on all the things other people took for granted. Which was exactly like her childhood had been. Why did that keep happening to her?

Was she doomed to always be on the outside?

But now, with Luke's arms around her, she realised what she had been missing. It was fun to be out as a couple, to drink and eat together and dance to great music. It was even more fun knowing Luke and she had a secret of their own. That no one suspected they weren't the real deal. *Yay!* She had actually pulled it off. She wasn't going to be shamed and mocked and humiliated after all. But not only that, their conspiracy added a level of intimacy to their relationship that was strangely exciting. Titillating even. Everyone in the ballroom believed them to be madly in love.

Everyone thought they were lovers.

It would be kind of cool if you were the real deal.

Abby blinked away the thought. Why would she want to be *actually* engaged to Luke? He was only with her tonight under sufferance. He'd even set a strict time limit on it—two hours. *Two flipping hours!* Which proved he wasn't her type. He had zero spontaneity. He was stiff and formal and never smiled, and he didn't have a romantic bone in his body. He was a die-hard workaholic. He probably worked in his sleep. If he ever slept.

But that doesn't mean you couldn't be lovers for real.

As soon as the thought entered Abby's head it clung there like a lint ball on a mohair sweater. That kiss was the problem. Luke kissed like a man who knew his way around a woman's body. He had awakened something in *her* body, something that wasn't going to be a good doggy and lie down and go back to sleep.

Luke was currently single and had been for five years. She hadn't even had a lover and she could hardly take one while she was pretending to be engaged to Mr Perfect.

So why not Luke?

Abby wasn't a casual sex type of person, especially since her mother's approach to sex had been not just casual but contractual and chaotic. But how would she ever feel normal if she were still a virgin when she was thirty? Or forty? Ninety, even? But if she slept with Luke the problem would be solved. She could tick the box marked Normal. The more she thought about it, the more she was sold on the idea. It was an ideal solution.

All she had to do was convince Luke.

Luke guided her out of the way of an enthusiastic couple, bringing her even closer to his body. 'How soon can we leave?' he asked.

Abby leaned back to look up at him. 'Aren't you having a good time?'

He gave her a twisted movement of his lips that might have passed for a smile...well, if you were standing in the next county, maybe. 'Your time is almost up, Cinderella.'

Abby bit down on her lip and lowered her gaze to his perfectly aligned bow tie. Why did he have to remind her he had a stopwatch going on their evening? What did that say about her?

It said she was resistible, that was what it said.

Some smoking-hot seductress I turned out to be.

'What's wrong?' Luke said.

Abby brought her gaze back up to his and, taking a deep mental breath for courage, asked, 'Do you think we could kick on and have some supper somewhere after this?'

A small frown creased his forehead. 'Why?'

'Because I'm still hungry.'

'We just had a four-course dinner and you ate my dessert.'

Abby looked at his mouth, her stomach tilting when she thought of his kiss in the car. How could she survive on just one kiss? She was hungry for more of his kisses. She wanted to feast on them. To gorge on them. To go on a massive binge on them and she wouldn't even feel guilty in the morning. 'I'm not ready to go home yet. I haven't been out in ages and ages and...well, neither have you so it kind of makes sense to make the most of it.'

'Abby.'

She closed her eyes in a slow blink and sighed. 'Okay. Okay. I get it. Time's up and you want to go home and work. Forget I mentioned it.' She began to pull out of his hold to go back to their table but his fingers around her wrist stalled her.

He brought her back to stand in front of him, his hips brushing hers with such heart-stopping intimacy she had trouble remembering to breathe. His eyes were as dark as deep blue ink and framed by a frown that was thoughtful rather than his usual disapproving one. 'Don't you want to stick around for the lucky door prize draw?'

'I can barely win an argument let alone a prize like that.' *As our earlier conversation just confirmed.* 'Anyway, it's just supper together. That wouldn't be breaking any of your rules, would it?'

His eyes went to her mouth for a brief moment. Then he seemed to gather himself and he tucked her hand over his arm. 'Supper it is.'

Luke took Abby to an exclusive bar/supper club a few blocks from where the ball had been held. He'd been there a couple of times for work things and liked the atmosphere. They served coffee and cake as well as the regular cocktails and beverages.

Abby gave a cursory glance at the menu and sat back in the plush velvet-covered armchair. 'I'm going to have Sex on the Beach.'

He lifted one eyebrow and allowed his latent sense of dry humour to make a brief appearance. 'Still a bit cold for that, don't you think?'

Her cheeks developed tiny twin flags of colour. 'Have you ever done it on the beach?'

Luke had spent most of the night trying *not* to think about sex, especially sex with Abby. 'Couple of times.'

She leaned forward to rest her hands on her knees, her voice coming out as a whisper. 'Can I tell you a secret?'

He tried not to stare at her mouth, tried not to imagine it kissing its way down his body. Tried not to get hard, but hey, he was only human. 'Go for it.'

She blinked a couple of times and then ran the tip of her tongue over her lips, and he got a whole lot harder. Her gaze flicked away from his and the colour on her cheeks deepened. 'Never mind. Forget I said that. I think I've had too much champagne.'

Luke's interest was piqued by the way she seemed to be avoiding his gaze. What secret did she have? Was it something even more cringe-worthy she'd made up about their 'relationship'? 'What were you going to tell me?'

She pressed her lips together for a moment and then swallowed. 'I've… I've never done it.' Then she did a shocked wide-eyed thing and slapped both of her hands over her mouth as if she regretted her words. 'Ohmygofh.' Her hands pressing against her mouth muffled the words. 'I can't believe I just told you that.'

Luke had to mentally rewind to their previous conversation about outdoor sex. 'You mean you've never had sex on the beach?'

She lowered her hands from her mouth and avoided his gaze. 'Anywhere.'

Luke frowned. 'You mean anywhere outdoors?'

She glanced either side of her to see if anyone was sitting near enough to overhear and, leaning forward again, whispered, 'I've never had sex.'

He looked at her blankly for a moment, trying to get his head around what he'd heard, or thought he'd heard. 'Let me get this straight... You're saying you've *never* slept with anyone? Is that what you're saying?'

She rolled her lips back inside her mouth and gave a single nod.

He leaned forward to make sure he wasn't mis-hearing her. 'You're a virgin?'

'Yup.'

Luke sat back as if someone had shoved him with the end of a telegraph pole. 'You're joking, right?'

Abby shook her head. 'Nope.'

She was a virgin? Abby Hart, the relationships and dating expert was a virgin? Why the hell hadn't she been intimate with anyone? She was twenty-three years old. Most modern girls lost their virginity well before then, unless they had religious reasons for being celibate.

'But why?' Luke asked, genuinely confused.

She shrugged and looked at the bowl of salted peanuts on the table between their knees. She took a peanut and popped it into her mouth and chewed and swallowed. She reached for another and another and did the same. 'Did you know it's virtually impossible to eat only one peanut? I've done extensive research on this. It literally cannot be done. Try it.'

Luke moved the peanuts out of her reach. 'Abby, look at me.'

She slowly brought her gaze back to his. Her tongue swept salt crumbs off her lips and he suppressed a groan. He couldn't stop thinking about her tongue doing that to him. 'I know it's a little weird, but I never really felt emotionally ready… I mean, before now.'

His heart slammed against his chest wall. 'Before…*now?*'

She tucked a loose strand of hair behind her ear and eyed the peanuts like a puppy looked at an out of reach treat. 'I sort of wanted to a couple of times, but I always put a stop to things out of fear I would make a fool of myself or…or something.' Her gaze met his. 'Anyway, I figure if we have sex anything like we dance then I think we'd be good together in bed.'

'That's another theory of yours, is it?'

'Yes, well, of course it's a theory because I haven't put it to the test yet, but that's the whole point of this conversation.' She gave him a smile that looked a little shaky around the edges. 'So, what do you say? Will you do it?'

Luke was having trouble getting his brain into gear. Other parts of his anatomy were well on their way, but his brain? No. Sleeping with Abby was the sort of trouble he could do without. Apart from the fact she was his kid sister's best friend, Abby was trouble, period. She wanted things he didn't want.

You want her.

He did. Badly. So badly he could feel the lust throbbing right here and now in his loins. Lust like he had never felt before. Not even as a horny hormonal teenager.

But it didn't mean he was going to have her.

He didn't get involved with virgins. Abby was the poster girl for the white knight and white wedding and white picket fence package. Everything she wrote in her column was about being in a secure and happy relationship.

Nothing he could offer her was anything near secure.

He didn't do commitment.

Luke leaned forward to take her hands in his to get her full attention. 'Listen to me, Abby—'

'We don't have to tell Ella,' she said. 'She doesn't even know I'm a virgin.'

He did a rapid blink. 'She doesn't? But I thought you two were best friends?'

She lowered her gaze to their joined hands. 'We are but we've only known each other for the last four years. There are some things you don't even tell your best friend.'

Luke could relate to that. There were things he

hadn't told a soul. Nor ever would. There was no point because talking about it would never take away his guilt. How could it? He gave her hands a little squeeze to get her to look at him again. 'Why didn't you feel you could tell her?'

A screen came down on her face and she pulled her hands away. 'Look, if you don't want to do it then let's leave it at that. I'll find someone else. Eventually.'

Luke's gut clenched. Which someone else? Some stranger she picked up in a bar? Or on a dating app? And why was she acting so closed-off all of a sudden? How well did his sister know Abby Hart? Did anyone really know her? Why had she got to the age of twenty-three without doing the deed? She was attractive and sexy and funny. She surely wouldn't have been short on offers?

Damn it, if he wasn't careful he'd be offering himself.

The waiter came to take their order and Luke was relieved when Abby ordered a simple cup of tea instead of the cocktail. A part of him was glad she wasn't having the sex-inspired cocktail but another part felt a twinge of disappointment he couldn't explain—didn't want to.

He waited until the waiter left to get their drinks before he spoke. 'I think you should think carefully before you pick up someone to sleep with either in a bar or online. There are some real creeps out there who might not be as nice as they seem on the surface.'

'Save your big brother lecture for your sister,'

Abby said and scooped up a handful of peanuts. 'I can take care of myself.'

Luke wished he felt more of a big brother to her than what he was feeling right now. He hadn't felt this degree of lust in years. It was as if it was taking over his body, his brain. His self-control. He couldn't stop thinking about her invitation. What exactly did she want from him?

Don't ask.

It was better not to know so he wasn't tempted beyond his endurance. Hell, he *was* already tempted beyond his endurance. His endurance better get back into shape quick smart or he was going to be in big trouble.

'You sure you don't want something to eat with your cup of tea?' Luke asked after the waiter delivered their drinks.

'I'm not hungry now.' She dusted the salt from her fingers. 'I've eaten too many peanuts.'

Luke had his own theory. Abby was exactly like eating a peanut. Making love to her once would never be enough.

Nowhere near enough.

Her phone made a pinging sound from inside her evening purse. She leaned forward to take it out and her gaze widened to the size of the saucer under her teacup. 'Oh, my God...'

'What's wrong? Is it bad news?'

She looked up from the phone and smiled. 'Guess what? You won the island holiday lucky door prize.'

CHAPTER FOUR

ABBY COULDN'T BELIEVE IT. Luke had won the prize *she* had been drooling over. How unfair was that? He could afford to pay for his own holiday. He could probably afford his own flipping island. Why had she sat in the unlucky seat instead of his winning one?

No doubt this was the universe's way of rubbing in her disappointment after Luke declined her offer of a fling. How could she not be feeling a little disappointed he'd rejected her offer? Had she made a mistake by telling him she was still a virgin? She still wasn't sure why she had told him—it had sort of slipped out in an unguarded moment. The combination of the magic of the evening in his company and all that champagne she'd drunk at the ball had loosened her tongue as if it was greased.

What had she been thinking?

She hadn't been thinking. She'd been feeling. Feeling things she had never felt before. Wicked things, like how exciting it would be to be Luke's lover. To enjoy more of those steaming-hot kisses and much more besides. Like having his hands caress every inch of her body, to have him possess her and take her to the heights of human pleasure—the sort of pleasure she had only ever experienced alone and never felt truly satisfied by.

Making love with Luke would be more than satisfying. How could it not be? His kiss had awakened a need in her body, a need that even now clamoured for attention. It was like he had set a primal beat thrumming in her flesh that only his touch could assuage.

Abby turned her phone around so Luke could see the message Felicity, her chief editor, had sent. 'See? Your seat number was the lucky one. They sent the message to me as they didn't have your contact details.'

He leaned forward to read the text. 'Can they redraw it?'

Abby frowned. 'You mean you don't want it?'

His expression was so difficult to read, hieroglyphics would have been easier. 'Clearly not as much as you did.'

Abby looked at the message again, vainly hoping they'd got the seat numbers wrong. But no, there it was in black and white. 'There's a time limit on the offer. You have to go within the next month.' She looked back at him to see him frowning at her. 'What?'

'Is it transferable?'

'Transferable?'

'Can I gift it to you instead of taking it myself?' Luke asked.

It was a nice gesture but how could she go alone?

Who went to a private island for a holiday on their own? How normal was that? It would make her feel even more of a pariah. Anyway, people from work would expect her to go with Luke and blog about the holiday and post pictures. It would seem odd if she didn't. And what would everyone say if she took a girlfriend instead of her fiancé? Luke had made it clear he wasn't interested in a fling so she was certain he wouldn't want to go with her.

She was facing the same dilemma all over again. If she went on the holiday on her own it would be like turning up to the ball on her own.

She would be outed as a big fat *abnormal* fraud.

Abby shoulders slumped. 'That's sweet of you, Luke, but even if it was transferable I won't be able to go.'

'Why not?'

She put the phone back in her purse with another sigh. 'I'd have to use it within the next month.'

'Why is that a problem?' Two horizontal pleats formed between his eyes. 'Can't you take some time off from work?'

'Taking leave isn't the problem,' Abby said. 'I have plenty of time owed me. It's taking someone with me that's the kicker.'

Something passed over his retinas like ripples on the surface of a lake. Then he frowned again, deeper this time. 'Stop that thought right there.'

Abby put on her most beguiling expression. 'What thought?'

'I'm not going with you on that damn holiday,

Abby. I told you the deal. Tonight for two hours—and we're over time as it is.'

'But it's only for a week,' she said. 'And I've always wanted to stay on a private island—any island, actually. I haven't had a proper holiday for ages and it would be so cool to stay in a luxury villa and—'

'Take a girlfriend,' he said. 'Take Ella.'

'Ella won't go during school term, she's way too dedicated a teacher to do something like that,' Abby said. 'And anyway, I can't take a friend. Everyone will be expecting me to go with you, especially since you won the prize. How will I explain it if you don't go with me?'

'Put that creative imagination of yours to use and think of something.' His sarcasm cut like a hunting knife.

'Are you only saying no because of what I told you?'

'I'm saying no because you and I getting it on is a crazy idea.'

'Why is it crazy?' Abby was trying to keep her ego from curling up in the foetal position and rocking in the corner. Was she so disgusting—so abnormal—that he couldn't bear the thought of making love to her? Had she misread his kiss and his touch?

His arousal?

'Abby…' His breath came out in a long whoosh as if he was trying to keep control and was only just managing to do so. 'I'm not denying I find you attractive. I do. But that doesn't mean I'm going to act on it.'

'But why not?' Abby was hoping she might win this argument as compensation for not winning the holiday. 'Why is my being a virgin such a big issue for you? I have to have sex some time. It might as well be with you—someone I know personally instead of a complete stranger.'

'You and me? That's crazy talk.' His voice had a gravelly intensity to it, as if he was digging deep to hold on to his resolve. 'You want marriage and all it entails. I'm not interested in going down that path, with you or anyone.'

'Is that because of your parents' divorce?' Abby said. 'Ella told me how awful it was.'

Luke's mouth thinned as if he had just eaten something bitter as bile. 'Yeah, well, it doesn't get much worse than when your dad suddenly announces he has a mistress and a baby on the way the night before your fifteenth birthday. But it's not because of that. I don't want the complication of a long-term relationship.'

'Where did you get the idea I'm asking for anything long-term from you?' Abby said. 'I just don't want to be a virgin any more. I feel embarrassed about it. Really embarrassed. That's why I haven't said anything to Ella. I feel like a freak for not having had sex yet.'

'I'm sorry but I can't help you with that.' He picked up his coffee and drained the contents, placing the cup back down with a definitive clunk.

Abby crossed her legs and folded her arms, her

lips pushed forward in a moue. 'Excuse me while I do some urgent CPR on my bludgeoned ego.'

A flicker of concern went through his gaze. 'It's not meant as an insult. Think about it. How would we explain it to Ella?'

'I think she would be thrilled you were finally taking a break from work.'

His features reminded her of a shuttered window. 'I run a global company. There isn't time for—'

'No wonder you get migraines,' Abby cut in. 'You push yourself too hard. I have a theory about people who are workaholics. They fill their days with work because they don't want to face what's missing in their life.'

'Yeah? Well, I have a little theory too.' His eyes were like laser pointers at a forensics lecture. 'People who pretend to be someone they're not do it because they're afraid people won't like the real version of them.' He rose from the chair and scooped up his jacket from where he'd left it. 'Come on. It's time to go.'

Abby remained silent on the drive back to her flat. Not that Luke addressed any comments to her. He was as taciturn as usual. What right did he have to analyse her? He didn't know squat about her. He didn't know how hard it had been for her growing up. How embarrassing it was to have grown up in foster homes, never knowing when you were going to be moved on to another family, another school, and trying to make friends with people who already had enough friends.

Her life had been one long struggle to fit in.

To be normal.

Luke might be a little screwed-up about his parents' divorce but at least his dad hadn't tried to kill someone. His mother hadn't slept with men for money while her little daughter was nearby. His mother hadn't then died of an overdose and left him in the deadlocked flat until someone found him the following day.

That was Abby's life story. The script she couldn't change, no matter how hard she tried. She was always being left to fend for herself.

What right did Luke have to criticise her? She liked who she was. She was a good person. She had friends, a job and a roof over her head.

But when Luke turned the corner into Abby's street she had to rethink the roof over her head bit. There were gas technician vans and two police cars with lights flashing and an ambulance outside her block of flats as well as a circle of nosy onlookers being ushered back by the police. 'Oh, my God, w-what's going on?' Her voice shook with shock.

Luke wound down his window when a police officer came over. 'What's happening?'

'There's been a major gas leak,' the officer said. 'The building's been evacuated until further notice. That section of the road is closed.' He pointed to a detour sign. 'You'll have to take a right over here.'

'But I live in that building!' Abby leaned across Luke to speak to the police officer.

'You can't go home until the problem's been

sorted,' the officer said so firmly it sounded like it had been underlined.

'How long will it take?' Abby asked.

The officer gave a shrug. 'There's been no announcement made as yet. You'll have to check the gas company's website for an update.'

'But I need to get some clothes and stuff.'

'Sorry. The area is cordoned off until further notice.'

Abby sat back in her seat with a slump of her shoulders. 'Great. Now I'm homeless. Go me.'

Luke wound up the window and drove to the detour. 'I'll book you into a hotel. You can stay there until things are back to normal.'

'I can't afford a hotel,' Abby said. 'And I absolutely refuse your offer to pay for it if that's what you're thinking.'

He pulled the car over to a parking bay further along the street they were on and turned to look at her. 'What about calling Ella? She might be able to put you up for a few days.'

Abby gnawed at her lip. 'I can't stay with her. It's too far to travel for work.'

'What about your family? Don't they live somewhere in London?'

Abby looked out of the window. It was at times like this that it hit her all over again how different her life was from everyone else's. She had no bolthole. No safe harbour to bunk down until a crisis was over.

She was totally alone.

'I can't stay with them. Their house is too small.'

Abby sensed rather than saw his frown. 'But I thought you told Ella they live in a big mansion in—?'

She sent him a sideways look. 'I lied, okay? They live in a council flat in Birmingham.'

'Why'd you lie about that?'

'Because…because they're not even my family…' Abby blew out a sigh. 'They're my foster family.'

There was a silence, broken by the rumbling of the car's idling engine.

'Your foster family?' Luke's voice was a mixture of concern and surprise. 'Where are your parents?'

She gave him a weary look. 'Believe me, you don't want to know.'

His frown was so deep his eyebrows made a black bridge over his eyes. 'How long did you live with a foster family?'

'The last one for six and a half years, and that was the longest I stayed anywhere,' Abby said. 'The ones before that, four and two years respectively, and the ones before that a few months at a time… I've been in the foster care system since I was five.' She didn't mention the six months she'd spent living with her father before she was taken into permanent care.

She preferred *not* to think about that.

Luke sat on an angle in his seat, looking at her as if he had never seen her before. But then in a way he hadn't. Abby had made sure no one in her present life knew anything of her past life. But now she had told him she felt a strange sense of lightness, as if something heavy she'd been carting around had slightly eased its load.

'Have you told Ella about this?' he asked.

Abby shook her head. 'I've thought about it… many times. But in the end I didn't see the point. It's not as if she's ever going to meet any of them.'

'She would be hurt to think you kept this from her.'

'I know… But you know how she worries over everyone. I didn't want her fussing over me, trying to compensate me for my crappy childhood. I just want to be like everyone else. Normal.'

'Whatever the hell that is.' His tone was wry.

There was another silence.

Luke started drumming his fingers on the steering wheel as if he was deep in thought, his gaze focused on the drizzle of rain sliding down the windscreen. He turned back to look at her at the same time he put the car back into gear. 'You can stay with me until your flat is ready.'

Abby looked at him in surprise. 'You wouldn't mind?'

Something at the back of his eyes indicated he minded a great deal but his voice was reassuring. 'It'll be fine. I'm hardly there in any case, other than to sleep.'

'It's very kind of you, Luke. Hopefully it'll only be for a couple of days. I promise not to disturb you too much.'

He gave a soft grunt as if the notion of her disturbing him was a given. 'But—just to be clear—you'll be sleeping in the spare room.'

* * *

A short time later, Luke unlocked his front door and followed Abby inside. Having her come and stay with him was a way to get to know her a bit more. To uncover more of the secrets she had kept about her background. Or so he told himself. He knew it was dangerous inviting her to sleep at his house. Sharing any personal space with her was dangerous. His house was large but it would need to be twice the size of Buckingham Palace for him to feel safe from the temptation she presented.

The stuff she'd told him about her background had shocked him. Why had she kept it a secret even from his sister, Ella? Who were Abby's biological parents and why had she been taken away from them so young? Had she been abused? Neglected? The thought of it was sickening. Was that why she was so determined to get to the ball tonight, to raise funds for underprivileged children? No wonder she couldn't bear not to go. He felt a heel now for making such an issue out of going with her.

Abby's past and the lengths she'd gone to keep it secret reminded him of the way he kept stuff to himself. He couldn't blame her for being a little hesitant to tell people things they might judge her for. People made judgements all the time on who your parents were, where you went to school, your accent, your income, the car you drove and where you lived. Even who your friends were.

Luke could understand now why she had been so taken with that luxury holiday. It was sad to think she had probably never been on a proper holiday with her parents. At least he had enjoyed some happy times with his family before his father dropped his bombshell the day before Luke's fifteenth birthday. Holidays after his parents' divorce had been pretty miserable. His mother would spend most of it crying or staring at couples walking hand in hand with a wistful look on her face. Ella, being nine years younger than him, had latched on to him in the absence of the father she'd adored and who no longer had any time for her, which meant Luke hadn't been free to do the things other teenagers his age did.

Luke closed the front door and looked at Abby's downcast expression. Her shoulders were slumped and some tendrils of her hair had fallen down around her heart-shaped face. It had been a big night for her, capped off by coming home to find her flat uninhabitable. A sudden wave of empathy swept through him and he had to stop himself from pulling her into a hug in case he was tempted to not let her go.

'Tired?' he said.

'Exhausted—but I can't help thinking what am I going to do about my clothes?'

Luke would be quite happy if she didn't wear any. Ever again. But that was a dangerous thought he shouldn't be allowing inside his head. 'We can sort that out tomorrow. Maybe they'll let you back in to fetch a few things even if they don't allow you to move back in.'

'What about Kimberley's clothes? Maybe I could—'

'You're a different size.'

A flicker of something passed through her gaze. 'Ella showed me a photo of her once. Kimberley was really beautiful and slim, wasn't she?'

'I didn't mean it that way.' Luke mentally rolled his eyes. What was it with women and their weight? Abby had a beautiful body—a gorgeous, luscious body he was having trouble keeping his hands off. Sure, her body wasn't stick-thin but he had always been annoyed by his ex's obsession with being reed-slim. It had been one of the reasons he'd ended their relationship. One of the many reasons. He couldn't face another meal out with Kimberley moving the food around her plate without eating a morsel. He'd found it cute how Abby had eaten his dessert tonight as well as her own.

'I only have a couple of her things anyway,' he said. 'I've been meaning to give them to her family but never seem to get around to doing it.'

Abby gave him a thoughtful look. 'Do you think it's because you're not ready to finally let go?'

Luke moved past her, undoing his bow tie as he went. 'I'll get you a toothbrush and show you which bathroom to use. Follow me.'

Abby followed him upstairs, where he opened the door to one of the spare rooms. It had a bathroom just down the corridor but she couldn't help noticing it was the furthest bedroom from his. It was another slap down to her ego. Did he think she'd come crawling into his bed during the night and try and seduce him? Clearly she had some work to do in the seduction stakes. A lot of work.

'Do you want something to sleep in? A shirt or something?' he asked.

'Don't worry. I can sleep in my… Actually, I'm not wearing any underwear. I didn't want any panty lines under my dress.'

Argh! Why did you tell him that?

His gaze flicked over her as if he were imagining her naked under her ball gown. But then he gave a rapid blink as if he was clearing his mental vision. 'Right, well, then. I'll leave you to get settled. Goodnight.'

Abby closed the door once he'd left and leant back against it with a sigh. Did he have to make it any clearer he didn't want her? Most men would have jumped at the chance for a bit of no-strings sex.

What was wrong with her?

Was she so hideous Luke couldn't stomach the thought of being intimate with her?

Or was it more about him than her? Was he still so hung up on the loss of his girlfriend he couldn't bear the thought of making love with someone else?

But he'd said he hadn't been in love with Kimberley. Why then would he remain celibate for so long?

Why was he still punishing himself?

CHAPTER FIVE

ABBY WAS SO tired she barely made it to the bed before her eyes closed. But during the night she woke with a start, wondering at first where she was. One of the legacies of her crazy childhood was a tendency to be a light sleeper. And all those years of sleeping at different foster homes made her jumpy whenever she woke in unfamiliar surroundings. She woke at the slightest sound, her heart racing, her legs feeling fizzy as the fight or flight reflex switched on.

She felt the mattress enveloping her like a hug and she breathed out a deep sigh of relaxation. At least it was the weekend tomorrow so she didn't have to front up to work still dressed in her ball gown.

But then she heard the sound again.

She sat upright, cocking her head to try and identify the noise. Was she imagining things? Had it been a dream?

Abby lay back down, remonstrating with herself for being so pathetic. Luke's house had top-notch security. Her fears of a masked intruder sneaking into her room were as likely as Luke himself coming in and saying he'd changed his mind about sleeping with her.

Not going to happen.

She closed her eyes again and tried to go back to sleep but her body felt twitchy and restless. And she was so thirsty her mouth felt like she'd been sucking on a stale gym sock. She threw off the covers and wrapped her naked body in the fluffy bath sheet towel she'd used earlier.

Abby tiptoed down the corridor but then she noticed a thin strip of light shining underneath Luke's bedroom door. She paused by the door, tilting her head against it to listen. She heard a groan and then the sound of something being knocked over and hitting the floor with a muted thud. 'Luke?' She rapped her knuckles gently against the door. 'Are you okay?'

There was the sound of a muttered curse and then footsteps padding across the carpet towards the door. The door opened and Luke looked down at her through squinted eyes, his features pinched and a ghastly shade of grey. He was wearing a pair of long grey cotton pyjama bottoms that were riding low on his trim hips. And, in spite of how unwell he looked, Abby had never seen anything so sexy.

'I'm fine.' His voice was in his gruff bear mode. 'Go back to bed.'

'You are so not fine,' Abby said, seeing the spasm of pain in his gaze. 'You look terrible.' How had she thought he was drunk six months ago? It was obvious he was unwell both then and now. She felt thoroughly ashamed. She had jumped to conclusions and misjudged him.

He leaned his forehead on the edge of the door as if he didn't have the strength to keep it upright on his neck. 'It's just a headache. It'll pass once the medication kicks in.'

Abby wasn't a sufferer of migraines but she'd read enough about them to know they could be crippling. Sufferers couldn't bear light or the slightest sound, and finding a quiet dark place until the migraine passed was usually the best solution. She took Luke's hand and ignoring his weak protest, led him back to the bed. 'Lie down,' she said in a soft voice. 'I'll get you a damp face cloth.'

Surprisingly, he did as she said and lay on his back on the bed, his long legs stretched out, his feet splayed outwards. Abby left him lying there while she went to his en suite bathroom and rinsed a face-cloth under the cold water tap. She squeezed it out and came back to him and, perching on the edge of the bed, laid the cool cloth gently across his clammy forehead. He made a low sound of appreciation but his eyes stayed closed.

After a while, Abby realised he was drifting in and out of sleep, his body twitching and his closed eyelids flickering as if trying to combat pulses of searing pain. She stayed beside him, reluctant to leave him until she was sure he was resting peace-fully.

Her eyes started to flicker, not from pain but tired-ness. She was still dressed in nothing but a bath sheet and, while it covered her adequately, she longed to slip between the sheets and close her heavy-as-dumb-bells eyelids.

Just for a few minutes.

Once the thought was inside her head it was impossible to resist the lure of the comfortable bed. It was a king-sized one, surely big enough for him not to even notice her there. Or maybe it was an emperor-sized one. Did such a thing exist? It was certainly big enough for a football team, plus some spectators.

He wouldn't even know she had been here.

She carefully peeled back the covers and slipped in, well away from Luke's sleeping form. Her head went down on the feather pillow and everything that was tense and tired inside her body began to slowly relax, as if she was a tightly wound ball of wool and someone was starting to unravel her.

Luke made a soft noise and rolled over to his side, facing away from her. Abby held her breath, her heart hammering until she was certain he was soundly asleep, and then she finally closed her eyes and the ball of wool in her tense muscles slowly and blissfully unwound the rest of the way...

Abby woke to find one of Luke's strong arms across her body and his legs brushing up against hers from behind. Slats of bright sunshine stole through the gap in the curtains, indicating it was well past dawn. What time was it? How long had she been sleeping?

Eek! She was sleeping in Luke's bed!

She suddenly realised she was naked and, even

though she moved a foot experimentally to search for it, there was no sign of the bath sheet she had wrapped around herself the night before.

How had she ended up naked in his bed with her limbs tangled with his?

Had they fooled around? Had she made a sleepy pass at him? Surely if they had made love she would remember it? She would most definitely remember it. She might occasionally forget to buy milk or bread or to pay the minimum payment on her credit card but she would never forget making love with Luke.

Abby closed her eyes again and tried to recall anything from the time after she'd slipped in beside him. Nope. Nothing but a blank…although there was that delicious little dream where someone had kissed the back of her shoulder. A prickly, stubbly sort of kiss followed by a lazy lion-like lick of the tongue that had sent a shiver over her skin.

Right now the back of her neck was being tickled by Luke's rhythmic breathing, and she could feel the rise and fall of his chest between her shoulder blades. She stayed perfectly still, not wanting to disturb him, mainly because she was sure he would spring away if he knew what he was doing.

How nice was this? How cosy and sexy and slightly wicked. She liked the feeling of being held, of being spooned as if she was treasured, special. She lay there quietly registering all the sensory hot spots on her body where it was touching his. The differences between their bodies, his hard-muscled frame and her softer one, made her feel womanly and feminine in a way she never had felt before. Even the scent of their bodies was different, but the thought of those intimate smells mingling with each other was strangely, excitingly arousing.

Luke made a sleepy sound that was part murmur, part groan and gathered her even closer, his face nuzzling into the side of her neck, the graze of his morning stubble making her skin shiver like a filly trying to shake off a fly.

Abby closed her eyes, feigning sleep, trying to get her breathing as rhythmic as his, which wasn't easy given her heart was stuttering like an old tractor engine.

One of his legs came over the top of hers and he pulled her against his morning erection. Abby had never felt anything so erotic and exciting in her life. Her girly bits clapped their hands in glee and her breasts tingled from the soft prickle of his masculine hair where his strong forearm was resting just below them.

'Mmm…' Luke's voice was a sexy hum against her neck that made her nerves fizz and flicker.

Abby was wondering how far she could push her luck when he suddenly jerked away from her with an expletive. 'What the freaking hell?'

She turned over to see him staring at her in abject horror. *So much for her self-esteem. Off to the corner with you to suck your thumb and rock.*

'What did I do?' Luke asked in a tone she hadn't heard him use before. It was strangled and hoarse as if he had swallowed a pineapple. 'Did we—? Tell me we—I didn't—'

'Nothing happened, Luke,' Abby said, letting out a frustrated sigh. 'I think we just somehow gravitated together while we were sleeping.'

He threw off the covers and stood up by the side of the bed, his expression dark and frowning. 'Why are you sleeping…*naked* in my bed?' His stress over the word 'naked' was like a skewer through the balloon-thin skin of her self-esteem.

Abby pulled the bed sheet over her body and sat up. 'I was worried about you. I didn't want to leave you until I was certain you were asleep. But somehow I—'

'Thought you'd whip off your clothes and jump into bed with me?' His tone couldn't have been more scathing than if he was reprimanding a rebellious teenager. 'For God's sake, Abby. I could have—' He scraped his hair back off his forehead, his mouth snapping closed as if he couldn't bear to say out loud what he could have done.

'I was wearing a towel—a big one—but it must have slipped off.' Abby glanced at the foot of the bed and saw a lump under the covers. 'There it is. See? It must have got pushed down there when we—'

'When we *what*?' His voice cracked like an egg on concrete. 'Damn it, Abby, I could have hurt you.'

'You didn't do anything I didn't want,' Abby said. 'I liked being spooned. No one's ever done that to me before. I liked the feel of your body behind mine. It was—'

'Stop.' He held his hand up as if he was stopping traffic. 'Stop it right there. This is not happening.'

'It is happening, Luke.' She clutched the sheet around her breasts to keep it secure. 'You want me.'

'It's a reflex,' he said. 'It happens to every man in the morning. It means nothing.'

Abby decided it was time to test a little theory of hers. She swung her legs off the bed and stood up and let the sheet slip so more than half of her breasts were showing. His eyes ran over her cleavage and the upper swell of her breasts, his throat bobbing up and down over a swallow.

'I'll just be going then.' She moved past him to leave the room but his hand reached for her and came down on her forearm. She stopped and turned to face him, her arm buzzing with sensation where his fingers lay. 'Am I really so unappealing to you?'

He frowned. 'God, no. I want you but—'

'Then why not have me?' Abby moved closer. 'I want you.'

His hand fell away from her arm. 'You want more than I can give.'

'I'm asking you to sleep with me, not marry me and have your babies. Why is having a fling with me so unthinkable to you?'

'I don't want what happens between us to get in the way of your relationship with my sister,' he said. 'Or for that matter for my relationship with her to be damaged.'

'It won't be,' Abby said. 'Ella knows you went to the ball with me. She's probably seen the photos of us last night all over social media. She'll be happy for you that you've moved on and she'll be happy for me as long as I'm happy.'

'And how long will your happiness last?' he said. 'I know how this works. The longer two people have sex together, especially if the sex is good, the harder it is to let go. Particularly for women.' Something about his expression made Abby wonder if there was more to that last comment than there appeared at face value.

'What if we were to set a time limit on it then?' Abby said. 'We could draw up an agreement so we both agree on the terms.'

His mouth opened and closed as if he were going to say something but changed his mind. Then he let out an exasperated sigh. 'Will you please get dressed? I can't think straight with you standing there like that.'

Abby stroked her hand down the length of his chest, stopping just above the waistline of his tented pyjama pants. 'Do you really want me to get dressed?' She channelled her inner sexy siren with a whisper-soft voice.

He swallowed again and took her by the hips almost roughly. 'No, damn it, I don't.' He brought his mouth down to hers in a blistering kiss that shot a bolt of lightning through her flesh.

She pressed closer, her barely covered breasts crushed against his chest, his sprinkling of hair intensifying the sensation like all her nerves were on the outside of her skin. The sheet was slipping but she didn't care. She was too caught up in the moment. The thrilling moment of feeling Luke's flaming lust. *For her.* His erection jutted against her as if his body was taking control, going on impulse not reason. His tongue came in search of hers in a smooth sexy slide and another hot spurt of longing darted through her.

He groaned against her mouth, a groan that sounded as if it had come from deep inside him. Somewhere deep and dark and closed off but now finally creaking open. His hands moved from grasping her hips to mould her to his body, one arm a steel band around her back, the other gliding up the back of her neck to splay his fingers into her hair, making her scalp tingle as if sherbet was trickling through her hair.

But just as suddenly as the kiss started, it was over.

Luke pulled back from her and released her, his expression a contorted mixture of lust and disgust. 'That should never have happened. I'm sorry.'

Abby wasn't one bit sorry. Her lips were buzzing, her inner core was fizzing and every cell in her body was clapping their hands for an encore. But there was only so much rejection her self-esteem could take. Was the disgust she'd seen on his face for him or for her?

She had offered herself and he had said an emphatic *no*. His body might want her but the rational part of him didn't.

Both parts of her wanted him. Every part.

Every throbbing, aching part.

Abby gathered the sheet more securely around her body, avoiding his gaze. 'I'm going to have a shower. I guess I'll see you downstairs.'

'I have to go in to work for most of today.'

'Do you usually work on Saturdays? No, don't answer that. I already know. Of course you do because you have no life other than work,' she said in a teasing tone, desperately wanting him to see how damaging it was to deny himself any longer.

'I took you to the ball as agreed, okay?'

'Which you enjoyed.' Abby eyeballed him. 'Didn't you? Go on, admit it, Luke. You had a good time.'

His gave an indifferent shrug. 'The ball was important to you so I took you. End of story.'

'What about that kiss?'

Something flickered over his features like a glitch in a film reel. 'What about it?'

'Actually, there were two,' Abby said. 'The one last night in the car and this one just now. You seemed to enjoy those too.'

He did something with his mouth, a sort of twitch and sideways movement of his lips, as if to remove the memory of those kisses. But his gaze was as shuttered as a beach house in winter. 'I'll be back around six this evening.' He took a couple of strides for the en suite bathroom.

'Aren't you forgetting something?'

He turned and frowned. 'What?'

She pointed to the sheet she was wrapped in. 'I don't have any clothes.'

'What about the dress you wore last night?'

Abby rolled her eyes like the ball bearings in a child's puzzle maze. 'Duh. That would be akin to the walk of shame to be seen out in public in a ball gown in broad daylight. Very morning-after-the-night before-ish. I hate feeling so...so vulnerable. So exposed.'

He seemed to be having some trouble getting his voice to work. He kept opening and closing his mouth as if he were having some sort of internal debate. 'Right, then I'll show you Kimberley's things and maybe there'll be something you could make do with until you go home.'

But when Luke pulled back the sliding door of his wall-to-wall wardrobe there were only a few female items hanging to one side, well away from his neatly ordered shirts and ties and crisply seamed trousers.

'Help yourself,' he said, stepping away as if even looking at the clothes was painful.

Abby worked her way through the half dozen or so coat hangers but it felt a little creepy to be handling a dead woman's clothes. They were beautifully made and she didn't have to peep at any of the labels to know they were all from high street designers. What must Luke think of *her* jumble sale assortment compared to these gorgeous things?

She sighed and stepped away from the wardrobe. 'I'm sorry but I don't think I can wear any of those.' She turned to face him. 'Why do you keep them there? Why not put them in another cupboard, or pack them up in a box or something?'

Luke slid the door back across, his expression as closed as the door. 'I haven't had time.'

'You've had five years, surely that's long enough to—?'

'I'll get to it eventually.'

'Like when you're moving into a retirement home?' Abby said. 'It's not healthy to keep that stuff for so long. It'll hold you back from—'

'I hardly think you're the one who should be lecturing me on how to live my life.'

Abby recognised his shot over the bow for what it was. A defence mechanism. She backed down. 'I'm sorry for prying, Luke. It's none of my business why you've still got those clothes there. And you're absolutely right. I have no right to be criticising you on how you live your life when mine is such a shambles.'

He drew in a breath and then let it out in a staggered stream. 'I keep them there to remind me.'

'Of…of her? Kimberley?'

He moved to the other side of the room to stare out of the window, his back turned towards her.

The silence was as intense as an unexpected music interval…the audience poised, waiting, waiting, waiting for the next note to be struck.

Abby wanted to prompt him, to encourage him to share whatever he was holding back, but she knew it would be better for him to be the one who broke the silence.

'Kimberley died the night I ended my relationship with her.'

Abby's heart gave a painful spasm and her breath caught on a thorn in her throat. 'Oh, no... I'm so sorry...'

He turned to face her, his expression a picture of regret and self-recrimination. 'I've thought about that night thousands of times, wondering if I'd said things differently, waited another day or two, a week even to call things off between us, if she would still be alive.'

Abby stared at him in shock. 'You feel...*responsible* for her death? But—'

His gaze was suddenly direct. 'Wouldn't you?'

She would. She very definitely would. Didn't she still blame herself for her mother's death? She still blamed herself for not being able to unlock the front door of the flat in time for help to be summoned for her mother, despite only being a child. 'Luke... I think it's perfectly understandable you would feel that way. I'm so sorry you've been carrying that guilt for so long. It must be unbearable.'

There was a slight relaxation of the muscles on his face as if her sympathetic words had eased some of his inner tension. 'It never goes away. The guilt of how I handled the breakup. How I handled the whole relationship, when it comes to that.'

'Were you ever happy with her?'

'Not particularly.' He let out a rusty-sounding sigh. 'We met when I was dealing with yet another one of my father's spectacular marriage failures and she was rebounding from a long-term relationship. With hindsight, I can see neither of us was in a good place. But we got on okay and we drifted into a relationship that probably looked more stable from the outside than it actually was. But I guess I wanted everyone to think that. I didn't want to be seen to be switching partners faster than I changed shirts.'

'But you were together for three years. No one would've accused you of being fickle if you'd ended things at two years or even at a year,' Abby said.

'I know, but there never seemed to be a good time,' he said. 'I almost called an end a couple of times earlier but then Kimberley got news of her ex getting married and then of him becoming a father. It was a tough time for her.'

'Oh, Luke, you sound like you were an amazing partner.'

'That's me.' His voice was both self-deprecating and bitter. 'A regular Mr Perfect.'

Abby decided it was time to share some of her own guilt, so he didn't have to feel so alone and isolated. Nothing was more isolating than guilt. She should know—she had graduated with Honours from the Academy of Guilt. 'I have a few regrets on how I handled things with my mother. I wish I'd been able to get help for her sooner but she died before I could.'

'I didn't realise she'd actually died. What happened?'

Abby let out a long breath, wondering if she was wise to reveal any more. People were funny about drugs and prostitution. Would it make him see her differently? Make her appear even more unacceptable to him than she already felt? But in the end she decided to tell him because of the trust he had shown in telling her about his guilt over his ex. 'Drug overdose. Heroin. She stuck the needle in her arm and died in the next room.'

Shock rippled over his features like wind through leaves. 'How old were you?'

'Five. But I remember it as if it were yesterday. I've always blamed myself. What if I was a difficult child? Too much for her to handle. What if I drove her to take that overdose?'

'You were five years old, for pity's sake,' he said. 'It was her responsibility to look after you. What could you have done anyway?'

'Maybe checked on her earlier...' Abby blinked, trying not to think of that day. Even though she had been so young, the image of coming out of her bedroom the next morning and seeing her mother lying on that threadbare-carpeted floor was imprinted on her brain.

Luke came over to her and placed his hands on her shoulders. 'Look at me, Abby.'

Abby slowly brought her gaze back to meet his. 'Even though I was young, I remember a lot about the night before she died. I was tired and hungry and my mother was agitated and insisted I go to bed earlier than usual. She would often lock me in there when... Anyway, she must have injected herself while sitting on the floor by her bed because that's where I found her the next morning. I would have got help earlier if I'd realised what she'd done. That's what I have to live with. I could have saved her but I didn't. The irony is my bedroom door wasn't even locked. I just

thought it was, like it had been so many times before. I went to bed and went to sleep, thinking it was
better than having a big showdown with her where
she would hit or slap me. When I came out in the
morning, I thought she was asleep but she wasn't…'

'Oh, Abby.' He gathered her close in a hug, his
arms warm and supportive and protective as if he
were holding that small, terrified child and comforting her.

That was all he said: *Oh, Abby*. But within those
two words was a message of understanding and empathy that she hadn't realised until now she had been
waiting all her life to hear.

After a few moments, he eased back to look at
her with a soft and tender look that made her heart
swell like bread dough. 'You mustn't blame yourself.'

'Ditto.'

He made a rueful movement of his lips and
stepped away from her again. 'Yeah, well, do as I
preach but not as I do. Hypocritical of me, I know,
but that's the way it is.' He walked into his en suite
bathroom and came out with his bathrobe. 'Here.
Put this on for now.'

Abby took the bathrobe from him and went into
the bathroom to put it on, expecting when she returned he would have left the bedroom, but he was
back over by the window, staring at the dappled sunlight coming through the leaves of the tree outside.

'Luke?' She took one step towards him and then
two and then four until she was standing with her
arms wrapped around his waist from behind.

His hands came down on hers and she braced herself for the moment he would push her away but it didn't come. Instead, he turned and his hands went to her hips, holding her close enough for their bodies to brush. 'This is crazy.' His eyes went to her mouth as if he had no control over his vision. 'Stupidly, irresponsibly crazy.' And then his mouth came down and covered hers.

CHAPTER SIX

A THRILL RUSHED through Abby at the undercurrent of passion in Luke's kiss. His lips moved with increasing urgency against hers, drawing from her a response that was equally passionate. Her body came alive at the determined thrust of his tongue, sending an electrifying shockwave of lust through her, making her bones shudder with the force of it like someone rattling a loosely assembled cage. His tongue found hers and played with such blatant eroticism her inner core contracted with greedy, hungry need.

This was why she hadn't made love to anyone before. No one had ever made her feel this level of arousal. No one had made her feel wanted for *her*. Not just for her body. He made her feel safe and understood. Desire shot through her with hot darting arrows, making her aware of every secret crevice of her body in a way she never had before.

The hollow ache between her legs became unbearable. A pulsing ache that begged for the possession of his hard body. An ache that could not be satisfied by anyone but him.

Luke walked her backwards to the bed, his mouth still fused to hers, the movement of his thighs brushing against hers making her insides quiver in feverish anticipation. No kiss she had ever experienced made her feel this level of excitement. Every one of her erogenous zones was eagerly awaiting his touch. She could feel herself swelling in her most secret place, the tingling sensation like a hollow spasm of part pain, part pleasure.

Luke laid her down on the bed and came down beside her, his hand going down her body in one slow stroke from her breast to her thigh and back again. When he came back to her breast he bent his mouth to it, circling his tongue around her tight nipple, stirring sensations in her that made her back arch like a cat enjoying a stroke.

He opened his mouth over her nipple, teasing it with his tongue, and then drawing on her with gentle little sucks that made her mouth drop open on a gasp of pleasure. He moved to the other breast, subjecting it to the same exquisite torture, sending riotous pulses of delight through her body.

'You're beautiful,' he said against her lips. 'Every inch of you is so damn beautiful.'

Abby wasn't used to receiving compliments and wasn't sure if he was just saying it to make her feel more comfortable with him. But she already felt amazingly comfortable with him. Why else had she stood half naked before him without a qualm? 'Careful,' she said with a self-effacing smile. 'You'll give me a big head.'

'That's not the only thing that's getting big around here.' His crooked smile made his blue eyes glint.

'I can feel it.' Abby reached for him, taking him carefully in her hand so she could explore the shape and heft of him. He was beading at the tip, the signal of high arousal, and it thrilled her to think she had done that to him.

He groaned and then let out a swift breath and eased her hand away, holding it captive in his. 'I don't want to rush this. To rush you.'

Abby was so aroused she couldn't imagine needing further stimulation. But when he brought his mouth back to her breasts her desire went up another notch, until she was breathing heavily as his lips and tongue and the gentle pressure of his teeth made her body sing like an opera diva.

He moved from her breasts to press soft just-touching kisses all the way down to her belly. He dipped the tip of his tongue into the shallow whirl of her bellybutton, setting off a racing fire of need further down her body.

'I want to taste you.' His voice had that honey and gravel combo thing going on. She hadn't realised it was possible to be so turned on by a man's voice.

Abby had read about this type of pleasuring but had never thought it was for her. She thought she'd be too shy or embarrassed at being so exposed to a lover. But, strangely, she felt none of that. All she felt was a sense of rightness, that this was what she wanted and needed, and somehow he did too.

He kissed her mound, allowing her time to get

used to him being so close to the most intimate part of her body. Then he gently opened her with a stroke of his tongue, the caress making her shiver from head to foot with a cascading shower of powerful sensations. He went deeper, his lips and tongue working on the swollen nub of her clitoris, sending lightning strikes of pleasure through her.

The sudden orgasm swept through her like a hurricane through a house of cards, spinning her senses, flipping and rolling and tossing them until her entire body was shaking with it. Ripples of aftershock pulsed through her flesh, leaving her breathless until every muscle relaxed as if her skeleton had been turned to liquid. 'That was…amazing isn't the right word,' Abby's voice came out as a whisper. 'Mind-blowing. Unbelievable. Magical. Wow. Wow. Wow.'

He came back to kiss her mouth, the musky taste of her on his lips exciting her in a way she would never have thought possible. It added another layer of intimacy that made her feel as if something had shifted between them.

Something unique and special that could not be undone.

Luke caressed her breasts again, lingering over each one as if he couldn't get enough of her.

'Aren't you going to—?' Abby said, feeling the hard ridge of his arousal against her thigh.

'I'm trying to slow down.'

'You don't need to. I'm ready.' She was more than ready. Her body was crying out for the physical connection that would finally join her with him in the most intimate embrace known to humankind.

He framed her face with his hands, his gaze searching. 'Are you sure about this. Really sure?'

Abby had never felt surer about anything. 'Make love to me, Luke. Please?'

He took in an uneven breath, his gaze dipping to her mouth, his thumb pad stroking along her lower lip. 'You have such a kissable mouth. I've thought about kissing it for a long time.'

A rush of pleasure ran through her. 'How long?'

'Remember when Ella first introduced us?'

'Yes.' Abby remembered it well. It had been four years ago when she was nineteen and still trying to find her feet. She had not long started a journalism degree because she couldn't decide what course to take and she'd met Ella while she had been working part-time in a bookshop to cover her study expenses. They'd struck up a conversation about the books they liked and within no time at all they were catching up for coffee and chatting as if they'd been friends since childhood. Not that Abby had told Ella the truth about her childhood. She wanted to maintain the image of herself she always projected, as someone who didn't have baggage or hang-ups or embarrassing relatives she would never have chosen if she'd had a choice. 'Ella brought me around to your house to meet you.'

'I wasn't in the mood for visitors.'

'I could tell that,' Abby said. 'I didn't like you at all. I thought you were standoffish and gruff.'

He stroked her bottom lip again, his gaze still trained on her mouth. 'I didn't always use to be like that... Well, not that bad, anyway. But when you smiled at me that day it made me feel about a thousand years old.'

She stroked her hand down his chest to his erection. 'You don't feel that old to me.'

He gave her a twisted smile. 'You're still way too young for me.'

'I'm only nine years younger and I'm mature for my age, or at least I like to think so.' Abby considered herself mature because for as long as she could remember she had been thrown on the mercy of her own resources. Nothing made you grow up faster than having no reliable adults around to depend on.

He kissed the end of her nose. 'You have an air of youthfulness about you. Like you believe life is meant to be fun and happy and you'll do anything you can to make it that way.'

'It's called positivity,' Abby said. 'Looking forward not back.'

His eyes did that searching thing again as if he was looking for something in her gaze. 'Abby...' He touched her face with a brush of a finger. 'You need to understand this is only for now. I can't promise more than that and even a short time frame is probably risking things.'

Abby wasn't sure what exactly he thought he was risking. Liking her too much? Enjoying being with her? Maybe even falling in love with her? But there was her risk assessment to consider. What if *she* fell in love with him? Was she flirting with danger by entering into a short-term affair that had no possibility of being for ever?

'We can set a date if you want,' Abby said, repeating her offer from earlier. 'We can programme it into our phones to give us a reminder. *Ping.*' She snapped her fingers. 'End of fling.'

A flicker of something passed through his gaze. 'You're joking, right?'

'I'm not joking,' Abby said. 'This is clearly creating a bit of stress for you so why not both of us agree on a breakup date?'

'It sounds a little…clinical.'

'It's more practical rather than clinical,' Abby said. 'We agree on a date and stick to it. Seriously, I should write a column about this. I could call it the no-nonsense guide to having a fling, or a fling without tears.'

His expression was shadowed by a frown and he started to ease away from her. 'Maybe this isn't such a great idea.'

Abby laid her hand on his arm. 'So you get to pleasure me but I don't get to pleasure you? How is that fair?'

He placed his hand over hers, his mouth set in a firm line. 'All right. One week from today, okay?'

One week? Abby had been hoping for two, possibly three. Months, not weeks. Years would have been even better. 'Agreed.'

He held her gaze for a long beat before he bent

his mouth to hers, kissing her with such passion her desire for him hammered and hummed in her blood.

He lifted his mouth and reached for a condom in the bedside drawer, but she found it incredibly touching he had to rustle around in there for a while before he located one. His long drought between lovers made her feel even more special. This was a big step for her and it was a big step for him. They'd made a commitment to have a one-week fling. It was as if they were equals, two people on a search for connection on a purely physical level.

He looked at the small foil packet a little doubtfully. 'I hope this isn't past its use-by date. Are you taking any contraception?'

'I take the Pill so I can regulate my cycle,' Abby said. 'I hate getting my period at inconvenient times. The Pill means I can plan it to fit in with my lifestyle.'

He unwrapped the condom and applied it to himself and then came back to settle between her legs, one of his positioned over hers, his weight propped up on his arms. 'Still sure you want to do this? It's not too late to stop.'

Abby took his face in her hands and eyeballed him. 'What part of *I want you* do you not understand?'

He gave her another crooked smile. 'Okay. I get it. You want me, but I don't think you want me half as much as I want you.'

'Try me and see.' She moved against him, offering herself to him, going on instinct as if her body knew what to do and when to do it and all she had to do was go with it.

He parted her with his fingers, and then he gently inserted one finger. Once he was sure she had accepted him without flinching, he inserted two fingers, moving them ever so carefully against her flesh as if she were something infinitely precious. 'Still okay?'

'Wonderfully okay,' Abby said on a shuddering sigh.

He moved over her, positioning himself so he could enter her, taking his time so she could get used to her body wrapping around him. She gasped with pleasure but he mistook it for pain and pulled away, his expression taut with concern. 'Did I hurt you?'

'No, I was just taken by surprise by how good it feels, how good *you* feel,' Abby said.

He moved back to her folds, slowing entering her inch by inch until she accepted him fully. Then he began moving, slow and gentle thrusts that sent waves of delight through her body. It wasn't as direct and intense as when he'd pleasured her with his mouth, but the rhythmic movement of him stirred a pool of longing into a whirlpool. She was almost there but not quite, her body straining to reach the summit but unable to find the point of no return.

Luke reached down between their bodies and caressed her with his fingers in a flickering movement that triggered an explosion in her intimate flesh. It radiated out in rippling waves that flowed through her body until she was half crying, half gasping from the ferocious impact of it.

He waited until she was done before he gave a series of hard, quick thrusts as if he was unable to control the tempo now he had finally allowed himself to let go.

And then there was silence—a silence unlike any Abby had experienced before. Peace descended on her like the feathery down of a luxury quilt, covering her body in a mantle of exquisite relaxation…

Luke couldn't tear his eyes away from Abby, sleeping next to him. Her body was once more entangled with his; one arm flopped limply over his waist, the other hand resting on the *thud-pitty-thud* of his heart. He was in two minds about berating himself for what had just happened. What he had allowed to happen. But he couldn't quite bring himself to fully regret making love to her. The experience of holding her in his arms, possessing her and leading her to her first orgasm with a partner was beyond anything he had experienced with any other lover.

Was that why it had been so different, because Abby had been a virgin? He wasn't sure, although it had definitely given their encounter a special context that made him feel privileged and honoured that she had trusted him to be her first lover. He knew one thing for certain; he would never forget the experience.

But this was as far as it could go.

As far as he would allow it to go. A brief fling and

then it would be time for her to move on and find her Mr Perfect—if such a man existed.

Luke had been so shocked to wake up with her spooned against him. Deeply shocked in his mind and yet his body had hijacked reason, sabotaged his resolve and made a mockery of his determination to keep away from her.

God only knew what his sister would make of his week-long fling with Abby. Ella had been at him for years—at least four years—to get back out there in the dating pool. Unbeknown to his family, he had gone on a couple of lukewarm dates over the last couple of years. But he didn't take them any further because he was unable to invest in a relationship where he would be responsible—accountable—for someone else's emotions.

He'd seen first-hand the emotional devastation of his mother when his father left. It had been gut-wrenching to witness and his sense of utter powerlessness had always stayed with him. Luke had worried for years she would never recover. He had an overwhelming sense of responsibility to keep the rest of the family together. To keep his mother in good spirits even though it had been a difficult battle to this day. She had never re-partnered and in a way he couldn't blame her. He too had been blindsided by his father's abandonment of the wife and family he had claimed so volubly and so publicly to love.

Abby nestled closer like a little cub. Luke began stroking her wavy chestnut hair in rhythmic strokes, breathing in the scent of her, of their lovemaking. Wondering again if he was a fool to have given in to the temptation of taking their relationship to this intense level of intimacy even if it was only for a week. He had always kept his distance from her— from anyone when it came to that. Whenever Ella had visited him with her in tow he had been formal and yes, a little gruff on occasion, but the way Abby's big brown eyes lit up when she smiled had done something to him—something he'd found immensely threatening.

She was open and he was closed. She was warm and he was cold. She was fresh and funny and optimistic and he was stale and moribund and staunchly, immovably pessimistic.

But somehow Abby had melted his resolve like a blowtorch blasted at butter. His body was drawn to her by an irresistible force, like lightning was drawn to metal, and his pleasure had been just as earth-shattering. Had he ever felt satisfaction like it? Or had it been too long between drinks to tell with any certainty? It was like making love for the first time and yet so much better, because his first time had been rushed and clumsy and over all too soon.

This time, his pleasure had lasted for ages inside his body. He could still feel the slight hum of it lingering in his flesh like the rumble of distant thunder.

Abby moved against him again, stirring his blood into a deep throb of longing. She opened her eyes and smiled at him. 'Hey, did that just happen or am I dreaming?'

Luke brushed an imaginary hair away from her face, keeping his own expression a little less open, stilling each facial muscle as if he was folding down the four top sections of a box. 'It happened.'

A frown flickered across her brow. 'You already regret it, don't you?'

He traced a fingertip over her bottom lip. 'I'm concerned you're going to think this is more than what it is.'

'You mean more than just sex?'

'A week-long fling is a week-long fling, it's not for ever,' Luke said, carefully gauging her reaction to his words.

She gave a soft laugh. 'Who are you really worried about losing perspective on our one-week fling? Me or you?'

That was exactly what he was worried about. He had already blurred the boundaries he had maintained for so long. Crossed a line he couldn't uncross. He had given in to the desire he had long suppressed or ignored or been too busy to allow to become a priority.

He could not undo their lovemaking.

It would always be something they had shared. Something unique and special, something she would never experience with anyone else and, he suspected, nor would he. The uniqueness of it encased it in an impermeable membrane of memory.

'Cute theory, but no,' he said. 'I know what I'm capable of and commitment is not something I'm interested in.'

'But we're going to be exclusive, right? While we're together this week?'

Luke was faintly annoyed she felt the need to ask. Did she think he was the type of man like his father? That it was a case of like father like son? He lived by very different principles from his father, who had worked his way through several partners since his initial affair. 'Of course we'll be exclusive. You have my word on that.'

'You have mine too,' Abby said with a smile. 'I think it's cowardly to cheat on someone. Why not be honest and say you're not happy with how the relationship is going? It seems only fair, in my opinion.'

'I couldn't agree more,' Luke said. 'When my father cheated on my mother she had no idea. No inkling anything was wrong. Only the month before, he had taken her to a nice restaurant to celebrate their seventeenth anniversary. He'd even bought her flowers the week before.'

Abby's frowning expression showed her disgust at his father's behaviour. 'That's nothing short of cruel. What type of man is he? A sadist?'

'Yeah, well, I don't have too much to do with him these days,' he said. 'I can't bear listening to him bragging about his latest conquest, especially when I know another couple of his exes took it badly when he dumped them.'

She stroked his cheek, her soft hand catching on his stubble, her eyes luminous. 'You're a nice man, Luke Shelverton. A decent man with standards that put other men like your father and mine to shame.'

Luke's ears pricked up at the mention of her father. What she'd told him about her mother had shocked him to the core. She had seemed reluctant to discuss either of her parents with him the day before. He couldn't help feeling touched she had let him in on such a painful secret. 'He's alive then? Do you ever see him?'

She looked down at his chest, where her fingertip was following the line of his right collarbone. It was as if she was mentally preparing herself—each stroke and glide of her finger against his collarbone was somehow building up her courage. 'I haven't seen him since I was five and a half.' Her gaze climbed back up to his. 'Family Services thought it would be good for me to have a connection with him after my mother died, even though they'd split up and he hadn't had anything to do with me for months.'

Five and a half years old. Luke couldn't get his head around it. What despair and fear had she felt to see her mother lying lifeless on the floor. And how terrifying to be handed to the father who hadn't been there for her for months on end.

His gut churned with anguish for her. For the senseless suffering she had endured because of the incompetent adults who should have been loving and protecting her.

Luke gently cradled her cheek, his eyes meshing with hers. 'I'm so sorry you went through that. I can't imagine how terrified you must have been.'

She gave him a flickering smile that seemed sad around the edges. 'I don't think about it much now.

It was a long time ago and in some ways it feels like it happened to someone else, not me.'

'Is that why you've not told Ella? Because you've rewritten your history to make it less painful?'

'Less painful and less shameful,' she said. 'My father is in jail and has been since I was six. He almost killed someone on a drug deal that went sour. He was the one who got my mother on heroin, I'm sure of it. It came out much later he was the leader of a drug gang. But back then he made everyone think she was the one with the problem. He painted himself as the poor pushed-aside father of his child. And the authorities fell for it, for a time.'

'Did you feel any connection with him when you went to live with him?'

Abby shook her head. 'I hated him. He was bad-tempered and treated the new woman he was with like a slave. And he made her do most of the looking after of me, which of course she resented and took out on me. He only wanted me because he thought it would whitewash his reputation with the social worker who used to do visits. I felt uncomfortable with him and would always end up in floods of tears when the social worker came. He made it sound to the social worker that I was crying because I was upset at the thought of being taken away from him and put into permanent care. I was too frightened to tell them the truth because I was worried they mightn't believe me over my father. He could be so convincing. And then, if they didn't believe me and left me with him after I'd said something, I knew he would punish me for speaking out. I felt so powerless.'

Luke pulled her close as if he could somehow make up for the shocking way she had been treated. He might have some issues with his own father, but at least he had never been passed like a parcel between foster carers. He had always had his mother and felt secure in her love. He had his sister, who always did her best to make their fragmented family work as well as it possibly could.

But Abby had suffered for most, if not all, of her childhood. How could she have turned out to be such an open and warm and positive person? She deserved much better than she had received. Could he in some small way make up for all the heartache and despair she'd endured?

The thought started as a seed in his mind and then started to spread its roots, tunnelling its way into every closed-off corner of his brain like a rampant vine. He could take her on the island holiday. He could spoil her and treat her like a princess for a week. He hadn't had a holiday in ages and it would be a good way of getting to know her even better. Besides, her flat was still uninhabitable and was likely to be for a few more days. This was a perfect solution.

A faint alarm bell sounded in the back of his mind, but he disregarded it. It was only for a week and they had both agreed on that. He wasn't promising a future with her.

He couldn't promise a future with anyone.

Luke picked up one of her wayward curls and wound it round his finger, holding her warm toffee-brown gaze. 'It would be a shame to forfeit that holiday I won.'

A light came on in her eyes. 'Are you saying what I think you're saying?'

He gave her a slow smile. 'I quite fancy a week in the sun. I'll have to juggle a few things in my diary but—'

'Oh, Luke, thank you, thank you, thank you.' She pressed her mouth to his in a series of kisses, making his lips swell and tingle for more. 'It'll be so much fun. A whole island to ourselves.'

'How soon can you pack?'

Her face suddenly fell. 'But what about my flat? I can't get to my clothes and I don't feel comfortable wearing—'

'No problem,' Luke said. 'I'll go and buy you something you can wear so we can go and get the rest. My treat.'

Her teeth worried her bottom lip and her eyes didn't quite meet his. 'I'm not sure I'm comfortable with you buying me stuff.'

He tipped up her chin so she met his gaze. 'Listen to me. I want to spoil you. I'll probably enjoy it more than you, so why not allow me this little bit of pleasure in my boring and stuffy workaholic life?'

Her eyes had a spark of wickedness. 'I'm all for giving you pleasure.' She wriggled closer and linked her arms around his neck, bringing her mouth within touching distance of his.

Luke closed the tiny gap between their mouths, his senses on fire at the way her lips moulded themselves to his. He stroked for entry and she opened to him on a sigh that made the base of his spine grow warm. Warmth that spread its way through the rest of his body, sending his blood on a fevered flood to his groin.

He caressed her breast, cupping it and then stroking his thumb over its peaking nipple. He took his mouth off hers to attend to her breast, licking around her areola and gently grazing the nub of her nipple with his teeth. She made a breathless sound of appreciation and moved restlessly against him, searching for him with her hand beneath the fabric of his sleepwear and finding him fully erect. The feel of her fingers wrapping around him made him even harder, the need pulsing through him in electrifying waves.

She kissed her way from his neck in hot little presses of her lips against his skin, all the way down past his abs.

Luke sucked in a breath and placed a hand on her shoulder. 'You don't have to do that—'

Abby glanced up at him with doubt flickering in her eyes. 'But you did it to me. Don't you want me to—?'

'Abby.' He cradled her cheek in his hand. 'I don't want you to do things with me because you think you have to. I want you to be comfortable with every part of what we do together.'

'But I am comfortable. I'm more comfortable with

you than anyone I've ever met. Talking about my childhood... Well, I've only ever told you that stuff. That's how comfortable I feel with you.'

Luke was touched she felt that way. Deeply touched. And so turned-on he was holding on to his self-control like someone trying to control a wild stallion with a silken thread. His thumb stroked the curve of her cheek, holding her shining earnest gaze. 'Are you sure you want to do this?'

She reached for him again, caressing him just the way he liked it as if she had some secret way of reading his body. 'I want to make you feel the way I did when you did it to me.'

A part of Luke insisted he stop right there, but another part—the caged part that was primitive and primal—wanted her mouth. Wanted her tongue. Wanted. Wanted. Wanted until he was throbbing with it.

Abby didn't wait for him to talk her out of it even if that sensible and civilised part of him had been on active duty. She reached across him for a condom and unpeeled it from its packet. She wriggled down and pushed away his sleepwear but, before she put on the condom, she breathed her warm breath over his engorged length. It was like being caressed by the breeze of a moth's wing and intensely, spine-tinglingly arousing.

'Give me the condom.' Was that his voice? That husky croak that sounded as if it came from the middle of a frog pond.

She held it just out of reach. 'I can do it. I did this

once in Sex Ed. But I have to tell you, you don't look anything like a courgette.'

'Good to know.'

Once the condom was on, she brought her tongue to him in soft little licks like a kitten lapping milk, making him shudder with fizzing pleasure that spiralled through his body. She opened her mouth over him, moving up and down his shaft with varying degrees of suction, and he groaned and groaned and fought to stay in control, wanting to prolong the thrill of watching her pleasure him.

Fight it or fly? Fight it or fly?

The mental chant was in time with his pounding blood.

And then he flew...

CHAPTER SEVEN

ABBY HAD NEVER seen anything so erotic as Luke totally at her mercy. His guttural groans and whole body shudders made her feel a wave of deep pleasure as if his orgasm was somehow tuned to a sensitive radar in her body. Triggering little electric shocks deep in her core at the realisation of her sensual power as a woman.

Luke was lying on his back, his breathing not quite back to normal, and he took her hand and brought it to his mouth, kissing each fingertip in turn, his eyes holding hers. 'That must have been quite some Sex Ed class,' he said with a wry smile.

Abby laughed and lay across his body, toying with the short and fine whorls of his dark brown hair at the sides of his neck. 'I like seeing you smile.' She traced her finger around his mouth, her skin catching on his stubble like silk on an emery board. 'You're really funny behind that stern façade you put up.'

He gave her a mock frown and rolled her on to her back and pinned her with his weight, his dark blue eyes gleaming. 'Stern? Is that how you see me?'

Abby shivered with delight at the hard press of his erection against her thigh, so close to where she ached and pulsed with longing. She traced each of his ink-black eyebrows, smoothing out the semi-permanent frown line that was etched into his forehead. 'I like it when you smile instead of frown. It makes you more approachable.'

He smiled and leaned across to get another condom. 'I am going to have to restock soon or we're going to have a problem.'

The only problem Abby could see was that she was going to get too emotionally involved in this fling. It was a risk she had been prepared to take, but had it been foolish to think she could keep her emotions separate? Making love with Luke was not a simple matter of two bodies joining for mutual release. There was so much more to it. A bond of intimacy developed and grew with each and every encounter.

She could *feel* it happening.

Each kiss, each stroke, each caress bonded her to him in a way she could never bond with anyone else. He was her first lover. The man who had taught her about receiving and giving pleasure. The man who responded to her as if her touch and her touch alone could unlock the primal desires he had suppressed for so long.

Luke leaned on one elbow to apply the condom, giving Abby a perfect opportunity to stroke her hand down his chest and sexily toned abdomen. He eased her back down and brought his mouth to each of her breasts, tending to them with licks and strokes and grazes of his gentle teeth that made every cell of her body hum with delight.

Abby was so ready, so full of need she couldn't stop a pleading whimper from escaping. 'You're taking too long. I want you *now*.'

He gently parted her folds and entered her with a groan that seemed to come from deep inside him. Abby welcomed him into her body, wrapping her legs around his hips so he could deepen his thrusts. The smooth, slick glide of his body within hers set off sparks in her nerves that swelled and sensitised her clitoris. But it wasn't quite enough friction to trigger the orgasm she could feel building like a rampaging storm in her female flesh.

Luke reached down between their joined bodies, caressing her with an expert touch like a maestro handling a Stradivarius. She soared off into the stratosphere, her mind partially blanking out as the ripples and shudders ricocheted through her body.

Abby floated back to reality just as he started to increase his pace, the faster, deeper thrusts triggering his own release. He gave a choked-off sound and then emptied in a series of pumps, finally collapsing over her, his head buried next to her neck.

She played with his hair in little lifts and tugs of the thick dark brown strands, listening to his breathing steadying, the rise and fall of his chest against hers making her feel closer to him than she had felt to anyone.

Luke turned his head to nibble at the sensitive

area below her ear, making her shiver all over. 'You're amazing. You know that, don't you?'

Abby turned her head so she was eye to eye with him, his breath mingling with hers. 'I was just thinking the same, but about you. My theory was right then.'

He sent his finger on a slow journey around her mouth. 'Which theory was that?'

'The dancing one,' Abby said. 'If a couple are good on the dance floor together, then they're likely to be good in bed together. We've just proven it.'

His smile did strange things to her insides, making them gooey and soft like melted marshmallows. 'Do you have any more theories you want to run past my sceptical scientific brain?'

Abby squinted her gaze. 'You think I'm nuts, don't you?'

He captured her mouth and pressed a hot, hard kiss to her lips. 'I think you're beautiful and funny and I'm going to make love to you all over again. That is, unless you'd rather dance?'

Abby pulled his head back down to hers. 'We can dance later.'

Later that morning, Abby had a shower and waited for Luke to come back with a casual outfit for her to wear and some underwear. It gave her a little thrill to think of him choosing knickers and a bra for her. Handling those intimate items with his clever hands, knowing he would be the one to take them off her when they next made love.

Abby wandered through Luke's house, a part of her feeling guilty at snooping, but the other part wanted to know everything about him. He was like a really gripping book she'd started reading and couldn't put down. She'd got him to open up about his girlfriend Kimberley…although she felt a little guilty her back story had overtaken the telling of his. Had that been deliberate on his part? Using her little trick by taking the searchlight off his life and shining it on hers?

Abby didn't regret telling him about her background. She'd thought she would but somehow she didn't. Luke was a safe person to tell. There hadn't been too many safe people in her life. But he was trustworthy and dependable, exactly like Ella, which meant Abby would have to tell her at some stage too.

But then, as if summoned by the thought of her friend, Abby's phone rang and she picked it up and saw it was Ella. 'Hi, I was meaning to call—'

'Is it true?' Ella said, excitement ringing in her voice. 'Luke actually went with you to the ball?'

'Yes, I finally got him to—'

'It was a rhetorical question, silly.' Ella laughed. 'I've seen the pictures of you from last night. They're all over Twitter. Don't you make quite the stunning couple?'

Abby wasn't sure she was ready to tell her friend *everything* about her and Luke. Like how her body was still humming from his lovemaking like a struck tuning fork. 'It was a fun night. Your brother is a surprisingly good dancer.'

'Oh. My. God.' Ella gasped. 'You got him to dance? Really?'

'Yes. We had heaps of fun and we even went out and had supper afterwards.'

'Are you serious?' Ella's voice was rich with delight. 'What else did you two get up to?'

Abby retreated into a protective silence. How could she just blurt out what had happened between her and Luke, even if it was to her best friend?

'Oh. My. God,' Ella said when the silence went on too long. 'Don't tell me you actually *slept* with my brother?'

'We—ell…'

'But that's marvellous!' Ella's voice wasn't far off a squeal. 'He hasn't slept with anyone since Kimberley. I'm sure of it. He hasn't even been on a date that I'm aware of. Well done, you.'

'You mean you…you don't mind?'

'Why should I mind? It would be a dream come true if you and he—'

'Don't get too excited.' A strange little pang struck Abby in the belly. 'We're just having a one-week fling.'

'Fling, *schming*,' Ella said. 'You're not the type of girl to have a fling. If you were, you would've had one by now. You certainly haven't had one since I've known you, otherwise I would have known about it. Are you sure you're doing the right thing? I mean it's great Luke's getting back out there, but a week isn't long enough for either of you to—'

'Ella…there's a lot of stuff you don't know about me…'

'You mean stuff about your childhood?'

Abby's heart missed a beat. 'What do you know about my childhood?'

'Just that you don't like talking about your family. You always change the subject or get me talking about myself instead. I see you doing it with other people too. You shift the focus off you.'

'Why haven't you said anything about it until now?'

'Because I figured you'd tell me when you were ready,' Ella said. 'You're not close to your family, are you?'

'That's because they're not my family.' Abby filled her friend in on most of what she'd told Luke. And, just like when she'd told him, a little more weight went off the burden she'd been carrying for so long.

'I wish you'd told me earlier,' Ella said. 'Poor you—having such a horrible childhood. But I can see why it would have been difficult for you to talk about, even to me. It's kind of nice you told Luke first, though. He's always been a good listener.'

'He's good at lots of things.'

'Speaking of which, fling or no fling, I think it's brilliant you and he are getting it on. It's what you both need.'

'Are you sure you don't mind?'

'Why should I?'

'But what if it makes things uncomfortable in the future?' Abby said. 'Like when I'm with you and

Luke is present once this week is over. It could be awkward for everyone.'

Most especially me.

'Think of it this way,' Ella said. 'Your fling with Luke will be a positive thing, no matter how it works out. It will help him move on.' There was a tiny pause. 'But you have to be careful, you know. Don't get your hopes up in case—'

'You don't have to worry about me,' Abby cut in with far more confidence than she felt. 'We've agreed it's only going to be for a week. No one is going to fall in love in that time.'

'I'm not so sure you can predict that with any certainty because—'

'Enough about me,' Abby said. 'How's school going? How were the parent teacher interviews?'

'I know what you're doing, Abby, but this time I'm going to let it slide,' Ella said. 'You don't want to talk about it, so fine. We won't talk about it. But please be careful. Luke has a thing about commitment. I think it comes from having a father like ours.'

'I'm sure Luke is nothing like his father.'

'He's not, but that doesn't mean he'll change his mind about settling down,' Ella's voice had a note of warning. 'I know what my big brother is like. Luke is so stubborn he could be conducting workshops and tutorials for mules.'

Abby couldn't help smiling. 'Believe me, I know.'

Luke bought an outfit and some lingerie for Abby at a boutique in Bloomsbury and walked back to his house, but he couldn't help feeling conflicted. Making love with her was amazing. Amazing and fulfilling and unlike anything he'd experienced before. But he couldn't quite dismiss the niggling worry he was stepping out of his comfort zone.

Way, way out.

Letting someone close, *that* close, was like peeling back the edges of a wound and preparing for the lightning strike of pain. So far it hadn't happened. So far. But how soon before it did? Letting someone into his life made him uneasy. As if he was walking over a lake of ice and not being sure where it was thick and where it was thin, every step a potentially dangerous one.

A potentially lethal one.

Abby had got under his guard like someone slipping under crime scene tape while the forensics team turned their backs. He had told her things he had told no one. But then so had she revealed things about herself to him that were painfully private.

Her disclosure made him feel…trusted. Yes, that was the word he was looking for. She trusted him with the truth about her difficult background. The shameful truth she had deliberately and desperately hidden behind a complicated web of white lies, like a magician using smoke and mirrors to fool the audience.

Abby's seemingly perfect life was exactly that—just an illusion.

So what the hell was he doing getting stuck in the middle of it? Pretending to be her Mr Perfect. Taking her on a luxury holiday for two like a freaking romantic honeymoon.

What was he *thinking?*

That was the trouble when he was around Abby. He didn't think. His body took over his mind and every primal desire in his system pumped and pounded and pushed against his willpower like a bulldozer against a cardboard box.

Because he couldn't resist her.

That first kiss had been his downfall, the second splintering his self-control like a sledgehammer on glass. Those kisses had flicked a switch inside his body, making every attempt on his part to withstand the potent lure of attraction a dismal failure.

Abby was his kryptonite. His peanut. He had to have more and more of her because it was impossible to resist her.

And for the next week he wasn't even going to try.

Abby had never been on a shopping spree before where someone else footed the bill. Shopping for herself was usually a tricky business of balancing her bank balance with her constantly overstretched credit card. She knew she couldn't really blame her background on her issues with money. In spite of her parents' woeful example, she had witnessed her various foster families balance delicate budgets and still provide meals and essentials, although not too many luxuries. She had great intentions of saving but something would always crop up—another bill, a friend in need, a charity she just had to make a donation to because she perceived their need to be greater than hers.

But when Luke took her shopping there was no question of her whipping out her credit card. He took care of everything and was a surprisingly helpful shopping wingman. And he was great at carrying all the bags.

Abby was in a boutique with him where there was swimwear as well as other casual fashion items. She ran her hand along the row of hanging bikinis and wondered if she had the courage to wear one. She had always worn a one-piece because it held in her less than toned stomach.

'Why don't you try one on?' Luke said.

Abby dropped her hand from the rack. 'I don't have the figure for it. I'd be too embarrassed.'

'There won't be anyone else but us on the island so what's to be embarrassed about?'

She turned back to the row of colourful bikinis in the section where her size was located and sighed. 'I don't know...'

'Here.' He reached past her shoulder and took three bikini sets off the rack: a black one, a vividly hot pink one and a bright canary-yellow one. 'You'd look great in any of these. Go on. Try them on.'

Abby took them from him but she was still feeling uncertain. 'Do you really think—?'

Luke bent his head to just near her ear. 'Personally, I'd prefer you totally naked, but yes, I think you'll look fabulous in all three of them. Now get in there and try them on.'

She shivered at the erotic promise of his words and the way his warm breath caressed her skin. She gave him a mock salute. 'Yes, sir.'

His dark eyes glinted and he gave her a playful pat on the behind. 'Cheeky minx.'

Abby went into the changing room and peeled off her clothes, trying to see her body in the mirror as Luke saw it. Since her early teens she had struggled with body image. The rush of hormones in puberty had turned her boyish figure into a lushly womanly one but she hadn't been emotionally ready for the impact it would have on the male gaze. Comments and leering looks from men had triggered some of the memories of her mother's clients and it had made her ashamed of her body instead of proud of it.

But when Luke looked at her she felt none of that shame. Almost from the first time she'd met him her body had been aware of him, but not in a threatening way. The way his gaze would drift to her mouth had given her a secret thrill that in spite of his standoffish demeanour he found her attractive.

Abby turned this way and that in front of the mirror, cupping her breasts in her hands, remembering how it felt to have Luke hold and caress them. Just thinking about him touching her sent another frisson through her.

She lowered her hands and tried on each bikini, unable to make a choice between them. She got dressed back in her clothes and, carrying the bikinis, came out to where Luke was waiting for her.

'How did you go?'

'I like them all but—'

'Good, then we'll take them all.' He took them from her and handed them to the hovering shop assistant. 'We'll take these.'

The young female assistant smiled at Abby once the bikinis were paid for by Luke and wrapped in tissue paper and placed in the shop's signature bag. 'Wow, he really is a perfect fiancé. I love your column, by the way. Your advice is always spot on.'

'Thank you,' Abby said, taking the bag's cream satin ribbon handle.

'Oh, is that your engagement ring?' The assistant peered across the counter at Abby's left hand. 'Can I see it?'

Abby lifted her hand for inspection but, looking at the ring, she realised it wasn't the sort of ring Luke would buy his fiancée if he ever had one. It was too flashy and cumbersome and it didn't really suit her hand. It was a *nouveau riche* type of ring— the sort of ring worn by someone trying too hard to impress. It was a status symbol, not a ring about the relationship status itself. She held out her hand and was excruciatingly conscious of Luke standing silently beside her.

'It's lovely,' the assistant said. 'I hope you'll both be brilliantly happy, but then of course you will. You're the perfect couple.'

Abby couldn't get out of there fast enough and was glad when Luke took her hand and walked her out of the shop. 'How about a coffee to finish up?' he said.

'I think I need something stronger than coffee.'

'That ring you're wearing is a cliché.' He turned the bulky setting around on her finger. 'And it's not even a real diamond.'

'How do you know it's not real?'

'It's a good fake, I'll give you that.'

Abby gave a self-deprecating grimace. 'I would've bought a real one if I'd had the money.'

His mouth tilted in a smile. 'You're a funny little thing, aren't you?'

'Yes, well, that's me—a living, breathing joke.'

A frown pulled at his brow. 'Hey.' He lifted her chin again, his intelligent blue gaze warm and darkly intense. 'I'm not laughing at you, sweetheart. I like your quirkiness. It's refreshing.'

Abby's heart gave a stumble. 'You just called me sweetheart.'

His hand fell away from her face. 'Wasn't that the deal? To call you terms of endearment in public? Honey and babe and sweetheart. Those were the correct words, right?'

'Yes…'

'But?'

She shrugged. 'I just didn't think you'd do it, that's all.'

His eyes held hers. 'Why's that?'

'You don't seem the type of man to say things you don't mean,' Abby said.

'You can thank my father for that.' He took her hand and continued walking with her down the street. 'He was big on words and small on action. I sometimes wonder what my mother saw in him. He doesn't seem her type at all.'

'I have heaps of readers who fall for the wrong men,' Abby said. 'It's like some women are programmed to choose the worst possible partner for them. And some do it repeatedly.'

'Thing is…' Luke paused. 'I think she's still in love with him, even after the way he humiliated her. I don't get it. Who does that?'

A woman in love.

'I guess there's no accounting for chemistry,' Abby said. *Isn't that the truth?* 'When it strikes it strikes and there's little you can do to stop it.'

CHAPTER EIGHT

THEY CONTINUED ALONG the street until they came to an exclusive cocktail lounge Abby had heard heaps about but never visited. Luke led Abby inside and they were soon seated at a velvet-covered sofa in a private corner.

Abby swept her gaze over the beautiful décor and wanted to pinch herself. She'd always wanted to come in here but it had always been out of her price range.

'What do you fancy?' Luke asked, handing her the drinks menu. 'A cocktail and peanuts or something more substantial?'

What I really fancy is you.

'Gosh, this place is amazing. Look at the list of food. And I've never heard of some of these cocktails. It makes me want to try them, just to see. I guess my diet can wait another day.'

He gave Abby a mock stern look. 'If I hear you say the word *diet* ever again I will not be answerable for the consequences.'

Abby gave him a quizzical look. 'You don't believe in diets?'

'Firstly, diets have a woefully high failure rate,' he said. 'Most people lose weight and as soon as they stop the diet they put it all back on again and more. And, secondly, you look fine just the way you are.'

'Thank you for saying that.' Abby reached across the table for his hand. 'I've struggled for years with body image.'

His warm, strong fingers wrapped around hers, sending a wave of longing through her. 'You have a beautiful body.'

She gave him an on-off smile and lowered her gaze to their joined hands. How nice would it be if a ring Luke had bought her was on her finger instead of that ridiculous fake?

After a while the waiter brought their drinks and a tasting plate of delicious food to share. Abby sat back and started on her cocktail, which seemed to go straight to her head, or maybe that was because of the way Luke kept looking at her as if he was reliving every moment of their lovemaking. She looked at the pattern around the edge of the tasting plate rather than meet his gaze. 'I guess not having parents around who loved me unconditionally has messed with my self-esteem.'

'Understandable, given what you've been through.'

Abby sighed. 'I've always been a bit jealous of Ella, you know. Growing up with two parents, well, at least one highly functioning one and a big brother to boot. That's why I made up so much stuff about my background and never told her the truth. As far as I'm concerned, that girl with the dodgy parents no longer exists.'

His eyes were warm with understanding. 'I think you underestimate Ella, but I hear what you're saying.' A shadow drifted through his gaze. 'I haven't told anyone I broke up with Kimberley that night. No one but you, that is.'

Abby put her cocktail glass down. 'Do you think she told anyone? I mean, before she got…?'

'Not that I'm aware of.' He shifted the base of his cocktail glass a quarter turn. 'There was a window of a couple of hours after she left my place and the accident. She might've just sat in her car and cried, for all I know.'

Abby could understand why he felt so crushingly guilty. How could he tell everyone they had broken up two hours before Kimberley's tragic death? What would it have achieved except more hurt for the poor girl's family? And, even if he had told them, wouldn't it have heaped even more blame on his shoulders that he didn't deserve? Couples broke up every day. Every minute or second across the world, people were ending their relationships. How could Luke have possibly known by ending his relationship with Kimberley she would be involved in a car crash a couple of hours later? It just wasn't possible.

And it certainly wasn't his fault.

But it made her realise how deeply sensitive Luke was underneath the gruff front he presented to the world. He'd thought deeply about how Kimberley's family would suffer even more heartache if they thought he had no longer wanted to be with her.

'Was she terribly upset when she left your place?'

His features clouded with the memory. 'That's another thing I've never really understood. She wasn't all that upset. I got the feeling she knew I was going to end things that day. I even thought she seemed... I don't know...relieved somehow. And yet...' He gave his head a little shake. 'Maybe I just wasn't good at reading her mood. I keep asking myself, did I *listen* to her? Did I hear what she wasn't saying instead of what she was?'

'Maybe in that two-hour window she talked to a friend,' Abby said. 'That's usually what women do when they're upset. They go to their girlfriends for support.'

'If she'd told anyone then no one mentioned it at the funeral or since,' Luke said. 'That's been one of the hardest things, apart from the guilt. Her family see me as the grief-stricken partner, unable to move on.' He gave a quick twist of his mouth. 'Thing is... It seems to help them to think that. They find it comforting that someone other than them is still devastated by her death.'

'But you are still grieving,' Abby pointed out. 'It's a process, not a timeline. You move through each of the stages when you're ready. Some people take years, others a lifetime and some never get through it. There's no right way of doing it.'

His smile was a wry slant. 'I can see why you

landed that job of yours. That's a wise head on those very beautiful shoulders.'

Abby shrugged off his comment and eyed the last olive on the tasting plate. 'Aren't you going to eat that?'

He pushed the plate across the table. 'It's all yours.'

Luke went to his London office first thing on Monday morning and shuffled his diary around and in the process gave everyone on the staff a minor heart attack at his uncharacteristic spontaneity. It was weird, but no one at his office seemed all that surprised that he was 'engaged' to Abby Hart. They bought it just like everyone else who had access to a phone or computer screen or newspaper.

'I always thought you were a dark horse, Luke,' Kay, his middle-aged secretary, said with a teasing smile. 'But I couldn't be happier for you. I love Abby's column. I read it every week. Her advice stopped me divorcing John last year.'

Luke frowned. 'I didn't know you guys were having trouble.'

Kay flickered her eyes upwards in a don't-get-me-started manner. 'I was going to leave him because he'd stopped helping me around the house and would just sit on the sofa in front of the TV while I buzzed around doing everything. But Abby pointed out in her column, most couples don't get divorced over a basket of washing. There are usually bigger issues that are hiding under the dirty laundry. She was bang on the money. Poor John had some financial worries from his business that were making him depressed and moody and tired. He was too ashamed to tell me about them, and if it hadn't been for Abby's advice I still might not know. That girl is a genius.'

Luke couldn't hold back a smile. 'She is pretty special, isn't she?'

Kay's beaming smile rivalled a set of sun-soaked solar panels. 'Well, look at you, smiling for the first time in I don't know when.' She leaned forwards and rested her forearms on her desk, her expression now sober. 'I guess you kept your relationship with Abby a secret out of respect for Kimberley's family. But they must be happy for you, surely? It's been five years.'

Luke's gut did its usual sharp claws clench when he thought of Kimberley's family. He'd called them to explain his engagement to Abby wasn't real, that it was just a favour he was doing for her. He hadn't told Abby he'd told them that because she was so insistent no one knew her fiancé was a fake. But he couldn't allow Kimberley's parents to hear about his 'engagement' from another source, especially in the press. 'Yes. I told them.'

'Well, even if you hadn't, you'd have to be a fossil hiding under a rock not to have heard about the outing of Abby Hart's Mr Perfect,' Kay said with another smile. 'Thing is, how on earth did you two keep it a secret for so long? That's taking dark horsemanship to a whole new level.'

Luke kept his expression safely in neutral. 'Believe me, it wasn't easy.'

* * *

Luke was on his way back to his house, where Abby was waiting for him before they headed to the airport, when he walked past a high-end jewellery store. He stopped outside and looked at the window display for a moment, realising it was totally out of character and that he was crossing a line he had never crossed before. But he couldn't stop thinking about her showing that shop assistant her ring the other day and how it had seemed to embarrass her. Why shouldn't he buy her something she wouldn't be embarrassed wearing? It was a way to make sure she was treated the way she deserved to be treated. It would also make him less conflicted about putting such a short time frame on their fling. He pushed open the door and asked to see the diamond pendant in the window. And once he had purchased the pendant he continued on his way home.

Luke was a little shocked at how much he was looking forward to this week on the island. Not just because he hadn't had a holiday in…when *had* he last had a holiday? It was so long ago he couldn't remember where he'd gone.

One thing he did know—he'd gone alone.

But a week with Abby on a private island was the stuff of fantasies. He couldn't help feeling excited about it. Hugely excited. Not just because their lovemaking was so freaking amazing, although he wouldn't be worthy of his testosterone if he didn't get hard just thinking about her in his bed. It was because Abby was fun to be around. She made him smile and he could barely remember the last time he'd smiled before she came barrelling into his life and demanding he be her Mr Perfect.

Luke was the last person to consider himself perfect, especially in an intimate relationship, but he couldn't help enjoying playing the role of her fiancé as it gave him the freedom to do and say things he wouldn't normally feel comfortable doing.

He wasn't a touchy-feely person. He wasn't the life-of-the-party loquacious type. He would rather design a robot than speak at length to a real person. At least he could program a robot to do what he wanted it to do.

But for some reason, with Abby, none of that mattered.

He liked the differences between them. He liked her laughter and her lightness of personality. He liked how she was positive and had such a can-do attitude. Her resourcefulness was a little wacky at times, like pretending to be in a relationship when she had never been in one before, and then giving everyone relationship advice that actually worked. Not to mention setting a date on when a fling should end. You didn't get much wackier than that.

Luke wanted this week on the island to be perfect for her. To make up for all that had happened in her childhood. He wanted to spoil her and make her feel like a princess for the next week.

Only a week?

He elbowed the thought away. A week was what they had agreed on.

And he was going to enjoy every smoking-hot second of it.

CHAPTER NINE

THE PRIVATE ISLAND and luxury villa were even better in the flesh than in the photographs, Abby decided when they arrived. Stunning views of the sparkling blue sea and the white sandy beach that fringed it could be seen from the sun-drenched terrace in front of the villa. A gorgeous infinity pool was set on the other terrace, which overlooked another fabulous view of the ocean. There were beautifully manicured gardens situated about the villa, and the slightly peppery scent of the scarlet pelargoniums that were in terracotta pots and hanging baskets filled the air.

The warm air with its hint of sea salt caressed Abby's face when she lifted it to the sun and she closed her eyes for a moment, taking in the distant cry of a seabird and the twittering of the birds in the nearby shrubs. She opened her eyes to see Luke smiling at her. 'What?' she said, suddenly embarrassed.

He gave her pony-tailed hair a gentle tug. 'You're so easily impressed.'

'Who wouldn't be impressed by this?' She waved her hand to encompass their surroundings. 'This

place is amazing. Pardon me for being a little overwhelmed but I've never been on a private island before. Nor have I seen a place as fabulous as this.
Apparently the villa has won several architectural
awards and I can see why.'

Luke gave a cursory look at the villa. 'It's not
bad.'

'Not bad?' Abby laughed. 'You're the master of
understatement. I would like to see something that
does impress you.'

'You in one of those bikinis I bought you would
impress me,' he said with a glint in his eyes.

Abby's core coiled and contracted with need.
'That can be arranged as soon as I unpack.'

Luke opened the front door of the villa with the
key he had been given by the person who had brought
them to the island by boat. She still couldn't believe
they had the island to themselves for the week. Not
even any of the household staff were on the island
this week. The housekeeper and gardener and pool
maintenance people were on leave. However, gour-
met food and boutique wines and champagnes had
been left as part of the prize package, and the boat
operator had informed them fresh fruit and vegeta-
bles would be brought in by boat mid-week.

Abby followed Luke inside the villa and couldn't
stop a gasp escaping when she saw the interior of the
foyer. The walls and floor were polished marble and
a Swarovski crystal chandelier hung from the ceiling
in prisms of glittering light like a fountain of shimmering diamonds. The large windows allowed the

view to come in from each side of the villa, making
it seem even more spacious and spectacular. Three
sides of the villa overlooked the sea but the fourth
side overlooked the densely wooded forest of the
hilly area on one side of the island.

Luke had a floor plan in the folder he had been
given by the boat operator, but Abby was too impatient for that. She went on her own tour of discovery,
calling out to him when she found another delightful
room or stunning angle of the house.

'Look at this, Luke.' She pointed to the well-ap-
pointed kitchen and the breakfast room that opened
on to a terrace where jasmine hung in a scented arras
from the side of the villa. 'I can't wait to cook in
there. And we can eat outside whenever we want.'

'It's a holiday. You're not meant to cook.'

'But I want to cook.' Abby all but drooled at the
luxury appliances and the acres of marble work-
spaces, which made her cramped kitchenette look
like a shoebox. A baby's shoebox. She opened a but-
ler's pantry. 'Goodness me, you could park a car in
here it's so big.' She closed the door and grinned at
him. 'Am I gushing too much?'

His slow smile made something in her stomach
drop. 'Come here.'

Abby walked across the kitchen to where he was
standing, her breath snaring in her throat when he
slipped a hand to the nape of her neck. His eyes were
so dark a blue his pupils almost disappeared. 'I don't
want to waste a second of this holiday with you slaving over a hot oven.'

She linked her arms around his neck and leaned into his hard frame, her body tingling at the erotic contact. 'So you'd prefer me slaving over your hot body instead?'

The glint in his eyes intensified. 'I couldn't have put it better myself.' His hands settled on her hips, holding her against the pulse of his body. His mouth came down and covered hers in a long, drugging kiss that made the backs of her knees feel fizzy. A hot pool of longing opened up inside her, creating a whirlpool deep in her core.

Abby sighed against his mouth, weaving her tongue with his, her body tingling with the need to get closer. Luke's hands were already working on her clothes, peeling them from her body as if he was unwrapping a present he had been waiting to open for a long time.

'I want you,' he said, moving his mouth against the sensitive skin of her neck, the caress of his warm breath sending shivers down her spine.

Abby was suddenly conscious of how hot and sticky she was from their travel. 'Maybe I should shower first...'

'I have an even better idea.' He took her hand and led her out to the sun-dappled infinity pool on the terrace.

There were towels in a hamper under a shelter and he took two out and laid them on two sun loungers. There was even sunscreen in a spray bottle thoughtfully placed nearby.

Then he undid the rest of his shirt buttons, looking at her with such explosive erotic intent her legs threatened to give way. 'Ever skinny-dipped before?'

Abby shook her head. 'I've always been too shy to do something like that.' Not to mention she was a hopeless swimmer. She only ever stayed in the shallow end because she hadn't learnt to swim with anything remotely near proficiency.

He stepped out of his trousers and shoes and socks and underwear before he came back to help her with the rest of her clothes. With each article he removed, he left a kiss in its place, his lips and tongue moving over her flesh in little nudges and licks that made her desire for him swarm through her body in a hot wave.

The sensation of the sun on her naked skin was so sensually arousing but, teamed with Luke's kisses and skilled caresses, she was breathless and aching with need within seconds. 'Are you sure no one can see us?' she said, sliding her hands down his muscular chest.

'We're totally alone.'

Abby glanced nervously towards the ocean in the distance. 'What about on the water? Maybe there's a yacht with a stonking big telescope that will—'

'Abby.' Luke's voice had a soothing quality to it that was like a caress in itself. 'You're safe with me. I wouldn't bring you out here if I didn't think it was private.'

Was she safe?

Safe emotionally?

Abby brushed aside the thought. She wasn't falling in love with Luke. That wasn't part of the deal.

How could she fall in love so quickly anyway? She was confusing phenomenal sex with love. Hadn't she written a column about that once? It was a classic mistake people made, especially women, confusing great sex with love, often being disappointed when the novelty wore off, to find there was nothing underpinning the relationship but physical lust.

Luke picked up the sunscreen and sprayed her back and shoulders and then handed her the bottle to do his. Once they were safely covered with sunscreen, he brought her back to the cradle of his body, his hands sliding down to cup her behind, his mouth fusing to hers in a searing kiss that made her toes curl against the sun-warmed flagstones. Then he lifted his mouth off hers to blaze a trail of kisses down to her breasts, subjecting each one to licks and sucks and gentle nips that made her gasp with delight.

After a moment, he lifted his mouth off her breast to nod towards the pool. 'Time to cool off?'

Abby glanced at the markings on the floor of the pool. 'Can we stay in the shallow end?'

'You're not confident in the water?' He framed it as a question but it sounded more like an observation, especially since he was looking at her in an understanding manner.

'Well, let's put it this way,' Abby said with a self-deprecating grimace. 'Every time I try and swim, someone throws me a flotation device and calls for a lifeguard. Swimming lessons weren't a priority at any of my foster placements.'

'Then that's something I can help you with while we're here.'

'Ella told me you won a heap of medals during your schooling but you stopped swimming when your parents split up,' Abby said.

A shadow passed over his features. 'Yeah, well, club training wasn't a priority after that.'

'Because you were always too busy looking after your mum and Ella?' Abby asked.

He made a twisted movement of his mouth. 'Don't get me wrong. I was glad to help with Ella. She was a good little kid and no bother. I just missed out on the stuff other teenagers my age were doing. It made me feel like an outsider. But I guess you know all about feeling like that.'

'Sure do. But I think what you did for Ella and your mum was amazing. They're so lucky to have you.'

He gave her a quick smile. 'Let's get you in the water before you melt, okay?'

Abby was so hot from his caresses she was expecting the water to sizzle when she entered it, holding Luke's hand for support. And the only melting she was going to do was when he looked at her with his dark blue eyes full of smouldering desire. The water enveloped her in a blessedly cool embrace that felt like silk against her naked skin. Maybe swimming wouldn't be so scary after all.

Luke brought her close to the aroused length of his body. 'There's only one problem with making love in water.'

'Putting on a condom?'

'Yep.'

Abby bit her lip. 'I guess we could go without…'

He looked at her for a long moment. 'No can do. Too risky.'

Abby knew he was being responsible about having safe sex. She was always insisting on her followers doing the same, but a part of her—a secret part—wished he would relax his rule for her. 'Because this is just a fling, right?' She tried to tone down the bitter note in her voice but didn't quite pull it off.

He let out a gust of a breath and slid a hand down one of her arms. 'Abby… Think about it. If you were to get pregnant it would—'

'I know, I know, I know,' Abby said. 'It would be a disaster for you.'

He frowned. 'And for you too, surely?'

Abby kept her expression blank while her mind suddenly raced off with images of her holding a baby—a little dark-haired angel with deep blue eyes. She blinked away the image and pasted a smile on her face. 'Of course it would be a disaster. I'm still building my career. I don't want to have kids until I'm in my late twenties at the earliest.'

Luke's expression was guarded, as if he wasn't sure whether to believe her or not. 'The Pill is mostly reliable but I don't want to risk it.'

'It's fine, Luke, really,' Abby said. 'I've written heaps of columns about this. It's too easy to get lost in the heat of the moment and then it's too late to undo. I've had heart-wrenching letters from followers who've had to deal with an unplanned pregnancy, more often than not to a guy they no longer want anything to do with. You're being sensible and responsible and I'm grateful for it.'

He gently tucked a wispy strand of hair behind her ear. 'So, swimming lesson first and then we'll finish this later.'

An hour later Abby wasn't quite ready for the Olympics but she could get from one end of the pool to the other without ending up with a lungful of water. The pool contained saltwater, which added extra buoyancy, and with Luke's excellent coaching she was reasonably confident she wouldn't drown if she stepped out of her depth.

She completed another lap and stood at the end and blinked the water out of her eyes. 'How many have I done now? I lost count.'

'You've done enough for one day,' Luke said. 'Besides, the sun is starting to pink your skin. The sunscreen's probably washed off by now.'

'I'll sit in the shade for a bit,' Abby said. 'You've been so patient with me but you must be dying for a swim yourself. Go on. I'll enjoy watching you. It'll be like watching a training video.'

Abby covered herself with a towel and sat on one of the sun loungers and watched Luke glide through the water with such economy of movement and graceful skill it was a delight to watch. He tumble-turned at each end with supple agility, and even more delightful was seeing all of his powerfully sculpted muscles coming into play. The strong back and shoulders, the long and muscled legs, the toned arms, the clever hands that were placed at just the right angle to maximise propulsion through the water. He had the sort of skin that tanned rather than burned, and even in the short time they'd been out here in the pool his skin had darkened.

After a few laps, Luke propelled himself out of the water by his hands on the edge of the pool. Abby sucked in a breath as the muscles in his arms and on his abdomen contracted at the movement. He wasn't the slightest bit uneasy about being naked, but then she wasn't uncomfortable being naked with him either. Physically or emotionally, which was even more surprising. She had told him more about herself than she had told anyone. Was it because he was a good listener or was it because he too had suffered? Whatever the reason, it gave them a common ground on which to communicate.

Luke came over to where she was sitting and perched on the end of her sun lounger near her feet. He shook his head like a wet dog and sprayed water droplets all over her legs.

'Hey—' Abby laughed and gave him a playful shove '—get away from me.'

He leaned over her, anchoring his arms either side of her waist, his eyes dark and gleaming. 'Are you sure that's what you want?'

Abby touched his lean tanned jaw with her hand, his dark regrowth grazing her fingertips. She looked into the bottomless blue of his eyes and knew in that moment the last thing she ever wanted was to have him away from her.

She wanted him close.

As close as she could possibly be to him. Wasn't she already closer to him than anyone? Her eyes fell away from his to study his mouth instead. She traced it with her fingertip, memorising it so she would never forget its sexy contours. 'You have a nice mouth. Strong and firm and masculine and yet soft too.'

He captured her finger with his mouth, drawing on it like he had suckled on her nipples. 'I'm rather fond of yours too,' he said once he released her finger. 'As you've probably noticed.'

Abby gave him a half smile. 'Do you think when this week is over we will still be able to be friends?'

A frown flickered over his forehead. 'I don't see any reason why not.'

'I know…but these things have a habit of becoming complicated…'

He pushed up her chin once more, locking her gaze with his penetrating one. 'Are you having second thoughts?'

Abby made sure her choice of words wouldn't betray her doubts. 'No. It's just it gets tricky running into exes at family gatherings and stuff. I mean, Ella is practically family to me and you too, so—'

'It won't be tricky, okay?' He stood from the sun lounger so quickly it nearly overbalanced. One of his hands scraped his damp hair back with such force it left deep groove marks along his scalp. 'I'll deal with it. We'll both deal with it like adults.'

'I don't see why you're so upset,' Abby said. 'I'm just expressing concern about how we're going to handle this going forward. We both have to be clear on how we're going to handle it.'

'Are you trying to ruin this holiday?' He glared at her so heatedly it made the bright sunlight seem dim by comparison. 'Is that what you're doing? Because if so it's working. We've only got a few days. Let's not waste them by worrying how we're going to look each other in the eye at Christmas and Easter, okay?'

Abby bit her lip. 'I'm sorry…'

He let out a long slow breath and came back over to sit beside her. He took one of her hands and brought it up to his mouth, pressing his lips against her bent knuckles. 'I'm sorry too.' His eyes were soft again. 'I shouldn't have spoken so harshly. Forgive me.'

'I shouldn't have pressed your buttons.'

He tucked another strand of her hair back behind her ear. 'Your nose is pink.'

Abby screwed up her face. 'I hate you for being able to tan without tears. I go pink and then I peel and get more freckles. Go me.'

He sent his fingertip down the slope of her nose. 'Your freckles are cute.'

She smiled and touched his mouth again with her fingertip. 'Are you going to finish what you started before we had a swim?'

He got off the lounger and pulled her to her feet. 'I'm all for a bit of alfresco sex but I don't want you to get sunburnt or the rest of our week will be ruined. Let's go inside.'

'Sounds like fun.'

He pressed a hot kiss to her mouth. 'I'll make sure of it.'

Luke woke from a relaxing post-sex snooze to find Abby had disappeared from the bed beside him. He could see the indentation of her head on the pillow and the tangle of the bedclothes from when they had made passionate love. He glanced at his phone on the bedside table for the time and was a little shocked to see a couple of hours had passed. He could hear sounds of activity in the kitchen downstairs and smiled to himself at the thought of Abby bustling about in there as if it was her idea of a good time. His approach to food was purely functional. He ate when he was hungry and he stopped when he was full. But he suspected that came from long years of living alone.

Luke's mind drifted back to his conversation with Abby by the pool. He wasn't sure what her motive was in talking about them running into each other in the future. Had she wanted him to consider the fact that she was bound to meet someone else and make him jealous at the thought of her bringing a new man home to meet his family? Why would he be jealous? She had a perfect right to get on with her life once their fling was over.

That was the deal—one week and one week only.

But the thought of running into her with a new partner made something in his stomach twist. Would he have to go to her wedding? Would he have to stand

and watch some other guy promise to love her and stay true to her for the rest of their lives?

Not going to happen.

Luke came downstairs to find Abby laying a table on the terrace overlooking the ocean. She was dressed in one of the casual outfits he'd bought her on their shopping spree and her hair was on top of her head in a loosely arranged knot that gave her a bohemian hippy look. She glanced up from folding a napkin and smiled. 'Nice sleep? I checked on you an hour ago and you were out for the count.'

'You should have woken me.'

She made a mock pout. 'Uh-oh, you're frowning. Maybe you should have stayed in bed a bit longer.'

It's no fun if you're not there with me.

Luke would never say it out loud because he didn't even like thinking it. It would be admitting he needed her. He didn't need anyone. He made sure of it. 'What can I do to help with dinner?'

'You can open the wine, or should we have champagne?'

'What would you like?'

'Champagne,' she said, eyes shining. 'This is my first ever private island holiday, well, yours actually since I'm gatecrashing.'

'I was happy to bring you,' Luke said. 'It's good to see you enjoying yourself.'

She gave her lower lip a nibble and started fussing with the flowers she had arranged in the middle of the table. 'Actually…there's something I need to ask you…'

'Yes?'

She turned from the table with a sheepish look. 'I got a text from Felicity. She wants me to post some pictures of us on our holiday on my Twitter and Instagram feed.'

Luke didn't even have to think about his answer. 'No.'

Her face crumpled with disappointment. 'But surely a couple of photos won't hurt? It will make—'

'You can post photos of yourself if you must but please leave me out of it. No way am I going to have my photo plastered all over social media.'

'You didn't seem to mind the night of the ball.'

'That was different,' Luke said.

'How is it different?' she asked. 'You were pretending to be my fiancé then and you're pretending now. What's a few more photos going to do?'

'None of this is real, Abby,' Luke said. 'You. Me. Us.'

Her brown eyes flinched as if he'd struck her. 'But our fling is real…isn't it?'

'Yes. For one week and one week only.'

'Fine. I'm okay with that,' Abby said, folding her arms across her body. 'I just don't see the problem with taking a few photos and sharing them online.'

'Look, you might be happy about sharing your life with the rest of the planet but I'm not,' Luke said. 'Once that stuff is out there you can't take it back. It's out there for ever.'

She chewed her lower lip as if she was thinking

about something. 'I guess it might be a bit awkward for Kimberley's family…'

Luke set his mouth in a flat line. 'It's not about her family. They know this is a fake engagement.'

Her eyes rounded in alarm. 'You *told* them about us?'

'I couldn't let them find out in the press,' Luke said. 'I thought it was better to give them the heads-up that it was a charade to spare their feelings.'

'But what about *my* feelings?' she asked. 'What about my job? What if they told someone it was a charade? What then? Did you think about that? My career will implode if they spill anything to the press. How could you do that without asking me first?'

Luke released a weary sigh. This was why he stayed out of relationships. He was rubbish at handling people's feelings. He hurt them without even trying. 'Look, I admit I should have discussed it with you first. But they're discreet and will keep it to themselves.'

'They'd better because otherwise I'm never going to forgive you if this blows up in my face.' She folded her arms and glowered at him. 'So…no photos. Is that your final word?'

'I just prefer to keep my life private. It's no one's business but mine.'

Worry flickered through her gaze. 'But what am I going to say to Felicity?'

'You could tell her the truth,' Luke said with a wry look.

Shock flashed over her features. 'I can't do that. I could lose my job.'

'You're going to have to tell everyone some time.'

She unlocked her arms and shifted her gaze. 'I know. I have it covered. I'm going to do a breakup blog. But don't worry; I won't make you sound bad. I'll make it that I broke it off because of my issues not yours.'

Luke came over to her and placed his hands on her shoulders. 'Look, how about I take some photos of you instead? How's that for a compromise?'

She seemed to mull it over for a moment before she let out a breath. 'They'd better be pretty damn good photos.'

He leaned down to press a kiss to her forehead. 'They will be.'

CHAPTER TEN

AFTER DINNER, ABBY sat with Luke in the moonlight on the terrace. He had taken several photos of her over the course of the evening and all of them were good. Some of them even brilliant. He had a good eye for lighting and with the golden and muted light during twilight and sunset he had made her look almost beautiful.

But she couldn't help feeling disappointed he didn't want to be in the photos with her. What harm was there in a photo or two? At least it would be something she could keep after this week ended. Would it have hurt him to allow her one little keepsake photo? She had no childhood photos to speak of. This was another reminder of how alone she truly was.

But she didn't want to be alone any more.

Not after this week. Not after being with Luke and experiencing the passion of being in his arms. Why couldn't they extend their fling? Why wouldn't he broaden the time frame to see how well they worked as a couple? Sure, they had little disagreements, but that was normal and even healthy. His refusal to be in the photos was a reminder of his unwillingness to commit to anything long-term and her stupidity in secretly hoping he would change his mind. How many times had she written about this in her column? Women always thought they could change men but it nearly always ended up in heartbreak. People could only change when they believed they had to change, when they felt the need to change. When they *wanted* to change. No one else could force you or coerce you.

'More champagne?' Luke held up the bottle.

Abby covered the top of her glass. 'Better not. I already feel a little tipsy.' Who knew what would come out of her mouth if she allowed her self-control to slip?

I'm in love with you. I want to be married to you and have your babies.

How could she have thought she could settle for a fling when all she wanted was for ever with Luke? She wanted to grow old with him, to bring up a family with him, to do all the things with their little family she had missed out on as a child. But how could she tell him that? It was the last thing he wanted to hear. The last thing he wanted was a permanent commitment. How could it have taken her this long to realise she loved him? Or had she been lying to herself all this time?

It was ironic but for years she had been telling lies. Heaps and heaps of little white lies and yet the one time she wanted to tell the truth she couldn't. If she told Luke how she felt about him he would be furious. Falling in love was never part of the deal. She had talked him into the charade and now she had to endure the clock ticking on their fling.

He sat back in his chair and looked at the wrinkled moonlit sea below. 'This place makes you wish you didn't have to go home.'

'Tell me about it,' Abby said, thinking of her cramped little flat and the thin walls where she heard her neighbours arguing or listening to their too-loud televisions. Out here in this paradise, all she could hear was the occasional cry of a seabird and the whisper of the wind through the cypress pines.

And that wretched ticking clock...

After a moment, Luke reached into his pocket and put a square box on the table between them. 'This is for you.'

Abby stared at the jewellery box, her heart beating so fast she was sure it was going to bounce out of her chest. 'What is it?'

'Open it and see.'

She picked up the box and prised open the lid to find a gorgeous diamond pendant winking at her from its bed of lush cream velvet. 'Oh, my goodness...'

She lifted the fine white gold chain and the diamond swung with sparkling brilliance as if someone had plucked a star out of the night sky.

'It's beautiful. I've never seen anything so gorgeous.'

She looked up from the pendant, trying to stop herself from getting emotional. No one had ever bought her anything so wonderful. It wasn't just that it was expensive, but more that he had gone out and bought it for her as if she was someone special to him. Someone he thought worthy of a beautiful, timeless diamond.

'But I don't understand… Why did you buy it for me?'

He gave a loose-shouldered shrug. 'I walked past a jewellery store and saw it in the window.'

Abby looked at the pendant and blinked back tears. But it was impossible for her to control the bubble of emotion in her throat. She gulped and clutched the pendant against her chest, trying to regain her composure.

Luke leaned forward and took her hand. 'Why are you crying? Don't you like it? We can exchange it for something else if you'd—'

'Oh, Luke—' Abby half-sobbed, half-laughed '—I adore it. I'm crying because no one has ever bought me something so gorgeous. I'm used to getting hand-me-downs or charity shop gifts. This is the most perfect present I've ever received. It's very generous of you, but you have to stop spending so much money on me.'

He rose from the table and came around to her side to help her put the pendant on. His fingers sent shivers through her body when he fastened the catch and then he dropped a light kiss to the top of her head before he came back to sit down opposite her. 'It's just a trinket. A keepsake to remember me by.'

A keepsake to remember him by.

The words were a wake-up slap to Abby's momentary slip into happy-ever-after dreamland. 'I'm not sure I'm going to forget you in a hurry.' She touched the necklace with her fingers. 'The last few days have been…the most amazing of my life.'

He smiled with one side of his mouth. 'I'm glad you're having a good time. You deserve it.'

'Are *you* having a good time?'

He took her hand and entwined her fingers with his. 'I'm having such a good time I'm going to have trouble getting back into gear for work.'

She squeezed against his fingers. 'Maybe you should schedule in a few more holidays.'

He turned her hand over and traced a lazy circle in the middle of her palm, his gaze following the movement of his finger, the gentle caress triggering a firestorm in her blood. 'Maybe I should.' After a moment, his gaze came back to hers. 'I used to love going on holidays before my parents divorced. But afterwards…well, it just wasn't the same.'

'It must have been so hard for you and your mum, trying to make things nice for Ella,' Abby said.

He released her hand and let out a jagged sigh. 'Mum tried her best but she found it hard to see other couples on holiday, other families doing all the things she used to do with us before my dad left. It was painful to witness her distress. I had to step up and do the man-about-the-house stuff—not that my father was any great handyman or anything—but on top of school work and looking after Ella, well, there wasn't a lot of time left over for hanging out with friends and doing normal teenage stuff.'

'You've been an amazing son and a wonderful brother, Luke,' Abby said. 'Your mum and Ella are always saying how much they adore you and wish they saw more of you.'

'I know I should see them more often but I'm always snowed under with work.'

'Maybe you allow yourself to be snowed under,' Abby said. 'You run a very successful business. Surely you can delegate or outsource a bit more so you can have a life as well as work? It's not healthy trying to do it all yourself.'

A frown knitted his brows. 'I enjoy work.'

'But you might enjoy other things too,' Abby said. 'But how will you know unless you free up some time to do them?'

He reached for her hand again. 'Okay, Miss Hart. We have the next few days for you to teach me how to kick back and relax. Are you up for it?'

Abby gave him a high five. 'Game on.'

Luke was having such a good time relaxing with Abby—and, yes, having fun…that word he'd almost forgotten existed—that he forgot to charge his phone until two days before they were to leave the island. But when he gave it some juice he was a little horrified to see all the missed calls from his office in London. He called to find out there was a crisis with one of the major projects he had going. But what was even more shocking to him was how close he had been to unplugging the charger and ignoring the long list of text messages and emails.

'You don't have to rush back,' his secretary Kay said. 'It can wait a day or two. We just thought you'd better know in case—'

'Of course I have to come back,' Luke said. 'I'm responsible for the project. I know all the codes and I can fix this in a snap. I can't allow anything to go awry at this late stage. I'll get the next available flight.'

'But what about your holiday with Abby? Don't you want to stay? You could do the recoding over the phone or on Skype or email them through.'

Luke did want to stay, which was the scariest thing of all. He never wanted to leave the damn island. He never wanted to leave Abby. But he had to. He was only making it harder on them both by allowing it to get this far. What had he been thinking? He couldn't just drop everything and hang out on a beach and have picnics and make love at sunset. That stuff was for other people. People who hadn't been stalked by tragedy and left to carry the guilt like an anchor in their gut. He had responsibilities and people relying on him. 'No,' he said. 'I'm coming back. This is far more important than a holiday.'

After five days of swimming and snorkelling and plunging into the sea from a rock face, Abby was constantly balancing the scales of having fun with the harsh reality the fun was going to end once the week was over. Making love on the beach, sunset picnics watching the night sky appear star by star, planet by planet, long candlelit dinners and lazy breakfasts had made the days pass faster than she wanted them to.

Luke had taught her to fish—something she had always wanted to do—and she had taught him to relax. They had two more days on the island before they returned to London, which meant their fling would be over.

But Abby had a feeling Luke might be rethinking the time frame. She'd seen him looking at her when he thought she wasn't watching with a thoughtful expression on his face. And he often toyed with the diamond pendant around her neck when he was lying beside her, letting the chain slip through his fingers and the diamond rest against his palm.

Was she imagining his change of heart? She didn't think so. She hoped not. She prayed not. Didn't the last few days prove how good they were together? She had never seen him smile so much and the tight lines bracketing his mouth and the creases on his forehead had all but disappeared.

Why wouldn't he want to stay in their relationship when they were so comfortable together?

Abby was putting the finishing touches to dinner when he came in carrying his phone and his overnight bag and frowning. 'What's wrong? That's the first frown I've seen you give for five days.'

'Sorry, Abby, but something's come up at work,' he said. 'I have to go back early. No one else can fix it but me and it's not something I can do over the phone. I've called the boat operator. He'll be here in half an hour.'

Abby's heart sank and the strings on her hopes severed. 'But what about me?'

'You can finish the holiday on your own. There's no point rushing back with me now, as I'll be stuck in the office for the next week by the look of things. You might as well make the most of the last couple of days.'

'But it won't be the same without you,' Abby said. 'What will I do with myself? There's no one else on the island.'

'I'll arrange for someone to be with you. A staff member or—'

'A *staff* member?' Abby stared at him. 'Why would I want to be here with a staff member when I only want to be with you?'

His features were set in tight lines. 'Look, I don't have time for this right now—'

'Make time, Luke,' Abby said. 'This is important to me. You can't just dash back to London as if the last few days didn't happen. Didn't they mean anything to you? Don't *I* mean anything to you?'

He let out an impatient breath. 'Look, if you're worried about what people are going to say then I can't see the problem. I'm not in any of the photos you post online so how will they know I'm not here with you?'

'But *I* will know,' Abby said. 'I'll be here wishing you were with me because…because I love you.'

He flinched as if she had hit him. 'Stop it. Stop it right now.'

'I won't stop it,' Abby tried to keep her tone calm. 'I can't hide it or pretend any more. I love you. The last few days have cemented it for me. I don't want our fling to end when the week is over. I want to be with you for ever.'

The frown between his brows brought all the tense lines back to his forehead. 'I told you what I was prepared to give you and a future wasn't a part of it.'

'But I think deep down you want what I want,' Abby said. 'You want it but you feel you don't deserve it because of what happened to Kimberley.'

'This has nothing to do with Kimberley,' he said. 'You're shifting the goalposts because you've had a great time playing in the sun and the sand, but it's not real, Abby. None of this is real. It hasn't been real from the start. It's just one big charade and I foolishly went on with it because—'

'If you say because you felt sorry for me I will scream loud enough to break all the windows,' Abby said. 'I don't want your sympathy. I want your love.'

Luke's phone rang and he put his bag down on the floor.

'Don't answer it,' she said. 'Surely this is way more important than a stupid phone call?'

He threw her an exasperated look and turned his back and answered his phone. 'Yes, I'm on my way. Yes. It's all under control.' He ended the call and turned back around as he pocketed his phone. 'I have to go.' He picked up his bag. 'There are people waiting for me.'

People far more important than her. He didn't say it but then he didn't have to. He had shown it by his choice to leave her here all alone. He hadn't asked

her to go with him. Why not? It wouldn't have taken
her long to pack. No, he wanted to leave without her
because he had never been here with her. Not willingly. Not wholeheartedly.

'You were never truly here with me on this island,
were you, Luke?' Abby said. 'Your refusal to be in
any of the photos is proof you weren't with me in
every sense of the word. I might as well have had a
cardboard cut-out of you because that's all you give
of yourself. The outer shell but not the innermost part
of you. The part that wants what everyone else wants:
love, connection, a future, a family. You've locked
that part of yourself away and thrown away the key.'

'Abby.'

'Don't use that lecturing voice with me,' Abby
said. 'I hate it when you do that. Why didn't you ask
me to go back with you? No, don't answer that. I'll
tell you why. You want out of this fling, don't you?'

'I never wanted to be in it in the first place.'

His coldly delivered statement was like a sledgehammer on the thin ice of her hopes. Each word
caused a deep fissure in her heart until she could
barely draw breath. 'Right, well, that's it in a big fat
crinkly nutshell,' Abby said. 'Sorry for all the trouble I've caused you.' She unclipped the pendant from
around her neck and handed it to him. 'Here. Take
it back. The box is upstairs. I don't suppose you'll
wait until I get it for you and pack up all the clothes
you bought for me?'

'I don't want the pendant or the clothes,' he said
through tight lips. 'They were gifts.'

'Oh, yes, for services rendered,' Abby said, casting him a look that could have frozen Mercury. 'Thanks, by the way, for helping me on that front. I'm sure my future partner will also be enormously grateful.'

There was a storm brewing at the back of his eyes but that was the only sign he was struggling with his anger. 'Enjoy the rest of your stay on the island.'

'Don't worry.' Abby inched up her chin. 'I will.'

Luke's flight was delayed heading back to London so by the time he got to his office one of his junior staff had solved the programming problem that had threatened his multimillion-pound project. He'd always thought Sanjeev had talent but this proved it beyond a doubt. He should've felt relieved everything was sorted, but with Abby's words still rattling around his brain like loose marbles he could feel another migraine coming on.

He didn't believe for a second she was in love with him. She was worried about her job and all the silly lies she'd told. They were two days from ending their fling and she was panicking about how she was going to maintain her reputation.

Well, that had nothing to do with him.

Not any more.

He shouldn't have stepped into the role as her Mr Perfect. That was his first mistake and the second was taking her to that island. A place like that, well, even he'd been a little set off course by all the fun they'd been having. He couldn't remember a time when he'd felt more relaxed.

But that didn't mean he wanted their fling to continue indefinitely. He'd toyed with the idea of extending it a bit. Sure he had. Why wouldn't he? But even if he had adjusted the time frame, ultimately he couldn't give her what she wanted. He hadn't been able to give it to Kimberley or any other woman he had dated in the past.

Why should Abby be any different?

He didn't want the fairy tale she wanted. She might carry on with that psychobabble she was known for, saying he was overcompensating with work or locking away parts of himself. Well, he was damn fine with locking away parts of himself. Those were the parts that had got him into trouble in the past.

He wanted none of it.

No wife.

No kids.

No commitment.

Abby had no right to insist he drop everything he'd worked so hard for just for the sake of the two days left of their holiday. He had responsibilities he took seriously. He had staff he had to provide income for and clients—important clients—and patients from all over the globe depending on him getting this exciting new project off the ground.

But you could have come back to London later...

Luke shut down the thought. That phone call had been a good excuse to cut short Abby's silly little fantasy. He'd done the right thing in coming back. Of course he had. Their fling had gone on long enough. He shouldn't have allowed it to start in the first place. He'd broken his own rule by allowing her to move in with him. And he never should have bought her that wretched pendant. What was it with women and jewellery? Abby had attached significance to his gift when all he'd wanted to do was give her something worth keeping instead of that fake stuff she wore.

Luke came out of his office just as his secretary Kay came in from a coffee break. 'Bet you wish you hadn't rushed back here now, eh?' she said. 'Sanjeev's a bright young man. We call him Mensa Man behind his back. You should let him do a bit more around here. He's more than capable.'

'I'm seriously thinking about it.' He turned back to go to his office.

'Was Abby terribly disappointed about having to come back early?' Kay asked.

Luke swallowed a tight knot. He wasn't ready to explain what had happened on the island. More to the point, he wasn't used to explaining his private life to anyone. That was Abby's forte. 'I left her to enjoy the last couple of days by herself.'

Kay looked at him as if he'd told her he had left Abby on the moon without a spacesuit. 'You left her behind? Alone?'

He shrugged. 'So? Only I needed to come back.'

'But why didn't she come back with you?'

'I didn't ask her to.'

'Why the hell not?' Kay asked. 'Did you have a tiff or something?'

Luke's throat was so tight he could have sworn he was wearing a tie but he still had on the casual shirt he'd dressed in on the island. He had to give it to Abby. She was a whole lot better at this lying gig than he was. 'It's…complicated.'

Kay crossed her arms and gave him the sort of look a mother did to a teenager who had failed an important exam. 'You've blown it, haven't you?'

Luke scowled. 'Can you quit the third degree? I pay you to work, not to pry into my private life.'

'You didn't have a private life before Abby,' Kay said. 'She's the best thing that's ever happened to you. Although I did wonder why she hadn't posted any photos of you from the island. That seemed a bit odd to me. I hope you weren't glued to your phone all the time. We tried to keep things ticking over here so you could relax, but then we hit that coding issue and—'

'What's odd about wanting my private life to be private?' Luke said with barely banked-down annoyance. 'I don't feel the need to tell everyone where I last had coffee or what I had for breakfast.'

'It's a way of connecting with people.'

'Yeah? Well, I prefer to do it the old-fashioned way.'

'Like that's been working a treat for you these last five years,' Kay's tone was so dry it almost crackled.

Luke drew in a savage breath and swung back towards his office. 'I knew I shouldn't have given you that last pay rise.'

'Do you want it back?'

He glowered at her over his shoulder. 'Keep it and your opinions to yourself. Understood?'

Kay saluted and clicked her heels. 'Yes, sir.'

Abby flew back to London the following day in such low spirits two of the flight attendants asked during the journey if she was all right. She mopped at her streaming reddened eyes and told them it was just an allergic reaction. When she came through Customs and saw all the couples being reunited it made her heart feel as if it was being crushed.

Why couldn't Luke love her? Why couldn't he want to be with her for ever? Why did he leave her to fend for herself like everyone she had ever loved had done?

There was no way she could have stayed on the island without him. Every corner, every space, every view contained a memory of their time together. All she had now was memories. She didn't even have any photos of them together because he'd been so darn stubborn about taking any. She'd sneaked a few of him when he wasn't looking, but there were none of them together. It was as if their time on the island hadn't happened, it was just a mirage.

Just like her life...

Abby couldn't avoid the truth any longer. For years she had been hiding behind a web of lies. Telling people who she wished she was instead of who she actually was. She wasn't the got-it-all-together girl of her blog and column. She was a lonely single young woman from a disadvantaged background who dreamed of having the fairy tale.

But her handsome white knight had locked him-self in his tower of guilt and there was nothing Abby could do to change him. She shouldn't have even tried. If she had just come out with the truth in the beginning she wouldn't have caused herself so much heartache. So many times she had given people advice in her column but she hadn't taken it herself.

There was no way she would have told someone to pretend to be engaged to save face. She would have told them a relationship based on a lie wasn't an au-thentic relationship. What right did she have to give advice? Her life was a mess. It had always been a mess. Her whole life was a lie. And it had to change.

Right here.

Right now.

She took out her phone and started typing a new column. Felicity might hate her or even fire her for it, but at least Abby would no longer be living a lie.

Luke couldn't stop thinking about the island. The sun, the sand, the beach, the bay, and the rock they had dived from. The way the island cut out the rest of the world, created a safe haven where they had been in touch with nature. He couldn't stop thinking about the amazing food Abby had cooked and the long lazy meals where they had sat under the stars sipping champagne.

But most of all he couldn't stop thinking about Abby.

She was in his thoughts every minute and every

second of the day and night. She was in his body. He would close his eyes and feel her soft little hands moving over him. He could feel her mouth, her lips, her tongue. Her smile was imprinted on his heart. Every time he pictured her smile his heart would contract as if it was being squished between two thick books.

Every time he went home from work his house seemed emptier and lonelier than it ever had before. Even work wasn't as enjoyable and fulfilling as before. Especially with Kay shaking her head and casting him rolled-eyed looks all the time.

She'd stopped lecturing him but as he was leaving work that day he found Abby's latest column open on her computer screen. Luke had so far resisted the temptation to read whatever lies Abby was peddling lately, but this time he couldn't stop himself from reading. It wasn't a long piece but it was heartfelt and honest. In it Abby shared how she had grown up through the foster system because her parents had had drug and alcohol issues. She spoke of how desperately she had wanted to fit in, to be normal—all the stuff she had told him during their time together.

His heart ached for her, revealing all that to the public. It was such a brave and dignified thing to do, for she crafted it in such a way to help people who were struggling with the same issues as her parents so they didn't feel judged, but rather to let them know help was at hand. She went on to say her pretence over being engaged to Mr Perfect was something she deeply regretted because there was no such thing as a perfect partner. The only thing you could wish for was to be the best partner you could be and that love would take care of the rest, if you were lucky enough to find someone who loved you.

Luke read that line twice because his vision had suddenly blurred.

If you were lucky enough to find someone who loved you.

Abby loved him. Why had he found that so hard to believe? Or had he been too frightened to believe it? Too worried it wouldn't last or would be snatched away from him. But he had been the one to sabotage it. He had found someone to love him and he had left her behind alone. He hadn't even asked her to come with him when work called him away. He had made his work a higher priority than Abby.

But his only priority was Abby.

Hadn't the last few days demonstrated that? He was walking through life like a ghost. His life was meaningless without her sunny presence casting out all the shadows that had doggedly surrounded him for so long. Why had he been such an emotional coward? Had he ruined any chance of a future with her?

He wanted to see her straight away but there was one thing he had to do first. He should have done it years ago. He raced home to pack up Kimberley's things, shooting her parents a text to say he would be around to drop them off as soon as he got a chance.

He folded the clothes and placed them in a cardboard box and gently closed the lid. It was like closing a chapter of his life.

His phone pinged with an answering text from Kimberley's parents to say they were in the area—could they drop in for a minute to pick up their daughter's things? Luke was desperate to go and see Abby but he couldn't fob off Kimberley's parents. Surely he owed them a few minutes?

He opened the front door an excruciatingly long hour later to find Peter and Tanya Norman standing there. 'Come in,' he said, greeting them as he normally did with awkward hugs and handshakes.

Tanya looked like she'd been recently crying, but then that wasn't unusual. 'Luke…there's something I have to tell you. I think it's time to tell you the truth about what happened the night Kimberley was… killed.'

Luke looked at Peter but he was doing his stoic father and husband thing, although he reached for his wife's hand and gave it an encouraging squeeze.

'The thing is…' Tanya swallowed. 'Kimberley was going to break up with you. She was interested in someone else but didn't have the courage to tell you. She didn't cheat on you. I know that for a fact. She was just finding it hard to bring things to an end with you because you were always so good to her. I think the only reason she didn't tell you about it that night was because she felt like she had betrayed you by allowing herself to fall in love with someone else while still in a relationship with you.'

Luke couldn't get his brain around the bombshell

news. Kimberley had been about to leave him? No wonder he'd thought their relationship was past its use-by date. But he'd always blamed himself. 'Why didn't you say something before now?'

Tanya looked ashamed. 'I felt it would hurt you too much to know she had fallen in love with someone else. You were always so good to her. So kind and patient when I know she wasn't always an easy person to be with. But I think that's because she wasn't in love with you. She'd been so hurt by her last relationship and you were a safe person, someone she trusted to take care of her. But in the end she wanted more. She wanted what everyone wants. True love.'

Luke wanted to be angry but somehow couldn't summon the energy. Kimberley's parents believed he'd been in love with her. He didn't think it served any purpose to tell them he hadn't been. 'Thank you for telling me,' he said. 'It was very courageous of you.'

'I was worried when I saw you and Abby Hart had broken up,' Tanya said. 'I was pleased you had found someone. Really pleased. I thought I wouldn't be when the time came but I was. But then I felt terrible when I saw you'd broken up. I wondered then if it had anything to do with what happened with Kimberley. I couldn't let another moment pass before I told you what I should have told you years ago. She might not have loved you as you loved her but she did love you. It just wasn't the right sort of love.'

Luke opened his arms and welcomed her into a

warm hug. He reached out with one arm and included Peter as well. No one said anything. They simply stood in a circle of three, honouring their memories of Kimberley.

And for the first time in five years Luke felt an enormous weight lift off his shoulders.

Abby had been mentally preparing for the fallout after her column went live but the opposite happened. Her inbox was filled with messages of support and encouragement, her Twitter feed went nuts and Felicity even mentioned something about a pay rise.

But, even so, it didn't make her heart feel any lighter.

Ella had phoned her every day since Abby had been back in London but she had been surprisingly tight-lipped about her older brother, saying only that she was reluctant to take sides as they were both adults and had to figure out this stuff on their own.

But Abby was worried Luke might never figure out his stuff. His stuff had put his life on hold for five long years. Would he end up an old lonely man with no one by his side?

Would she end up alone?

Who else did she want but Luke? He was her Mr Almost Perfect. The man who had stolen her heart with his first frown.

Sabina came into Abby's office cubicle carrying a huge bunch of red roses. 'These are for you,' she said.

Abby's heart gave a stumble. 'For me?'

'Yep and there are more. Like heaps more.' Sabina nodded towards Reception. 'It's like a florist's shop out there. And a fruit shop.'

Abby frowned. 'Fruit?'

'Strawberries,' Sabina said, eyes twinkling. 'Chocolate-coated ones and champagne. A dozen bottles of it.'

Abby's legs were shaking so much she could barely stand and it was a moment or two before she could get her voice to work. 'Who's it from?'

Just then a tall figure appeared outside Abby's cubicle.

'They're from me,' Luke said and then proceeded to go down on one knee in front of her. 'Darling, please forgive me. I've been a stupid fool. I can't believe I left you on that island all on your own. It was such a crass and hurtful thing to do. Please say you'll forgive me. I'll do everything in my power to make it up to you. I'll even buy the damn island so we can go back there and have a proper holiday without me acting like a jerk and storming off as if work is the only thing I care about. I care about you. I love you.'

Abby could barely see through tears and threw her arms around his neck. 'Oh, Luke, of course I forgive you. I've ached to hear you say those three little words. I love you so much I'm just about bursting with it.'

He smiled at her with such tenderness her heart squeezed. 'You are the love of my life. I'm only half a person without you. Will you marry me and make me the happiest man on the planet?'

Abby choked back a happy sob. Could there have

been a more heartfelt proposal from a man in love? 'Oh, darling, of course I'll marry you. But what changed your mind? I thought you were—?'

'I'm ashamed of how I pushed you away when all I've ever wanted from the moment I met you was to hold you close. I love you, my darling. I think I've probably loved you from the first time you smiled at me.'

'I can't believe you just proposed to me in front of all these people,' Abby said, glancing at the assembled crowd outside her office cubicle, including Sabina, who was looking all dewy-eyed as if she'd been watching a romantic movie.

'I don't care who's watching,' Luke said. 'They can stream it live on Twitter or wherever else for all I care. I want everyone to know how much I love you.'

Abby hadn't thought it was possible to feel such happiness. Luke loved her. He wanted to marry her. It was a dream, a fairy tale come true. 'Ella is going to be beside herself. *I'm* beside myself.'

He stood up and then held her close. 'You're beside me and that's where you're going to stay for the rest of our lives.'

Abby stroked his face, her heart feeling so full when she saw the love shining in his gaze. 'I was so sad when you left me behind. But I realised when I got back to London I had to stop lying about how perfect my life was when it was anything but.'

He held one of her hands against the deep thud of his heart. 'I can't promise you a perfect life, I can't even promise to be a perfect partner but I can promise to love you and protect you for as long as we both shall live. Now, I think these people are waiting for us to seal this promise with a kiss.' His eyes glinted. 'Shall we get on with it?'

Abby smiled and lifted her mouth to his. 'Yes, please.'

EPILOGUE

One year later...

ABBY CAME OUT to the sun-warmed terrace at the villa on the island, where Luke was waiting for her to come back from the bathroom. *Their* island—Luke's and hers. Luke insisted it was his gift to her but he had already given her so much.

She hadn't thought it possible to be so happy and contented. They weren't a perfect couple by any means but their love for each other more than made up for that. Her lonely childhood felt so far away now. The love Luke showered her with more than compensated for the disadvantages she'd suffered as a child. Not a day went past without him telling her he loved her. He always said it first, not just when she said it to him. He showed it too in thousands of ways. Little things he did for her, like ignoring his phone when it rang when she was telling him something important, or even when she was telling him something unimportant. He made *her* feel important. He made her feel the most important person to him and that was something she was so grateful for.

Abby kept the pregnancy dipstick behind her back and came over to where he was sitting on a sun lounger with a book resting on his lap. 'What are you reading?' she said, leaning down to plant a kiss on his head.

He captured her by the hand and brought her down on to his lap, quickly shoving his book aside. 'Work stuff, but you're way more interesting.' He suddenly frowned. 'Hey, what's that you're hiding behind your back?'

Abby smiled and brought her hand from behind her to show him. 'Guess what? We're having a baby.'

Tears shone in his eyes and he swallowed deeply. 'Oh, darling, that's wonderful. I can't believe it. We're having a baby.' He gave a delighted laugh and gently cradled her head to kiss her. 'You'll be the most amazing mother, I'm sure of it.'

Abby looked lovingly into his eyes. 'And you will be an amazing father. I'm so proud of the way you've worked on your relationship with your dad since we got married.'

His broad smile warmed her heart. 'I know he's not perfect, nor ever likely to be anything close to it, but he's making an effort so the least I can do is make one too.'

Abby kissed him on the lips again. 'Maybe he'll make a much better grandfather than a father. Some people are like that.'

Luke stroked her cheek, his expression so full of

love it made her breath catch. 'You've taught me so much about relationships, my darling. You make me a better person. More understanding, more accepting, more forgiving.'

'You've taught me heaps too,' Abby said. 'Like how to be honest about what I want. And right now, I want you.'

Luke brought her mouth back down to his and gathered her close. 'Perfect, because I want you too.'

* * * * *

If you enjoyed Melanie Milburne's 75th book,
A VIRGIN FOR A VOW,
why not explore some more stories
by the same author?

THE TYCOON'S MARRIAGE DEAL
A RING FOR THE GREEK'S BABY
WEDDING NIGHT WITH HER ENEMY

Available now!

'Where am I to sleep?' Laurel asked.

'There's a guest bedroom across the hall.'
Cristiano pushed open the door opposite his own.

She turned to glance at him and that was her
mistake. Her breath came out in a rush as heat
flared between them. He put his hand on her
wrist.

'Don't, Cristiano,' she whispered.

'Don't what?'

'Don't touch me.'

'Don't tempt you?' He stroked the silky skin of
her inner wrist with his thumb. 'Is that what you
mean?'

Laurel remained frozen, her pulse hammering.

'Why deny what is between us, *bella*?'

'There's nothing between us.' She had to nearly
gasp the words out.

'Your body begs to differ.' Cristiano could see the
indecision in her fractured gaze…the desire as
well as the doubt. 'Stop worrying so much. What
are you afraid of?' he murmured, his lips very
nearly brushing hers.

'This…' she whispered, and then Cristiano
kissed her.

After spending three years as a die-hard New Yorker, **Kate Hewitt** now lives in a small village in the English Lake District with her husband, their five children and a golden retriever. In addition to writing intensely emotional stories, she loves reading, baking and playing chess with her son—she has yet to win against him, but she continues to try. Learn more about Kate at kate-hewitt.com.

Books by Kate Hewitt

Mills & Boon Modern Romance

Moretti's Marriage Command
Inherited by Ferranti

One Night With Consequences

Engaged for Her Enemy's Heir
Larenzo's Christmas Baby

Seduced by a Sheikh

The Secret Heir of Alazar
The Forced Bride of Alazar

The Billionaire's Legacy

A Di Sione for the Greek's Pleasure

Secret Heirs of Billionaires

Demetriou Demands His Child

The Marakaios Brides

The Marakaios Marriage
The Marakaios Baby

Rivals to the Crown of Kadar

Captured by the Sheikh
Commanded by the Sheikh

Visit the Author Profile page
at millsandboon.co.uk for more titles.

THE INNOCENT'S
ONE-NIGHT
SURRENDER

BY

KATE HEWITT

First Published in Great Britain 2017
By Mills & Boon, an imprint of HarperCollins*Publishers*
1 London Bridge Street, London, SE1 9GF

© 2017 Kate Hewitt

ISBN: 978-0-263-93516-5

Our policy is to use papers that are natural, renewable and recyclable
products and made from wood grown in sustainable forests. The logging
and manufacturing processes conform to the legal environmental
regulations of the country of origin.

Printed and bound in Spain
by CPI, Barcelona

THE INNOCENT'S ONE-NIGHT SURRENDER

To Jenna,
Thanks for spurring me on with this book!
Love being able to chat with you.
Love, K.

CHAPTER ONE

LAUREL FORRESTER burst from the hotel room like a bullet from a gun, aiming for the lift down the hall. Her breath came in tearing gasps and she stumbled in the heels she wasn't used to wearing—stupid, sky-high stilettos her mother had insisted on.

She heard the sound of the door to the executive suite being wrenched open behind her and then heavy footfalls.

'Come back here, you stupid little—'

With a mewling gasp of terror, Laurel put on a burst of speed, racing around the corner. The gleaming black doors of the lift shimmered ahead of her, a promise of freedom.

'Wait until I…'

She closed her mind to Rico Bavasso's threats and stabbed the button for the lift with a shaking finger. *Please, please open. Save me…*

Bavasso came round the corner, moving swiftly for a man pushing sixty. Laurel risked a glance back and then wished she hadn't. Three diagonal cuts slashed one of his lean cheeks, where she'd scratched him, blood oozing down his face in crimson, pearly droplets.

Please, please open. If the lift doors didn't open, she didn't know what she'd do. Fight for her safety, for her life. Go down kicking and screaming, because go down she would. Bavasso might be older but he was big, strong and angry, and she was five-foot-four and just a little over a hundred pounds soaking wet.

With a glorious ping the doors opened and Laurel threw herself inside, bruising her shoulder against the far wall before she scrambled upright. She pushed just about every button she could, anything to get her away from the hell that had erupted with Bavasso's demands and grabs, his insistence that he would get what he'd paid for. What her mother had promised him.

Bile rose in Laurel's throat at that memory and she choked it down. She didn't have the luxury of memories or even thoughts in this moment. This was about basic survival. She pushed the 'door close' button repeatedly as Bavasso stumbled towards the lift, a smile of triumph curving his cold mouth, his glowering face thrust forward. His bow tie was askew, his tuxedo shirt straining against the buttons as he reached one hand forward to keep the doors from closing. Laurel shrank back against the lift wall, her heart beating in her chest like some wild, winged thing.

'I've got you, you little slut.'

Laurel kicked off one of her wretched stilettos and swung it at Bavasso's grasping hand. He let out a howl of outrage and yanked it back, his palm impaled by the dagger-sharp heel. The doors closed and then the lift was soaring upwards and Laurel was safe, *safe*.

She let out a sob of both terror and relief, her senses overwhelmed by what had happened—and what had almost happened, but thankfully hadn't. Her trembling legs felt weak and watery and she sank onto the floor, drawing her knees up to her chest as shudders wracked her body. *That had been so close*.

But she wasn't out of danger yet. She still had to get out of this hotel, out of Rome. Bavasso had her handbag in his hotel room, as well as his security detail waiting down in the foyer. Laurel had seen them when he'd been playing baccarat, standing around like stony-faced gorillas, eyes darting around the casino floor, looking for threats. And now she was one.

What would he do? Over the last two days' acquaintance he'd been sleek and charming, although admittedly paying her more attention than she'd have liked, considering he was her mother's latest love interest. He also seemed arrogant and entitled, and she feared he might not let this lie. And what about her mother? Was Elizabeth safe? Would Bavasso turn on her—or had she really been part of it all along, as he'd implied? *I'm only taking what your mother promised me.*

Surely not? Surely her mother wouldn't have sold her off like a cow at auction? With another cry Laurel covered her face, the tumult of the evening too much to bear. She should never have agreed to come to Rome, to play a part so she could get what she wanted. And yet she had. She'd weighed it up in her mind and she'd decided it was worth it. One last favour and then she'd finally be free. Except she wasn't free now. She didn't feel remotely free.

The doors opened and Laurel lifted her head, shrinking back, half-expecting Bavasso to be there, waiting. But, no; the lift opened directly into what looked like a private suite, twice as elegant and spacious as the one Laurel had just fled.

She scrambled to her feet, pulling on the hem of the short sparkly dress of silver satin that had also been her mother's choice. *Bavasso wants to see a lovely young woman in her prime, not some dowdy wallflower. He's a discriminating man, Laurel.* Now she was afraid she understood all that had meant.

Laurel knew she couldn't stay in the lift; the doors would close and then the lift would start heading down again, back to Bavasso or his goons, somewhere she definitely didn't want to be. Cautiously Laurel took a step out, onto a floor of polished black marble. Floor-to-ceiling windows were visible in every direction, giving a panoramic view of the Eternal City, lights shimmering in the darkness.

Modern-looking sofas of black leather and gleaming chrome were scattered around, the soaring space lit only by a few minimalistic table lamps, so it took Laurel a stunned second to realise there was someone in the room with her.

A man stood at its centre dressed in black trousers and a charcoal-grey shirt that was open at the throat. His hair was black and cropped close to his head, his eyes a piercing grey, the same colour as his shirt. His arms were folded, emphasising impressive biceps, and everything about him radiated power. Control. *Danger.*

Laurel's breath hitched and she froze where she stood, dawning realisation, relief and fear colliding inside her with an almighty crash. *Could it be...?*

Then he spoke, a voice like molten silver, pitched low. His tone was both authoritative and sensual, winding around her shattered senses, pulling them tight.

'Hello, Laurel.'

She gave a little gasp of surprise even though she'd known, deep inside, that it was him. That it had to be him. The awareness she felt of him didn't make sense, considering they were near strangers, yet she wasn't surprised by it at all.

'Cristiano.' She let out a little laugh of relief; the adrenalin still coursing through her body made her feel shaky and weak. Or maybe he was making her feel shaky and weak, standing there like a rock-solid pillar, arms still folded, face expressionless in the dim light. 'Thank God.'

He arched one dark slash of an eyebrow, his gaze travelling to her tiny, torn dress. 'Things get a little out of hand?'

Laurel glanced down at her dress, an embarrassed flush sweeping over her along with all the other overwhelming emotions. The dress was practically indecent, a spangled slip that revealed far too much thigh and cleavage. One of the straps had torn from the bodice, so the dress gaped even more. She wasn't even wearing a bra, only a tiny scrap of a thong. And, from the hard look in her stepbrother's eyes, Laurel suspected he knew it—and wasn't impressed.

She took a deep breath, trying to gather her scattered wits. Her head was spinning from everything that had happened, and her legs still felt weak. She longed to sit down, to *breathe*, to figure out how she'd got here and what on earth she was going to do next. 'I didn't even know you were here.'

'Didn't you?'

'No, of course not...' Laurel frowned, belatedly registering Cristiano's cool tone, the look of mocking censure in his iron gaze. And then she remembered the last time she'd seen him, ten years ago, when she'd been a silly fourteen-year-old to his manly twenty-three, and when she'd practically thrown herself at him as part of a stupid teen-aged dare.

'I don't even know where I am,' she said, trying to smile, but her lips didn't seem to be working properly. They just wobbled.

'You're in the penthouse suite of La Sirena. My private home.'

'Oh.' So she'd pushed *that* button? But how had she been granted access? 'Well, I'm glad the doors opened up here. Very glad.'

'I'm sure you are.' There was a note of sardonic amusement in his voice that Laurel felt too scatter-brained to understand at the moment. It sounded as if he was referencing something she was meant to know about and didn't. Unless he was referring to her stupid schoolgirl crush all those years ago. Laurel doubted that. She doubted her one clumsy attempt at a kiss—he'd pushed her firmly away before she'd so much as made contact—had stayed in Cristiano's memory for more than a millisecond. He'd been that unimpressed.

'Do you mind if I clean myself up?' she asked. 'I feel...' Dirty. She felt dirty. But Cristiano didn't need to know that. He was already looking at her as if he thought she was, a realisation that made heat scorch Laurel's face once more. She knew she was wearing a slinky, slutty get-up, but did he have any right to judge her? Although, considering her actions tonight, perhaps he did.

'Be my guest.' Cristiano gestured towards a corridor that led to the suite's bedrooms. 'You'll find everything you need in one of the bathrooms.'

'Thank you,' Laurel answered, her tone turning a bit haughty to cover her confusion—and her guilt. If she could have picked the circumstances in which she ever saw her stepbrother again, these would not have been them. Not by a million awful miles.

Was it just the way she was dressed or was there another reason he was being so cold? Not that they'd ever had much of a relationship, or one at all. Her mother had been married to his father for three years, but in that time Laurel had only met Cristiano twice. Once after the wedding, when he'd had a blazing argument with his father, Lorenzo Ferrero, and then stormed out. And the second time when he'd come home for some reason and she'd attempted, in pathetic, girlish naivety, to impress him.

Six months later Lorenzo had divorced Elizabeth and Laurel and her mother had high-tailed it back to Illinois, with nothing but a pocketful of jewellery to fund Elizabeth's often exorbitant lifestyle. Ferrero had had a watertight pre-nup, and her mother did like to spend money…

Cristiano was still staring at her, arms folded, the emotion in his silver eyes fathomless. What had she expected him to say? Do? He'd never expressed any familial concern or even interest in her before.

She was a stranger to him, or near enough to it, just as he was to her—or should be, except for the fact that out of idle curiosity—or perhaps, shamefully, something a little deeper than that—she'd followed his exploits on social media and scanned the many tabloid articles about his playboy lifestyle. She'd always been fascinated by this man who had loomed on the periphery of her life, dark and powerful, when she'd been an innocent teenaged girl emerging shyly from her chrysalis of gawkiness into uncertain womanhood.

It truly stunned her that she was in his penthouse now, although she supposed, if she stopped long enough to think rationally about it, she shouldn't have been that surprised. She'd known the hotel where they'd met Bavasso was owned by Cristiano. She just hadn't expected actually to see him.

Cristiano's mouth curved in a smile that held neither humour nor warmth. His eyes glittered like burnished mirrors, reflecting nothing. 'You said you wanted to clean yourself up?' he prompted.

'Yes.' Laurel realised she was staring but it was hard not to stare at a man who was so starkly beautiful, so arrogantly attractive. The silk of his shirt clung to his well-defined pectoral muscles and the narrow trousers emphasised lean hips and powerful thighs. But beyond the impressive musculature of his body was the aura he possessed, the lethal authority and latent sexuality he emanated from every perfect pore—and that was what made Laurel stare. And not just stare, but *imagine*, shadowy, vague thoughts and images that danced through her mind, awakening longings that been dormant for her whole life. Thankfully they remained shadowy, falling back and leaving a streak of restless heat in their wake.

Staring at him now, taking in the arrogant tilt of his head, the dark, winged eyebrows, the sculpted mouth formed into a hard, hard line—he looked just the same as he had ten years ago. Perhaps he was a bit more muscular now, a bit more powerful. He'd made his own millions in the last decade, she knew, in property, casinos and hotels, at the highest end of the market.

He'd also, according to the tabloids, had dozens and dozens of mistresses—Hollywood actresses and European supermodels who graced his arm like the most expensive accessories, and, if the papers were to be believed—and Laurel suspected they were—were discarded after a matter of days.

It seemed incredible to her that she'd actually tried, in a clumsy, desperate way, to make him like her gawky teenaged self. The realisation made her cringe even now—especially now—yet surely Cristiano didn't remember that? He'd swatted her away like a fly.

Just the memory made flustered confusion sweep through her and quickly she turned away, afraid that Cristiano would see her uncertainty. He'd seen too much already, starting with this skimpy dress.

'Thank you,' she mumbled again and then, not wanting to prolong her agony, she hurried down the hall.

Cristiano watched Laurel scurry down the hall like a frightened rabbit. A sexy frightened rabbit, wearing far too little clothing for his comfort, and only one shoe. He turned away, his jaw tightening, the flare of sexual attraction arrowing through him annoying him further. He hadn't expected to feel it quite so strongly, especially now that he knew what she was like.

When he'd seen Laurel Forrester swan into La Sirena this evening, dressed like a hooker and on the arm of a man who made his skin crawl, he'd felt shock slice through him. It was ten years since he'd last seen her; she looked a whole lot more grown up now, yet he'd recognised her. Instantly.

That second of stunned amazement had morphed into a deep, sick disappointment that settled in his gut, a leaden weight that was absurd, because if he'd had to think about it for a second he'd have known Laurel would be just like her mother—a craven, amoral gold-digger playing for her best chance. She'd shown her true colours at just fourteen years old, after all, and heaven knew the apple didn't usually fall far from the tree.

Which was why he had been so determined to cut off all his ties with his own father. The last thing he wanted to do was make the mistakes Lorenzo Ferrero had, chasing after some ridiculous and ever-elusive happily-ever-after and becoming increasingly more desperate to find it. Letting himself be used, hurt and humiliated, and for what? An amorphous emotion that didn't really exist, or at least shouldn't. Love.

Cristiano strolled towards the window, shoving his hands deep into his trouser pockets as he mused on what lay in store for Laurel...and for him. He'd watched her on the casino floor, draped on Bavasso's arm, her attempts at flirting cringingly over the top and obvious. She might be many things but what she definitely wasn't was a good actress.

Bavasso, of course, had lapped it up and demanded more. A lot more, apparently, because after Cristiano had left the floor he'd stayed by the bank of security cameras in his flat, watching her, waiting—but for what? He was acting obsessed, which was stupid, but he hadn't been able to keep himself from doing it.

He'd told himself it was because of their past—because he knew her mother was a thief and he had no intention of letting her fleece any of his customers, even one as unpleasant as Rico Bavasso. He'd told himself that, but he didn't completely buy it.

Then everything in him had frozen and clenched hard when he'd seen her leave the casino floor, Bavasso holding her hand, practically dragging her towards the lifts. But she'd gone. She'd been *smiling*. For some reason that smile had reached a vulnerable place he hated the thought of even possessing.

Cristiano didn't know what had happened upstairs in the

hotel suite but he could guess all too easily. Still he'd stayed by the cameras, which was why he'd seen her running for the lifts, as if the hounds of hell were chasing her—or just one lascivious one. Whatever game she was playing, she'd decided not to see it to the finish. And, while Cristiano certainly believed in a woman's right to say no whenever she chose to, it didn't change his opinion of Laurel Forrester one iota.

On the cameras he'd watched her hit all the buttons, including the one for the penthouse. The lift doors to the penthouse were always locked, but with one flip of a switch Cristiano had sent Laurel straight up to him.

And now here she was.

The only question that remained was, what was he going to do with her?

He narrowed his gaze as he looked out of the window, the Colosseum lit up at night, a beacon to the city. He'd brought Laurel up here because she'd needed rescuing and he was a man of honour.

But honour only extended so far. And now, with the lift doors locked again, the only person Laurel needed rescuing from was him.

CHAPTER TWO

LAUREL PEEKED INTO the first room on the left, a sumptuous bedroom with an *en suite* bathroom, and then she tiptoed over thick, white pile carpet, past a huge king-sized bed on its own dais with a rumpled black satin duvet. This was where Cristiano slept, and she sensed him in every sleek and powerful line of the room. She smelled him too—that spicy aftershave and something else, something infinitely more male that wound through her senses and ignited fireworks in her belly. Fireworks she was going to do her best to ignore.

Her curious gaze took in the room's stark elements—bed, bureau, view. No personal objects or mementoes, no photographs or knick-knacks. Not even a book. No sign of a woman, either, so perhaps he was between mistresses. But why was she looking? Laurel bolted for the bathroom, locking the door behind her.

The bathroom was just as elegantly stark as the bedroom, and almost as big. An enormous sunken black marble tub with gold taps, a separate infinity shower bigger than her bedroom back home and double sinks. Laurel registered the heat coming through the quarry tiles beneath her feet and let out a shuddery sigh, the events of the last few hours slamming into her all over her again.

The endless evening at the casino, while Rico had played baccarat and given her lascivious looks that Laurel had told herself were in her imagination. They had to be. Bavasso liked her mother. Her mother had said she was hoping for a ring, for goodness' sake. He wouldn't look at her. The only reason she was meeting him was to give her mother her blessing.

Wasn't it?

Then the moment when he'd asked her to go upstairs, and Laurel had given her mother a frantic look. Elizabeth had smiled and had told her she'd be along in a few minutes and they'd all have champagne to celebrate. And Laurel had believed her. Of course she had believed her. Elizabeth was her mother and, while she'd done some questionable things over the years, she'd never done anything like this.

Laurel closed her eyes as she tried to will back the pain of the betrayal. Although, betrayal wasn't the right word, not really, because Elizabeth hadn't promised anything but the cold, hard cash she knew Laurel needed... And Laurel had been willing to take it. Did that make her any better than her mother, a woman who was always on the prowl for a man to fund her lifestyle?

Taking a deep breath, Laurel opened her eyes and then shrugged off the satin slip of a dress. It pooled at her feet and, overcome suddenly with a remorse so strong it felt like a physical illness, cramping her stomach and making her gorge rise, she kicked the offending garment into the corner of the room.

But that wasn't enough—Laurel could still see the dress, a rumpled pile of silver, and with a little cry she snatched it up and pulled. The thin fabric tore easily, and within seconds the dress was in bright, glittering ribbons that she stuffed into the bin. Then she realised it was remarkably unwise to destroy the one piece of clothing she had. Was she meant to go confront Cristiano in nothing but a lacy thong? *That* would go over well.

With a groan, Laurel turned on the shower. She needed to wash and scrub off the scent of the expensive, cloying cologne that Rico Bavasso wore before she thought about what could she do—or what could she wear.

She stepped under the powerful jets, letting the water stream over and wash away her regrets...if only it could.

She never should have agreed to her mother's plan. Never should have sold her soul for a flimsy promise her mother now might not even keep. And if she didn't…

Laurel's heart lurched. It didn't feel fair that she wanted so little, worked so hard and might still end up with nothing. But she knew there was no point in whining or crying about it. She'd made her own choices, and they hadn't all been good ones. Some of them had been extraordinarily bad. Somehow she had to rescue what she could from the rubble of the last few hours.

She stayed in the bathroom for as long as she could, first under the soothing spray of the shower, and then brushing her hair. Thankfully there was a thick navy terrycloth robe hanging on the door and she swathed herself in it, grateful that it covered her from her neck to her toes. She needed the armour, flimsy as it was.

She also needed time to figure out a plan—and how to present it to Cristiano. She had, unfortunately, extremely limited resources or options. She'd left her handbag behind in Bavasso's hotel room, with her money, driving licence and hotel key. Her passport, at least, was in the safe back at the shabby *pensione* where she and her mother were staying. But how was she going to get there? What if Bavasso was waiting for her?

Taking a deep breath, she decided it was time to face the music. Face Cristiano…a prospect that made her insides lurch with alarm even as a little ripple of anticipation shivered through her. She was looking forward to seeing him, even sparring with him, although heaven knew she shouldn't be.

The relief she'd felt at being rescued, however accidentally, from Rico Bavasso's clutches had dissolved, replaced with an uncomfortable realisation that there was no love lost between Cristiano and her, or Cristiano's father and her mother. A bitter divorce had put paid to any family reunions, and if he remembered Laurel's schoolgirl crush he certainly didn't do so fondly. But surely he'd help her, a woman so obviously in distress and need? Cool and remote he might be, but he was—she hoped—a man of honour.

With nothing left to lose, Laurel headed back out to the suite's sitting room. Cristiano was stretched out on one of the sofas, his long, muscular legs propped on a glass-and-chrome coffee table, his high-tech smart phone in one hand as he scrolled through messages. He slid it into his pocket and stood up, all graceful, fluid urbanity, as she came into the room.

'Feel better?' he asked with a sardonic lift of one eyebrow.

'Yes, thank you. Your shower is amazing.' Her voice sounded thin and wavering, the voice of a girl rather than a woman. Laurel straightened. Cristiano might reduce her insides to quivering jelly—it was hard not to be affected and, yes, dazzled, by a man who exuded so much potent, masculine sexuality—but she could still take control of this conversation. 'I need to ask a favour of you.'

Cristiano looked unsurprised. 'Oh?' His voice was mild and enquiring, yet something dark pulsed underneath that innocuous tone, something that made Laurel feel even warier than she already did.

'Could you please send someone—one of your staff, perhaps—to my hotel? I need my things—my clothes and my passport.' She lifted her chin, forcing herself to meet his sardonic, silvery gaze. 'I'm intending to leave Rome as soon as possible.'

He cocked his head. 'Things not work out to your satisfaction here, then?'

She couldn't miss the mocking note in his voice and a flush swept over her. Still she kept his gaze. 'No.'

'Rico Bavasso doesn't like to be thwarted, you know,' Cristiano said after a moment when he continued simply to study her, an inspection so thorough Laurel felt as if he could see beneath the big, bulky robe she wore.

'I guessed as much, which is why I'm planning on leaving the country.'

'You think it will be that easy?'

Unease tightened in her gut and flared through her insides. 'What do you mean?'

'Bavasso is a powerful and unpleasant man,' Cristiano stated flatly. 'You chose the wrong mark, *bella*.'

She stared at him, that one work reverberating through her. *Mark.* So he thought she was a con artist, one step up from a prostitute, perhaps. She shouldn't care. She shouldn't even be surprised. She'd been acting like one, more or less, all evening, even if she'd never meant things to unravel the way they had. Shame burned deep, singeing her conscience, her soul. Why had she been so stupid; so desperate?

And as for Bavasso being both powerful and unpleasant…having it confirmed was the last thing she needed right now.

'He's not my mark,' she said. Cristiano merely looked disbelieving. 'You have no right to judge me,' she snapped, her nerves strung tight. Cristiano was hardly the person to be angry with, but no one else was available, and frankly she could use a tiny bit of sympathy right then. 'So what do you suggest I do?'

'Lie low for a while,' Cristiano stated carelessly, as if it was all of very little concern to him. And, of course, it was. She might have been semi-cyber-stalking him for the last ten years but Laurel very much doubted he'd given her so much as a thought. She was half-amazed he'd even remembered her name.

'Lie low,' she repeated, and she was the disbelieving one now. 'How? And where? I left my handbag in his hotel suite and all my belongings are back in the *pensione*.' She drew a quick, sharp breath. 'Will you *please* send someone to fetch them? It's a small favour...'

'A small favour? I'm hardly about to send one of my staff into a very difficult situation, *bella*.'

'Don't call me that,' she returned tightly. She knew he didn't mean it and it felt mocking. A sneer she couldn't stand when she already felt scraped raw, everything about this situation making her feel intensely, painfully vulnerable.

'Why not?' Cristiano challenged, his voice turning soft, seductive. 'You are very beautiful. I am merely stating fact.' His gaze lingered, caressing her, making her respond. She felt heat unfurl in her belly and pool between her thighs, a treacherous and most inconvenient heat she was doing her best to deny.

'Why is it difficult?' she persisted, trying to pretend he wasn't affecting her. That a blush wasn't sweeping in a scorching tidal wave over her entire body.

'Because Bavasso is an unpleasant man and he is likely to make things difficult for anyone who helps someone who thwarted him. I have no doubt he will have his security detail waiting at your hotel. If someone shows up asking for your room key, they'll know.'

'But couldn't you...couldn't someone be discreet?'

Cristiano's eyes narrowed. 'You might feel entirely at ease with putting an innocent person in such a situation, but I am not.'

Laurel swayed as she was hit afresh by what an awful mess she'd managed to get herself into. Feeling as if her legs might give way beneath her, she walked to the sofa across from Cristiano and sank onto it. 'What am I going to do?' she whispered, more to herself than to Cristiano. She dropped her head into her hands and closed her eyes. 'What am I going to *do*?'

* * *

Cristiano suppressed the pang of sympathy he felt for Laurel. The sight of her sitting there with her head in her hands, her hair falling in a golden-brown waterfall around her face, her robe gaping open to reveal slender, golden thighs... What man wouldn't be affected? Not just by sympathy, but by desire. He suppressed that too. It was inconvenient at the moment, although he'd noted Laurel's obvious response to him with interest. He'd also noted her attempt to cover it. For whatever reason, she didn't want him knowing how he affected her, and she hadn't made any attempt to ask to stay, so what game was she playing?

'The answer seems fairly obvious,' he remarked as he strolled to the window and gazed out at the view of Rome's skyline by night. 'You stay here.'

He glanced back at Laurel; she raised her head, her aquamarine eyes wide with shock, the exact colour of the sunlit Aegean Sea. Her hair hung in damp ringlets around her heart-shaped face and her robe—his robe, actually—had slid off one shoulder, revealing its perfect curve.

'Stay here?' She frowned, her expression of confusion almost comical and definitely suspect. She was putting it on quite thickly for his benefit, and why? This was surely what she'd wanted. What she'd been hoping for. He was a far better bet than Bavasso. So did she think her reluctance would somehow earn her brownie points or, heaven help him, trust?

He trusted no one, especially not a woman like Laurel Forrester.

'Yes,' Cristiano answered, his voice clipped, touched with impatience. 'Stay here.'

'For how long?'

'As long as is necessary.' He paused, letting his gaze sweep over her once more. The robe gaped at her chest and he could see the shadowy vee between her breasts, almost glimpse their sweet, apple-like curves. 'As long as I want you to stay.' She drew in a quick, sharp breath, colour flooding her face. She almost looked outraged. 'You don't need to look quite so bewildered,' Cristiano drawled.

'Why shouldn't I be bewildered?' Laurel demanded. 'It almost sounded as if…'

'As if what?' Cristiano prompted silkily. She bit her lip and looked away.

'Nothing.'

Cristiano almost laughed at that. She didn't want to overplay her hand. She was so obvious, it amused him. Almost. The trouble was, he hated game playing. All his liaisons had been conducted with discretion and honesty, from their businesslike beginning to the expected end of the transaction. This would be no different, but he'd humour her for a little while…just to see where she'd go with this. What exactly she was trying to get? How much?

'So how long would that be?' Laurel asked, straightening as she drew the robe closed at her throat, every inch the outraged virgin. 'Because I don't even have any clothes.'

'A day or two at most. Bavasso will have moved on by then, no doubt.' He let his gaze linger. 'As for clothes… I'm not at all sure they'll be necessary.' She gasped and he laughed. 'Relax, *bella*. I'm only joking.' Sort of. 'I'll arrange for some clothes to be brought up to you.'

'Thank you,' she said stiffly and looked away. Cristiano propped one shoulder against the floor-to-ceiling window, taking the time to study her. The puppyish roundness of her teenage years had melted away, leaving behind a lithe yet curvaceous body. She was slender, verging on petite, yet her legs seemed endless and golden, her hair a cascade of colours, from chestnut brown to tawny orange to pure gold. She must pay her hairdresser a fortune.

'So where is home, out of interest?' he asked. 'Since it's obviously not Rome.'

She darted him a quick, suspicious glance before answering, 'Illinois.'

'Illinois?' That surprised him, although he knew she and her mother were American. His father had picked up Elizabeth Forrester in a third-rate casino in Miami and had married her just four days later. 'Chicago?' He would have expected Los Angeles or New York, somewhere where she could be seen and admired—and where she could find a sugar daddy.

'No, a small town you've never heard of.' Her tone was repressive. 'Are you going to order those clothes?'

'You're being quite demanding, for a woman who has nothing to offer… Unless you do have something to offer?' He intentionally let a note of innuendo into his voice and saw how her pupils flared in response. This was so *easy*.

'My gratitude,' Laurel bit out. She turned her head away, refusing to look at him.

'Ah, well, the question remains, how is one's gratitude expressed?' He enjoyed toying with her, enjoyed the way her breasts rose and fell with every agitated breath. A rosy blush swept across her collarbone. She had the most delectable skin, all golden cream and roses. He couldn't wait to touch it. Taste it.

'I would hope a simple thank you would do.' In one abrupt movement she rose from the sofa, pulling the huge robe more tightly around her slender frame. 'I don't understand you, Cristiano. An hour ago I was attacked. Why are you toying with me like this? Do you enjoy being cruel?'

Annoyance sparked. 'You call this cruel?' He took a step closer to her, noting the gold sparks in her eyes, as well as the ones firing between them. 'How, *bella*, am I toying with you?'

'You know.' She kept her face averted, her breath coming

in quick, ragged bursts. She didn't want to say it. Admit it. And Cristiano realised he very much wanted her to.

'I don't know, actually. I need you to enlighten me.'

She drew a tortured breath, looking anywhere but at him. 'Fine. You're almost sounding as if…as if you expect me to…something to happen between us.'

'Something is already happening between us, *bella*,' Cristiano answered softly. 'Can't you feel it?' He certainly could. He felt it in the tautening of the air, the heightened awareness he had of her: of every draw and tear of her breathing; the pearly sheen of her skin; the way his loins tightened when she touched her lips with her tongue.

'I just want to go home,' she said, her voice low. 'This isn't my world. I don't belong here.'

'You were certainly acting as if you belonged here earlier in the evening.'

Finally she looked at him, horrified realisation and hurt flashing in her aquamarine eyes. 'You saw…?'

'I saw everything. You on the casino floor with Rico Bavasso—practically sitting in his lap, laughing at his jokes, letting him paw you while your mother watched. She taught you well, I suppose.'

She shook her head, curls bouncing. 'It wasn't like that…'

'It was exactly like that and you know it,' he answered, a hint of steel entering his voice. 'Now what I'm wondering is, why are you acting like an outraged virgin now?'

She let out a cry and whirled away, stalking towards the lift doors. Cristiano watched her, darkly amused, as she pushed the button.

'You intend to go down to the lobby, to face Rico Bavasso and his security, in my dressing gown? Because that is not a tactic I'd recommend you employ. It will end badly for you. Very badly indeed.'

'I'll take my chances,' she said, her whole body taut and quivering, his robe trailing the ground.

'That's quite a risk you're willing to take, then.'

'And one I prefer.'

Her games were getting tiresome. What on earth did she possibly hope to gain from them? She had his interest already. Playing hard to get, or as if she were some offended innocent, was both pointless and aggravating. 'Unfortunately it's one I do not prefer,' Cristiano said lazily. 'The lift is locked, *bella*. You're not going anywhere. Not until I say so.'

CHAPTER THREE

LAUREL WHIRLED AROUND, the breath leaving her lungs in one almighty whoosh. Cristiano lounged against the window, his hands in his pockets, looking for all the world as if he were out for a summer stroll. Not as if he'd just threatened her. Not as if he'd just intimated that she was as captive in this hotel suite as she would be in Rico Bavasso's.

'Out of the frying pan and into the fire, it seems,' she managed, trying to keep her voice from shaking. Cristiano was not hiding the heat that simmered in his eyes, but she could hardly believe it. Ten years ago he'd batted her away like an annoying inconvenience. So now he wanted her, and she had no say in the matter?

'Fire has much to recommend it.'

She stared at him, caught between confusion and outrage. Was he teasing her? She couldn't believe that he wanted her badly enough now to keep her captive in his penthouse. She couldn't believe he wanted her at all. He had his pick of the most beautiful and glamorous women in the world, and she was an inexperienced hick from nowhere, Illinois. What could he possibly see in her?

'What do you want, Cristiano?' she asked slowly, not entirely sure she wanted to hear the answer.

He lifted his chin, his silver-grey eyes blazing, but with ice. Cold and hot at the same time—but didn't it feel like a burn, when you touched something icy and incredibly cold? That was how Cristiano felt to her. A cold blaze of danger.

'It's simple,' he said. 'I want you.'

He couldn't put it more plainly than that, yet still she was sceptical. 'Why me? You could have any woman you wanted.'

'Thank you.'

'Why should either of us pretend otherwise? You're in the celebrity gossip magazines often enough.'

'Why, *bella*, are you keeping tabs on me?'

'It would be hard not to, considering how often you feature in the press—and *please* don't call me *bella*.'

'All right. Laurel.' He spoke quietly, with a sincerity she hadn't heard before, his tone of voice low and heartfelt, affecting her in a way that his barely leashed looks had not. That tone left her feeling unsteady. Uncertain. And, shamefully, wanting.

'Well?' she demanded unsteadily. 'Why?'

'Why do I want you?'

'Yes.' She could hardly believe they were having this conversation. Cristiano's tone made it sound as if he were chatting about the weather.

'Why not?' Cristian answered with a shrug.

'That's it? "Why not"?' She stared at him, trying to fathom what was going on behind that inscrutable face, the negligent shrug of his powerful shoulders. Was it simply that a woman was available, a woman who he obviously assumed made free with her body, so of whom he intended to take advantage? The thought made her feel physically sick.

'You take issue with my response?' he enquired.

'Yes. You're practically threatening me—'

'There are no threats, Laurel.' Cristiano's voice cut across her, quick, lethal and very, very sure. 'Nothing I have said or done is a threat. And nothing will be.'

She flung one arm towards the lift doors. 'And the locked doors?'

'The last thing you want is for anyone to have free access to my flat.'

'Because of Bavasso?'

'I believe you underestimate him. Admittedly, he is able

to turn on the charm when he wishes, but he can be a vicious man.'

She suppressed a shudder as she recalled Bavasso's hands on her, reaching, grabbing. 'I believe you,' she said. 'But I still don't appreciate feeling like a prisoner.'

'For your own safety, as well as my own, I must take precautions. I'm sure you understand.'

He was so smooth, so aggravatingly assured, that Laurel felt her protests falling away, unspoken. Cristiano had locked the doors, yet here she was, the one who felt as though she was being unreasonable.

'And if I insist on leaving?' she asked. 'What then?'

Cristiano shook his head slowly, his expression one of patently mock regret. 'But you see, I could not live with putting a woman into potential danger on my conscience. Especially one I was once, however happenstance, related to.'

'We were never related.'

He inclined his head in a regal nod. 'It is as you say, of course. Stepsiblings hardly count as blood relations.'

'And surely you exaggerate?' Laurel persisted. She had to believe that. 'Rico Bavasso isn't *that* dangerous.' When she'd first met him, he'd seemed charming, just as Cristiano had said: silver-haired, hazel-eyed, all smooth urbanity. Admittedly something about his assured manner had made Laurel uneasy, but her mother had seemed happy, and Laurel had just wanted her money. Shame licked through her again at the thought.

Cristiano dropped his expression of fake regret as his gaze turned startlingly serious. 'Do you really want to take such a risk?'

Wordlessly Laurel shook her head. Bavasso had been so angry. She had no desire to run into him again, especially not any time soon.

'How well do you know him?' Cristiano asked. His voice

was mild, even friendly, but with a ripple of darkness underneath that nearly made Laurel gulp again.

'I don't know him,' she said quickly. 'That is, not very well at all.' She didn't really want to go into the how and why of her acquaintance with Rico Bavasso, yet it seemed Cristiano had already assumed the absolute worst.

Which wasn't all that far from the truth, unfortunately— yet it felt different. It was different, at least to her. She hadn't thought Bavasso had been interested in *her*.

'You seemed as if you knew him quite well while you were on his lap, whispering in his ear,' Cristiano said in that same awful, mild tone.

'I wasn't on his lap,' she snapped.

'Close enough.'

Laurel shook her head. 'It wasn't what it looked like.'

'Funny, I think it was exactly what it looked like.'

'You would.' Clearly Cristiano was going to think the worst of her. And Laurel knew it had looked bad. How could she explain that she had never meant to lead Bavasso astray; that when he'd started cosying up to her she'd frozen inside, appalled and uncertain? And, with her mother smiling and nodding the whole while, she'd assumed it was all in her head, that she was being paranoid and over-sensitive. If only.

'I believe you, as a matter of interest,' Cristiano drawled. 'I don't think you know him well. If you had, you would not have tangled with him so precipitously.'

'No, I wouldn't have,' Laurel agreed. Had her mother known what Bavasso was capable of? Had she been in on it? Had she realised that, if Laurel had known what Bavasso really wanted, she never would have agreed to set foot in all of Italy, much less a casino in Rome? Cristiano's casino. 'Can I have some clothes, please?' Her voice sounded high and thin, as if she was scared.

And she was scared—of everything, at the moment.

Scared of a future she couldn't even begin to fathom, a freedom she longed to grasp but which felt further away than ever. But she wasn't, Laurel realised, actually scared of Cristiano. Despite his determination, his desire, she believed him. She had to believe him, believe that he wouldn't threaten or force her to do something she didn't want to do.

But the trouble was, he wouldn't be forcing her. Already she felt a dark, honeyed ribbon of longing wind its way through her, melting her resistance. Already she was imagining the feel of his lips on hers. Already she was anticipating the delicious, icy burn of his touch. His caress.

'Of course you can have some clothes,' Cristiano answered smoothly, thankfully distracting her from her fevered imaginings. 'As a matter of fact, I already ordered them while you were in the shower. You seem to think I am some sort of brute, Laurel, which I confess I find a bit ironic, considering the man you just fled. I hope the contrast between us is more than apparent.'

It was. Oh, it was. Laurel didn't trust herself to answer so she turned away, walking towards the windows, taking in the incredible view.

She heard Cristiano move and then she felt him come up behind her. Her breath froze in her lungs and her heart felt suspended in her chest. Every nerve was strung tight, every sense on overload. And he wasn't even touching her.

Then Cristiano laid a hand on her shoulder. Even through the thick terrycloth robe she felt the press of his palm like a brand, a burn, and it took everything she had not to respond—although she didn't even know how she would. Move closer or further away? Her body would betray her.

'I should tell you now,' he said in a soft voice, 'That I abhor game playing of any kind. Every transaction I've had with a woman has been straightforward and intensely pleasurable. So, if you think you can gain something more from me than what I have already offered by playing the coy miss, think again.'

He squeezed her shoulder lightly, a warning, while Laurel's mind spun. Everything he'd said was offensive, appalling. She didn't even know how to begin to respond. A transaction? Intensely pleasurable? Coy miss? She nearly choked with affront at it all.

'What exactly are you offering?' she finally asked in a shaky voice when she'd managed to kick her mind back into gear and could form at least one coherent sentence. 'Out of curiosity?'

At last, a straightforward question. And he would give a straightforward response. Finally they were getting somewhere.

'My protection,' Cristiano said as he stepped away from her, deciding he needed a little space to stay cool and level-headed. When he'd been standing behind her he'd inhaled her scent, something light and fresh, a hint of lemon and violets. He'd felt her heat, warm and seductive, and the desire to slip the robe from her shoulders and feel the silky skin underneath had been so strong his palms had itched. His body had ached.

'Your protection?' she repeated. He couldn't quite gauge her tone, veering between tremulous and infuriated.

'From Bavasso.'

She stayed where she stood, staring out at the darkness, a slight, slender figure swathed in dark blue. 'Do I really need protection?'

'For a short time, yes.'

'And how can you protect me? By keeping me here?'

'Initially, yes. Bavasso is like a child with a toy when it comes to women. The best way to get him to forget you is for you to be seen to belong to someone else.' He paused, waiting for that to sink in, then continued, 'Bavasso enjoys the use of my hotels and casinos. If he discovers that you are with me, he will not pursue you.' Bavasso was a vicious man, but only with those weaker than him. Cristiano was confident Bavasso would not bother with Laurel once he realised she was off-limits. And he very much intended her to be off-limits…to anyone but him.

'*With* you?' Laurel's jaw hardened, her mouth set in a line as she continued to stare out into the night. 'Is that a euphemism?'

'It is fact.' Their affair was only a matter of time. Surely she realised that? Surely she felt it in the desire that shimmered and pulsed between them, an energy force neither of them could deny?

'And so I exchange one man's unwanted attention for another.' She spoke flatly and Cristiano prickled with irritation. He did not believe his attention was so *unwanted*.

'Again you are comparing me with Bavasso, and I will remind you of the contrast.'

'Oh, you're certainly more attractive,' Laurel said as she turned around, true bitterness spiking her words. 'I'll grant you that. Although, Bavasso is good-looking in that "silver fox" kind of way.' She tossed the words out, but beneath the blaze of anger he felt they'd cost her. 'And your…seduction would no doubt be far more assured and deft,' she added. 'But it still amounts to the same thing.'

'It does not.' His whole body was twanging with both indignation and awareness. How dared she compare him to sly, sleek Bavasso? And how could he want her now, more than ever, when she was verbally repelling him as best she could?

Laurel lifted her chin, her eyes flashing blue-green fire. 'Tell me how it doesn't, then.'

Cristiano stared at her for a long moment, his jaw clenched, fists too. He felt angry, aware and *wanting*. 'I told you before, I do not threaten. I certainly do not force. Trust me on that, Laurel.'

'Why should I trust you on anything?' she challenged. 'And, in any case, there are different kinds of coercion.' She looked away, a flush staining her cheeks, her teeth sinking provocatively into her full lower lip. Realisation dawned and bloomed inside him, making him smile. She wasn't afraid of him forcing her. She was afraid she wouldn't need to be forced.

'Coercion?' he asked softly. 'Or seduction?'

She drew a shuddering breath, lifting her chin and tossing her hair back, forcing herself to meet his knowing gaze. Because he did know—he knew that she wanted him, just as he wanted her. Why she was fighting the attraction, however, remained a mystery. Was she holding out for more? 'What else do you offer?' she asked. 'Besides protection?'

'Pleasure.' He watched her eyes flare, but to her credit she held his gaze. 'Of that you can be certain.'

'You are appallingly arrogant.'

'Merely sure.'

She shook her head slowly. 'And how long would this… arrangement between us last?'

'As long as I want it to.' He felt the first flickers of triumph, mingled with a strange and unsettling disappointment. After all her maidenly outrage, Laurel was acting exactly as he'd expected her to, needed her to…and he found he didn't quite like it.

'And how long would that be, do you think?' she asked. Her eyes flashed and her lips trembled, fury and fear mingled together. 'Judging from what I've read in the tabloids, your mistresses don't last more than a week. And we are talking about me becoming your mistress, aren't we? That's the position I'm being interviewed for, isn't it?'

'Call it what you like.' He'd had straightforward discussions with previous mistresses, but for some reason they hadn't felt quite like this: so cold and mercenary. Although, mercenary was exactly how he'd always wanted to be, especially when it came to women. Any softer emotion, never mind actual love, was for fools. Fools like his father, who had been both fleeced and heartbroken by grasping women like Laurel's mother and the wife before her. As for his own mother...

'So for how long?' she asked, a catch in her voice. 'Roughly?'

Cristiano's eyes narrowed. 'For as long as it takes for Bavasso to be satisfied that you're off-limits.' And as long as he still wanted her.

'It's my safety you're thinking of, is it?'

Now he was getting seriously irritated. 'Among other things.'

'How kind of you,' she drawled, and he could not mistake her sarcasm. He watched her walk across the room, the sash of his robe trailing the ground, her long, wavy hair cascading over her shoulders. She looked like a young, hesitant queen and, in spite of everything, or perhaps because of it, for a moment he admired her.

'Your safety is important to me,' he said, 'whether you believe it or not.'

'Why should it be? I doubt you even thought of me once in the last ten years.'

'Then you thought wrong.'

She stilled at his tone, which was quieter and more sincere than he'd meant it to be. 'Any thoughts you've had of me can't have been good ones,' she said, her tone as quiet as his, and equally sincere. 'Can they?'

'Some were...interesting.'

'Interesting?' She turned around to face him. 'I thought you might despise me, Cristiano.'

'*Despise* is a strong word.'

'Your father despises my mother.'

'I am not my father and you are not your mother.'

'No.' She drew a quick breath. 'But you've judged me just as you've judged her. Tarred us both with the same brush.'

'And I have had obvious reason to do so. Are you telling me differently?'

She looked away. 'You wouldn't listen.'

Cristiano could not imagine any scenario that could excuse or explain her behaviour with Bavasso on the casino floor. 'I'd listen,' he said mildly, 'but whether I believed you or not is another matter. In any case, why do you care what I think of you? Emotions have no place here, *bella*. This is about something else entirely. Something basic and very, very pleasurable.' He started walking towards her slowly, and she stilled, trapped, mesmerised by his lazy yet purposeful words. Perhaps now it was time to show her just how pleasurable it all could be.

'You paint such an appealing picture,' Laurel said huskily. She didn't move. 'No emotions, no concern for feelings, just sex. For maybe a week.'

'Sounds perfect to me.' He kept walking until he was standing right in front of her. She hadn't budged, and he knew he had her. 'Stop playing your games,' he whispered as he reached for the sash of her robe—*his* robe—and tugged her towards him. She came, reluctantly, perhaps, but her pointless act of protest was already being revealed as the masquerade he'd known it was. Her hips nudged his and heat flared bright and white-hot inside him. He sucked in a hard breath and tugged again at the sash. Her eyes widened as she felt the evidence of his arousal.

He touched her chin with one fingertip, tilting her face to his. 'This can really be very simple.'

'To you.'

'And to you. Why not?' He stroked her cheek and she closed her eyes. A shudder went through her. 'See how you respond to me?' he murmured. 'And I haven't even kissed you yet.' He stroked her cheek again, enjoying the silky feel of her skin, the tremor that went through her whole body. 'We are going to be very, very good together, *bella*. I feel it. I know it.'

She let out a shuddering gasp and then opened her eyes, wrenching herself away from him as if she had to break steel bonds to be free. Her eyes shot blue-green sparks at him as she clutched the gaping robe together with one hand.

'What I know, Cristiano, is that you're an arrogant, manipulative bastard and I have no intention of making any sort of deal with you, now or ever. So why don't you practise your so-called charms on some other woman who wants them?' With another gasp that sounded halfway to a sob, she turned from the room and ran down the hall, slamming the bedroom door behind him and then turning the lock with an audible click.

CHAPTER FOUR

LAUREL FELT AS if she needed another shower. She paced Cristiano's bedroom, her heart racing, her whole body tingling despite the storm of indignation raging through her. No matter what big words she'd just thrown at him, she'd been tempted—seriously tempted—and for one glorious second she'd been sure he was going to kiss her, had imagined the sensuous slide of his lips along hers…

What was happening to her? How had she fallen down this rabbit hole of manipulation, sex and greed? She lived a quiet life in a small town in Illinois, working as a nurse, possessing a handful of casual friends, and no boyfriends, ever. For a second she pictured her grandfather's farmhouse—its floorboards of weathered, honeyed oak, the view of rolling fields from the kitchen window, the friendly glimmer of the pond in the distance. She ached to go home, for things to feel familiar and safe again. Boring, even. She didn't want this. She didn't want any of this—not her mother, not Bavasso, not Cristiano.

Liar.

She silenced that taunting inner voice by sheer strength of will and tried to think practically about what she should do now, since she seemed intent on burning her bridges both left and right.

She couldn't leave Cristiano's penthouse, not yet anyway. She took his warning about Bavasso seriously…just as she took his offer of no-strings sex seriously.

Why wouldn't you become the man's mistress?

Frustration bubbled inside her and she paced the room, feeling both frantic and caged. She wouldn't become the man's mistress because she had more self-respect than that.

More pride. And more of an instinct of self-preservation. Sex with Cristiano would burn her up, leaving nothing but cinders. She felt that in her very bones, knew it from the way she'd reacted to his hand on her shoulder, the merest brush of his hips against hers…

Heat flared through her at that potent memory and she whirled away from the window, pacing the room to the bathroom and back. At this rate she'd wear out the thick pile carpet.

A knock sounded on the door and she stilled, every muscle tense, every sense on high-octane alert. 'Yes?'

'Your clothes have arrived.'

She couldn't tell anything from Cristiano's tone. Warily Laurel opened the door. He stood there, one hand outstretched with several luxury shopping bags dangling from his long, lean fingers.

'Thank you,' Laurel said stiffly, taking the bags. 'You didn't have to get so much.'

'Who knows how long you will be here, *bella*?' Cristiano answered lazily.

'Not very long, if I can help it,' Laurel retorted. 'I'm going to get dressed and then we need to talk.'

'Excellent. I've ordered some food, so we can talk as we eat.'

It all suddenly seemed so civilised, Laurel thought with a savage twist of humour as she closed the door. Almost as if Cristiano wasn't keeping her captive, intending for her to be his mistress. To keep her here for *sex*. It seemed ridiculous, laughable, yet she felt the seriousness of the situation all the way through her body, right down to her toes.

She emptied the bags on the bed, blinking at the sight of the elegant clothes, which included several outfits, including undergarments. How on earth had he managed to know her bra size? she wondered as she picked up a push-up bra in nude lace and coffee-coloured satin. Although, on second thoughts, Cristiano no doubt could gauge a woman's bra size from across a crowded room.

She chose the most conservative outfit, a swishy knee-length skirt in pale blue and a matching silk T-shirt top. Now that she was finally dressed in something that was neither revealing nor inappropriate, she felt a little more restored to herself. Almost as if the last seventy hours had never happened. Almost, but not quite.

In addition to the clothes, Cristiano had thoughtfully provided a bag of luxury toiletries, and Laurel took advantage of them, putting on a little discreet make-up, brushing her hair and twisting it up into a knot.

Taking a deep breath, she headed out of the bedroom. She found Cristiano in the dining area on the far side of the living room setting out food on a table that looked as if it had been carved from a single piece of ebony.

Laurel inhaled the tantalising scents of basil and lemon, and realised she hadn't eaten anything since lunch. All evening Bavasso had plied her with cocktails she'd tried not to drink and no food.

Her stomach growled audibly and Cristiano looked up, humour glinting in those silvery eyes. Laurel managed a little laugh. 'I'm hungry.'

'So I hear.' He gestured to one of the chairs, made of gleaming black wood. 'Come sit down.'

Laurel hesitated, discomfited by this apparently new normal. Then she decided she would take what civility Cristiano offered, and she slid a chair out and sat down as he lifted the silver domes off several dishes.

'What would you like?' Cristiano asked as he lifted a plate. Laurel glanced at all the different dishes of Italian specialities, from *fiore di zucca*, a Roman dish of courgette fritters, to pasta carbonara and several delicious-looking salads.

'It all looks good to me.'

'Then I shall give you a bit of everything.'

Laurel watched as he ladled the different dishes onto her plate, feeling as if she'd fallen down yet another rabbit hole. Why had Cristiano changed his tune so drastically? Why was he being so *nice*?

'Thank you,' she murmured as she took her plate from him. Cristiano filled up his own and sat down on the opposite end of the table.

'Dig in,' he said in the same mild tone he'd been using since she'd emerged from the bedroom. 'I'm glad the clothes fit,' he said with a nod to her skirt and top. 'That colour of blue was a good choice. It brings out your eyes.'

'Um, thank you?'

He arched a dark eyebrow. 'Can you not accept a compliment?'

'It just sounded…' Laurel hesitated, wondering if she was being hypersensitive. 'Proprietary.'

'Proprietary?' His smile and eyes both gleamed. 'About you or the clothes?'

'Both.'

Cristiano sat back in his chair. 'Stop fighting it, *bella*,' he said, his tone turning lazy. 'It would be far more pleasant for both of us if you did.'

'Stop fighting it? Or you?'

'Both.'

They stared at each other, a stand-off, and one that made fireworks fizz in Laurel's middle. There could be no mistaking the, yes, *proprietary* gleam in Cristiano's silvery-grey gaze. And definitely not just about the clothes. But, instead of feeling outraged and objectified as she knew she should, Laurel felt…excited.

Excited to know the heat simmering in those silvery depths was for her. She might be no more than a convenience, the expedient option, but he still wanted her. And,

Bavasso's odious groping aside, Laurel had precious little experience with being wanted.

So why *was* she fighting it? Her body battled with her brain, with both sense and self-preservation. The look stretched and lengthened between them and Laurel fought to hold onto all the reasons why she should not engage in some temporary, tasteless affair with Cristiano Ferrero.

Because this was his world, not hers, and she was already out of her depth. Because she had enough experience of people who loved and then left you, starting with her own parents—as well as Cristiano's father, Lorenzo. She didn't need another reminder. Because she was too innocent, too naïve, and too darn hopeful to survive the kind of arrangement Cristiano was suggesting.

Because he was dangerous, as dangerous as holding a firework in your hand and letting yourself be mesmerised by the fizz and spark. It wouldn't take long for it to blow up in your face. To ruin your life.

Laurel dragged her gaze away from Cristiano's simmering, steady one. 'I want to ask about my mother,' she said when she trusted her voice to sound normal. Her body was still reacting, little electric pulses going off in the strangest of places. Low in her belly. Between her thighs.

'Your mother?' Oh, that mild, enquiring tone. Already she knew to suspect it.

'Yes. If Rico Bavasso is as unpleasant as you say, then I'm worried for her.'

'*Bella*, if there's one thing I know, it's that your mother can take of herself.'

Laurel glanced up sharply. 'What's that supposed to mean?'

'Let's not pretend when it comes to your mother,' Cristiano answered. Gone was that mild tone, replaced by something far harder. Something that hinted at the unrelenting steel she knew lurked beneath his smooth urbanity. 'We both know what she is.'

'Which is?' Laurel threw at him. She wasn't under any illusions about what Cristiano Ferrero or his father thought of her mother, but some perverse, determined streak in her still wanted to hear him say it out loud.

'She is a craven, amoral, shameless, gold-digging liar,' Cristiano stated with flat and final authority. Laurel opened her mouth but nothing came out. She hadn't expected him to state it quite so plainly. So coldly. 'And,' he continued, 'I have no reason not to think you are the same.'

Cristiano watched the colour drain from Laurel's face and wished he didn't feel guilty for speaking so plainly. Aggravatingly, at every step it seemed he had to remind himself to act in the manner to which he'd become accustomed—matter-of-fact to the point of ruthlessness.

Anything else smacked of weakness or want and was completely unacceptable. He would never succumb to either option, as his mother did, or manipulation and lies, as his father did, letting himself get ensnared in a sticky web of a woman's deceit.

No man was an island, but he was doing his damnedest to try. But Laurel didn't have to look so *wounded*. As if he'd sucker-punched her when he'd been stating the obvious.

'Well.' Her voice was shaky as she placed her napkin next to her plate of barely touched food. 'Don't sugar-coat it.'

'I see no need to sugar-coat anything,' Cristiano replied shortly. 'Surely we are both aware of the facts surrounding our parents' divorce?'

'If you mean, did Lorenzo Ferrero cut my mother and me out of his life without so much as a goodbye, then yes, I'm aware.' A bright spot of colour appeared on each glorious cheekbone, enflaming and annoying him in turns.

'You almost sound as if you were the one who was betrayed.'

'I was.' Laurel pressed her lips together, as if she'd revealed too much with that statement. She looked away, blinking hard. 'But clearly you don't think I have any right to that feeling. Clearly you think, even without knowing me at all, that I am one step up from a prostitute.'

For a second Cristiano paused. He could see Laurel was battling intense emotion, and he didn't think she was faking it. 'I accept that you were young at the time of our parents' divorce,' he said after a moment. 'You might not have been aware of your mother's actions.'

'And yet you said you judged me as you judged her,' Laurel returned. Her lips were white, her eyes huge, the only colour in her face those two bright spots.

'I said I had no reason to think you were different. Prove me wrong if you can.'

'Why should I bother?' she flung back at him. 'You're… you're disgusting.' She rose from the table, her body taut and trembling. 'You disgust me. You act so superior, as if you're standing above everyone, judging their actions when you have no clue, no *concept*, of what our lives are really like. And meanwhile your actions are just as reprehensible as my mother's, or even those of Rico Bavasso.'

'Don't compare me to that man,' Cristiano warned in a low voice.

'Why shouldn't I? You trapped me here—'

'I rescued you.'

'You propositioned me and still you refuse to let me go. At least I managed to escape Bavasso's clutches.' She shook her head, her lip curling in genuine disgust. She was *repulsed* by him. The realisation was shocking and deeply, deeply unsettling. For the first time Cristiano didn't wonder what game she was playing, but whether she was playing one at all. And right now he didn't think she was. He'd been trying to get her to be honest, and it seemed he'd succeeded in that goal. It just hadn't turned out at all as he'd expected.

'Your mother doesn't matter to me,' he said swiftly. 'We never should have talked about her in the first place. She is not relevant to our discussions.'

'We talked about her because I'm worried for her safety, no matter what you think of her or her actions of ten years ago. Can you please see that she is all right? Regardless of what you think of her, surely you have that much honour?'

Elizabeth Forrester had always struck Cristiano as the kind of woman who knew exactly on which side her bread was buttered, but for Laurel's sake he nodded tersely. 'Very well.'

'Thank you.'

A truce, then, of sorts. Laurel glanced down at her plate and then, her chin tilted at a haughty, proud angle, she sat down and started to eat again. It seemed Laurel Forrester knew on which side her bread was buttered as well.

'How did you feel betrayed by my father?' Cristiano asked abruptly. The remark had niggled at him.

Laurel looked up warily. 'Because one minute we were all playing happy families, and the next my mother and I were on the plane back to Illinois, and I never even saw him again. Not so much as a text.'

'And your mother had two million euros in her private bank account,' Cristiano reminded her flatly.

'Two million euros that your father got back,' Laurel retorted. 'Thanks to his water-tight pre-nup agreement. She didn't see a penny of it.'

'That makes it better, then? Just because she was caught?'

Laurel had the grace to look away. 'Caught doing what, exactly?' she hedged. Did she think he didn't know?

'Caught stealing from my father,' he snapped, annoyed

that she was practically defending her mother's indefensible actions. 'Taking his money and squirreling it away.'

'Is it stealing, when they were married?' Laurel asked quietly. 'She took money from a joint bank account. Technically it was hers too.'

'Technically,' Cristiano agreed, the word bitten off and spit out. 'Fortunately the law did not consider it a technicality.'

'Still,' Laurel persisted. 'What's yours is mine and vice versa, isn't that right? Or do you not believe in marriage vows?'

Cristiano sat back, starting to fume. He really hadn't wanted to rake up old memories of Elizabeth Forrester's betrayal of his father, but Laurel was forcing his hand. 'She was stealing from him, *bella*, no question.'

'I admit it might have *looked* like that, but she didn't mean it the way you—'

'She was siphoning money from various accounts and putting it in an offshore account under a different name!' Cristiano cut her off, his voice like the snick of a blade. 'Are you actually defending her?'

'Not defending,' Laurel answered, a flush rising to her face. 'I know she's…' She stopped and shook her head, clearly at a loss, because she couldn't defend her mother even if she wanted to. Elizabeth Forrester was so clearly indefensible.

'And what was that money for?' Cristiano continued, relentless now. 'The day when she left him for some toy boy? Considering her behaviour since then, it seems likely.'

Laurel's face went pale again. 'What do you know of my mother's behaviour since then?'

'Tonight was not the first time she has come into La Sirena.' He didn't make a point of following Elizabeth Forrester's romantic entanglements, but he'd seen her enough times over the last ten years—usually on the arm of some puffed-up aristo, fawning, flirting and making Cristiano nauseous—to know that she lived by her wits and fading beauty. Every time he'd seen her he'd felt vindicated in telling his father about the private account he'd discovered ten years ago.

'Tonight was the first time I came into La Sirena,' Laurel said quietly. 'Or had that escaped your notice?'

Cristiano stared at her, trying to decipher what she was really trying to say. That she was different from her mother? Or perhaps just more discreet. 'So why did you?' he asked. 'Out of interest?'

He waited, bracing himself for some spun-out sob story about desperate times and hard circumstances. But she just pursed her lips and shook her head. 'It doesn't matter.'

And Cristiano told himself that was fine, because it didn't. He wasn't interested in getting to know Laurel, yet against his better judgment, and all common sense, he was curious. What had she been doing for the last ten years? Living the way her mother did? It was the utterly obvious assumption, and yet...

Something in him resisted that assumption, which was stupid as well as pointless. Laurel toyed with her fork and then pushed her plate away. 'I'm sorry. I'm not hungry any more.'

'You should eat.' She was slender enough for a breath to blow her away. She just shook her head.

'I... I think I'll go to bed. It's late and it's been a very long day. A very long couple of days.' She rose from the table, pausing uncertainly. 'Thank you,' she said. 'For the clothes and the food and the place to stay.'

As if he'd given it all to her out of the goodness of his heart. As if their arrangement, the one he still most definitely wanted, didn't remain on the table, needing to be discussed. Cristiano rose too.

'I'll see you to your room.'

Her pupils flared. 'That isn't necessary.'

'Oh, but I assure you,' he answered softly, 'It is.'

Laurel stared at him for a beat longer and then word-lessly turned from the room. Cristiano followed her to the door of his bedroom, where she hesitated, her back quivering with tension.

'Where…where am I to sleep?'

'There is a guest bedroom across the hall.' He pushed open the door opposite his own. She turned to glance at him, and that was her mistake. Her breath came out in a rush as heat flared between them. Cristiano put his hand on her wrist, felt the leap of her pulse beneath his fingers. Laurel pressed her lips together.

'Don't, Cristiano,' she whispered.

'Don't what?'

'Don't touch me.'

'Don't tempt you?' He stroked the silky skin of her inner wrist with his thumb. 'Is that what you mean?' He ran his thumb gently down to her palm and then up to her inner elbow. Laurel remained frozen, her pulse hammering beneath his questing fingers. 'Why deny what is between us, *bella*?'

'There's nothing between us.' She nearly had to gasp the words out.

'Your body begs to differ.'

'Ten years ago you shoved me away as if I disgusted you.'

'Ten years ago you were a child. What was I supposed to do?'

She turned to face him, her breast brushing his arm. 'Don't pretend you felt anything for me then.'

'The point is what I feel for you now. And what you feel for me. It's real, *bella*, what is between us. Why shouldn't we enjoy it?'

He could see the indecision in her fractured gaze, the

desire as well as the doubt. All she needed was the tiniest bit of incentive, the merest push to tumble her into temptation…and he was more than willing to give it.

'Stop worrying so much,' he murmured as he dropped his head so his lips were a fraction away from hers. He could hear her breaths, uneven and ragged. 'What are you afraid of?' he added, his lips very nearly brushing hers.

'This,' she whispered, and then Cristiano kissed her.

CHAPTER FIVE

It felt as achingly wonderful as she could ever have imagined. Better. *Far* better. Sweet and dark at the same time, and so very intense. Cristiano was entirely in control, commanding her response. Demanding it.

Laurel's head fell back as Cristiano's lips moved on hers and he deepened the kiss, his tongue plundering the soft depths of her mouth, taking ownership, sending pulses of pleasure through her whole body.

It was just a kiss, yet it felt life-changing. Soul-shattering. He put his hand on her waist, his fingers splaying over the dip of her hip, his palm burning her through the thin silk of her skirt, another brand. In this moment he owned her and they both knew it.

Laurel couldn't have broken that kiss even if she'd wanted to, which, to her own shame, she did not. She craved his touch, the explosion of sensation inside her an excitement that was impossible to contain or deny, licking through her veins, making her stand on tiptoe to give him greater access, to reach more of him.

Cristiano pulled her to him, fitting her body intimately to his so need roared through her veins and heat flared deeper and hotter.

He kissed his way from her mouth to her neck, his tongue teasing circles against her fevered skin; his hands stroking her hips, her thighs, making everything inside her coil so tightly. She felt as if she was about to explode, as if she needed to break apart. She arched against him, unable to help herself, her mind a haze of need as she craved the kind of release she'd never experienced with a man before.

Cristiano growled low in his throat and he skimmed his

fingers underneath her skirt, running the tips along her inner thigh, teasing the sensitive skin before his thumb nudged the edge of her underwear and then slipped beneath, making her gasp at the shock of the tender invasion.

For a few blissful seconds Laurel couldn't even think. She'd never been touched so intimately, so knowingly. And with such expertise. Cristiano knew exactly how a few lazy strokes sent her spinning, all her muscles clenching, her nails digging into his shoulders, everything in her straining as she fought for both control and release. She couldn't have both—there was a battle raging inside her, and she didn't know which side she wanted to win.

Her eyes fluttered open and through the daze of desire she caught sight of her own reflection on the mirrored wall—her flushed face, her swollen lips, her half-lidded eyes, her arched hips. But as for Cristiano—he didn't look half as affected as she did. His expression was shuttered, his lips slightly pursed as he continued to touch her in such an intimate way. He looked almost clinical, dispassionate, a scientist conducting an experiment with guaranteed results. He was working her body. Manipulating her.

With a cry Laurel jerked out of his arms. Cristiano's startled gaze clashed with hers and his eyes narrowed.

'What…?'

'Don't,' she said raggedly. Her body pulsed with unfulfilled desire—and shame. She'd fallen right into his arms. Into his trap. 'Don't,' she said again, and stumbled into the bedroom, slamming the door in his face.

She flipped the lock, letting out a shuddering breath, her body still pulsing with pleasure—and frustration. Pushing her tangled hair away from her face, she paced the room that was just as sumptuous as Cristiano's own. What on earth was she going to do now?

Wait seemed like the only option. Laurel washed her face, combed her hair and then slumped into a leather armchair by the window overlooking the Tiber, gleaming in the moonlight. It had to be at least three in the morning, and her body ached with exhaustion, yet she knew she wouldn't be able to sleep. She tried to make her mind empty out, but it seethed with worries and memories. Bavasso's leering face. Her desperate flight. Cristiano's kiss.

She must have dozed off, because a knock on the door startled her awake. She'd been dreaming...dreaming of Cristiano. Hands...lips... Her body tingled as if he'd been touching her.

'Yes?' she called, her voice sounding hoarse and scratchy.

'I checked on your mother,' Cristiano called through the door, his voice gruff. 'She's all right.'

Laurel swallowed. 'Where is she?'

'She went back to the *pensione* where you were staying. Bavasso shouted at her, but that was all. It's you he's angry at, not her. Who knows? They might be able to patch things up.'

He spoke sardonically, and Laurel could hardly blame him. Bavasso wasn't the first boyfriend of her mother's to behave in a way that should have had Elizabeth sending him packing. Trouble was, if there was still something to be had, she never did.

'So he's still angry at me?' she asked after a tense pause.

'I'll take care of you, Laurel.'

The throb of sincerity in his voice shouldn't have affected her. Definitely shouldn't have made her eyes sting. 'I'm not sure I want to know what that means.'

'I won't let Bavasso bother or hurt you.'

But you'll hurt me, in an entirely different way. She thought of his cold, clinical face in the mirror. He'd known exactly what he'd been doing. Laurel blinked hard and didn't reply. 'Get some sleep,' Cristiano said roughly. 'It's nearly dawn. We'll talk later.'

'Okay.' A moment passed, silent, endless. Somehow Laurel knew he was still there. 'Cristiano?' she asked softly.

'Yes?'

'Thank you.'

Laurel had left her clothes and toiletries in Cristiano's bedroom, and so she stripped off her skirt and slept in her T-shirt and panties. The night was warm, and she opened the windows, breathing in the sultry air. Already the moon was waning, the horizon the pearly grey of early morning. Her body ached and her eyes felt as if they were full of grit. She needed to sleep.

She curled up on the bed, scrunching her eyes tight and wishing herself back home. Back in her single bed with the patchwork quilt her grandmother had made, the pure, golden light of an Illinois summer streaming through her window. She'd give just about anything to be able to re-wind the last three days, go back to the moment where her mother had showed up at her grandfather's farmhouse—Laurel should have closed the door in her face.

Instead she'd let her in. Let her speak. Because stupidly Laurel was always hoping her mother wanted her, not just something from her.

'Darling, you'll never guess,' Elizabeth had announced in a flurry of air kisses and perfume. 'I've met someone.'

Laurel had just stared. This was hardly news.

'He wants to meet you. I want you to meet him.' Elizabeth had smiled mischievously, but Laurel had detected a desperate glitter in her mother's eyes. She was forty-six years old and her days reeling in wealthy businessmen and minor celebrities were surely numbered. 'There might be a ring in my future.'

'Really?' Laurel had said, unsure how she'd felt about that, or anything to do with her mother. She hadn't seen her in two years. Her mother had been in Monaco for her grandfather's funeral three months earlier.

Elizabeth had strode into the living room with its rag rug and faded sofa, and a shudder had gone through her. 'I always hated this place.' She'd looked around, her lip curling. 'Goodness knows why you keep staying.'

'I love it here,' Laurel had said quietly. She placed one hand on the warm, satiny wood of the newel post. 'It's the only home I've ever known.'

Elizabeth's mouth had tightened. She hated any hint of her deficiencies as a mother. 'I'm sorry I couldn't provide you with a more stable upbringing,' she said stiffly. 'If your father—'

'I didn't mean it like that.'

Elizabeth had turned to look at her directly. 'So will you come to Rome, to meet Rico? It should only take a few days.'

'Rome?' Laurel had boggled at the suggestion. 'Why would I go there? I mean…can't he come here? And why does he have to meet me?'

'Family is important to him. And I need this to work, Laurel.' The desperate look in her mother's eyes had intensified. 'If you do this, I'll give you the only thing you've ever wanted, I promise.' She'd glanced around the worn living room. 'All I'm asking is for you to show Rico that we're a family, that you're pleased to have him in your life. Is that so much to ask?'

Cristiano stretched out on the bed, as far from sleep as he could possibly be, his body still pulsing with the aftershocks of kissing Laurel. Her skin had felt like the supplest silk under his hands. He shifted, trying to suppress the ache in his groin, the flicker of regret whispering through him on dark wings.

He hadn't heard a sound from the bedroom across the hall, not so much as a creak of a floorboard. He hoped Laurel was asleep. She had to be exhausted, after everything she'd endured tonight.

Including him.

Guilt, Cristiano reflected, was a very inconvenient emotion. It was one he wasn't used to feeling. He'd always prided himself on his plain speaking, his honesty. He never pretended to care. The women he chose to be with knew what he was willing to give, and all that he wasn't, up front. That, in his view, was something admirable. Honourable.

So why did he feel as if his actions tonight hadn't been? As if he'd used Laurel, just as Bavasso had used her? She'd responded to his touch, heaven knew. He'd felt it. He'd certainly felt it in himself, a raging fire he'd struggled to control, the strength of which had alarmed him—because, when he'd taken Laurel in his arms, it had been to prove something to her as well as to himself. Yet he'd had to use all his self-control, all of his deeply ingrained self-discipline, to keep from giving in to the tidal roar of need inside him and drowning in her kiss.

And when Laurel had jerked out of his arms she'd looked…horrified. And hurt. As if he'd damaged her in a way he didn't like to think about.

Restless now, Cristiano rose from his bed and pulled on a T-shirt and drawstring pyjama bottoms. Pale pink morning light seeped along the horizon as the sky lightened to a luminescent grey. He wouldn't sleep. And, he decided as he grabbed his laptop and strode out to the living room, he needed to know more about Laurel Forrester.

Cristiano made himself a mug of strong coffee and then stretched out on one of the sofas, his computer on his lap. He typed her name into the search engine and waited for the results.

He scrolled through pages obviously about other people—a physics professor in Colorado, a housewife in South Carolina—before finally hitting on one that snagged his interest, simply because it was from Illinois. Laurel Forrester, on the page of the website for a hospital in Canton Heights. He frowned, not quite believing this could be his Laurel—because Laurel, whether she acknowledged it or not, was most definitely his. For now, at least.

He clicked and scrolled down the staff directory until he found Laurel Forrester, RN. She was a *nurse*? That so didn't fit the profile of the woman he'd seen totter into La Sirena only a few short hours ago on the arm of one of Rome's shadiest businessmen. Surely that wasn't her?

Cristiano raked a hand through his close-cropped hair, fingernails grazing his skull. He went back to the search results and scrolled through several pages. Then he clicked on images, but not a single one came up that looked like Laurel. Her Internet footprint was light indeed, unlike her mother's.

Just to prove a point to himself, Cristiano typed Elizabeth Forrester's name into the search engine. It didn't take long to find dozens of photos of his former stepmother, usually on the arm of some Z-lister, always looking a little defiant, as if she was daring her audience to ask if she was happy.

Cristiano leaned his head back against the sofa, replaying the moment when he'd seen Laurel come into the casino yesterday evening. He'd been standing by the roulette table, keeping a discreet eye on the heavy betters, making sure nothing got out of hand. His establishments were high class and respectable, where gambling was a dignified pastime rather than a desperate sport.

He'd seen a flash of silver in his peripheral vision, and he'd turned, the nape of his neck prickling, although he hadn't even known why. He'd seen Elizabeth Forrester first, wearing a crimson cocktail dress that was far too tight and short for a woman of her age, although she still had the body to pull it off. His insides had tightened, his mouth turning down in disgust at the sight of the gold-digger who had just about ruined his father's life. And then he'd seen Laurel.

He'd recognised her instantly, even though it had been ten years. It hadn't taken a moment of mental gymnastics, not even a second. He'd looked at her and he'd known. And he'd felt, in that moment, a pang of something deeper than desire—the need to possess, to consume, a craving so overwhelming he struggled to control it.

And then he'd seen whose arm she was on. He'd taken in the skimpy dress and sky-high heels, the bright make-up and hair shellacked with hairspray, and he'd felt as if he could be sick. He *had been* sick, sickened by her obvious tactics, and his stomach had cramped when Bavasso had pulled her onto his lap. She'd perched there, her smile frozen in place, determined to endure…and for what? Had Bavasso paid for the sycophantic attention…and worse? Far worse.

Cristiano had stayed on the fringes of the crowds, watching Laurel and Bavasso out of the corner of his eye, his gut churning. Bavasso went for the baccarat table as he always did, flanked by two of his bodyguards—and Laurel. Elizabeth lurked in the background, looking anxious and trying not to. Clearly this was Laurel's game, but Elizabeth had some stake in it. A mother and daughter team. Had they always been like that? Probably.

He hadn't been able to keep from looking at Laurel, noticing the tiny dress, the slender yet generous figure poured into it. He hadn't thought of Laurel Forrester once in the last ten years, but he realised then that, on some level, it had been a conscious decision. Not thinking of her had taken effort, a matter of will. And he was certainly thinking about her now.

It had taken all his self-control not to stride over to Bavasso when the odious man had pulled Laurel onto his lap. Cristiano had seen the flash of disgust cross Laurel's face but then she'd lifted her chin, her smile firmly in place, and Cristiano hadn't known whether to feel admiration or contempt. She hated this, but she still chose it. That was the kind of woman she was.

So why now was he starting to wonder, even to doubt? He was a man who dealt in certainties. And the certainty he'd seen last night was Laurel agreeing to go up to Bavasso's hotel room. The only reason she'd been in Cristiano's casino with that man was because she'd chosen it. Because she wanted something from him.

Right?

With a sigh Cristiano opened his laptop again and once more he scrolled through the search results for Laurel Forrester. He clicked on the page for the hospital in Illinois again, and went through every page of the website to see if he could find anything more about Laurel Forrester, RN. After half an hour he came across a page of thank you messages and photographs from patients—and there was a photo of Laurel, standing next to an elderly woman and her adult children, looking tired but smiling. He hadn't seen her smile like that all night. It was a genuine smile, full of warmth and kindness, and Cristiano stared and stared at it, unable to look away. Who was the woman in the photo? And who was the woman who had locked herself in his guest bedroom, defiant and afraid?

Cristiano shoved his laptop away. His eyes were gritty, his head starting to pound. Outside sunlight was spreading across the city sky like melted butter, pearly grey giving way to pale, fragile blue. Cristiano opened the sliding glass doors to the private terrace and breathed in the summer air, fresh this early in the morning, yet already imbued with heat.

He curled his hands around the railing as he gazed down at the city starting to wake up, lorries and motorbikes filling the narrow, ancient streets. Laurel would wake up soon too, and then what? They needed to have a conversation, something he hadn't anticipated. He'd expected a simple transaction, and one that was welcome on both sides. That was what he always got, what he demanded. Instead tonight he'd encountered resistance, animosity and doubt—as well as desire. He needed to figure out what was going on, and who Laurel was, before he made his next move.

A sound from the penthouse had him stilling. Over the muted roar of early-morning traffic far below he heard it again, a sound almost like a moan or a cry. Quickly Cristiano strode from the terrace, closing the doors behind him. In the sudden, muted stillness of the penthouse he froze, straining to listen.

There it was again—an anguished moan, coming from Laurel's room. Was she hurt? In pain? Every protective instinct Cristiano had rose to the fore, propelling him across the living room and down the hall.

He knocked sharply on the bedroom door. 'Laurel?'

Silence—and then a whimpering cry. Cristiano tried the handle, rattling it uselessly, as he knew the door was locked. '*Laurel*. Answer me. Are you hurt?'

The only response was a shuddering sob. Cristiano didn't think—he just acted. Backing up a few steps, he rammed the door with his shoulder. It took a few tries, and would create a few bruises, but the lock finally busted and the door sprang open.

With the curtains drawn against the dawn light it took Cristiano's eyes a few desperate seconds to adjust, and then he saw Laurel lying in bed, the sheets twisted around her slender body, her eyes clenched shut, her face an agonised grimace. She was in the throes of a nightmare.

'*Laurel.*' Cristiano spoke gently now as he crept towards the bed and touched her shoulder. 'Laurel, you're dreaming. It's all right. Wake up.'

Laurel's body shuddered with the force of emotion he

could see on her face, twisting her features as if she were in agony. 'Don't...' she murmured brokenly. 'Please don't... I don't want to...' Another cry and she pressed her face into the pillow.

It took Cristiano a few shocked seconds to realise, with icy horror, that she was reliving Bavasso's attack. He felt sick—sickened not just by Bavasso, but by himself. His arrogant self-assurance that Laurel would welcome his attention. Hell, that she'd be grateful.

'Laurel.' His voice was soft as he gently touched her shoulder again. 'Laurel, *cara*. Please wake up.' He shook her shoulder, carefully, not wanting to startle or scare her.

And then she did wake up with a sudden gasp, as if she were coming up out of water, as if she'd been drowning. Her face was pale and shocked, her eyes wide and unfocused.

Relief pulsed through him, stronger than anything he'd felt in a long time. 'Laurel, *cara*, you're okay. It was just a dream.'

She blinked a few times, and Cristiano couldn't tell if she had fully come conscious or was still in the hazy throes of her nightmare.

'It wasn't a dream,' she whispered, and she let out a broken little cry. 'It was real.'

'Oh, *cara*.' Cristiano reached for her, not even thinking about what he was doing as he hauled Laurel against his chest, moving onto the bed so she could snuggle against him. The feel of Laurel in his arms—her head burrowing into his chest, her body curled into his—felt supremely right, touching him deeply in a place he'd thought didn't exist. A place he'd excised long ago. 'It's okay,' he whispered. 'You're safe here.' And he knew he meant it.

CHAPTER SIX

THE VESTIGES OF the nightmare clung to her like a grey, snaking mist, obscuring her vision. Obliterating rational thought. Laurel felt Cristiano's arms close around her and they were warm and strong, encasing her in a way that made her feel safe. Protected. *Cherished.*

Some small part of her brain whispered for her to resist this new offensive of his but the nightmare was still too strong—the memory of Bavasso's sneering face, his hands pawing at her—and Cristiano was murmuring to her, his voice steady and low, a humming in her chest. Then he gently shifted her over so he was lying on the bed and she was in his arms, her body close to his, and that felt so very right.

Laurel nestled against him and closed her eyes, not wanting to move. Definitely not wanting to think. The nightmare was still there, lurking, like the monster under the bed, the skeleton in the cupboard. She shuddered and Cristiano's arms tightened around her.

'It's okay,' he whispered. 'You're safe here.'

Even in the grip of her nightmare she knew she shouldn't believe him. She shouldn't trust him. And yet she did, because right now she needed someone to trust. Someone to hold her and tell her she was safe. So she burrowed deeper into the strong wall of Cristiano's chest, closing her eyes and her heart to the memory of his cold, flat statements; to that awful, clinical look on his face in the mirror as he'd touched her body.

Cristiano stroked her back, her hair, whispering soothing words in Italian. It sounded like water rippling over stones, like music. She closed her eyes and tried to make the monster retreat. But Bavasso was still there, lingering on the edges of her mind. It had all happened so *quickly*.

After his assurances that they would all go upstairs for champagne, that this was a family celebration, it had turned into something else in the space of a second. The door to the hotel suite had closed behind her and, before Laurel had so much as been able to blink, he'd been grabbing her, his mouth on hers, his hands on her body. She'd frozen, unable to process what was happening; then, when she'd felt Bavasso squeeze her breast, she'd started to fight, kicking and screaming, nails contacting with flesh. Bavasso had let out an agonised roar, and that had only spurred her on. It had been make or break. Life or death. Eventually she'd made it out through the door, with his hot breath on her neck, his curses renting the air.

'Laurel. *Laurel.*' Cristiano's hands cradled her face and Laurel realised she was weeping, silent tears streaking down her face. She tilted her face up to his as he gently wiped her tears away with his thumbs. It was a gesture so tender and intimate, it made everything in her yearn.

No one had ever touched her like this, yet this was *Cristiano*, a man who had shown her very little understanding or compassion. A man who seemed to think she was little better than a whore. A man whose caress made her feel as if he were touching her with sweet fire, warming and burning her all at once. And suddenly she wanted to be burned.

The distant part in her brain that had been reminding her how stupid this all was, how dangerous, fell silent. Her lips parted. Cristiano's compassionate gaze stilled, fastening on her mouth. The whole room seemed to shimmer.

'Laurel…'

She liked the way he said her name. She liked it far better than *bella*. When he said her name, she felt he knew her. She felt known, and that felt wonderful. Her body arched, just a little, towards his. It was enough.

Cristiano let out a tiny sigh and then he lowered his head, his hands still cradling her face, and brushed his lips against hers. This kiss was entirely different from the calculated and passionate assault in the hallway. This was a balm, a gift—one she accepted, her lips parting under his, her hands coming up to clutch handfuls of his T-shirt. Cristiano's breath came out in a shudder and the kiss deepened, turning both hungry and yet still so achingly sweet. She wanted to be kissed like this for ever—and yet already she wanted more.

Cristiano's breathing was harsh and ragged as he shifted on the bed, pulling her closer to him so their legs twined together and their hips nudged, the press of his arousal against her stomach electrifying. Pulses of desire were zinging through her, short-circuiting her thoughts. Gone were reservations, regrets, resistance. She slid her hands under his shirt, felt the taut muscles and satiny skin of his abs, and let out a shuddering sigh. Cristiano drew his breath in sharply as she let her hands drift across his chest, revelling in the hot, hard feel of him.

'Laurel...' This time her name was a warning. She didn't like that quite as much.

'Please,' she whispered, her eyes fluttering closed. 'Please touch me.'

She wanted to be touched. She needed to feel desired and treasured and loved, just for a little while. She knew it wasn't real; of course she did. She wasn't that naïve, that *stupid*. But just for a few hours, a few moments, even, she wanted this. Him. She wanted pleasure and closeness and touch. And she didn't want to think about the consequences.

'You make me feel beautiful,' she whispered as his lips moved over her skin, from her jaw to her throat. Her hands bunched on his arms, her palms rounding over his taut biceps. 'You make me feel desired.'

'You are desired,' Cristiano said, his voice a husky

growl, his lips brushing her heated, over-sensitised skin.
'I promise you that.'

Laurel let out another shuddering sigh as Cristiano's
mouth moved lower. He slipped his hands under the silky T-
shirt she'd slept in, and when his palms cupped her breasts
she moaned out loud. How could this feel so impossibly
good? So wonderfully right? But it did. It did… And yet
the aching restlessness surging through her body and settling between her thighs made her realise even this wasn't
enough.

She wanted it all.

Cristiano slid her T-shirt higher and then his mouth was
on her, teasing, tormenting, touching her in a way she'd
never been touched before. Laurel arced off the bed, her
hands clutching his head, anchoring him to her. Still needing more.

'Cristiano…' She gasped out his name and his head
moved lower, his tongue teasing her navel, then moving
even lower, lips brushing the tender skin of her belly. He
was going to touch her—kiss her—*there*. It seemed like
the most intimate, sacred act. The most revealing and vulnerable. Laurel's whole body tensed as taut as a bow, waiting, straining…

And then Cristiano hesitated, his lips pressed to her
stomach, just below her belly button. 'Are you sure about
this…?' he began, and Laurel let out a ragged laugh.

'Yes.'

'You've just been through an ordeal…'

Now he mentioned that? Now he showed compassion
and understanding? 'Don't you dare develop a conscience
now,' she said, her voice coming out in ragged pants. 'Don't
you *dare*.'

He laughed softly. 'Very well. I won't.' And then his
mouth moved lower, his tongue knowing exactly what to
do, how to send lightning streaks of pleasure ripping jag-

gedly through her, and Laurel let out a sound she'd never made before—half-scream, half-sob. Her body felt as if it were splintering into crystalline fragments, a rainbow of sensation arcing through her. She let out another shattering sob, and then Cristiano was on top of her, a heavy yet comforting and necessary weight that she welcomed utterly, and then, yes—finally, amazingly—he was sliding inside her, the sensation both so unexpected and wonderfully right.

She felt a twinge of pain, a chafing sensation as he moved within her, and Cristiano paused. Cursed. That, Laurel suspected hazily, wasn't supposed to happen.

'You can't be…' he breathed, his body poised over hers, the muscles in his arms corded, a sheen of sweat on his brow.

She tilted her face up to his, her body pulsing with need, pulsing around him. A strong, sweet craving made her arch her hips as she tried to draw him deeper into herself, searching for an elusive something she couldn't even articulate but knew she needed. 'I can't be what?'

Cristiano's face was contorted, his teeth gritted with the effort of holding back. *'Vergine,'* he bit out. 'Tell me you're not.'

She didn't know much Italian, but that word was pretty self-explanatory. For a second Laurel thought about lying. Cristiano hardly seemed like a man with many arrows on his moral compass, but perhaps this was one of them: deflowering virgins. Yet, when it came down to it, she didn't think she could lie. And in any case she didn't think such a lie would be believable. Her body told its own truth.

'Does it matter?' Laurel asked softly, because to her it didn't. She'd needed this. Asked for it. Demanded it, even. So why was Cristiano looking so anguished? This had been her choice, not his. 'Remember what I said about that conscience?' she gasped out.

'I remember.' His expression had turned grim, and Laurel faltered. He was *inside* her, for heaven's sake. Was he really going to stop now? It was a little late for regrets.

'Cristiano…' She put her arms around his shoulders, smoothing her palms down his back, drawing him closer to her. Gasping as, his jaw still clenched, he slid deeper inside, filling her up. And then, with a groan, he started to move.

And the slightly strange sensation of being filled up exploded into something else entirely. Something huge and wonderful and soul-changing as Laurel started to match his rhythm and then began to fragment all over again.

A virgin. He never would have guessed. Certainly hadn't expected it. With his body still pulsing with the aftershocks of the most explosive orgasm he'd ever had, Cristiano rolled onto his back and stared at the ceiling. Tried to untangle the churn of what he felt—guilt, pleasure, anger and a deep, primal pride because he'd been her first. Her only.

He gave up the task because the feelings were too tightly twined to separate. And he needed to figure out what to do now.

He glanced at Laurel, who was also staring at the ceiling, a pensive look on her face. Her body was flushed and rosy, her lips swollen, her hair spread on the pillow in a glorious, golden swirl. Looking at her made him want her all over again, even as the sweat dried on his skin and his heart still thudded.

A virgin. What was he supposed to do with that?

'Well.' She let out a soft, satisfied little sigh that, impossibly, made him smile. 'I'm glad I experienced that.'

As if he were a tourist attraction, a Ferris wheel or a rather interesting museum. He didn't know whether to be annoyed or flattered. She turned to him, her eyebrows raised, a small and endearingly uncertain smile on her face. 'Are you?'

Was he? Most definitely. Sex with Laurel Forrester had

been…mind-blowing. The best sex he'd ever had, and he'd had a lot. But she'd been a *virgin*. And he shouldn't have taken advantage. She'd been having a nightmare, remembering an attack only hours earlier. And he'd just stolen her innocence.

Laurel might doubt it, but Cristiano had a code of honour and his behaviour just now—hell, his behaviour since Laurel had stumbled into his flat—violated it. That was not something he could accept.

And, as for how she'd made him feel, the places she'd reached inside him, well, that was something he could not even begin to think about.

'It's taking you a while to answer, so I'm guessing not.' Laurel's voice wobbled a little and she sat up, reaching for the T-shirt Cristiano had tossed over her head at some point. He couldn't even remember when. The last hour felt like a golden blur of exquisite feeling. He hadn't been in control of anything, and that was something else he couldn't accept.

This wasn't who he was—someone controlled by desire, motivated by lust. Unable to keep from wanting a woman. Just like his father.

'I did enjoy it,' he said, his voice coming out flat. 'Obviously. But you should have told me you were a virgin earlier.'

Laurel shrugged the T-shirt on and then turned to him, one golden-brown eyebrow raised. 'And you would have believed me?'

No, he wouldn't have. Not in a million years. 'Still,' Cristiano said, because he couldn't think of anything better and, damn it, she *should* have told him. He should have known.

'I think it's my decision whether I release that information or not,' Laurel said a little coolly. 'Not yours. It's my body, after all.'

'But I have a responsibility—'

'No, I have a responsibility.' Laurel cut him off. 'To myself. And I chose to have sex with you so, guess what, Cristiano, you're off the hook. Although why you've put yourself on the hook, I have no idea. You didn't seem to be so consumed by morals earlier in the evening when you were suggesting one of your *arrangements*.'

He deserved that, but it still chafed. 'This is completely different.'

'Is it? Why? Because I'm not who you thought I was?'

He thought of the photo of her with those patients. No, she wasn't who he thought she was. At least, it seemed she was more than that. 'Why were you with Bavasso tonight?' he demanded. 'Why were you acting like…like his trollop?' The words burst out of him unfairly, but he was jealous. And angry.

Hurt flashed across her face, then her expression shuttered and she looked away. 'I don't want to talk about that.'

'I do.'

'Too bad.'

'Damn it, Laurel,' he snapped, his temper starting to fray. 'I deserve to know.'

'Why? Just because you slept with me?' She lifted her chin, eyes flashing. 'I doubt you demand such rights of the legion of women you've slept with.'

'You don't know anything about me.'

'And you don't know anything about me,' she answered, rising from the bed. She tugged the T-shirt down in a useless attempt to cover her bottom. 'So we're even. Now, if you don't mind, I'd like you to go.'

'I do mind.' He settled against the bed, arms folded. He still didn't know exactly what he wanted from this situation, but it definitely wasn't to be kicked to the kerb. He was the one who decided when things ended. *If* they ended.

Laurel stared him down, her lower lip pushed out, her eyes narrowed. 'What do you want from me?' she demanded in a low voice.

Hell if he knew. 'Why are you a virgin?'

'Why?' She stared at him incredulously. 'Why do you care?'

'Humour me.'

She shook her head slowly. 'There's no pleasing you, is there? You branded me a whore and, now you know I'm a virgin, you so obviously aren't happy with that either.'

He didn't need his unreasonableness pointed out to him. 'Why?' he gritted.

'Why not? Is there a law that says twenty-four-year-olds can't be virgins?'

'Practically. Most women…'

'I am not most women.'

She was an utter enigma, and he didn't like that. He needed things to be straightforward. Women to be what they seemed. He needed Laurel to be what she'd seemed, what he'd assumed, because the alternative made his stomach cramp with acidic regret for the way he'd behaved. The things he'd said—and done.

She drew herself up, all haughty dignity, and then ruined the effect by tugging again on her T-shirt. Her legs looked endless and golden, and he couldn't keep from remembering how silky her skin had felt.

'So you're just going to stay here?' she asked in a chilly voice. 'In my bed?'

'My bed, actually.'

She pressed her lips together, looking suddenly far more vulnerable than proud, and Cristiano wished he hadn't tried to score such a petty point. He was above such tactics, surely? And yet… Laurel had unsettled him so much. He felt completely wrong-footed. Wrong everything.

He glanced out at the sky, now the palest of blues. It was

a little past seven in the morning after the longest night of his life. 'Perhaps you should get some more sleep,' he said, rising from the bed in one fluid movement, then reaching for his drawstring bottoms. 'We can talk later.'

Laurel folded her arms, a movement meant to make her look strong, but she looked as if she was holding herself together. Literally. 'About what?'

'Everything,' Cristiano said, then he strode from the room.

CHAPTER SEVEN

LAUREL LISTENED TO the door slam shut behind Cristiano and let out a weary breath. That had been exhausting. Her body was still tingling with the memory of his touch, her heart thudding from the sharp words they'd just exchanged. She'd acted far more assured and confident than she really felt. The truth was she felt like a quivering bowlful of jelly inside.

She'd known sex with Cristiano would rock her world. Burn her up. And here she was, feeling utterly singed.

With a shudder, Laurel sat on the bed, drawing her knees up to her chest. The last she'd wanted after her first experience of sex was an interrogation about what she'd been doing with Bavasso and why she'd been a virgin.

Cristiano had almost seemed angry, and so unmoved by what they'd just done. Yet how could that surprise her? The legion of women he'd had…his face in the mirror. No, the only surprise was how stupid she was. Again. And yet even now she couldn't regret it.

The feel of his hands on her…his body inside her… Laurel shuddered again, this time with longing. She'd never felt anything so intimate or intense or…incredible before. It felt far more *important* than she'd expected. Of course, it wasn't important to Cristiano. It definitely didn't mean anything. She knew that, yet…she couldn't keep from feeling changed, as if something inside her had shifted for ever. She would have a tie to Cristiano now, no matter what happened in the future. An unbreakable tie, at least for her, even if he forgot her name in a few weeks.

Beyond all that, experiencing such pleasure made her

want to know it again. To feel Cristiano's hands on her, his body…

Yet she knew she wouldn't. For her own health and sanity. And in any case she doubted Cristiano would ask. He'd got what he wanted. She was undoubtedly out of his system now, and he would be on to the next woman, another conquest. She'd fallen so easily.

With a sigh Laurel curled up on the bed, fatigue crashing over her. She'd barely slept all night, her one attempt tormented by nightmares. She'd sleep now, if she could, and then she'd deal with Cristiano. No matter what had happened between them, she needed to find a way forward. A way back home.

When Laurel awoke bright, lemony sunlight was spilling through the windows and the room was warm. It was midday, and she'd been asleep for hours. Feeling muddle-headed, Laurel took another shower, and when she came out she saw Cristiano had moved all the clothes to this bedroom. They lay on the end of her freshly made bed in neat piles, making her feel vaguely uneasy. If he was sending a message, she didn't know what it was.

She dressed in a simple sheath dress of lavender linen, which felt too fancy, but there wasn't anything more casual. Then she put her damp hair up in a twist, took a deep breath and headed out.

Cristiano wasn't in the living area as she expected, and she wandered through the sprawling space before she found him in a glassed-in alcove on the far side, clearly a study area. He was seated at a desk, his laptop open in front of him, wearing a black button-down shirt and charcoal-grey trousers. He turned as she approached, and Laurel had to suppress a stab of desire at the sight of him freshly showered and shaven, his hair still damp, his silvery eyes as piercing as twin blades.

'Good morning.'

'Good afternoon, actually,' she returned with an attempt at a laugh. 'I didn't expect to sleep so long.'

'I'm glad you did.' He turned back to his laptop, pressed a few buttons and then shut it with a decisive snap. 'So.' He swivelled back to face her, his gaze coolly appraising.

'So.' Laurel took a deep breath and buoyed her courage. 'I think I can brave Bavasso.' She kept her voice light but firm. 'I'll risk it, anyway. I want—I need—to go home.' Her voice wobbled a little at the last, but she kept her gaze steady on Cristiano's inscrutable face. Why did he have to be so beautiful? He was all sharp angles and clear, hard lines, the purity of his silver eyes a perfect foil to his olive skin and inky dark hair. It made it hard to keep his gaze. Hard too to keep her nerve.

'Where is home, incidentally?' He'd reverted to that mild voice that hid so much. Made her wary.

'I told you, a small town in Illinois.'

'Canton Heights?'

So he'd done an Internet search on her. 'Yes.'

Something flickered across his face like a ripple in water and then was gone. 'You work as a nurse.'

'You've done some homework.' She lifted her chin. 'Yes. Does it matter?'

'Not particularly.' Now she heard disinterest, and for some stupid reason it stung. 'But you can't go home just yet.'

'I think you're overreacting about Bavasso.'

Cristiano arched an eyebrow. 'And how could you possibly make such a judgement?'

'It's just…' She couldn't make such a judgement, but she had to try. Had to get out of here, for her own sake, and she didn't have any other options besides the obvious one: leave. 'He'll get over it, surely? He barely knew me. And he cares about my mother…' she trailed off, afraid that wasn't true.

'Cares about your mother? Where on earth did you get that idea?'

Of course, Laurel would rather her mother broke things off with Bavasso, but she questioned whether she would, even now.

'He attacked you last night, Laurel, and he would have done far worse if you hadn't escaped. Surely you haven't forgotten that already?'

Anger leaped inside her at his admonishing tone. 'Of course not.'

'Or the ensuing nightmare you had?'

Memory shimmered in the air between them, memory of her nightmare and also how he had comforted her. Laurel looked away, hating herself for being so affected by him. 'Of course I remember everything, Cristiano. It was only a couple of hours ago. But surely it's my decision, not yours, about whether I risk Rico Bavasso's fury?' She hadn't meant to make it a question.

'As I have said before, it is not. Not when you have no idea what you're asking.'

'Stop treating me like a child,' Laurel snapped, and Cristiano's eyes flashed like a glint of light on metal.

'I am not treating you like a child,' he said in a low, lethal voice that slid inside her like a cold blade. 'I am treating you as someone who is out of her depth and experience, which you cannot deny. I don't know how or why you got involved with someone like Bavasso, Laurel, but trust me, you are in over your head.'

More than he knew. She was in over her head not just with Rico Bavasso but with the man in front of her. Cristiano Ferrero felt far more dangerous to her now than the sleek silver fox staying several floors below. She could hardly say that now, however.

'So what are you suggesting? That you keep me captive in your penthouse until Bavasso moves on?'

'That would hardly accomplish our purpose.'

'Which is?'

'To show Bavasso that you are mine.' Cristiano spoke coolly but heat flared in his eyes, turning them nearly to gold. *His.* She'd been his only hours ago, marked for ever by every touch of his hand, every brush of his lips. Laurel fought not to blush.

'And how are you going to show that?'

'By appearing with you tonight, as I mentioned before. Perhaps you have forgotten?'

Last night was a blur of panic and disbelief. She recalled him saying something along those lines, but she hadn't taken him seriously. Had she? Now she did. Now, judging by the feeling of icy dread seeping into her stomach, she took him very seriously indeed.

'Tonight? That's it?'

'We'll see how it unfolds.'

'So tomorrow I could go home?' she pressed, eager for a deadline. A finish line.

'Not quite.' He paused, his mouth compressing, his silvery gaze flicking over her in cool assessment. 'I believe your stay here will be for two weeks, perhaps a little longer. That should be sufficient.'

'Two *weeks*?' Laurel goggled at him. 'But you said Bavasso would be satisfied in a day or two.'

'It's not Bavasso I'm thinking of.' Cristiano dismissed the man who had loomed like such a threat with the snap of his fingers. 'After our appearance tonight, he will no longer be welcome in any of my establishments. I do not harbour criminals.'

Laurel gulped. 'Okay. Then why two weeks?' She'd only taken a week off work. Laurel swallowed. 'I can't hang around here for two weeks. I have work…'

'I'm sure they'll understand.'

'They're depending on me.'

'Even so.' Cristiano's tone and expression were both implacable. Laurel knew nothing she said would have any effect at all. He was utterly immoveable, untouchable, yet mere hours ago she'd been writhing underneath him, arms and legs wrapped around him, as close to him as she'd been to anyone, ever. She had to stop thinking about that.

'I still don't understand why you want me to stay here for so long.' For his own pleasure? The possibility brought a swift intake of breath, a stupid rush of pleasure, a flash of alarm. Surely not...?

'Don't you?'

'Stop playing games, Cristiano.' Laurel started to get annoyed. 'You can't keep me a prisoner for your own—your own pleasure.'

'That's not why I want you here.'

Ouch. Laurel willed herself not to flush with the humiliation of that flatly spoken assurance. 'You still haven't told me why.'

'I want you here because in approximately fourteen days I'll know whether or not you are carrying my child.'

Cristiano watched with dispassion as shock drained the colour from Laurel's face, turning her eyes into huge, aquamarine pools. Innocent as she was—or rather, had been—she hadn't thought about birth control.

'Judging from your expression,' he said dryly, 'I can assume you are not on the pill?'

'No.'

'Or have taken any other precautionary measures in terms of birth control?'

'No,' Laurel snapped. 'Why should I? I was a *virgin*, in case you've forgotten.'

'I assure you, I have not.'

She took a quick, sharp breath. 'It is very unlikely I'm pregnant.'

'Is it?' Cristiano's calm tone belied the churn of anger, regret and anxiety he felt inside. 'Do you have information of which I am not aware?'

'I don't think I was in that part of my monthly cycle.' Her eyebrows rose in challenge. 'You are knowledgeable of such basic biology?'

'I believe I am.'

'Then you know that the only way I could be pregnant now is if I was ovulating in the last twenty-four hours.'

'And that is a possibility, is it not? You are fertile, I assume? No problems there?'

Her cheeks went pink. 'Not that I know of.'

He spread his hands. 'So we wait.'

She stared at him. 'Two whole weeks?'

'You're the nurse, Laurel. Isn't that how long it takes to get a positive result?'

'Around that, yes, from ovulation.' She spoke reluctantly. 'But I really don't think this is an issue, Cristiano.'

'We'll find out soon enough, won't we?'

'You speak so knowledgeably about all of this.' Laurel's lip curled. 'You have some experience in these matters, I suppose?'

'Actually, no. None of the women I have ever been with has become pregnant.' He'd always taken precautions. Laurel was the only woman with whom he'd lost control—and he had no intention of telling her that. He had no intention of it happening again, either.

'Never?' She looked sceptical and for some reason it annoyed him.

'No, never.' One woman had faked a pregnancy, and Cristiano had insisted she perform a test in his presence. Unpleasant but necessary, and the matter had been resolved quickly. He was not a man to be duped. Not the way his father had been.

'So we wait two weeks. And then what?'

'What happens next depends on whether you are carrying my child.'

The words fell into the stillness, rippled like stones cast in a pool. Laurel stared at him, her eyes hard and shiny, like glass. 'I'm not pregnant.'

'You don't know that.'

'But if I am,' she continued swiftly, '*I* will decide what to do about my baby.'

Anger fired through him, a clean, burning sweep. He rose from his chair, the movement controlled and precise. 'This child, should it exist, belongs to me as much as it does to you. *We* will decide, *bella*, make no mistake.'

Her jaw tightened, her eyes sparking at him. Cristiano's fists clenched. It was entirely inappropriate that he was turned on at this moment, yet he felt it all the same. Desire, hot and strong, coursed through him, making him want, even now, to take her in his arms and kiss her useless protests away. He took a quick, controlled breath. Now was not the time to indulge in such feelings. He'd already decided he wouldn't touch Laurel Forrester again. She was too tempting. Too dangerous…to his shame.

'You really are a control freak, aren't you?' she said in a low voice that vibrated with fury. 'A heartless one. You'd insist on making the decision about whether I could keep my own child.'

'What?' He stared at her in disbelief. 'What is that supposed to mean?'

Confusion flashed and she bit her lip. 'I assumed you'd want me to have an abortion.'

He felt a deep surge of an emotion he couldn't identify—and then he realised it was hurt, and he hated that he felt it. That he'd let a woman, a woman he barely knew, make him feel it. 'I would never do that,' he said in a low voice. '*Never.* If I really wanted you to get an abortion, I would procure a morning after pill right now.' He'd thought of it, but with the amount of time it would take to get one it seemed risky, and the idea of it repelled him. 'If you are pregnant, I would want you to keep the child. My child.' His throat worked and his chest felt tight. 'Our child.'

'Okay.' She looked surprised, even a little winded, by his vehemence. And he was surprised too. He'd never wanted children. Had never anticipated getting married or having a family. Having those ties that bound and choked. And yet…if, by the hand of Providence, Laurel was pregnant with his baby, there was no question what he would do. He would marry her.

Not that he intended to tell her that now. She looked shell-shocked as it was.

'So…' Laurel licked her lips. 'What would happen, then? If…?'

'We'll discuss that if and when it occurs,' Cristiano answered swiftly. Laurel was still looking flummoxed.

'And for the next two weeks…?'

'You stay with me.'

She cocked her head, a question in her eyes that he knew she didn't dare ask. And he decided to leave the question as to what the nature of their relationship would be unspoken and unanswered. He'd made a decision not to sleep with her, yes, but he wasn't about to reveal that information. He wasn't at all sure if he'd stick to that decision.

Cristiano reached for his mobile phone and thumbed a few buttons. 'I will arrange for the necessary wardrobe, cosmetics and stylists.'

Laurel's mouth dropped open. 'What?'

'You have no clothes.'

'You just got me some clothes, and I have more back at my hotel—'

'Appropriate clothes,' Cristiano amended. 'As my…companion, you need to be dressed and styled in a certain way.'

Laurel's mouth pursed. 'Like a doll, you mean.'

'No, like an elegant, beautiful, accomplished woman. The only kind I have on my arm.'

She laughed at that, a hard note to the sound. 'So those supermodels are accomplished?'

'In their own way.' Admittedly, intelligence or wit had not been high on his list of desirable qualities for a sexual liaison. 'I can hardly have you traipsing about in a dress like the one you wore last night,' he added.

She flinched and looked away. 'You seem to like reminding me of that.'

'"Like" is not the word I'd use.'

'Isn't it?' She swung back to challenge him with a glare. Heat flared deep inside again. He didn't usually like to be questioned or challenged, but something about Laurel's attempts to stand her ground, the innocent bravery of it, made him admire her as well as want her. Both emotions were inconvenient at the moment.

'I accept that you were playing a part,' he said levelly. 'Or something like that. And I will find out why soon enough.'

'Will you?' she scoffed.

'Yes,' Cristiano said, and his voice vibrated with the force of his feeling. No matter what the next two weeks held, he fully intended to get to the bottom of the enigma that was Laurel Forrester. 'I will.'

CHAPTER EIGHT

CRISTIANO WAS AS good as his word. Within an hour of the calls he'd placed, people started arriving—women dressed all in black, with heels higher than the ones Laurel had worn last night, carrying expensive-looking garment bags, glimpses of silk and satin visible on the padded hangers.

A team of white-coated beauticians came in as well, wheeling in cases and equipment and making Laurel blink. She'd never had so much as a manicure in her entire life, and it looked as if they were setting up an entire beauty salon in her bedroom.

She glanced at Cristiano; his expression was impassive, almost bored, as he watched the parade of experts march in. But when he caught her eye he gave her the tiniest glimmer of a smile which, inexplicably, made her heart lift.

'I know you're about to tell me how ridiculous this all is,' he said in a low, lazy voice. 'But why don't you enjoy being pampered for a bit?'

There were a lot of reasons why she shouldn't enjoy anything about this. He was making her over because she wasn't good enough. She didn't even want to be here. And as for the chance that she was pregnant...

Well. There was nothing she could do about any of it. One of the army of women pressed a glass into her hand and, bemused, Laurel glanced down at the green drink.

'What...?'

'Spinach, kale, almond and banana smoothie,' the woman said. 'With flax seeds and Omega 3 oils. Does wonders for your skin.'

And actually tasted surprisingly delicious. Over the rim of her glass Laurel caught Cristiano's eye again. This time he was smiling properly, and it made her realise she hadn't actually seen him smile—a real smile, not that cold curving of his lips—since she'd first stumbled into his penthouse.

'I'll leave you to it,' he said softly, and disappeared in the direction of his study while Laurel let herself be ushered back into her bedroom.

The next few hours were a whirl of treatments as beauticians slathered every inch of her body with some unguent, oil or scrub, and others worked on her fingers and toes, filing, buffing and polishing. A woman gave her a head massage while some kind of seaweed mask dried on her face and Laurel decided that this was a rabbit hole she would happily disappear down for a while. She'd never felt so pampered or relaxed, and she forced herself not to think about all the 'what if?'s that still loomed, or what the next two weeks were going to look like.

She'd called the hospital, and with they'd been relaxed about her taking the time off, given all the vacation time she had saved up. So maybe, just maybe, she could enjoy *some* of this enforced holiday.

After her hair, face and body had all been dealt with she was swathed in an enormous robe of the softest terry cloth and shown gown after gown after gown. Not that she was actually given a say. One of the assistants whisked a gown away before she'd even had a chance to touch the satiny material.

'Wrong colour,' the woman said briskly, thrusting the dress back in the wardrobe.

Laurel ended up trying on several evening gowns, all haute couture, incredibly well made and even more expensive.

'This one for tonight,' one of the women declared when Laurel tried on an emerald-green gown with a diamanté halter top. The stylist was tall and thin, dressed all in black, her dark hair pulled back into a bun so tight her eyes were nearly watering.

'Tonight…?' Laurel stared at her blankly even as those *what ifs* started creeping into her consciousness, dread curdling her stomach.

'Yes, tonight.' The woman pursed her lips. 'Signor Ferrero was very specific about what he wanted.'

'Was he?' The enjoyment Laurel had been feeling at being pampered, the relaxation that had seeped like honey into her very bones, drained away. 'What did he want?'

The assistant didn't hear, or pretended not to hear. 'Now your make-up and hair,' she said, and led Laurel to a chair, where a band of women armed with hairdryers and straighteners was waiting.

An hour later Laurel was ready—although, for what, she didn't even know. Her hair had been straightened and then pulled back into an elegant chignon. Diamond teardrop earrings dangled from each ear, and as for her face…

When she finally got to examine her reflection, Laurel was amazed and more than a little disconcerted. She looked like a stranger. A very elegant, glamorous and, yes, even beautiful stranger. Discreet eye shadow and mascara made her eyes look huge. Bronzer and contouring made her cheekbones stand out like blades. Crimson lipstick made her mouth look plump, full and blood-red. She didn't know whether to be pleased or horrified by what she saw. In any case, she just felt numb.

'Signor Ferrero is waiting,' the woman with the tight bun announced and, with her fingernails digging into Laurel's elbow, she led her out of the bedroom and back into the living area of the penthouse.

Twilight was stealing over the city, lights beginning to twinkle far below, the sky the pale violet of a bruise. Laurel minced her way across the slick marble floor; the silver-heeled stilettos she wore were even higher than the ones she'd had on last night, and the dress puddled around her ankles, making her feel as if she were in some sort of elegant strait jacket.

'Signor Ferrero is on the terrace,' the woman murmured, then headed back to the bedroom. Laurel could hear the other assistants starting to pack up all their equipment. She took a deep breath and carefully made her way across the floor to the open doors on the far side of the living room. She hadn't even realised the penthouse had a terrace, but now she could see Cristiano standing on a wide balcony framed with potted plants, gazing out at the city.

She paused on the threshold, the balmy summer breeze blowing over her. Her heart was stuttering in her chest for all sorts of reasons. She had no idea what was going to happen tonight. What she would be expected to do. And as for Cristiano...

He looked magnificent in a tuxedo, the jacket encasing his broad shoulders to perfection, the crisp snowy whiteness of his shirt the perfect foil to his dark hair and olive skin.

Then he turned and Laurel caught her breath, because the heat flaring in Cristiano's eyes made her remember last night in all its exquisite detail. She didn't want the reminder, didn't need it, to complicate what already felt fraught. With what felt like superhuman effort she banished the memory and stepped out onto the terrace.

'So here I am, all dolled up with nowhere to go.'

His eyes simmered like liquid silver, his mouth a compressed line. Laurel had the sudden urge to run her hand along his chiselled jaw with its hint of sexy stubble. To feel his skin under her fingers again. 'On the contrary. You have somewhere to go.'

Her heart stuttered in her chest. 'Where?'

'Down to the casino. With me.'

Laurel swallowed dryly. The last time she'd been on that casino floor... 'Tonight? I mean, so soon? If I'm going to be here for two weeks...' She trailed off, a desperate note entering her voice. She didn't want to go down there. Didn't want to see Bavasso again, or be another ornament on someone's arm, even Cristiano's. Especially Cristiano's.

'Of course so soon,' Cristiano answered in a clipped voice. 'Why wait? The sooner Bavasso realises you're mine, the better.'

'Maybe I don't want to be anyone's.'

'Too late, *bella*, and too bad. You don't have a choice any more.' Cristiano's smile was hard, the kind of smile she was used to, the kind she really didn't like. 'You should have thought of that before you tangled with Bavasso. Fortunately, I think this can be resolved quickly. The sooner Bavasso is off my property, the better.'

'Fine, let's go,' Laurel said, and held out her hand.

Mistake. Cristiano's palm slid across her, jolting her senses. Reminding her of...everything. Lips, tongues, hands, legs, bodies. Skin...smooth and hot and hard. *Stroking...*

She really had to stop thinking like this.

Cristiano's fingers tightened on hers, reminding her that she was under his control. She was his...at least for the next two weeks. And in spite of everything, against all sense and odds, Laurel felt a lick of excitement through her veins. Anticipation fizzed in her stomach and she decided not to suppress it for once. She needed the hit to make it through this evening.

They rode in silence down the lift, its speed making Laurel feel dizzy. Or perhaps Cristiano was the one making her feel dizzy, with her hand still in his, the spicy scent of his aftershave, the heat of his body, the overwhelming maleness of him, dominating her senses. She couldn't think, could barely breathe.

'So what happens when we go into the casino?' she asked, her voice breathy with nerves.

'Follow my lead.' Cristiano's voice was grim. 'And, for the love of heaven, do a better job of playing a mistress with me than you did with Bavasso.' He glanced at her, eyes and teeth both glinting. 'That shouldn't be too hard, since you *are* my mistress.'

The doors opened before Laurel could make a stinging comeback and, with his careless remark still thudding through her, she followed him out onto the crowded casino floor.

Nothing about this felt as he'd anticipated. Needed. Laurel was stunning, but she wasn't Laurel. When she'd appeared on the terrace, Cristiano had fought the nonsensical urge to take the pins from her hair, to grab his handkerchief and wipe the crimson lipstick from her luscious mouth. To strip her of her dress and heels and put her back in the plain T-shirt and skirt she'd worn earlier, or preferably nothing at all. He didn't want her like this, looking like all his other mistresses, glamorous, edgy and hard.

But that was exactly how he'd wanted her to look. Exactly what he'd told the army of assistants to make her look like, because she needed to look like his mistress. She was his mistress…of a sort.

Not liking it didn't make sense. It made him feel angry and strangely vulnerable, two emotions he despised. So he wouldn't feel them. Cristiano paused on the threshold of the casino as a cold, steely calm came over him. He was here to show Bavasso that Laurel was his, for Laurel's sake as well as his own. The reputation of his hotel and casino, of his professional status, rested on keeping men like Bavasso in check, or preferably off the premises. The sooner this irritation was dealt with, the better.

Bavasso was certainly unpleasant, but Cristiano wasn't really worried about him. And he might have overplayed Bavasso's reputation in order to secure his own interest in

Laurel. He felt a qualm of guilt about that and shoved it away. He'd deal with Bavasso tonight and tomorrow, and the next two weeks, would be his and Laurel's.

Raising his chin, Cristiano coldly scanned the room with its baccarat and blackjack, poker tables and roulette wheel. Diamonds glinted and the buzz of conversation, glasses clinking and dice being rolled, filled the room.

Cristiano had never gambled. He hated the thought of it, the desperate need for the adrenalin rush, the loss of control, the craven craving. Casinos were a necessary part of a luxury hotel chain, but he'd never placed money on a bet. Never held his breath for the roll of the dice. It wasn't the kind of man he was.

So why did bringing Laurel onto this heaving floor feel like a risk?

Next to him she shifted nervously, and he caught the scent of her perfume, something unfamiliar and cloyingly expensive, not the scent of lemon and violets he'd smelled earlier.

'What exactly am I meant to be doing?' she whispered. The pulse leapt in her throat as her gaze darted around the crowded room.

'All you have to do is look beautiful and smile,' Cristiano said. 'I think you can manage that.' He glanced at her, his mouth curving in what he intended to be a reassuring smile, but she didn't look as if he'd put her at ease at all.

Her face was pale, her eyes wide, her slender hands clenched into fists at her sides. 'Relax,' Cristiano murmured. 'We have to be convincing.'

'Why?'

'Because I would like to deal with Bavasso and be done with him. If he suspects he's being played, he'll continue to annoy the both of us.'

'You make him sound like a fly.'

'And I will swat him away.' Cristiano reached for her

hand. Her palm was icy cold in his as he pulled her deeper into the room and the throng of curious onlookers. He was used to being looked at, the owner of La Sirena and notorious in his own right. Women eyed Laurel up and down, mouths twisting in disappointment or derision. Men eyed her lasciviously, making everything in Cristiano tighten. She was his, damn it. *His.* He didn't even want them looking.

This was starting to feel like a very bad idea.

He pulled Laurel along, deeper into the crowd. She stumbled slightly, muttering under her breath, almost making Cristiano smile. She disliked the dressing up almost as much as he did.

'Now what?' she whispered.

'Enjoy.' He slid his arm around her waist, splaying his fingers along her hip. He felt her react, and it afforded him a flare of primal pleasure. Yes, she was his, whether she acknowledged it or not. Whether she wanted to be or not. They had a connection, a bond, forged in desire. She couldn't break it, and he didn't want to. Yet.

Laurel's body was tense under his arm as he moved her towards his usual place by the roulette table. Bavasso hadn't come in yet, although Cristiano expected him. He'd heard from his staff that he was still in Rome, and when he was he came to La Sirena nearly every night.

Idly Cristiano stroked Laurel's hip and her body twanged in response. 'You look like you're at the dentist,' he murmured, leaning closer so his breath fanned her ear. She shivered. 'I told you, relax.'

'I can't.'

'You're safe here, Laurel. I won't let anyone hurt you.' That was a promise he was absolutely sure he'd keep.

She just shook her head a fraction, her expression as pained as if she were having a filling done. Annoyance sparked inside him.

'You were a better actress with Bavasso,' he growled, further annoyed that he felt irritated and, yes, even a little hurt by how difficult she was finding this. *Him.*

'That was different.'

'How?'

Her tongue darted out to lick crimson lips. 'It just was.'

'Maybe you need a drink.' He snapped his fingers and a waiter came scurrying. 'Champagne,' Cristiano ordered. 'And two glasses.'

'Very good, sir.'

His narrowed gaze continued to survey the room as he stroked Laurel's hip, willing her to soften. 'Is it so very difficult,' he murmured, 'for you to appear as if you enjoy my company? Because you enjoyed it last night.'

'I wonder,' she breathed, 'how long you're going to keep reminding me of that.'

'As long as it takes for you to begin to relax.'

'Reminding me of my complete and utter folly is hardly going to get me to relax,' she snapped. 'Surprisingly.'

'Perhaps I'll remind you in a different way, then,' Cristiano answered, and he turned her around to face him. Her eyes widened, lips parting instinctively as she gazed at him warily. Cristiano lowered his head, sensing every eye in the room upon them. Then he stroked that crimson mouth with one fingertip, felt Laurel's shuddering breath and smiled.

CHAPTER NINE

LAUREL FELT CRISTIANO's finger on her mouth and, despite her desperate determination not to react, to yield, fireworks started going off in her body. His other hand remained on her waist, fingers splayed over her hip, and she was more conscious of his hands touching her than she'd been of anything in her life.

She couldn't keep from responding, tilting her head back as he traced the outline of her lips, a move so seemingly innocent and yet so overwhelmingly sensual. Distantly she heard the ripple of murmurs around them, like waves breaking on a faraway shore.

Cristiano dropped his finger from her mouth, looking, of course, utterly unmoved besides a faint flush on her high, sharp cheekbones. 'Good girl,' he murmured and Laurel wanted to weep.

This felt so much worse than those awful moments with Bavasso, when she'd felt trapped and frozen by shock, caught in a drama in which she'd had no intention of acting. This felt as if her soul was being slowly and inexorably crushed. Every moment she stayed down here—draped on Cristiano's arm, 'mistress' practically branded on her forehead in scarlet letters—felt like a sacrifice, a slaying, of everything she was.

Because this wasn't who she was. Who she wanted to be. And the fact that she'd actually given herself to this man, and it had meant something to her, made her want to curl up in a ball and cry.

'Chin up,' Cristiano said, touching her chin with his finger. 'And smile.'

Laurel couldn't summon a smile. She turned away from

him, conscious of the whispers, the murmurs, the looks. Was she imagining the derision? The contempt? A woman's lip curled and Laurel blinked back tears. She *hated* this.

'Drink,' Cristiano ordered, and handed her a flute of fizzing champagne. Laurel took a long swallow, needing the alcohol to dull her senses, which were heightened to a painful point.

'Easy,' he said, and her fingers tightened around the stem of the glass.

'Stop ordering me around,' she hissed. 'I'm an adult— not a puppet, not a doll, despite what you and everyone here believes.'

And, because she desperately needed some space, she stalked away from him, her dress swishing around her ankles, her head held high as she met no one's gaze.

She couldn't do this. She certainly couldn't do this for two whole weeks. Laurel took another sip of champagne and willed herself to get a grip. Two weeks and she could have her life, or at least most of her life, back…as long as she wasn't pregnant. And she couldn't be pregnant. She just couldn't be.

Out of the corner of her eye she saw a flash of red and her whole body stiffened. It was her mother, Elizabeth, standing alone in the corner of the casino. Laurel walked towards her, a mix of despair and relief churning inside her.

'Elizabeth.' Her mother had never wanted her to call her Mom, or Mother, not even when Laurel had been small, although occasionally the endearment slipped out. It didn't now.

'*Laurel.*' Elizabeth's gaze was as conflicted as Laurel's, a mix of guilt and relief. 'I'm glad to see you safe.' Her mother's gaze raked her up and down. 'And it seems you landed on your feet.'

For a moment Laurel couldn't speak. Her chest burned with indignation and hurt and she simply stared, battling emotions too intense to verbalise. 'You call this *on my feet*?' she finally squeezed out. 'Did you…did you know Rico Bavasso was going to attack me?'

'Of course I didn't.' Guilt flashed across her mother's face again. 'Do you think I'd have let you upstairs if I'd known what he planned? I was expecting him to propose!'

For a second Laurel almost wanted to laugh. Her mother sounded outraged…on her own behalf.

'You must have suspected something,' she insisted in a low voice. 'The way he was acting on the casino floor…'

'What old man doesn't like to flirt with a beautiful young woman? Do you think I liked it? That I welcomed such an occurrence? He was mine.'

'He's not now?'

'I haven't seen him since. He wants nothing to do with me.' Elizabeth sounded more resigned than bitter. 'It was a bad idea, bringing you along. It just showed me up.'

'That's your takeaway from all of this?' Laurel let out a hollow laugh. Her mother had always been foremost concerned with herself. The only saving grace was that she was up front and unapologetic about it. *I spent the first twenty-four years of my life living for other people, wearing myself out. It's time I started thinking about myself.* And it seemed she'd never stopped.

Laurel shook her head, weary now. 'I never should have come here.'

'Who are you with now?' Elizabeth asked, ever pragmatic. 'Someone worth it, I hope?'

Laurel closed her eyes briefly. 'I'm with Cristiano.'

'Cristiano?' Elizabeth boggled at that bit of news. 'I thought he'd never have anything to do with either of us ever again.'

'And with good reason.'

'You know I never would have left Lorenzo.' Elizabeth's voice was tight. 'That money wasn't…'

'I know,' Laurel said tiredly, because she'd heard this all before. 'But it was still stealing.'

'We were married.' Elizabeth struggled to contain her bitterness, even after all these years. 'Can you blame me for wanting a nest egg?'

The trouble was, Laurel couldn't. Not exactly. But she couldn't justify it, either. So she said nothing, and Elizabeth's scarlet mouth twisted bitterly. 'Watch your back, that's all I have to say. Cristiano sold me down the river and he'll have no compunction doing the same to you.'

'Wait—what?' Laurel stared at her mother in surprised confusion. 'What do you mean, he sold you down the river?'

Elizabeth shrugged. 'He told Lorenzo about the bank account, fired him up and made it all seem far worse than it was.' She took a sip of her drink, a shadow of sorrow passing over her features. 'I did love him, you know—Lorenzo. No matter what his son or anyone else thought.'

'I know you did.' She'd doubted many things about her mother but not that. But Laurel hadn't realised it was Cristiano who had blown the whistle on her. Did it make a difference?

'Be careful,' Elizabeth said in a low voice. 'About Cristiano and about Rico. This isn't your world, Laurel. You're far too naïve for it. I shouldn't have dragged you into this, but I was desperate. I wanted to please Rico. I should have realised he'd prefer you.'

'I'm going to leave this world as soon as I can,' Laurel promised. 'All I want is to go home.'

'It won't be home for much longer, I'm afraid,' Elizabeth stated bluntly. 'I'll need my half.'

Cold crept into Laurel's bones, even though she'd been expecting this. Of course she had. 'But you said—'

'Laurel, I only agreed to give you my half of the house because I thought Rico was going to propose! I'm sorry, but I need the money.'

Laurel swallowed tightly. 'Please, Mom,' she whispered, using the endearment her mother never liked. Sometimes it slipped out, because she'd always wanted a mother. A proper mother, who cuddled, kissed and cared. 'Please. That house is the only thing...'

Elizabeth's expression turned sly. 'Maybe you can get something out of Cristiano. If you can, then we'll talk.'

Something out of Cristiano? He might have bought her these clothes but he wouldn't give her a penny. And she wouldn't ask for one. Laurel swallowed. 'You know that's impossible.'

'Then the house will have to be sold. Your grandfather left me half that house in his will. It's my inheritance as much as yours.'

'I know it is, but...'

A hand closed around Laurel's arm like a steel band, making her nearly drop her drink. 'As much as I hate to interrupt this little chat, we have places to be and people to see.' Cristiano inclined his head towards Elizabeth, his gaze glittering, before he steered Laurel away.

'You didn't have to—' she began, only to be cut off by his clipped voice.

'Bavasso is here.'

'Is he? Where?'

Cristiano nodded towards the baccarat table and Laurel's blood felt as if it had frozen in her veins as she caught sight of the man who had assaulted her last night: neatly dressed, the silver thatch of hair, the glinting eyes. A handsome older man, charming when he wanted to be, yet he made her skin crawl and her stomach heave.

The reaction was visceral, instinctive; she couldn't have controlled it if she'd tried. 'I think,' she whispered, 'I'm going to faint.'

Cristiano's arm came around her waist as Laurel sagged against him. 'Not yet, *bella*,' he murmured and then, as

Bavasso turned to watch, he kissed her in front of everyone, his mouth moving over hers with possessive thoroughness, causing desire to flow through her, a molten river of want. Another moment and she'd be reduced to a puddle on the floor.

'Please,' Laurel whispered when he finally broke the kiss. 'I can't… I can't handle any more of this. Please get me out of here.'

Cristiano glanced at Bavasso and then, seemingly satisfied, he started walking towards the lifts. 'Very well. I think we've made our point.'

Laurel managed to keep herself upright as she walked past the staring crowds and saw Bavasso's tight expression, the bodyguards on either side of him. The lifts. All she needed to do was get through those gleaming black doors.

They opened and Laurel practically hurled herself inside. When they'd closed again she let out a sound that was halfway to a moan and crumpled against the wall, her knees buckling beneath her. It was the second time in the space of twenty-four hours that she'd fled to a lift. Her dress pooled around her as she slowly slid to a seated position, resting her head on her arms.

'Was it really so terrible?' Cristiano asked dryly. 'Being seen on my arm?'

'Everything about it was terrible.' Laurel drew a ragged breath, willing herself not to cry. She didn't think Cristiano would be impressed by her tears. 'I felt cheaper than I ever have in my life right then.'

'Cheaper than last night?' Cristiano demanded in disbelief, sounding annoyed. Laurel looked up, conscious of the tears pooling in her eyes and starting to streak down her cheeks. It seemed she was going to cry after all.

'Yes, Cristiano, cheaper. Because, although you'd never believe it, I wasn't trying to impress Bavasso. He wasn't my *mark*.' Her voice hitched and she forced herself to continue. 'I was there to meet my mother's boyfriend, possibly fiancé, and when he started treating me… Well, you know how he treated me. I didn't know what to do. How to respond. And so I froze and I let it happen, and it made me feel awful, but *this*…' She swiped at her cheeks. 'I gave myself to you last night. I know it didn't mean anything to you, of course I do, but it meant something to me. Maybe it shouldn't have, but it did. And to be treated like your mistress, your possession, your *plaything*… I hated it. I hated every minute of it.'

She'd said way too much. Far more than she'd ever intended to reveal. Anything she said could and would be used against her, no doubt. She'd just given him ammunition, but she felt too weary and heartsick to care.

The doors opened and Laurel started to scramble to her feet, hampered by the long, narrow skirt of her gown. Cristiano reached a hand down to help her but Laurel jerked away.

'I don't need your help—'

'Don't be ridiculous,' he snapped, and helped her up. 'I don't think Bavasso will bother you, at any rate. If it's any consolation, I think he received the message we wanted him to.'

'It isn't,' Laurel tossed over her shoulder, and stalked into the penthouse.

Cristiano watched as Laurel kicked off her heels, her whole body trembling, and then started yanking the pins from her hair. It was what he'd wanted to do earlier, to dismantle the elaborate costume she was wearing, but now that she was the one doing it he felt annoyed somehow. There was no pleasing him when it came to this contrary woman, it seemed. And there was no pleasing her.

'I don't really understand what you're so upset about,' he said levelly as Laurel shook out her hair. She grabbed a tissue from the box and wiped at her lipstick, tears now drying on her face, leaving raccoon-like circles under her eyes.

'Of course you don't.'

'This is what we agreed on. The most expedient way to get you out of the mess you got yourself into. I'm *helping* you, Laurel.' And he wouldn't think about what she'd said about Bavasso flirting with her, how she'd frozen. It made sense, yet Cristiano resisted trusting Laurel, even that far. Trusting anyone.

'I know, I know.' She scrubbed at her lips until they were raw looking. 'You're a prince.'

He couldn't miss the sarcasm. As for the other things she'd said in the lift—about what they'd done last night meaning something to her—well, she'd been a virgin. Of course she was going to dress up what had been nothing more than a very pleasurable physical act. He'd been expecting it, but it didn't make it any easier to deal with.

Sighing, Cristiano reached for his phone. 'Why don't you change, since you apparently find that haute couture gown so abhorrent? And shower, if you like. I'll order us some food.'

She stared at him, a storm of emotion in her eyes, and then without a word she turned on her heel and stalked into the bedroom, slamming the door behind her.

Women. Muttering a curse, Cristiano dialled for room service.

Twenty minutes later the food had arrived and Laurel emerged from her bedroom dressed in a pair of loose linen pants and a silky T-shirt, her damp hair curling in ringlets about her face and shoulders. Cristiano liked her better this way, not that he would say it out loud. The last thing he wanted to do was give Laurel any hope for what could be between them.

Laurel's face was composed, nothing showing in her eyes. The emotional, distraught woman from before was replaced with someone who thankfully was calm and hopefully going to be sensible.

'What would you like to eat?'

'Anything is fine.' Laurel sank onto the sofa, curling her bare feet under her as she gazed out at the night sky. Her expression was pensive, and she didn't even look at Cristiano as he handed her a plate of food.

'Thank you,' she murmured.

'You're welcome.' Cristiano sat opposite her. 'What did your mother say to you down there, anyway?'

She turned to glance at him. Still nothing in her eyes, in her face. 'She wanted to know what had happened to me.'

'And what did you tell her?'

'Not much.' She leaned her head back against the sofa, looking so weary Cristiano had the impulse to comfort her. To reassure her—yet about what? 'Your kiss told her all she needed to know.' She spoke lifelessly, without any interest or spark.

'And last night with Bavasso?' He took a careful, even breath. 'Was it really…was it how you said?'

Laurel shrugged. 'Believe what you like.'

'Last night you said it wasn't what it looked like. Is that why?' Her gaze slid away from his and Cristiano felt in his gut that there was more she wasn't saying. Laurel wasn't quite as innocent as she wanted him to think. 'Tell me the truth, Laurel.'

She sighed and picked at her food, her hair falling forward to hide her face. 'About a week ago my mother came to me and asked me for…for a favour, I suppose. We hadn't seen much of each other in recent years, or really at all. She'd been dating Rico Bavasso and she said he wanted to meet me.'

'What I saw last night was hardly your mother introducing you as her daughter to her boyfriend.' Cristiano couldn't keep the scepticism from his voice. He didn't even want to.

'I know. She said he was feeling his age and it would do him good to flirt with a younger woman. It sounded innocent, but maybe it was just me being naïve.' Laurel gulped. 'I can't believe my mother would...'

'Set you up?'

'She wanted him for herself.' Laurel shook her head. 'When I talked to her tonight, she was annoyed that Bavasso had been interested in me at all.'

'Charming.'

Laurel sighed. 'That's just how she is. I've accepted it.' She glanced up at him, something in her expression hardening. 'You don't know anything about my mother or me, for that matter. So please don't judge.'

'It's hard not to judge from what I saw and continue to see,' Cristiano returned coolly. 'What I don't understand is why you agreed to come at all, if there has been no love lost between the two of you.'

'Because I suppose I'm always hoping it will be better between us this time.' Laurel hesitated, and Cristiano waited for the other shoe to drop, because surely it would? 'And,' Laurel admitted quietly, 'Because she offered me something I wanted very much.'

There it was, just as Cristiano had known. His instincts hadn't been wrong. 'And what did you want so much?' he asked.

'A house. My house.' Cristiano stared at her, nonplussed, and Laurel continued, 'I spent a lot of my childhood at my grandfather's house in Canton Heights. It's a small farmhouse, nothing special, but I love it. It's the only place besides... Well, the only place I think of as home.'

'Besides?' Cristiano honed on that revealing word. 'Besides what?'

Laurel shrugged, her gaze sliding away. 'Besides the villa in Milan when we lived with your father. That felt like home, for a little while.'

Three years. He stared at her, trying to gauge what she was feeling. How much she was feeling. 'And so this house...' he said after a pause. 'Your mother agreed to... what? Give it to you?'

'Her half. My grandfather died three months ago and he left the house, the only thing he had, to both of us equally. I think he was hoping she'd come back, settle down.' She let out a humourless laugh. 'She'd never do that. My mother hates the place. But she agreed to sign over her half to me if I...met Bavasso and was nice to him. So I agreed, because the only thing I've ever wanted in life is my own house. My own home.' Her voice wobbled and she looked away.

'Why didn't you just offer to buy her out?'

Laurel let out a shaky huff of laughter. 'Because I don't have a hundred grand just sitting around,' she returned. 'Even farmhouses in rural Illinois cost money, you know. Money I don't have.'

Cristiano remained nonplussed. 'Still, you were agreeing to a rather large unknown just for a house.'

Laurel sucked in a breath, swinging around to stare at him, her face pale, her eyes narrowed. 'Says someone who has no idea what it's like not to have one.'

'What do you mean?'

'Oh, come on, Cristiano. You're rich. You've always been rich. You have absolutely no idea what it's like not to be. To be *poor*.'

He opened his mouth to make some suitably stinging reply and then closed it. She was right. He didn't know. He never had. 'That's true,' he said evenly. 'I don't.'

Laurel let out a tired laugh. 'But it doesn't excuse making reprehensible or at least stupid decisions. I know.'

'I didn't say that.'

'It was on your face. You might as well have shouted it.'

Could she read him so easily? Because, yes, he had been

thinking something along those lines. He didn't particularly like Laurel knowing, though.

'If it makes any difference, it happened in increments,' Laurel said. 'I agreed to meet Bavasso as no more than my mother's boyfriend. And then we got to Rome and my mother was telling me to dress up for him. Okay, fine. And then it was "be nice to him", and I didn't even know what that meant. I think she felt trapped. She wanted him for himself, but she realised she'd lose him altogether if I wasn't…well.' She shook her head. 'She didn't mean for me to be hurt, that I do believe. Things got out of hand for both of us. But I'm not excusing any of it, trust me.'

'All right.' Cristiano absorbed all that for a moment before continuing, 'Tell me about your childhood.' Because he realised he wanted to know. 'Before your mother married my father. Where did you grow up?'

She looked surprised, then a little wary. 'Why do you want to know?'

'Perhaps it will help me to understand who you are and why you've made the choices you have. That can only be a good thing, surely, since we have to spend the next two weeks together?'

'By your decree.' Laurel sighed. 'Fine. Where should I begin?'

'Why not at the beginning?' Cristiano gave her a mirthless smile. 'It's the very best place to start.'

CHAPTER TEN

LAUREL SHIFTED ON the sofa, unsure how to deal with Cristiano's request. He wanted to know about her? Why? To use whatever she said against her? And yet she was so tired of staying suspicious. Being so careful all the time with him. And that tactic hadn't worked out all that well so far, so why not tell him everything? Who cared what he thought? He'd already shown her tonight what he thought of her—just another mistress. A prop.

Being seen on his arm—knowing what people were whispering about her, knowing what she and Cristiano had done together—it had been worse than anything she'd endured with Bavasso. More shameful. And she knew Cristiano would never understand that.

'My mother was born in rural Illinois,' she began. 'My grandfather was a poor farmer and they didn't have much money. She married a local boy and they had me.'

'Sounds like a fairly normal story so far.'

Oh, that even tone. The mildness. 'It was,' Laurel agreed, trying to match his tone. 'They struggled, but so did a lot of people. But then my father lost his job on the assembly line of a local factory. He started drinking too much. Things started to get ugly, or so my mother tells me. I was only four at the time, when he left.'

'Four? Do you remember your father?' He was looking at her closely, but she couldn't tell anything from his tone or his expression.

'Vaguely. The smell of chewing tobacco, the scratchiness of his shirt. Sitting next to him in his truck.' She shrugged, trying to ignore the tightness that had started in her throat and chest. 'It all feels like parts of an old dream. Foggy fragments, no more.'

'Yes.'

Something about the way he spoke, the contained feeling underneath the words, made her ask, 'What about your mother? Do you remember her?'

'Yes, of course. She died when I was nine.' Cristiano spoke dismissively, looking away, making Laurel wonder. 'So what happened after your father left?'

Laurel shrugged. 'My mother tried to get work but it was hard. Not much was going on in that part of Illinois, and of course she had me to take care of. My grandfather needed to work on the farm and my grandmother had died before I was born. We moved to Chicago and while she was waitressing she met someone.'

Her first 'daddy'. Laurel had always hated how Elizabeth made her call the men she'd entertained her father... except for the ones who weren't interested in kids. More than one boyfriend had never known about her at all. Laurel had been very good about staying quiet, hiding in cupboards, pretending she didn't exist.

'And that's how it began? Elizabeth funding her lifestyle through a series of men?'

'Yes, you could put it that way, I suppose.' Laurel sighed, disliking how scornful he sounded, although she couldn't really blame him. 'It was hard for her, you know. More than one of her boyfriends was bad news. Seriously bad news. Sometimes we had to run.'

And sometimes her mother would leave her with her grandfather in Canton Heights, which had been the sweetest relief, as well as a disappointment. No more dank hotel rooms or temporary apartments, no more late nights crouching in corners or under the covers. No more drama and endless uncertainty. And no more Mom.

But then her mother would always collect her again,

and in her mother's sudden, desperate hug Laurel had believed Elizabeth did love her and want her with her. Why else would she come back for her? And there had been moments when Elizabeth had seemed, if not quite maternal, then at least a little caring. She'd given Laurel plenty of advice, a lot of it bitter, and when she'd landed Lorenzo she'd promised Laurel things would be better for her too. It wasn't much, but Laurel believed her mother loved her, in her own way. At least, she wanted to believe that.

'So you had ten years of this and then she hit the jackpot with my father.'

Laurel flinched a bit at his tone but then she lifted her chin and met his cool gaze head on. 'Yes, but you know she didn't even realise how rich he was when she met him.'

'She just got lucky, then.'

'Yes, I suppose she did. I know what it looks like—and, trust me, I know my mother is selfish and self-serving— but I do believe she and your father loved each other, Cristiano.' Her mouth twisted. 'Obviously that isn't something you can understand.'

He leaned forward, his eyes sparking gold fire. 'They loved each other? That's why she siphoned two million euros into her own private bank account?'

'She was trying to protect herself.' Laurel held up a hand. 'I *know* it was wrong. I'm not justifying it, just trying to make you understand. This is a woman who grew up dirt poor, who had men treat her badly time and time again. She was trying to give herself a little security—but, yes, I realise it was stealing.' Memory sharpened inside her. 'I didn't know you were the one who told your father, though.'

Something flickered in Cristiano's eyes. 'Why shouldn't I have?'

'I'm not saying you shouldn't have. Only…you could have asked her first. You could have tried to figure out what was going on.'

'It was fairly obvious, *bella*.'

'Don't call me *bella*!' Laurel snapped. 'Not now. Not ever.'

'I did what was right. Surely you can't deny that?'

'I just wished you'd talked to her first. I don't think she would have ever left him. She's lived her whole life on the edge. With Lorenzo we'd both finally found a haven. Your father was a kind man, Cristiano. If he'd been told another way, he might have understood.' Ten years later she still remembered her mother's resignation, felt her own numb shock at Lorenzo's cold treatment of them both. He'd taken her for rides in his sports car. He'd slipped her pocket money and tousled her hair. He'd bought her a dress for a school dance. He'd been more of a father to her than anyone, save her grandfather, and he'd cut her off without so much as a conversation. But that was a pain too deep and personal to share with Cristiano, especially when he was looking at her with such disdain.

'I cannot believe,' Cristiano said, ice in every word, 'That you are blaming me for what happened when your mother is so clearly a gold-digger and a thief.'

'I'm not blaming you. I just wished it could have been handled differently—'

'And,' he cut her off with even more arctic tones, 'I cannot believe you are defending the woman who as good as sold you to a man twice your age just twenty-four hours ago.'

Laurel looked away, blinking hard. She couldn't argue with what he said. Her mother had treated her badly, no matter what protestations she'd made earlier. Even if she believed what her mother had said… It was just that Laurel had always wanted to see the best in her mother. Wanted to believe her mother loved her, deep down. *Because if your own mother didn't love you…* 'I've already told you, I'm not defending her,' she said after a moment, her voice low. 'Just trying to explain things. Not that you'd accept any explanations.'

'Like I said, actions speak for themselves.'

'They do, don't they?' Laurel risked a look back at him, noting the flinty eyes, the granite jaw. He was completely unmoved. 'And yours do too. What made you so suspicious of people, Cristiano? Of women? Because you were suspicious of my mother from the moment you met her.'

'Of course I was. My father picked her up in a cheap casino in Palm Beach. They married in four days. Who wouldn't be suspicious?'

'A whirlwind romance.'

He let out a huff of humourless laughter. 'That's one way of putting it.'

'Still, it's more than that,' Laurel insisted. 'You're suspicious of everyone. Every woman, myself included. Why?'

He stared at her for a long moment. 'Life experience.'

'What life experience?'

She didn't think he'd answer but then he shifted restlessly on the sofa and bit out, 'After my mother died my father had several mistresses. They all took him for a ride. They were so patently false: the cloying way they spoke; pretending to be interested in me, a sulky ten-year-old.' He shook his head, the movement terse, angry. 'They were just out to get whatever they could—money, jewels, cars, clothes. They raked it in until my father realised they were using him and then he cut them off.'

'So we both endured a parade of other people in our lives,' Laurel said quietly. 'It's hard, but it doesn't need to make you cynical.'

'Cynical?' Cristiano challenged. 'Or smart? Before your mother my father married a woman. Jade. She was twenty-three, a bombshell. A *bomb*—and she detonated right in the middle of our lives. She took my father for nearly everything he had. He hadn't bothered with a pre-nuptial agreement, because he was so sure it was love.' Cristiano shook his head, his features twisting with the memory. 'Fortunately a lot of his money was tied up in property and unreachable to her. But she left him as destitute as she possibly could, and ran off with her boyfriend, who had been in on the whole thing.'

'I'm sorry,' Laurel said quietly. She heard the hurt in his voice but knew he wouldn't want her to try to comfort him. He'd hate the thought of her offering sympathy. Pity. Yet she understood him more than she ever had before. 'That's terrible,' she continued. 'But not everyone is like that.'

'None of this matters,' Cristiano dismissed. 'It has nothing to do with us.

'Us?' Laurel forced herself to ask, meeting his gaze directly, even though the look in his eyes felt as if it could freeze the blood in her veins. 'There is no "us".'

'There is if you're carrying my child.'

'Don't talk about that as if it is a probability.'

'It is a possibility.'

'Barely, and in any case you said we'd cross that unfortunate bridge if we came to it.'

'Very well,' Cristiano said evenly. 'Let's talk about the next two weeks.'

Laurel resisted the urge to shudder at the prospect of more evenings like the one she'd just endured. 'Are you going to drag me down to the casino again? Night after night?'

Cristiano's mouth twisted. 'You make it sound like a fate worse than death.'

'No, but it's not something I'm looking forward to in the slightest.'

Cristiano sat back, his gaze turning worryingly speculative. 'No, I don't think we'll go down there again,' he said slowly. 'I don't think Bavasso is a threat any more. He knows you're mine.'

Laurel eyed him warily, hating how arrogant he sounded. How possessive. She really was just a thing to him. An object to be used. 'What, then?' she asked.

'We'll go to France.'

'France?' Laurel's eyes widened almost comically. Cristiano sat back and smiled, glad to have surprised her. Because she'd surprised him too much already, with her anger and her hurt, and then her revelations about her childhood. Cristiano had told himself not to feel sorry for her, not to be moved by what was really a common-or-garden sob story, but he did. He pictured a very young Laurel hiding from one of her mother's abusive boyfriends and felt a boiling anger surge through his veins. And that was a very inconvenient thing to feel.

'Why would we go to France?'

'Because I have a new manager at my hotel in Paris and I want to check up on her. Also, there is a charity gala I am meant to attend. You can come as my date.'

'Your date?' Laurel was still goggling at him. 'But why? Bavasso won't be there.'

'I don't care about Bavasso any longer, and you shouldn't either. I need a date, and you're here. It's convenient.'

'So glad to be of service.' Laurel sat back, looking nonplussed by the change of plans. Cristiano understood her surprise. He'd only just decided to take her to Paris tonight. To escape the oppressive feeling here, with Bavasso below, her mother in attendance, all the bad memories swirling around them.

They'd go somewhere new, somewhere different, where the past didn't dog them. Where they could simply be and enjoy each other. Because all evening a realisation had been coalescing inside him—he wasn't done with Laurel Forrester. Their affair *would* be real, and therefore all the more convincing. But first he needed to explain the parameters.

He gazed at her now—the long, golden-brown curls, the

shadowed eyes, the way she nibbled her lip. She was nervous, uncertain, maybe even afraid. He needed to reassure her. He also needed to convince her.

'Laurel.' She jerked her startled gaze towards him, eyes wide with wary apprehension. Cristiano leaned forward, his attention fully focused on the woman before him. 'What you said in the lift—about sex meaning something to you.'

Colour flared in her cheeks. 'Don't use that against me now,' she said. 'I didn't mean it like that.'

'Like what?'

She lifted her chin, a brave attempt at haughtiness. 'You don't need to worry that I'm going to fall in love with you, Cristiano. Trust me on that.'

This was unexpected, and for some reason her lofty assurance rubbed him the wrong way. 'What a relief.'

'I'm sure it is, since you seem to have an allergic reaction to love or commitment.'

'An allergy suggests something that isn't a choice,' Cristiano returned lightly. 'And trust me, Laurel, it is very much a choice.'

'Is it? Or is it just a reaction to your childhood, all those women of your father's?'

Cristiano sat back against the sofa and folded his arms. 'My, what a stunning little piece of psychoanalysis.'

'Actually, it seems fairly obvious to me. We're all products of our childhood, aren't we?' Laurel shrugged. 'I know I am.'

And now, even though he knew he shouldn't be, he was curious. He needed to know more. 'What do you mean by that?'

'People leave,' Laurel stated starkly. 'Don't they? Some by choice, some not. It's one of the reasons why I won't fall in love with you, Cristiano. I don't want to fall in love with anyone.'

'One of the reasons?'

A faint, sardonic smile curved her lush mouth. 'It's not exactly as if you've been Prince Charming, is it?'

'I... I...' He was actually stuttering in his shock. Suddenly she looked so smugly confident, sitting curled up on his sofa, acting as if the prospect of her falling for him was the remotest of possibilities. And yes, that was fine, that was what he wanted; of course it was. Yet he still found it seriously annoyed him.

'Thank you for putting me so much at my ease,' he said dryly when he'd thankfully recovered his composure. 'What, then, did you mean in the lift?'

She didn't pretend to misunderstand. 'Sex is important. You're giving yourself to someone, making yourself vulnerable. I mean, just being naked is being vulnerable, isn't it?' Cristiano shrugged a non-answer. He was, he realised with a pang of unease, out of his depth. He didn't talk about this kind of stuff. He didn't even think about it.

'And then the things you do together...' Her cheeks were going from pink to fiery red and Cristiano knew she was recalling all they'd done together. All he intended they do again. And again. 'Well, it means something. Not love, necessarily, but there's a bond of sorts. A shared memory. I know men seem able to dismiss it as just some kind of physical workout, but it didn't feel that way to me.'

'So,' Cristiano asked after a moment, the restless ache of desire surging through him as her words sparked memories of deep kisses and golden skin, 'what did it feel like to you?'

'Like I said, there's a bond.' Laurel's face was still red as she looked away. 'No matter what—even if I never see you again after these two weeks, which is the most likely scenario—there will be a bond. You...you were my first.'

The simply spoken words pierced him with guilt. Her first, and so far her only lover. It was a responsibility he hadn't wanted but, now he had it, and he wasn't going simply to throw it away.

'Then there's no reason not to make the most of these two weeks,' he said, and Laurel jerked around to face him, her mouth dropping open in shock.

'What…?'

'We gave each other a great deal of pleasure, Laurel. Surely you won't try to deny that?'

She gulped. Audibly. 'No, I can hardly deny that part of it.'

'And you have so kindly assured me that there is no risk of an emotional attachment. The bond we have is physical, and it's one we should both enjoy for as long as we can. Don't you think?'

'I…' She licked her lips and Cristiano could not keep from groaning at the sight.

'It seems you are doing your best to convince *me*,' he said, and her gaze widened, pupils flaring.

'I'm not trying to…'

'You don't need to try, *bella*.' He slipped off the sofa and came to kneel before her. 'It just is.' He slid his hands along her legs, over her knees and across her thighs. Laurel shuddered in response. 'This thing between us—it just is. Why should either of us fight it?'

She stared at him, her pupils dilated, her breathing ragged. 'So two weeks of…of being together? That's what you want?' She breathed.

'It's very simple, isn't it? We enjoy each other and we both walk away satisfied.' He stroked her inner thighs lightly. 'Very satisfied.'

She stared at him, transfixed, a rosy flush sweeping over her whole body. Cristiano slid his hands higher, splaying his palms across the tops of her thighs, keeping her in place. Laurel let out a breathy little sigh, the sound of acceptance. Of victory.

Cristiano leaned in. 'We both want this, Laurel.'

Her eyes fluttered closed, her body trembling under his light touch. 'I… I know.'

'There's nothing to fear or regret here,' he added, compelled to reassure her even now. 'Nothing but pleasure for both of us.'

She nodded, the movement jerky, and Cristiano closed the space between their mouths. The kiss was deep and endless, branding them both. His hands tightened on her thighs, and hers gripped his shoulders, both of them steadying and anchoring each other.

Eventually, breathless and wanting, Cristiano broke the kiss. 'Yes?' he demanded, his voice raw with need.

Laurel opened her eyes and gazed at him, her expression both dazed and resolute. 'Yes,' she whispered.

CHAPTER ELEVEN

LAUREL WOKE UP to dazzling sunlight and an empty bed. She stretched, muscles aching that had never ached before. Hours later and she still felt sated and boneless. One thing was inarguable—Cristiano was an attentive, thorough and excellent lover.

Not, of course, that she had any way to measure his performance besides her own breathless satisfaction. She rolled onto her side, tucking her knees up to her chest and fought the expected rush of guilt and doubt. She'd made a decision last night, a foolhardy and potentially dangerous decision. Cristiano Ferrero was way, way out of her league. She didn't have any experience with dating, with men, with relationships.

But this wasn't a relationship.

A timely reminder, and one she would have to give herself constantly over the forthcoming days. No matter what she'd assured Cristiano last night, it would be all too easy to fall in love with him, or at least believe that she had. Because she might have told Cristiano she didn't want to fall in love with anyone, but that wasn't strictly true. It was simply that she hadn't yet found anyone to fall in love with. Anyone to take that almighty risk for—the risk of offering herself wholly with the possibility of being pushed away. People left. It was the one truth she'd learned over and over, yet she still kept hoping there was someone out there who wouldn't. Someone who would think she was worth staying for. She believed it because she wanted to believe she was lovable.

But she knew Cristiano wasn't the man who would convince her of that. So she'd take these two weeks and get out of them what she could. Because fighting Cristiano was a lost cause, especially when she was fighting herself as well, her own impossible desires and dreams. Far easier, and far, far more enjoyable, to give in.

And what a sweet surrender it had been.

Sighing, she stretched and then sat up in bed. She didn't know what the day held, or what Cristiano would act like now she truly was his lover. His mistress.

The door to the bedroom opened and Laurel stilled, before drawing the sheet up to cover herself. Cristiano stood in the doorway freshly showered and dressed with two cups of coffee.

'Good morning.'

'Good morning.' Laurel took the cup of coffee he handed her, cradling the warm mug between her palms.

'We leave for Paris in a couple of hours.'

'So soon?'

'I need to meet with my manager before the gala tonight.'

Laurel nodded slowly and took a sip of coffee. 'All right.' She was excited to go to France, to escape the confines of Rome and its recently made memories. She wanted to be somewhere new with Cristiano.

He turned away, his eyes narrowed as he gazed out at the bright sunshine of a summer's morning, at the light glinting off the windows and roofs of Rome; he looked so impossibly beautiful, the stark lines of his body and face gilded in sunlight.

'Cristiano.' Laurel's voice wavered and he turned, dark eyebrows raised in query. 'Thank you.'

A tiny smile quirked his mouth. 'Now, that was unexpected.'

'I know I haven't been particularly grateful for your intervention,' Laurel allowed with a small, answering smile. 'But I am. I don't know what I would have done if you hadn't stepped in.'

Something flashed across Cristiano's face, an emotion Laurel couldn't gauge, and then he gave a little nod. 'You should get dressed,' he said, and walked from the room.

An hour later Laurel stepped into the lift that would bring them to the lobby and the waiting limo to take them to the airport. She wore a shift dress in aquamarine linen and a pair of taupe open-heeled sandals, her hair caught back with a sapphire clip—and Laurel suspected the sapphires were real. It had come with a drawerful of jewellery that she was afraid to touch. Was this how Cristiano treated all his mistresses—with jewels, clothes and careless expense? She'd been telling herself all morning just to go with it, enjoy the over-the-top craziness, but she still found it hard.

She'd paid her own way since she was eighteen years old, working her way through her nursing degree with part-time jobs, insisting on paying rent—admittedly, a minimal one—to her grandfather. She didn't like feeling bought.

And yet she couldn't keep a warm glow from spreading through her when Cristiano saw her, a slow smile stealing over his features as his gaze swept over her. 'You look lovely.'

'Thank you,' Laurel murmured.

They now had a relationship of sorts and, while it felt far better than the constant battling, it was still…odd. Considering she'd never even had a boyfriend, Laurel was not at all sure how to navigate a love affair, and a temporary one at that.

Cristiano helped her into the limo and Laurel slid into the sumptuous leather luxury, amazed all over again at the turn her life had taken. In Illinois she drove an old pick-up truck.

'You look so surprised,' Cristiano remarked as he sat next to her, sliding out his phone and thumbing a few buttons.

'It's been a long time since I've been in a limo.'

He looked up, arching an eyebrow. 'How long?'

'Since our parents were married,' Laurel admitted. 'Those three years were like a dream to both of us. I think we knew it couldn't last.'

'Because your mother got greedy.'

'Let's not rehash this, Cristiano,' Laurel said on a sigh. 'I know what she did was wrong, okay?'

She couldn't help but wonder about the *what ifs*, though—what if he hadn't said anything about that bank account; what if Lorenzo and Elizabeth had stayed married... It beggared belief how different her life might have been now.

Except here she was in Italy, in a limo, living a life of luxury, if only for a short time,. So it seemed she had that life, albeit temporarily, after all.

'So what exactly are we doing in Paris?' she asked once they were settled in the first-class section on the plane, their seats forming a private nook.

'As I told you, I have a business meeting this afternoon, and then the charity gala tonight. After that...' His slow smile was like a burn, the wicked glint in his eyes a hiss. 'After that we can do what we like,' he murmured, his gaze lowering to sweep meaningfully over her.

And even though part of her felt she should resist the innuendo, the expectation, Laurel couldn't keep from re-acting. Heat flared, need tightening inside her into sharp, aching points.

She smiled and looked away, trying to regain her composure. A flight attendant brought them both glasses of fizzing champagne, and Laurel took a much-needed sip. She wasn't much of a one for alcohol, but right now she needed the distraction.

'Relax,' Cristiano murmured as he lounged back in his seat and sipped his drink. 'Bavasso has been dealt with.'

But it wasn't Bavasso making her feel as if everything inside her was on edge. It was this man right here, his silvery gaze slipping inside her, stirring things up, making her restless, wanting and afraid. After years of living a small, calm life, it felt like too much. Maybe, Laurel reflected wistfully, she just wasn't mistress material.

Cristiano watched Laurel fidget out of the corner of his eye and wondered why she was so nervous. It couldn't be Bavasso, so it had to be him and the new status of their relationship—although he used that word with caution.

Still, the last twelve hours had been some of the most enjoyable of his life. Not just the sex, which had been as incredible as before, but—dared he even think of it?—the company. He was starting to *like* Laurel—her feistiness, her sense of humour, her easy-to-read emotions and limitless compassion—something he'd never felt for any of his other mistresses, whose personalities had been of zero interest to him.

'What is the gala tonight in aid of?' Laurel asked. 'Which charity?'

'A children's hospice, I believe.'

'Really?' Interest sparked in her eyes. 'I'm a hospice nurse. Palliative care.' Which meant she helped people in the last days and weeks, even hours, of their lives.

'That must be difficult sometimes,' he said quietly.

'Yes, it can be. Sad, of course.' She gave a sorrowful smile. 'But it's often an overlooked part of the medical profession. People are so focused on getting better, they don't want to think about what happens when you can't.'

'Of course,' Cristiano murmured. He was disconcertingly moved by the thought of her helping people at such a hard time in their lives. The selflessness of it, when there was so little reward. The patients she dealt with were never going to get better. 'So how did you choose that particular field of nursing?' he asked, even though his gut was telling him to stop asking questions. *Stop being interested; stop caring, for heaven's sake.*

'My grandfather.' Laurel was quiet for a moment, her expression pensive and a little shadowed. 'He was diagnosed with dementia while I was doing my degree. I was living with him, working during the day and taking classes at night. My grandad really wanted to be able to stay at home as long as he could, and so I went even more part-time to make that happen. After all he'd done for me over the years...' She pressed her lips together, her gaze distant. 'It was the very least I could do.'

The very least, and yet so much. And, Cristiano reflected, the opposite of what he'd assumed. When she'd walked into the casino he'd decided right then that she was a shallow, mercenary, experienced gold-digger like her mother. Instead he was discovering how innocent she was, how *pure*. A woman who'd been willing to put her own ambitions aside to care for an elderly man; to dedicate her life to easing the burdens and sorrows for others.

It was an uncomfortable realisation.

'And you said your grandfather died three months ago?' he asked after a moment.

Laurel nodded. 'Yes, in the hospice where I work, so I could see him every day. That was a great blessing.' She let out a soft, sad sigh. 'And it was a great loss. The last year of his illness, he was very confused. And the last few months, he didn't even know who I was.' Grief flashed across her face and then was gone.

Cristiano felt a tightening in his chest, an overflow of emotion. He was discovering depths to Laurel that amazed and humbled him. And, damn it, he still wanted her to be shallow. He needed her to be, because that was so much simpler. So much easier.

'I'm sorry,' he said again, the words heartfelt, but feeling useless.

'Thank you. I still miss him. I suppose I always will.' She turned to him with a small smile. 'Enough of my sob story,' Laurel said, injecting a note of brightness into her voice. 'What about you?'

What about him? What could he say? He was a sinner to her saint. At that moment, he felt he'd done nothing of note in his life whatsoever. Cristiano shifted in his seat and took a sip of champagne. 'What do you want to know?'

'How did you get started in the hotel business? Your father is in finance, isn't he?'

'Yes, he was. He's retired now.'

'So why hotels instead of the family business?'

'Because I wanted to be my own man, on my own terms, not just follow in my father's footsteps.' He hadn't wanted to follow in his father's footsteps in any way—not the business, not the three marriages, not the endless loop of love and heartbreak that had left his father alone and wistful in his villa in Capri, still hoping for some kind of silver years romance.

'Fair enough,' Laurel answered. 'So why hotels?'

Cristiano shrugged. 'I got my start by buying up a run-down *pensione* and turning it into an exclusive boutique hotel.' He shrugged. 'A combination of luck, risk and a small amount of skill.'

'I'm sure it was more than a small amount,' Laurel said, smiling, and Cristiano looked away.

'Maybe.' The truth was he'd been in the right place at the right time, and had been willing to take a risk on a big vision no one else had shared. It didn't feel like that much, all of a sudden.

'And from that one little *pensione* you now have how

many hotels?' Laurel asked, and Cristiano turned back to her.

'An even dozen. Most are in Europe, but I'm expanding into North American and Asia.'

'With one in New York and one in Hong Kong.'

Cristiano arched an eyebrow. 'You're well informed.'

Laurel blushed and ducked her head. 'I read about it in the papers.'

'Did you?' That was interesting. Had she been keeping tabs on him? That schoolgirl crush from ten years ago had perhaps lain dormant. Once that information might have alarmed him, but now he felt strangely pleased by the thought.

'You are in the tabloids a lot, you know,' Laurel said, clearly trying to recover. 'With whatever supermodel or actress you're with at that nanosecond.'

'Nanosecond?' Cristiano leaned forward. 'That's insulting to my sexual prowess.'

Laurel's blush, which had faded to a lovely, dusky pink, now returned to red. 'I didn't mean it like that.'

'I know you didn't. You couldn't possibly have.' He leaned a little closer, so his leg nudged hers and his breath fanned her ear. 'But perhaps I need to remind you of it anyway.'

Laurel's lips parted soundlessly and her gaze darted around the first-class area. Their seats formed a private alcove, but it wasn't *that* private. Not private enough to do what Cristiano was now aching to do.

And yet… He trailed one hand up Laurel's bare leg, skimming the sensitive skin under her knee before sliding his fingers under the hem of her dress.

'*Cristiano.*' Laurel looked scandalised but also excited. He saw it in the flared pupils, the parted lips, heard it in her uneven breathing. And felt it in himself. He was barely touching her, yet it felt like the most wildly exciting thing he'd ever done.

He stroked the silky-smooth skin of her inner thigh, listening to her breathing hitch and feeling his own painfully intense reaction as lust arrowed through him.

'Someone will see,' Laurel whispered, her breath hitching, but she didn't move.

'See what?' Cristiano stroked her thigh again, letting his fingers slide just that little bit higher. Her skin felt like cool silk. 'We're just sitting here, chatting.' And, from the outside, that indeed looked like all they were doing. Their bodies blocked the view of Cristiano's hand where it was inching inexorably higher.

'Maybe, but...' Laurel shifted, giving him greater access—intentionally or not? Cristiano didn't know and he wondered if Laurel even knew. This was new territory for her and, he was realising more and more, new territory for him. Which made him all the more determined to put their relationship back onto familiar footing. Incredible sex and nothing more.

'But what?' Cristiano prompted softly. His fingers climbed higher, to the warm apex of her thighs, and Laurel let out a shuddering gasp as he stroked her knowingly.

'But...' Her voice trailed away as her eyes fluttered closed and she slouched in her seat, helpless to do anything but respond to his touch. Desire and triumph roared through him in a primal, possessive wave.

'But nothing,' Cristiano murmured as he continued to stroke. 'Nothing but this.'

'May I refresh your champagne?'

The bright, chirpy voice of the flight attendant had Laurel freezing, her eyes snapping open as she stared at the woman in shock, sprawled in her seat, her legs parted.

Cristiano withdrew his hand and straightened, giving the woman a smile as he reached for his glass. 'Why not?'

he said. They could finish what they'd started when they reached Paris. Although his body ached with the need to slake himself with Laurel, he knew the few hours of delaying satisfaction would be a delicious torment for them both.

Laurel straightened, pulling her dress down, then taking a sip of her champagne, clearly trying to restore her composure. 'Do you do that kind of thing very often?' she asked unsteadily, and Cristiano hesitated.

Was she going to be jealous about the other women he'd had, insecure because of his experience and the lack of her own? But if he admitted that he hadn't done this before—that he never did anything that threatened his control of a situation, that she was the only one who made him act in a way he never would have expected—would she then assume that she was different from all the rest? That he would be different with her?

'Not very often,' he answered with a wicked smile and took a sip of champagne. Laurel nodded and sipped her own champagne, and Cristiano could tell his answer disappointed her, if just a little.

But it was important to remind her that this was an affair, two weeks of fantastic sex and absolutely no strings. Hell, Cristiano acknowledged moodily as he drained his glass, it seemed he needed the reminder as well.

CHAPTER TWELVE

LAUREL GAZED OUT of the window of her bedroom in the hotel suite of La Sirena, Paris as twilight settled softly over the City of Lights. They'd arrived several hours ago, and from the moment she'd stepped off the plane to now she'd been pampered, indulged and, yes, made love to.

They'd taken a limo from the airport to the hotel, and then the concierge had personally escorted them to the luxurious suite that Cristiano reserved for his personal use. As soon as the door had closed behind him, Cristiano had reached for her, kissing her hungrily as if it had been months rather than mere hours since they'd last been together.

And yet Laurel was hungry for him, ravenous, especially after the appetiser he'd teased her with on the plane. Just the memory of his knowing fingers climbing higher while people near them read newspapers or sipped champagne made Laurel blush and fidget. It had been utterly thrilling.

In the hotel suite he'd backed her towards the bedroom, tugging down the zip of her dress in one fluid movement and then helping her step out of it without missing a single stride. Laurel had walked backwards slowly, wearing only her bra and pants, her eyes glued to Cristiano as he unbuttoned his shirt and shrugged out of it.

She didn't think she'd ever tire of looking at him: the ridged muscles of his abdomen; the bronzed, burnished skin; the flare of heat in those silvery eyes. She could hardly believe that a man like this, a man who radiated such a powerful sexual charisma, wanted *her*.

Yet as he'd stalked her towards the bedroom, a predator intent on his more than willing prey, she knew he did.

He'd caught her up as she crossed the threshold, her breath coming out in a whoosh as their bodies made exquisite contact, hard against soft. Cristiano had made short work of her bra and pants, and then neatly hooked his leg behind her knees, so she'd had no choice but to fall onto the bed with a tremulous laugh.

He'd fallen with her, his body covering hers, so hot and hard and muscular. Legs, lips, hands, hips—all tangling, pressing, invading, *consuming*.

Just the memory of it all made Laurel's whole body tingle. If she'd known how fantastic sex could be, she'd have had it a whole lot sooner. Except, of course, she'd never met anyone she'd been remotely interested in taking that step with. She'd never met anyone like Cristiano.

A light knock sounded on the door. 'Ready, *bella*?' Cristiano called and Laurel turned to inspect her reflection in the mirror one last time.

She wore a royal-blue evening gown with off-the-shoulder straps and a diamanté belt encircling her waist, the gauzy material falling in a perfect column before pooling about her feet. A stylist had done her hair in an artful updo, with a few curls resting provocatively on her shoulders, and another assistant had done her make-up, making her eyes look smoky, her lashes endless. She looked elegant but also sexy, and not, she hoped, like nothing more than Cristiano's latest. Tonight she did not want to be dismissed as the eye candy on Cristiano's arm. And she didn't want him to treat her that way, either.

Yet…she couldn't quite banish the memory of the rest of the afternoon—the way Cristiano had quickly rolled off the bed, pulling on his trousers and shirt while Laurel had lain there, dazed and naked, the last of her climax still thrumming through her.

'Where are you going?' she'd asked sleepily.

'I told you, I have a meeting.' Cristiano had reached for

his neck tie without looking at her. 'You can relax here. Feel free to order anything you want from room service.' He'd shot her a glinting smile. 'Too bad I'm not on the menu.'

And then he'd gone, the door clicking shut behind him, leaving Laurel alone for the rest of the afternoon. There was no reason to feel lonely, she'd told herself as she'd strolled through the sumptuous suite and then indulged in a long, lovely bubble bath. No reason to feel as if Cristiano was fobbing her off, putting her in her place. This was what she'd signed up for, what she'd agreed to. She was his mistress. This was what mistresses did.

But for a little while, sitting in the suite alone, picking at the sandwich she'd ordered from room service, she'd longed to go back to Illinois—to her grandfather's house, to her job, to a life that made sense and made her feel useful and important—admittedly, in a small way, instead of lounging about like some useless ornament, waiting on Cristiano's pleasure.

'Bella.' Cristiano's voice was lazy with a hint of laughter as he rapped on the door again, startling Laurel out of her reflections. 'At this rate we're going to miss dinner.'

Laurel took a deep breath and banished those memories. Two weeks. Two weeks and then she would go back to that life, small and important as it was. She just needed to enjoy what she had and not ask for more. Not expect it to be different. 'I'm coming.'

Laurel opened the door, a purely feminine pride stealing through her at the look of blatant heat in Cristiano's eyes. It still amazed her that she affected him this way, just as he affected her. As always, he looked devastating in a tuxedo, the perfect foil to his ink-black hair and olive complexion.

'You look wonderful,' he said, the thrum of sincerity audible in his voice, then he took her hand and led her to the lifts.

The charity gala was being held in the hotel's opulent

ballroom, a room with frescoed walls and giant crystal chandeliers, now filled with a crowd of the most elegant people Laurel had ever seen. For a second she hung back, overawed by it all, but Cristiano tugged on her fingers and brought her into the room.

'Remember,' he murmured. 'You're with me.'

He joined a group of business associates, wealthy men and women and their partners, everyone speaking in flawless French that Laurel couldn't follow. She spoke a smattering of Italian, thanks to her three years living in Milan, and a bit of schoolgirl French, but that was it. Everyone here seemed as if they spoke several languages with ease.

A middle-aged man turned to her with a friendly smile. 'Are you English?' he asked in accented English and Laurel smiled, grateful for someone making a friendly overture.

'American, actually. And I'm sorry, but I don't speak much French.'

'I speak English,' the man replied with a very Gallic shrug. 'So it is okay. You are with Monsieur Ferrero?' His inquisitive gaze flicked to Cristiano, who was engaged in a discussion with another businessman, but Laurel had the sense that he was listening intently to their conversation, even though he didn't so much as look at them.

'Yes. But I'm interested in hospice care,' she said, determined to be there on her own terms as much as she could. 'Back in the US, I work as a nurse in palliative care.'

'Do you?' The man's eyes sparked with interest. 'I would love to hear your thoughts about rehabilitative palliative care. Do you practise that where you work?'

'We are beginning to,' Laurel said with real enthusiasm. It was invigorating to talk to someone about issues that mattered, to feel useful again, with more to contribute than simply being an accessory or a clothes horse. 'It's difficult, because of course you have to reach patients earlier, before they're referred to hospice care.'

'Exactly. We are pioneering a new method, of consultants giving us referrals of anyone with a non-curative diagnosis.'

'But most people don't want to hear they have a non-curative diagnosis,' Laurel said quietly. 'They want to believe they can get better.'

'Yes.' The man nodded and then extended his hand. 'Michel Durand, consultant at the Institut Curie.'

'Laurel Forrester. A nurse at Canton Heights General Hospital.' She gave a self-conscious smile as she shook his hand.

They chatted for a few more minutes, with Laurel becoming increasingly animated as Michel asked her opinion on various new initiatives in palliative care happening in America. Then he glanced at Cristiano, eyebrows raised.

'Do you mind if I steal your lovely companion away for a few minutes? There are a few people here I'd like her to meet.'

Cristiano's expression was suspiciously bland as he smiled and nodded. 'Of course.'

With one quick, questioning look which Cristiano returned just as blandly, Laurel went.

Cristiano tracked Laurel's progress across the crowded ballroom as he half-listened to one of his associates drone on about an investment opportunity in Bucharest.

'It's ripe for tourist venues, and there's a lovely nineteenth-century building perfect for renovation, right in the heart of the Old Town…'

'La Sirena Bucharest?' Cristiano dragged his gaze away from Laurel to give the man a small smile. 'I'll think about it.'

Then he turned back with narrowed eyes to watch Laurel laugh and chat with several men who, improbably, were not staring at her cleavage but actually listening to what she was saying.

And she must have been saying something important, because she looked so passionate—eyes sparkling, mouth curving, her hands moving in graceful arcs as she described something. Cristiano had no idea what, but he couldn't look away from her. And neither could any of her listeners.

What was the emotion churning like acid in his gut? Was it a simple matter of jealousy? His mistresses were *his*. They devoted their time and attention to him. It was so obvious that he'd never needed to articulate it in one of his arrangements. But his arrangement with Laurel was like no other.

'Who is she?'

Cristiano turned to see the man who had suggested the Bucharest hotel—Niko Savakis—nodding towards Laurel. 'Your latest *amour*,' he clarified, making Cristiano inexplicably want to punch him. 'Who is she?'

'Her name is Laurel Forrester.'

'She's different from your usual blonde bombshells,' Savakis remarked.

'Oh?' Cristiano's voice was dangerously quiet. 'How is that?' He did not like Savakis looking at Laurel as if she was something one purchased in a shop. He didn't, he realised, like Savakis thinking of Laurel as simply his mistress, here today, most likely gone tomorrow.

None of this made any sense.

'She's intelligent and articulate, for one,' Savakis replied mildly. 'She's beautiful, but not in a showy, obvious, clearly fake way.' He gave Cristiano an amused glance. 'Not to disparage your previous mistresses, of course. But Miss Forrester certainly seems like a cut above. Perhaps you'll hold onto her for a while.'

'Perhaps I will.'

Savakis registered Cristiano's even tone with a little amused smile. 'And if you don't... I'm sure there are plenty of men who would happily take your place.' His considering gaze flicked back to Laurel; she was laughing, looking incandescent and so very happy. 'Myself included.'

'Don't even think about it,' Cristiano warned him in a low growl. His fists bunched at his sides. Savakis looked surprised, and then he smiled.

'So she is different,' he murmured, and moved away.

Cristiano forced himself to relax. *What was going on here?* This was not how he conducted relationships. Affairs. *Arrangements.* He didn't care about the women he was with. He barely thought about them beyond what they could provide in bed.

Laurel was different. And, even more alarmingly, he was different with Laurel.

Since she'd stumbled into his penthouse just three days ago she'd shaken him up. Reached him in a way no one else had, and certainly not a woman he'd slept with. He didn't understand it. Didn't understand himself. And he hated not feeling as if he was in control—of the situation and of himself.

But one thing he knew more than any other was that he was not happy with her across the room, chatting and laughing, looking as if she was having the time of her life. Without him.

With each step cementing his purpose, Cristiano strode across the room to join Laurel.

'Ah, Ferrero.' Michel Durand, the doctor who had spirited Laurel away, gave Cristiano what seemed a too-knowing smile. 'Where did you find such a charming and intelligent woman? She is far from your usual date.'

Did everyone have to keep mentioning the attributes, or lack thereof, of his usual paramours? Cristiano smiled tightly. 'She found me, as it happens.'

Laurel blushed and Durand glanced between them both, intrigued. 'Is that so? It sounds as if there's a story there.'

'There is,' Cristiano agreed smoothly, inserting himself into the little circle and sliding his arm around Laurel's waist. 'But it is not one I am going to tell you.'

'Ah.' Durand looked again between them, his gaze sliding speculatively from Laurel to Cristiano and then back again. 'Very intriguing. We have been having a most illuminating conversation about rehabilitative care.'

'A very important topic, I am sure.' And one he knew nothing about. After a tiny pause the conversation started up again, swirling around him. He could hardly contribute, save for the generous cheque he would write for the hospice—that was something he was good for, at any rate.

But after a few moments of battling his own petty irritation Cristiano started to listen. He listened to Laurel's impassioned plea for dignity in end-of-life care, and was amazed—although he acknowledged there was no real reason to be so surprised—at how articulate she was. How determined and passionate. And he felt something stir inside him, something that had been long and purposefully dormant.

It was strange and unsettling, this awakening inside him, parts of his soul stirring to life, his atrophied heart stretching and seeking. It was strange and deeply alarming, because he didn't want to start caring about Laurel. Yet since she'd catapulted back into his life he'd been battling against just that.

If he was smart, he would let her go. Tell her to have a nice life and send her back to Illinois. But Cristiano knew he couldn't do that. First, because she might be pregnant, and second, because he didn't want to.

The second reason trumped the first by a long shot.

During a lull in the conversation, Laurel caught him looking at her and she smiled uncertainly. 'Why are you scowling at me?'

'Am I?' He reached for her hand, twining her fingers

with his and tugging her gently towards him. He craved the contact even now, felt his heartbeat start to slow as her hip brushed against his leg. 'I suppose it's because I'm thinking how I'd rather be alone with you upstairs than in this stuffy room listening to people witter on.'

Laurel smiled slightly but he saw a flash of something close to hurt in her clear, aquamarine eyes. 'I rather enjoy the wittering, actually.'

Of course she did. And Cristiano felt a pang of shame for dismissing what he knew was an incredibly important topic. Too much of tonight was putting him off balance, out of sorts. And the only way he knew to rectify it was to put things back the way he was used to having them. Laurel in his bed. End of story.

'How about this?' he suggested in a lazy murmur. 'Fifteen more minutes of wittering, we say our goodbyes and then we head upstairs?'

Laurel was eyeing him thoughtfully, in a way Cristiano didn't particularly like. As if she saw through his suggestion to something underneath that he tried to hide, and hell if he even knew what it was.

'We'll miss dinner.'

'I don't care.'

There was a pause as she looked at him, seeming to see far too much. 'All right,' she said softly. 'If that's what you want.'

'It is.' It had to be. And yet, as he watched Laurel begin to make her farewells to the people she'd been talking to, he also felt that it wasn't.

Somehow he wasn't getting what he wanted out of this deal, yet at the same time he was getting far more than he'd ever expected or asked for.

Ten minutes later they were leaving the ballroom. Laurel was silent and pensive as they stepped into the lift and soared up to their private suite, and although he wanted to

Cristiano couldn't quite make himself take her in his arms. Turn this into the simple physical exchange he'd told himself he wanted it to be.

What was keeping him from it, damn it? Every nerve felt scraped raw, every sense on high alert as the lifts opened into the suite.

Laurel walked into the suite ahead of him, looking so elegant and lovely, and something in Cristiano broke, the fragments hardening into crystalline points. He took a step towards her and she stilled, perhaps sensing the danger in him. The emotion he couldn't express or suppress, the emotion he couldn't afford to feel.

'Cristiano…?' She turned to him, eyebrows raised in uncertain query.

'Turn around,' Cristiano said, his voice low and hard, a demand that brooked no opposition.

Laurel stared at him for a moment, a faint frown drawing her eyebrows together, and then wordlessly she turned around.

Cristiano stepped towards her and with one swift tug he unzipped her dress.

CHAPTER THIRTEEN

LAUREL FELT THE cool air brush her back and drew in a sharp breath. Cristiano pushed the gown off her shoulders and then slid it down so it pooled about her waist. He didn't speak, and she felt the tension and something inexplicably like anger rolling off him in powerful waves. Felt a tremble of both fear and excitement in herself because, no matter how he treated her, it seemed she couldn't get enough of his touch. But what was going on?

'Cristiano, what—?'

'Don't talk.' He spoke flatly, and Laurel fell silent, even more apprehensive now.

Cristiano stepped behind her, so she felt his powerful frame practically pulsing into hers. He reached up and covered her breasts with his palms, the touch possessive and sure, making her ache. She sagged a little against him as his thumb teased the aching peaks of her breasts and he dropped a kiss onto the curve of her shoulder. And, even though she didn't want to, even though something about this felt completely off, Laurel responded.

A shudder ripped through her as Cristiano rocked against her and her dress slid into a gauzy pool about her feet. She was wearing nothing but a thong—the style of the dress had prohibited a bra—and Cristiano was fully dressed. Fully in control. Everything about this felt unequal. *Wrong.*

'Cristiano…'

'I said, don't talk.' He trailed his hands along her rib cage and then anchored her hips against him. Laurel couldn't keep a moan from escaping her as he pushed against her, and a blaze of pleasure pulsed between her thighs. She threw out a hand towards the hall table to brace herself and Cristiano laughed softly.

'You're not going to fall. Trust me, *bella*.'

She heard the sound of him unzipping his trousers and then taking a condom from his pocket and, with a strength she hadn't expected, she wrenched away, stumbling over her dress before she righted herself. Her breath came in ragged pants as she turned to look at him.

Colour slashed his sharp cheekbones and his eyes glittered with silvery, metallic intent.

'I may be your mistress,' Laurel gasped out, 'but I am not your whore.' And then, not trusting herself to say anything more, she stalked towards the bedroom, slamming the door behind her.

A shudder went through her and Laurel forced herself to blink back tears. What a way to ruin what had been a happy evening. What a way to make her feel excruciatingly cheap. Laurel searched for comfort clothes, but she didn't have any. Sexy nightgowns, provocative lingerie, coordinated outfits, evening gowns. Not a T-shirt or pair of comfy yoga pants to be found.

With a sudden cry she tipped a drawer out and let the silky garments spill onto the floor. For good measure she kicked them, lobbing them into the corner of the room. She hated everything about her situation here, and even herself, for responding to Cristiano even when he treated her like the trollop he seemed to think she still was.

With another cry she yanked the evening gowns off their padded hangers and threw them in the corner with the rest of the slinky clothes and lingerie.

They might have cost a fortune, but she didn't want them. Didn't want any of it. Ten more days, she told herself. Ten more days and then she never had to see Cristiano again.

Damn it, why did that thought hurt?

A knock sounded on the door. 'Go away,' Laurel called raggedly, the words ripped from her. 'Go *away*, Cristiano.'

She reached for the terrycloth dressing gown hanging on the bathroom door and shrugged into it. Then she pulled the pins from her hair, flinging them on to the dressing table. She'd really been looking forward to tonight. Excited to talk about something that mattered, to feel like more than a mistress. But Cristiano seemed determined to remind her of her lowly status.

Why?

'Laurel,' Cristiano called, his voice low. 'I'm sorry.'

She stilled at the words, which sounded surprisingly heartfelt. She didn't open the door, though.

'Laurel? Did you hear me?'

'Yes. I'm not sure I care, though.' Which was a lie.

'Please open the door.'

'Why? So you can finish what you started? I'm not interested, Cristiano, and, no matter what our *arrangement*, I'm not available on demand.' She choked out the words, hating herself. Hating everything.

'I'm not... I just want to talk. Please.'

Laurel hesitated, then, because she was so angry and she wanted someone to yell at, never mind what Cristiano wanted to say, she stalked to the door and threw it open. 'Fine.'

He turned and walked into the living area and, after a few seconds where she struggled to control her temper and regain her composure, she followed him.

Cristiano stood with his back to her, having shed his tuxedo jacket and bow tie. Laurel tightened the sash on her dressing gown and stiffened her shoulders. 'Well? What did you want to say to me?'

'I am sorry.'

'You said that already.' She was in no mood to be soft and understanding. 'Although I actually question what you're even sorry for. You have the uncanny ability to make me feel cheap without even trying.'

'Actually,' Cristiano said as he turned around, 'I was trying.'

'Oh.' Laurel blinked, absorbing that awful statement. 'Is that somehow supposed to make me feel better?'

'No.' Cristiano rubbed his jaw. He looked haggard suddenly, the stubble glinting on his jaw, his eyes shadowed. Haggard and yet still so impossibly sexy, with a few studs on his tuxedo shirt undone, revealing the lean column of his throat, the bronzed perfection of his chest. But she couldn't think about that now. 'I was just stating a fact,' he said.

'Thanks for that.' She shook her head slowly as tears threatened once again. But, no, she would *not* cry. She wouldn't let Cristiano see how he affected her. Hurt her. And yet she needed to know. 'Why?' she whispered.

Cristiano raked a hand through his close-cropped hair. 'I… I don't know.'

'I was having a good time tonight, you know,' she told him, forcing her voice not to wobble. 'Talking about things that mattered. Feeling important. A small thing, no doubt, and probably pathetic, but it mattered to me. I'm not… I don't want to be your…your sex toy.'

'You're not,' Cristiano insisted in a low voice.

'Your convenient mistress, then. You pulled me from the gala before it had hardly started, and with everyone watching you took me upstairs and treated me like a—like a—' Her voice choked and she struggled to go on.

'Laurel, please. Don't.' Cristiano sounded genuinely anguished. 'I shouldn't have… I'm sorry.'

'So you say. But I still don't understand why you treated me like that.' She drew a shaking breath. 'Do you get your kicks from humiliating women?'

'Of course not.' He sounded angry now, colour slashing his cheekbones. 'I wasn't trying to humiliate you.'

'Just making me feel cheap, then. As usual.'

'Just reminding you of our relationship!' he exploded. 'Reminding myself.' He turned away, raking his hands through his hair again, leaving them on top of his head as he blew out a long, weary breath. 'And you were enjoying it, so don't pretend otherwise.'

'I can't help how I respond to you,' Laurel returned with as much dignity as she could muster. 'I wish I could.'

'Do you?' He let out a humourless laugh.

'*Yes.* I know what you think of me, how little you think of me, and yet I still melt like butter when you so much as crook your finger. That's humiliating.'

'You have no idea what I think of you,' Cristiano said, and dropped his hands.

'Your actions give me a pretty good idea.'

'No.' He turned around to face her. 'Because the truth is I think you're amazing. Smart and driven, kind and compassionate.' Laurel's mouth dropped open as she stared at him in complete shock. 'And that's the reason I took you from the gala, Laurel. That's the reason I brought you up here and tried to remind us both that this is just about sex. Because I'm starting to care about you, and I don't want to.'

He hadn't meant to say all that. And now that he had Cristiano fought the urge to retreat or lash out, either one, something to mitigate the damage he'd just inflicted on himself. Laurel was staring at him, her mouth hanging open, looking completely gobsmacked, and no wonder.

'Wow,' she said finally, and she shook her head. 'Wow. Am I supposed to be touched? *Thankful?*'

The scorn in her voice shocked him. He hadn't been expecting it. He had, he realised, been expecting her to be surprised and moved and—hell!—pleased. He'd given her more emotion, more of *himself*, than he had any other woman. Yet Laurel didn't seem to appreciate that fact.

'No,' he said after a moment, his voice stiff. 'Of course not. I was just trying to explain.'

'Trying to explain how you behaved like a complete bastard? Thanks. I feel so much better now.'

He stared at her, anger crystallising inside him. 'Glad to hear it,' he bit out. This is what he got for being honest. He supposed it was better than having her go all dewy-eyed on him, although right now he wouldn't have minded a little softness. Laurel was all hard, glittering edges, filled with a fury he didn't fully understand.

Then, abruptly, she deflated. She walked slowly to an ornate sofa, all gilt curlicues and striped silk, and sank onto it. 'I don't understand you,' she whispered. 'You start to care about me and you treat me even more like you don't?'

Cristiano felt the stirrings of shame and even embarrassment. When she put it like that, it sounded ridiculous and infantile. 'Basically, yes,' he said, and sat opposite her. 'That's what happened.'

'Why?'

Cristiano didn't answer for a long moment. He already felt flayed raw, exposed in a way that made him want to both cringe and attack. 'Remember when you said you didn't want to fall in love with anyone?'

Laurel's eyes widened and Cristiano silently cursed. He had *not* meant to say the dreaded L-word. 'Yes…'

'In a similar way I don't want to care about anyone,' he clarified swiftly. 'Never mind actually fall in love.'

'Because the women you've known, your father's women, were untrustworthy?'

'Yes.' That wasn't the whole truth, but it would suffice for now.

'But you seem to get angry when I show I'm not like those women,' Laurel pointed out with infuriatingly clear logic. 'When I'm acting differently, like tonight. You got angry because I was talking about nursing, not because I was being as shallow and mercenary as you once assumed me to be.'

'That's not why I got angry.'

'Why, then?'

Cristiano stared at her in frustration, his jaw locked so tightly he felt as if he could break a tooth. This conversation wasn't going anywhere good. Laurel was far too persistent and smart to be fobbed off with some vague half-truths.

'Because you're too good for me,' he said finally, the words ripped from him. 'I want you to be shallow and mercenary, because then this makes sense. A sexual arrangement, nothing more. But when you talk about nursing or your grandfather—or listen to what people say or *laugh*— then it turns into something else, and I don't want that.' He injected a grim note of finality into his voice. 'At all.'

Laurel sat back against the sofa, looking a little winded. Then she straightened and said, 'I didn't ask you to want it.'

'I know,' Cristiano said shortly. He hardly needed the reminder, and it rubbed raw, especially now.

'But,' Laurel continued slowly, 'Is it such a bad thing— to care about someone? Because if I'm not like those other women…your father's…then what's the problem? The risk?'

And just like that she got to the painful, beating heart of it and Cristiano had no idea how to answer. So he told her the truth. 'This isn't about me thinking you're like them,' he said. 'It's about losing control.'

Laurel's eyebrows rose. 'Losing control? How?'

Cristiano shifted restlessly in his seat and then in one abrupt movement he rose from the sofa and paced the spacious room, feeling caged by his memories.

'Any serious relationship—a loving marriage, anything—involves a loss of control. A giving up. And that's something I can't stand. And, yes—' he cut across her before she could say anything '—it's because of my childhood. We're all products of our growing up; you were right there. But it's not because of my father's mistresses, or his second wife, or your mother. It's because of mine.'

The silence between them felt both heavy and taut. Laurel was gazing at him steadily, a softness to her expression that made him want to bury himself in her arms. Seek comfort when he had given her none.

'What about your mother?' she asked when the silence had stretched to snapping point.

'She loved my father. And he loved her.' Cristiano felt his throat working as he swallowed hard. 'Very much.'

'Was that such a bad thing?' Laurel asked softly.

'Yes, because their love was…turbulent. Passionate. They were always fighting and falling back in love—throwing vases, breaking plates, what have you.'

'Not every loving marriage is like that.'

'No, but the loss of control is still there. Being enslaved to your emotions and at the mercy of another person.'

'A person you trust.'

'Maybe.' Cristiano continued pacing, his head down, teeth gritted. 'But maybe you shouldn't trust anyone that much.'

'What happened to your mother, Cristiano?' The question was soft and sad, so full of compassion, that it nearly broke him.

'She and my father had an almighty row. I think they enjoyed arguing, the intensity of it, and of course the passionate making up. This time she flounced out of the house. She'd done it before; I remember watching from the window as she'd speed down the driveway in her little red convertible. I never knew if she was going to come back or not.' The memories were hitting him now, wave after relentless wave, reminding him of the turmoil and tumult of his childhood. The arguments, the shrieking voices, the feeling, as a boy, that he never knew what to expect. Who to trust. Or what it meant truly to love someone.

'That must have been very hard on you,' Laurel said quietly. Her eyes were filled with a sorrowful compassion that Cristiano feared would be his undoing. Perhaps her fury and scorn would have been better to deal with. He could have matched them. But this…

'There's no shame in it, you know,' she said. 'In feeling hurt.'

Oh, but there was. Because it revealed a weakness in him, a gaping, bleeding need that felt like the very life were draining out of him.

'Anyway,' he resumed after a moment, when he trusted himself to speak normally, 'that time, that argument, she left in her convertible and she didn't come back. She died,' he explained succinctly. 'Crashed her car straight into a tree.'

'Oh, Cristiano…'

'The thing is,' he continued, determined to say it all now. 'It was a straight, flat road. No other cars were involved. And the tree was about ten feet away from the road. So why did she crash? How?'

Laurel's face paled, her eyes wide and dark. 'You mean you think she did it on purpose?'

'It seems likely, doesn't it?'

'I don't know…'

'That's what love does to you,' he finished flatly. 'It kills you.' When he said the words out loud they sounded melodramatic, even childish, yet he knew he meant them. Utterly.

'Oh, Cristiano.' Laurel's face was suffused with sadness. 'It doesn't have to. I have to believe that.' She let out a sad little laugh. 'Not that I would really know.'

'What do you mean?'

'The people I've loved have always left. My father, my mother, your father.' She gave him an almost apologetic look. 'You might not want to hear that, but I loved him. He was like a father to me for those three years—showing up to school concerts, taking me for a ride in his fancy car. The only father I've ever really had, my mother's parade of boyfriends aside.'

'I… I didn't realise.' He hadn't given Laurel's feelings so much as a thought when he'd told his father about Elizabeth's secret bank account—and she'd only been fourteen. How could he have been so thoughtless? So selfish? Yes, Elizabeth had been a thief. But Laurel had been collateral damage, and he hadn't even cared. 'I'm sorry.'

'It was a long time ago. I didn't say all that to make you feel sorry for me. I just wanted to say that I understand, at least a little bit. But I guess I'm still hoping that it can be different for me some day, with someone new. They won't leave.' Her lips trembled and she forced them into a smile. 'They won't want to leave.'

'Laurel…'

'And it can be different for you, Cristiano, one day. One day maybe you won't believe that love kills or even hurts. You'll see that it can heal and restore and strengthen.'

'You have a lot of faith,' Cristiano said in a low voice. He was unbearably moved by her hope, when she had so little to hope for. So many people had left her.

'Not really,' Laurel admitted with a shaky laugh. 'I talk a big game.'

Cristiano nodded slowly. He felt weary and aching, yet, strangely, cautiously hopeful—although about what, he couldn't quite say. Wasn't willing to verbalise.

'Thank you,' he said after a moment. 'For listening. For understanding. And I am sorry for…before.' He paused, weighing his words, his feelings. Truth versus safety. Caring versus control. 'The question is,' he said slowly, 'what do we do now?'

CHAPTER FOURTEEN

LAUREL SHIFTED WHERE she stood, trying to ease the ache in her feet. Stilettos were not for the faint of heart, and she'd worn them five days running. For the last week she and Cristiano had been touring his hotels across Europe—first Paris, then London, Milan and now Barcelona. He'd been checking on his managers, doing business, and she'd been enjoying seeing places in Europe she'd never thought she'd have the opportunity to see.

Ever since their surprisingly honest conversation after the charity gala, things had shifted between them. They weren't in love, and Laurel knew better than to start painting rainbows in the sky or building fairy-tale castles. She didn't even want to, because she knew dreaming of a happy ending with Cristiano was foolish to the extreme. But she'd started to relax and enjoy their time together, and he had as well.

They'd chatted, laughed, teased and talked. And made love. Sex was no longer a transaction, but a sharing, an expression...but of what? That was a question Laurel didn't let herself ask, much less answer.

They might have made some much-needed strides in their love affair, but Cristiano was still a man who guarded his back and his heart. Trust didn't come easily, and love didn't come at all. But at least Laurel was going in with her eyes wide open; she had no intention of falling in love with Cristiano Ferrero. The trouble was, he was starting to make that rather difficult.

'Just another few minutes,' he murmured as he came to her side at the cocktail party they were attending—yet another social occasion that doubled as networking for Cristiano. 'You look like your feet are killing you.'

'They are,' Laurel admitted. 'I'm not used to wearing high heels this much. For work, it's usually sensible lace-ups.'

'I'll give you a foot-rub later,' Cristiano promised, and her stomach swirled with pleasure and pure, simple happiness. Yes, Cristiano was giving her far too many reasons to fall in love with him.

They made their farewells a few minutes later and stepped outside into a balmy Spanish night, the scent of orange blossom on the evening air.

A limo was waiting for them, as it always was, and Laurel slid into the sumptuous leather interior with a contented sigh. A week of this and she'd become accustomed to luxury.

Cristiano settled in next to her and reached for her leg, lifting her foot onto his lap. He slipped off her stiletto with a wince.

'You could kill someone with one of these things.'

Laurel leaned her head back against the seat, revelling in the feel of his powerful thumbs rotating circles on the balls of her feet. 'I practically did. I embedded one in Rico Bavasso's palm.'

'Did you?' Cristiano let out an admiring laugh. 'Served him right. No wonder he was rather put out, though.'

'Do you think he's really got the message?' Laurel asked, even though the last thing she wanted to talk about was Rico Bavasso.

'Undoubtedly. He's attached himself to a French singer—some wannabe pop star.'

'He has? That was quick.' She frowned. 'Although I don't particularly like the thought of him inflicting himself on some other woman. Do you think…is he really dangerous?'

'He attacked you, didn't he?' Cristiano's thumbs paused on the balls of her feet. 'But I might have exaggerated his need for revenge.'

She nearly jerked her foot out of his grasp. 'What?'

'I had some real concern, but...' Cristiano's smile was unrepentant. 'I wanted to keep you to myself for a little longer, and Bavasso provided a convenient excuse.'

She laughed, relaxing against the seat. A few days ago she would have been outraged by his confession. Now, in the security of their relationship—and, yes, she used that word with care—she only felt amused. 'I'm glad to know that now.' Cristiano continued his massage and Laurel let out a groan of pleasure.

'I will never wear heels like these again, ever.'

'What about the event in Madrid tomorrow?'

'There's another event?' She couldn't keep the disappointment out of her voice. The last week had been a lovely whirlwind, but she was *tired*.

Cristiano looked surprised. 'Are you telling me you don't like parties?'

'I'm getting weary of them,' Laurel admitted. 'Tiring of being "on" all the time, getting dressed up, and the hair and make-up and the posing...' She sighed. 'I just want a return to some kind of normality. To be able to relax and be myself.' *With you.* Admitting that might be a step too far.

Cristiano slid his hand from her foot to her calf, trailing his fingers along her skin meaningfully. 'I can think of a way to relax.'

'I'm sure you can.' Laurel's breath hitched as he smoothed his hand from her knee to her hip. Over a week and she still hadn't tired of his touch, not remotely. A single fingertip trailed along her skin and, yes, she still melted. Just like butter.

'Perhaps we could go somewhere quieter,' Cristiano

said, his hand sliding up and down her leg. 'Somewhere… relaxing.'

'You know,' Laurel murmured, watching his hand move up and down, 'you can make anything sound like an innuendo.'

'It's a gift.'

'It must be.'

The limo pulled up in front of their hotel and Cristiano helped her out. Laurel's body tingled with anticipation. Every night this week they'd left a party and gone to Cristiano's private suite. Every night he'd taken her in his arms, taken her to bed, and she still felt the fizz of excitement, the sizzle of desire.

They rode the lift in silence, and then when the doors opened Cristiano turned to her, as he always did. His teeth gleamed in the darkness.

'Come here,' he whispered, and Laurel came willingly. Eagerly.

She woke up the next morning tangled in navy satin sheets, sunlight spilling through the floor-to-ceiling windows, a sleepy smile on her face. Cristiano was gone, but he usually rose early to work on his laptop, then woke her up by bringing her coffee and croissants. More than once they'd made love amongst the crumbs.

Now he appeared in the doorway, freshly showered and shaven, wearing a pair of charcoal trousers and an open-necked button-down shirt in deep blue. As always, he possessed the power to steal her breath.

'Good morning.' He handed her a steaming mug of coffee which Laurel accepted gratefully. 'I thought we'd do something different today.'

'Oh?' She took a sip, her eyebrows raised in expectation.

Cristiano braced one shoulder against the doorframe. 'You said you were tired of the social whirl, and I think we could both use a break.' He paused, his gaze resting thoughtfully on her. 'So I thought we could go to Capri.'

'Capri?'

'Yes, the island in the Bay of Naples—do you know it?'

'I've heard of it, but I've never been there.'

'It's a lovely place. We can take a short flight to Naples and then a ferry to the island.' He paused, and Laurel tensed, for she could tell there was something more he was going to say. Something important. 'It's where my father lives.'

Her eyes widened as realisation shot through her. 'Your father…? You mean we're going to—to visit him?' She could hardly believe it. Cristiano rarely talked about his father, and when he did it was with reluctance, and perhaps even disdain. Their relationship hadn't been close ten years ago, and it didn't appear to be any closer now.

And yet…

'Yes, I thought you might like to see him.' Cristiano took a sip of coffee, his gaze on the windows and the view of the city stretched out before them. 'Since you seemed close to him all those years ago.'

'I was.' She swallowed, nerves fluttering in her middle. 'But I don't actually know if he'd like to see me.' Lorenzo had sent her and Elizabeth away without so much as a backward glance. Even now, the memory had the power to sting and wound.

'I've already called him,' Cristiano answered, moving his gaze back to her. 'And he does.'

Cristiano watched as Laurel's lips parted and tears filled her eyes. 'Oh…he does?' She sniffed. 'That's… Well, that's wonderful. Thank you, Cristiano.'

He nodded, not trusting himself to say more. He still wasn't comfortable with this kind of emotion, but he was trying to get used to it. For the last week he'd been living in a limbo of deep enjoyment and relentless discomfort, pain and pleasure mixed. Because being intimate with someone—physically, emotionally—was a whole new realm of experience, and one he wasn't entirely sure about. The vulnerability, the intensity, the *risk*. And yet the more time he spent with Laurel, the more he wanted to.

He also wanted to make amends as best as he could. More and more over the last week he'd realised what a disservice he'd done Laurel when he'd told his father about her mother's bank account. Yes, Elizabeth was a gold-digging schemer and a thief, but that hadn't been Laurel's fault, and she'd suffered as a result. If he'd handled the situation differently, if he hadn't been determined to paint the grimmest picture to his father, maybe things would have worked out differently. At least perhaps Lorenzo would have stayed in touch with his stepdaughter.

'I can't believe it,' Laurel said as she hugged her knees, her golden-brown curls tumbling about her shoulders. 'To see him again... Are you sure he wants to see me?' She glanced at him, eyes full of apprehension as she nibbled her lower lip.

Guilt pierced Cristiano with poison-tipped arrows. He hadn't told Laurel the extent of his involvement in their parents' divorce. At first it hadn't seemed relevant and now he knew it would hurt her and, more alarmingly, jeopardise their fledgling relationship. Because he was already thinking about ways to keep her around after the two weeks were up...assuming she wasn't pregnant. Sometimes he found himself half-hoping she was.

'I'm sure,' he said firmly. 'He was thrilled to hear we'd been in contact.'

Laurel raised her eyebrows. 'Does he...does he know how much contact we've been in?'

Cristiano smiled. 'I didn't give him details, but I think he guesses.' He paused. 'Is that a bad thing?'

'No. I just…' She hunched her shoulders, her gaze sliding away. 'We've less than a week left,' she said quietly, and Cristiano felt as if the breath had been punched from his lungs.

'What does that matter?' he asked when he trusted himself to speak normally. To sound unconcerned.

'I don't want your father to get his hopes up,' Laurel explained. 'To think something more might be going on.' She gave him a direct look, her chin slightly lifted, showing courage and determination and a hint of vulnerability.

'Don't worry,' he said, wondering how he was meant to reassure her. Should he tell her his father wouldn't get his hopes up, or that perhaps he should? When, if ever, should he tell her he wanted more from this relationship than another week?

The question, of course, was how much more. Cristiano had tried to envision different scenarios in his head, and most of them involved Laurel being his permanent, full-time mistress. He wasn't ready to countenance anything more, yet he knew instinctively she'd resist such a role. So he waited, saying nothing, hoping things would be clarified for both of them in time.

'We should get going,' he said as he turned from the room. 'Our plane leaves in a few hours.'

A short while later they were leaving the suite for the airport. Laurel was dressed in a cheerful polka-dot sundress—after she'd thrown all the clothes Cristiano had given her onto the floor, he'd offered to buy her new ones. She'd happily gone out to far more modest shops and picked up a couple of casual outfits. She'd insisted on paying for them herself, but Cristiano had insisted more, and eventually she'd acquiesced.

As the limo took them to the airport she gazed at him speculatively. 'When was the last time you saw your father?'

Cristiano shrugged. 'A year or so.'

'You don't see him very often.'

Another shrug; her perception still possessed the power to rub him raw. 'I'm very busy.'

'But you're not close,' Laurel persisted quietly, and Cristiano sighed.

'No,' he agreed, 'I suppose we aren't.'

'Why not?'

Cristiano gazed out at the blur of buildings streaming by. 'Because I don't respect him,' he said at last. 'And it's difficult to have a relationship, at least a positive one, when there is no respect involved.'

Laurel considered this for a moment. 'Does he respect you?'

'I have no idea, and I really don't much care.'

'Why don't you respect him?' She was like a dog with a bone, worrying away at it, getting to the bloody marrow.

'Do we really have to talk about this?'

'We're about to go visit him, so yes, I think we do. Why don't you, Cristiano?' She asked the question softly, her voice filled with compassion. She was ready to understand him, and it made him answer reluctantly.

'Because he's thrown his life away on love.'

'Ah.' She nodded thoughtfully, not looking as disappointed in his answer as he'd expected, and perversely wanted her to be. 'So you're angry at him for wasting his life.'

When she put it like that... 'I'm not angry,' he said tersely. 'Not exactly.' Except, he realised as he said it, it wasn't true. He *was* angry, but it seemed childish somehow. An emotion he wanted to rise above.

'It must not have been easy,' Laurel said quietly, 'to lose your mother the way you did. And then to see your father fall in love with women who weren't in love with him.'

'Do you count your mother in that number?' Cristiano

asked more sharply than he intended but, damn it, he felt so raw.

'No,' Laurel said softly. 'I don't. But I understand why you would.' She reached for his hand and Cristiano threaded his fingers through hers, taking a deep breath to compose himself. These honest, emotional conversations still felt new and difficult. Painful. But he was trying, because he knew Laurel wanted more from him, and amazingly, alarmingly, he wanted it too. He was tired of the superficial, sex-only arrangements he'd had before.

And yet that question niggled at his mind—*how much more do you want?*

The rest of the journey to Capri passed pleasantly enough; Laurel stood at the railing of the ferry and gazed out at the blue-green sea, jewel-bright under the afternoon sun.

'It's so lovely,' she murmured. 'I'd forgotten how lovely it was in Italy.' She tilted her face to the sun, her whole body seeming to drink in the light. If Cristiano could have painted her like that, he would have. She was the essence of happiness, of joy and freedom, a faint smile curving her lovely mouth, her hair blowing in the wind.

They walked from the ferry landing to the funicular, the cable railway that went to the town centre. From the *piazzetta* they walked to Lorenzo's villa, which was on the outskirts of the town. Laurel gazed round at the white villas with their brightly painted shutters and pots of trailing bougainvillea, delighting in everything.

And then they were there, standing in front of the steep, winding steps that led to his father's villa, a tall, white building near Capri's old town, its terracotta roof tiles blazing under the late-afternoon sun.

Laurel paused, nervousness flitting across her features as she gazed up at the steps, and then shot Cristiano an anxious look.

'Do you really think…?'

'I know,' Cristiano said, and took her hand. They climbed the steps together, then stepped into the airy, sun-lit foyer. A housekeeper bustled in with a cheery stream of Italian…and then there he was, Cristiano's father, standing in the doorway, looking older and frailer in the year since he'd last seen him, but also far happier, his face wreathed in smiles as he held his arms out to Laurel.

'Cara,' he said in a voice full of welcome and warmth, and with a little stifled cry Laurel ran into his arms.

CHAPTER FIFTEEN

LAUREL STRETCHED OUT on the sun lounger, her heart brimming with happiness. It had been three days since they'd arrived in Capri, and they'd been the best three days of her life.

Seeing Lorenzo again...having him welcome her with open arms and tears in his eyes... Laurel hadn't even realised just how much she'd missed him, the gaping absence he'd left in her life, until she'd ran into his arms and he'd whispered how sorry he was ever to have let her go.

Being with Cristiano out of the public eye, with no fanfare or spectacle, no socialising or small talk, was another wonderful blessing. Finally they could simply *be* with each other, enjoying lazy mornings and lovely, long nights, strolls around Capri and afternoons lounging by the pool. Laurel knew it couldn't last—in just three more days the requisite two weeks would have passed since that first, fateful night. Three more days and she could take a pregnancy test.

And what if she *was* pregnant?

It was a question she hadn't let herself think too much about. In those first difficult days she hadn't wanted to think about it. Hadn't possessed the strength to imagine that dreaded *what if?* scenario.

Now...now she dared not think about it for an entirely different reason. Because part of her, an increasingly large part, was hoping she was pregnant with Cristiano's child.

Logically she knew she probably wasn't pregnant. She was fairly regular and her period wasn't due for at least another week. And in any case she knew a pregnancy wasn't a good idea. She wanted Cristiano to choose to be with her for her own sake, not just to provide for their child. And yet…she wanted Cristiano to choose to be with her.

That was the truth she had to force herself to face, the reality that crowded in during quiet moments. They most likely had only a handful of days left together, yet in the quiet of her mind she dreamed of for ever.

'You look deep in thought.' Lorenzo walked slowly towards the lounger next to Laurel's and sat down carefully. Laurel had noticed, over the last few days, how slowly he moved, how cautiously, and it made her wonder. Worry.

'Not too deep,' she said with a smile and then leaned her head against the lounger. 'It's too beautiful a day for deep thoughts.' The infinity pool shimmered in front of them, surrounded by orange and lemon trees, the roofs of Capri and the sparkling sea in the distance.

'Yes, perhaps it is.' Lorenzo settled himself against his lounger with a slight wince, causing Laurel another pang of worry. 'And where is my son this morning?'

'Catching up on some work, but he promised to join us for lunch.'

'I've never seen him look so happy,' Lorenzo said quietly. 'Thank you.'

Laurel smiled wryly. 'I don't know if it's my doing.'

'Oh, it is, Laurel, I'm sure of it. He's in love with you, even if he doesn't want to realise it.'

She let out a laugh at the older man's perception, hope struggling with fear inside her, a torment of emotion. 'That's the nub of it, isn't it?' she asked, trying to sound light. 'He doesn't want to.'

'Cristiano has always had a deep suspicion of any emotion, particularly love.'

'Yes.' She took a deep breath and let it out slowly. 'He told me a little bit about you and his mother. How much you loved each other.'

'Did he?' Lorenzo nodded slowly. 'Of course, he is only remembering it as a child.'

'Was it different than he said?'

'I don't know what he said, but I can imagine.' Lorenzo sighed, his face looking pale and drawn and old. Again Laurel felt that pang of worry assail her. Lorenzo did not seem a well man. 'My marriage to Gabriella was tempestuous, to say the least,' he continued. 'She thrived on it, all the passion and anger and energy. It made her feel alive, but it drained me.'

'That doesn't sound entirely healthy,' Laurel ventured cautiously.

'No, it wasn't. It was exhausting at the best of times, and incredibly dispiriting at the worst. When she died...' Pain flashed across his face and then was gone. 'I blamed myself. I shouldn't have let her run out the way she did. I knew she was in a temper, and the maddening thing now is I can't even remember what we argued about. That feels wrong, don't you think—to die for something that you've forgotten about? And yet she was in such a rage at the time.'

'That doesn't seem like it was your fault.'

'Perhaps.' Lorenzo was silent for a moment. 'Still I regret it. I regret many things.' He squinted at the horizon, sunlight sparkling off the sea. 'I fear Cristiano is the way he is because of me.'

Laurel knew it to be true, by Cristiano's own admission, but she was interested in Lorenzo's perspective. 'What do you mean, the way he is?'

Lorenzo shrugged. 'What I said before. His deep suspicion of emotion, of love. His determination to be an island, which no man is.' He gave her a small, wistful smile. 'While I am quite the opposite, always searching for something more. The one person who will make me feel connected and whole. I thought I'd found it with your mother.'

Emotion clogged in Laurel's throat. 'She thought she'd found it with you.'

'Did she?'

Laurel forced the words past the lump in her throat. 'I know she stole from you, Lorenzo, but it wasn't… She didn't…'

'In the years since,' Lorenzo said slowly, 'I've thought often about the money your mother took. Money I would have given her freely, but I wonder if she knew that.'

'She lived in fear of being poor,' Laurel said quietly. 'Poor and abandoned. She always has.'

'In any case, I regret sending you both away so precipitously, without so much as a discussion.' Lorenzo shook his head sorrowfully. 'I have regretted it for a long time, especially how you, one so young, must have felt.'

Laurel blinked hard. 'It was…difficult,' she admitted, and Lorenzo's face crumpled a bit.

'I'm so sorry, my dear. I felt so betrayed, you see, because of the experience with my second wife. Did Cristiano tell you about that?'

'Yes, a little.'

'He convinced me that Elizabeth would leave, and in my weakness and self-doubt I believed him. She was so lovely and vibrant and young. I often wondered how she could possibly love me—me, and not just my money.' He shook his head, sadness creasing the already deep lines of his face.

'I suppose it's a problem any rich man faces,' Laurel said carefully. 'And I am not blind to my mother's faults, Lorenzo. She had a hard childhood and money is important to her. She's become used to a certain standard, and she'd lived her life to make sure she has it.'

Lorenzo smiled. 'I am well aware of Elizabeth's faults as well, my dear. But we all have them, don't we? No one is perfect.'

'No.' And her mother was far from it. Even now Laurel wondered why she defended her. Her mother had used her to win favour with Rico Bavasso, whether she'd meant things to go as far as they had or not. That was kind of hard to forgive, yet Laurel still wanted to forgive her. But that, she realised, was the stark difference between her and Cristiano—despite the mistakes and sorrows of the past, she strove to find forgiveness, redemption, hope. She wanted to believe in love, craved to know it was possible. Cristiano didn't.

Sighing, she settled back against the lounger, her heart twisting inside her. She was falling in love with Cristiano, with his kindness, honesty and sudden, surprising tenderness. The sensitive soul that hid beneath his hardened exterior. She was falling in love with him, but she knew it wasn't a good idea. It would only end in tears. Hers.

Lorenzo reached over and touched her hand. 'Give it time,' he said quietly. 'Give him time. He does love you, you know. He just has to stop fighting it.'

Laurel gazed down at Lorenzo's veined, arthritic hand and blinked back tears. 'Thank you,' she whispered. 'I hope you're right.' It was the closest she'd come to admitting she loved Cristiano.

Lorenzo smiled and removed his hand. 'Living without love is such a waste. Cristiano will realise that in time. And time is something both of you have.'

Laurel couldn't ignore the wistful note of sorrow in Lorenzo's voice. 'Lorenzo,' she said carefully. 'Do you know I work as a nurse? In palliative care?'

He didn't pretend to misunderstand what she was getting at. 'Ah.' He leaned his head back against the lounger and closed his eyes. 'I see.'

'How long have you been ill?' Laurel asked softly.

Lorenzo didn't speak for a long moment. Laurel waited, hoping even now that he might dismiss her concern, tell her he was just an old man who became tired. But, no. He opened his eyes and gazed out at the horizon, lemon-yellow sun and bright blue sky. 'I was diagnosed with cancer of the kidney three months ago. It had spread to my stomach and lungs. There's no stopping it.'

'Oh, Lorenzo.' Laurel gazed at him in deep sadness and sympathy. To have found each other again only for him to be taken away... 'How long?' she asked.

Lorenzo gave a little shrug. 'The doctors do not like to discuss dates. I refused treatment...there was no point, and I do not wish to spend my last days in a hospital, on machines and in great pain.' He sighed. 'A few months, they said, maybe more, maybe less. A year at the most. I have medication for the pain.'

'It doesn't seem like enough. I've noticed you wincing.'

He shrugged again, and Laurel pressed her lips together. 'Pain management is a very important part of end-of-life care, Lorenzo,' she said gently. 'You want your last days to be as pleasant and pain-free as possible, and research shows that you do better physically as well as emotionally if your body doesn't tire itself fighting the pain all the time.'

'Thank you for the advice.' He smiled and touched her hand. 'The medication makes me feel loopy. I don't want to take too much of it.'

'I understand.' And she did, all too well. She dealt with her patients' concerns about the effect of pain relief on their quality of life all the time, and the most important part of palliative care, in her opinion, was letting patients make their own choices for as long as they could. 'Does Cristiano know?' she asked after a moment. Her throat still felt thick and tears crowded at the backs of her eyes. For Lorenzo's sake she didn't want to give in to her own emotion, but she felt unbearably sad at the thought of losing him all over again. And what about Cristiano?

'No,' Lorenzo said after a pause, which was no surprise to Laurel.

'Why haven't you told him?'

Lorenzo shrugged. 'I suppose I wanted to spare him the pain when there is nothing he can do. Cristiano has never been one to accept inaction.'

'True.' Laurel managed a small smile. 'But I think he would want to know.'

'Yes and, now that you are both here, I will tell him. At least he will have you to comfort him, *cara.*' Lorenzo gently touched her cheek, and Laurel smiled through her tears.

Cristiano gazed out at the bright-blue sky and golden sunshine and clenched his jaw so hard it felt as if he might break a tooth. Anger was a far better emotion to feel than grief.

'How long have you known?' he asked.

From behind him Lorenzo stirred and sighed. 'A few months.'

'And you didn't feel the need to tell me?'

'There's nothing you can do, Cristiano.'

'Even so.'

'I suppose I wanted to wait until we were face to face.'

'I would have come sooner if I knew it was important.'

Lorenzo sighed again, the sound soft and sad. 'Would you have?' he asked quietly.

Cristiano turned around, his fists clenched, his heart racing, as if he was preparing for a fight. Spoiling for one, maybe, but he didn't want to antagonise his father now, not when he was so ill. But he didn't know how to be, how to feel. The natural emotion—grief in all of its dark, unrelenting mess—was anathema to him.

'Of course I would have,' he said, but even as the words left his mouth he wondered. Doubted. He'd avoided his father for years, ignored the ways Lorenzo had reached out. Why? Because of his contempt for his father's choices, or for a deeper, more revealing reason?

Because loving someone always hurt.

'Well, I am not quite at my end yet,' Lorenzo said lightly. 'There is time, Cristiano. Time, perhaps, for us to heal old wounds.'

'What old wounds?' Cristiano tried to sound dismissive but the words stuck in his throat like shards of broken glass, and his voice came out sounding strangled.

'I know you harbour anger towards me for my choices.' Lorenzo took a deep, steadying breath. 'In my search for love I let a lot of women into your life. A lot of uncertainty and confusion.'

'I'm a grown man,' Cristiano dismissed. 'And in any case, I survived.'

'But we all want more out of life than survival, don't we? And I fear you have sworn off love because of my experiences.'

Cristiano just shrugged. He didn't trust himself to speak. He didn't know what he'd say, in any case. Yes, he'd sworn off love, and for good reason. And, although the last week and a half had been the best of his life, he still wasn't ready to make that kind of commitment to Laurel. Couldn't open himself up to all the risk and pain. Did that make him an emotional coward? Maybe. But at least he stayed strong. Solitary.

He left his father a short while later, because Lorenzo was clearly tiring, and went in search of Laurel. Twilight was settling over the terrace, the air holding a hint of coolness, as Cristiano stepped outside. Laurel was standing by the balcony, her hands resting on the ornate stone railing, her face tilted to the last dying rays of the sun.

'You spoke to your father?' she asked softly.

'You knew.'

'I guessed.' She turned to him, a world of sorrow in her eyes. 'I spend all my time with people who are dealing with terminal illness. You get to know the signs.'

'I wish he'd told me.'

'I know.' She moved towards him, all fluid grace, and put her arms around him. For a second Cristiano resisted. Part of him wanted to stay strong, separate. But the pain he felt was too much for him to bear on his own, and the sweet, pliant warmth of her body was the balm he so desperately needed.

He pulled her close, burying his face in her fragrant hair. 'I've always tried to live my life so I have no regrets,' he muttered against her hair, his eyes clenched shut. 'I thought that was the best way to be, and yet now I feel awash with regret. Too many things to feel sorry for. To atone for.'

'Regret isn't a bad thing, Cristiano,' Laurel said gently. 'It doesn't have to be about guilt or shame. It's a strong and brave thing to feel, because it allows you to take responsibility for your actions and make a positive choice for the future.'

'That sounds very wise.'

'I've talked a lot to people who are dealing with regrets. It's something you think about as your life comes to an end. And,' she added, a tremor in her voice, 'I've had regrets of my own.'

He eased back, searching her face. 'What do you regret?'

'Letting my mother talk me into coming to meet Rico Bavasso, for one.'

'But, if you hadn't, you would never have met me again.'

She smiled, but it wavered on her face, as uncertain as a shadow slipping away. 'You don't regret meeting me, do you, Laurel?' Cristiano asked with more urgency than he meant to reveal or even feel. 'Do you?'

'No.' Still she sounded uncertain, and that hurt him more than he expected.

'Why? Why would you?' Of course he knew the reasons, yet still he asked. Torturing himself because he couldn't help it.

'It's not as if this is going to last,' Laurel said after a moment, her voice so quiet Cristiano strained to hear it, even though he was standing right next to her. 'You don't have a monopoly on pain, Cristiano.' She spoke without rancour, merely stating truth. 'I don't want to get hurt, either.'

'I don't want to hurt you.' He meant it more than he'd ever thought possible.

She gave him a sad, wistful smile. 'Sometimes we don't have a choice in these things.'

'But if you're pregnant…' It was a possibility he'd considered unfortunate mere days ago, but now it opened up a whole new realm of choice to him. To them. 'If you're pregnant, I will marry you.' He didn't know whether it was a threat or promise. Both, perhaps.

'And if I'm not?' She gazed up at him, her face cast in silvery light from the rising moon, her eyes large and clear, hiding nothing. The choice was his, to stay or to go, to risk or to hide. To love or to leave.

Cristiano's mind spun. He thought of his father wasting away in bed, alone after so many years and still heartbroken. His mother, storming out in a fearsome rage, only to go to her death, and for what? *For what?* 'We don't have to make any decisions right away,' he said, and disappointment flickered across Laurel's face before she nodded.

'No,' she agreed. 'I suppose not.'

It wasn't the answer she'd hoped to hear, that much was obvious, and Cristiano could hardly blame her. Who wanted prevarications at a moment like this? She wanted him to sweep her up into his arms, kiss her and tell her he loved her. He couldn't do that, but two out of three wasn't bad, was it? It was all he had to offer. All he had to give.

He pulled her closer and pressed a kiss to her forehead, then to her lips. Gentle kisses that were meant as promises, although of what he could not say.

And Laurel accepted them, her arms coming around

him, her soft, warm body fitting to his. Desire flared inside him, along with something stronger—a soul-deep craving to connect in this moment, not to feel alone. Not to be solitary, even if that meant admitting weakness. In this moment he needed it. He deepened the kiss, driving his hands through her hair, searching for her and branding her. Seeking solace as much as satisfaction, and finding both in this. In them.

Laurel answered him kiss for kiss, their breathing turning harsh and ragged, their bodies coming together in a connection so piercing and deep it felt exquisitely painful. She didn't protest when he held her by the hips and hoisted her up onto the balcony railing. She wrapped her legs around his waist as he stroked her, finding her ready for him.

It was a matter of mere moments as he slid the condom from his pocket, fumbling with it in his haste, then thrust into her, the sense of completeness, of rightness, overwhelming him so that tears came to his eyes.

Laurel arched closer, drawing him in further, matching every thrust as they both found their release.

Cristiano cried out, the sound splintering the still night air, his heart thudding against Laurel's as he rested his forehead against her and drew shuddering breaths.

His body felt sated, drugged with the aftermath of pleasure, yet something deep inside him still ached and yearned. This, which had always been enough, wasn't any longer.

CHAPTER SIXTEEN

HOLDING ON TO happiness felt like trying to cup water in your hands. No matter how you tried, it still trickled out. Two days passed, lovely, golden days, yet they possessed an urgency, a fear, that they hadn't before. Laurel felt it in herself, and she also felt it in Cristiano. Time was running out.

And, even though it didn't have to be this way, even though Laurel knew if Cristiano asked her she would stay, she would try, she would risk it all, she knew in her bones, in her very soul, that he wasn't going to ask.

He thought about it. She saw it in his eyes—the faraway look that came over him, followed by a hardening of his features into an unwelcome resolve she wanted to scream and fight against. She wanted to rail and weep—to demand why he thought staying safe was so important, why he didn't think risking life and love with her was worth it—but she didn't because, when it came down to it, she was afraid too.

The possibility of a face-to-face, outright rejection from Cristiano, of pushing for answers and then getting ones she didn't want, kept her silent. She didn't care about her dignity or her pride, but she didn't think her heart could take one of his crushing set-downs. Not after all they'd shared.

As for the possibility of pregnancy... With every passing day Laurel wondered and hoped, even though logic told her it was unlikely. And yet...as a nurse she knew it wasn't out of the question that she might have fallen pregnant on that first night, no matter how she'd once scoffed at such a notion.

It still seemed crazy to hope for such a thing, yet she feared it was the only way Cristiano would commit to her. She could hardly believe she'd fallen into that age-old trap of wanting a baby to snare a man. Was she that weak? That desperate?

Twelve days after Laurel had first stumbled into Cristiano's penthouse, she lay in his bed, her head resting on his shoulder, her fingers trailing a light path down his muscled chest. She didn't think she'd ever get tired of touching him. She'd spent a good part of the last two weeks touching him, smoothing the satiny, muscled perfection of him, learning the planes and angles of his well-defined body.

And yet so much more than that too… With a pang she thought of the laughter they'd shared, the surprising conversations, the simple pleasure of being in his company. Yet the next two days pressed down on her, an unbearable weight. Was it really going to end so soon?

'The day after tomorrow it will have been two weeks,' she said softly, because she couldn't not say it. Underneath her hand she felt Cristiano tense.

'So it will.' An answer that gave nothing away, of course. He never did, especially in moments like these. She recalled that deceptively mild tone from their first days together and feared its return.

'Shall I take a pregnancy test, then?' she asked.

'That was always the plan.' Just in case she'd needed the reminder, which she didn't. He paused, his body still tense next to hers. 'Do you think there's a possibility…?'

'I don't know.' But she hoped. She'd taken to wondering if the slightest queasiness, the faint cramping, meant anything. Stupid, she knew, because even if she was pregnant it was too early for noticeable symptoms. Yet, just like with her mother, with everything in her life, she hoped for the best. She wanted to believe that she and Cristiano could be together—but did it really have to take a pregnancy to make it happen? It seemed her hope didn't stretch to Cristiano himself, to him changing and learning to love her, being willing to make that jump and take that risk.

'We'll find out soon enough,' he said, his tone repressed, and Laurel feeling she had no choice, let the matter drop.

The next morning Lorenzo summoned her to his bedroom, where he was resting. He spent a good part of each day in his bedroom, making Laurel wonder if he had as much time as the doctors had said.

'Are you feeling all right?' Laurel asked, trying not to let anxiety creep into her voice.

'I'm fine.' Lorenzo smiled. 'Just a bit tired, which is nothing unusual in my condition. But I have a favour to ask of you. Quite a large favour, as it happens.'

'Oh?' Laurel came to sit on the edge of his bed, taking his papery hands between hers. 'If it's within my power, I'll do it.'

'I want to see your mother.' Lorenzo held Laurel's gaze as she tried to hide her surprise. 'I never stopped loving her, and with so little time left, I'd like to spend what there is of it with someone I love.' His questioning smile wavered a little. 'If you think she'll have me?'

'I...' Laurel had no doubt her mother would jump at the chance of finding a secure position, though she hoped Elizabeth would want—and feel—more than that. Was the love still there? Laurel hoped it was for Lorenzo's sake... as well as her mother's. This could be a much-needed re-union and reconciliation for both of them.

'I know you can't really answer that question,' Lorenzo assured her. 'But could you talk to her? Prepare her, a little? And if you could give me her phone number, if you find she would welcome a call...'

'Yes, of course.' What other answer could she give? Yet with a heavy sensation in her stomach Laurel feared how Cristiano would react to her involvement in getting Elizabeth and Lorenzo back together. At best, he'd be coldly contemptuous of such doings. At the worst…completely furious.

Yet looking at Lorenzo's tired, lined face, seeing his wan smile, Laurel knew she couldn't refuse his request. Not for any reason at all.

She called her mother a few minutes later, sitting on a bench in the terraced garden, away from the house and anyone who could listen in.

'*Laurel.*' Her mother sounded genuinely glad to hear from her, which was unusual in itself. 'How are you? Where are you? I've been so worried!'

'I'm sorry I haven't been in touch,' Laurel said, although her mother was rarely in touch with her. Still, the apology came of its own accord, as it always had.

'Well, where have you been?'

'With Cristiano.'

Elizabeth drew her breath in sharply. 'Still? He usually tires of women after a week at most.'

Laurel tried to suppress the flash of annoyance and even hurt she felt at her mother's matter-of-fact tone. 'He'll tire of me soon, I suppose.' Sooner even than she'd expected, no doubt, after he found out about this phone call.

'I'm glad to know you're all right.' Elizabeth sniffed. 'I was worried, you know, although I doubt you'll believe me. I never meant things to happen that way with Rico.'

'I know.'

'I thought he just wanted to flirt. I hoped that was all it was, for both of our sakes. I know I've been far from the world's greatest mother, but I don't think I'm that bad.' She let out a wobbly laugh, and then sighed. 'The truth is, I'm too old for him. I'm too old for most men these days. All washed up at forty-six. I'm sorry.'

'I know.' Laurel believed her mother, even if Cristiano would think it was foolish. Her mother never thought out her slap-dash plans, her desperate bids for the life of luxury and security she'd always craved.

'I'm sorry,' Elizabeth said after a moment. 'Truly. But I will need the money from the sale of that house.'

'I know,' Laurel said again. She hadn't deceived herself that her mother would suddenly have an attack of generosity and give her her half of her grandfather's house free and clear. And she'd decided, after everything, that a house was just a house. She couldn't afford a similar place; in fact, on her salary, she'd barely be able to afford a one-bedroom apartment in town. But after everything it didn't seem to matter quite so much. Home wasn't a farmhouse in Illinois any more. It was wherever Cristiano was, and that was a place she most likely wasn't going to be able to be.

'I'm calling for a reason, though, Mom,' Laurel said, determined to say what she needed to. 'Cristiano and I are staying with Lorenzo.'

Elizabeth drew her breath in again, a quick, audible hiss. 'Oh, yes?' she asked cautiously.

'He'd like to speak to you, on the phone. He asked me to call you first, to see if you'd welcome a call from him.'

Elizabeth didn't speak for a long moment, and when she did her voice was thick with unshed tears. 'Yes,' she said, and cleared her throat. 'Yes, I would very much welcome a call from him.'

Fury boiled through Cristiano's blood like black tar, rising up and choking him. He strode through the villa, glaring into empty rooms in search of the woman who had orchestrated his father's destruction. *How could she?* And without consulting him!

Moments ago he'd left his father's bedroom, stunned past all sensibility. He'd managed to moderate his tone with his father, but Cristiano didn't think he would be able to show such self-control when it came to Laurel.

He found her in the library, a pleasant, book-lined room with views of the side garden, adorned with its orange trees and hibiscus. Laurel was curled up on the sofa, a book lying open next to her, her expression both pensive and wary. She'd been waiting for him, waiting for him to confront her, because she knew what she'd done was wrong.

Cristiano closed the door carefully behind him and stared her down. Laurel lifted her chin, meeting his narrowed gaze with something close to defiance, infuriating him all the more.

'How could you?' he stated quietly, not even a question. 'How *could* you?'

'I assume you're talking about helping your father to be in touch with my mother.'

'She is arriving here tomorrow morning.'

'I know.' Laurel's chin went up another notch. 'I helped to book the flight, a red-eye from New York.'

Cristiano shook his head, trying to keep a rein on his anger. He felt like throttling her. 'My father is in his last months of life, and you want to bring Elizabeth Forrester back into his life?'

'He asked.'

'Of *course* he asked.' Cristiano raked a hand through his close-cropped hair, nails grazing skin, the brief flash of pain an outlet for his frustration. 'He's feeling lonely and vulnerable. He is an eternal optimist when it comes to matters of the heart. And, in every single case, every romantic attachment he's ever made has ended in disaster.'

'What are you afraid of, Cristiano?' Laurel asked quietly. 'Because in this case the disaster is going to happen, no matter what. Your father is going to die. Why shouldn't we—yes, *we*—help to make his last days and weeks a little bit happier?'

He stared at her in disbelief. 'And you think having Elizabeth here will achieve that aim?'

Something flickered in Laurel's eyes but she kept his gaze. 'I don't know,' she admitted. 'But I hope so.'

'Do I need to remind you that this is the woman who, only two weeks ago, as good as sold you to a very unpleasant man and did nothing while he attacked you?'

'No,' Laurel answered stiffly. 'You don't need to remind me. And it wasn't quite like that—'

'The woman who,' Cristiano continued relentlessly, 'Has been seen with several dozen Z-listers over the last decade? Who is so clearly only with a man for what he can provide for her financially?'

'Is that what you're worried about?' Laurel flung back at him. 'That my mother will take Lorenzo's money? Your inheritance?'

'Hardly.' The single word was scathing. 'I have no need of my father's money, and he obviously won't need it in the long term.' He pressed his lips together. 'No, Laurel, I'm worried about my father's health. His mental and emotional health. How do you think he'll feel if and when Elizabeth abandons him in his greatest moment of need? Don't you think there is a significant chance of her coming here, taking what she can and hightailing it to heaven knows where?'

Laurel pressed her trembling lips together. 'That's a rather cynical view.'

'I have reason to be cynical,' Cristiano snapped. 'Many reasons. I have yet to see a romantic relationship that has actually worked.'

'Not even ours, obviously,' Laurel returned, bitterness spiking every word. 'Not that we have a romantic relationship. Of course I don't dare to presume such a thing.' She rolled her eyes, and Cristiano glared at her, his fists clenched, his chest heaving.

'This isn't about us.'

'Of course it isn't.'

'If you're trying to say something, why don't you just spit it out?'

Laurel took a deep, steadying breath. When she spoke, her voice was quiet, even sad, the bitterness and anger gone. Too bad they were still out in full force in Cristiano. 'The difference between us, Cristiano,' she said slowly, 'Is that I choose to hope and you choose to doubt. And that is a chasm that neither of us seem able to cross.'

'How poetic,' he practically sneered. 'If I'm doubting, it's because I have very good reason to doubt. I've watched your mother swan into one or another of my hotels over the last ten years, always on the arm of some man, always out for herself. That is not the kind of person I want to introduce into my father's life at this point.'

'Too bad you don't have a choice,' Laurel returned evenly. 'He's a grown man, and he can make his own choices. He *asked* me,' she emphasised, her voice throbbing with emotion now. 'He asked me to call her and see if she'd welcome a phone call from him. And she did. There were tears in her voice when she realised he wanted to be in touch.'

'I'm sure there were,' Cristiano dismissed. 'She's a passable actress.'

Laurel shook her head. 'Does it make you happy?' she asked. 'To feel so bitter and superior all the time? Does it feel good to tear down every possibility of hope and love that you can? Because, if it doesn't, you must be a wretched, unhappy man, and then I would feel very sorry for you.'

Cristiano felt a muscle tick in his clenched jaw. 'The last thing I need,' he ground out, 'is your pity.'

'You have it anyway,' Laurel snapped. Tears shone in her eyes and she blinked them away fiercely. 'Would you really deny your father a chance to be with the woman he loves?'

Yes. Everything in him shouted it. But he stayed silent, because to admit such a thing seemed both callous and cruel. Laurel took a step towards him, one slender hand outstretched.

'What is it you're really afraid of, Cristiano?' she asked softly.

Afraid? He wasn't afraid. Not for himself, anyway. For his father. This wasn't about him, about them, even though Laurel kept trying to make it seem as if it was.

'I'm not afraid. I just don't want to see my father get hurt.'

'If he's willing to take the risk, then you should be as well.'

Cristiano just shook his head. His anger had started to dissipate, replaced by a weary acceptance. He knew Laurel was right; he couldn't keep his father from inviting Elizabeth here, into his life, if he wanted to. He couldn't even keep him from getting hurt. And blaming Laurel for helping a grown man make his own choice was, he knew, unfair.

So all that was left to feel was something close to despair, a deep and unwelcome understanding that Laurel was right. They *were* different. She held onto hope and he couldn't find it anywhere. He didn't even know how to try.

The last two weeks had been amazing, but they'd been just that. Weeks out of time, apart from reality. What happened if and when it turned out Laurel wasn't pregnant? She'd go back to her life in Illinois and he'd go back to Rome.

He could ask her to stay with him as his mistress, but he knew instinctively that Laurel would reject such a possibility. Perhaps it was better to have a clean break, a swift separation. Perhaps then they could both move on as they needed to.

'Fine,' he said, his voice clipped. 'She can come, and tomorrow you can take that pregnancy test. For both our sakes, I hope it's negative.'

CHAPTER SEVENTEEN

LAUREL STOOD ON the front terrace of Lorenzo's house and watched her mother mount the steps. She'd taken the ferry from Naples, and then the funicular to the centre of Capri, then walked the rest of the way, insisting she didn't need anyone to collect her.

It took Laurel a few moments to realise her mother looked nervous. Her lips, devoid of her usual scarlet lipstick, were pressed together; and, instead of one of her picture-perfect outfits, complete with jewellery, heels, and a face-full of make-up, she wore a simple, loose sundress and sandals. She looked lovely, and every one of her forty-six years.

Laurel started down the steps. 'Mom.' She didn't use the endearment often, but it slipped out now naturally. Elizabeth looked up at her, her face creasing into a smile.

'Laurel.' They embraced, the hug unfamiliar in its rarity, yet still so welcome. The last twelve hours, since her confrontation with Cristiano, had been some of Laurel's worst. After their argument he'd disappeared into the study, and he hadn't come to their bedroom all night. This morning he'd closeted himself again, which Laurel supposed was just as well, as she doubted his presence would add to the happy reunion.

And yet…everything in her ached. Her relationship with Cristiano was as good as over, and she couldn't stand the thought.

'Come on—let me bring you to Lorenzo,' she said, taking her mother's arm.

'How is he?' Elizabeth asked quietly. 'He told me about his illness on the phone. And that…' her voice wavered '…that he doesn't have very long. A few months, maybe.'

'He's perked right up since you told him you were coming. He's missed you.'

'And I've missed him.' Elizabeth shook her head. 'He was the only man I ever really loved, you know. I know I've made a terrible mess of my life in so many ways, but Lorenzo…' Her voice quavered, her eyes bright with tears. 'If only I hadn't squirreled away that stupid money.'

'Don't think about that now—'

'I didn't think of it as stealing. Just…security.' She shook her head. 'If I could go back in time…'

Laurel patted her arm in quiet comfort. 'Let me take you to him.'

She led her mother through the villa to a small sitting room where Lorenzo had been resting and waiting. Now as Laurel opened the door he stood slowly, his face creased in expectation and anxiety.

'Elizabeth.' The single word had a world of meaning, a wealth of memory.

'Lorenzo.'

Laurel didn't need to see or hear any more. The way her mother looked at Lorenzo, and the way he looked at her, was more than enough to assure her she'd done the right thing.

She only wished Cristiano could see it, but then she doubted he would believe even then. He didn't want to believe. She'd come to that realisation during the long, sleepless hours of last night. When it came right down to it, Cristiano was making a choice. He wasn't enslaved to his emotions or lack of them any more than she was. He was making a choice—one he made every day. To live alone. To stay separate. To choose not to love. And somehow, although she couldn't see how now, she was going to have to come to terms with that.

'Laurel.'

Laurel stilled, everything in her tensing with both yearning and alarm as she saw Cristiano standing in the front doorway of the villa. He looked rumpled, sexy and gorgeous in faded jeans that clung to his muscled legs and a T-shirt that lovingly caressed his pecs. His eyes looked silver in his tanned face, a hint of stubble on the clean, hard line of his jaw.

'Yes?' Laurel managed, practically stuttering in her nervousness. She ached for him so much, and she couldn't believe he was simply going to walk away from her. From them.

'I went out and bought this.' He held up a small white paper bag, the kind that came from a pharmacy. Laurel didn't need to ask what the bag held.

She licked her dry lips. 'You want me to take it now?'

Cristiano shrugged. His face was impassive, giving nothing away. 'You might as well.'

Laurel made no move to take the bag. Now that the moment was here, she didn't want it. Would rather keep not knowing. 'You know, two weeks isn't a magic number,' she said, her voice uneven. 'Some women don't test positive for longer than that.' And there were more sensitive tests that showed a pregnancy at only ten days after conception. Laurel knew that, knew she could have taken a test days ago, but she'd remained silent.

Cristiano arched a dark eyebrow. 'Why don't you take the test and then we'll discuss possibilities?'

With no other option, Laurel took the bag from him and headed upstairs. Cristiano followed.

'I'll wait here,' he said when they were in the bedroom they'd shared since coming to Capri, save for last night. 'It should only take a few minutes.'

Wordlessly Laurel nodded and then barricaded herself

in the bathroom. She turned the lock and let out a shuddering breath. The moment of truth.

Fortunately the test came with instructions in English and, squinting to make out the fine print, Laurel read them and then did what was necessary. She turned the test over so she didn't have to look at it and sat on the edge of the bathtub, her heart rollicking within her. Three minutes had never seemed so long.

Outside the bathroom door she could hear Cristiano pacing the bedroom and she wondered what he was thinking. Hoping for. Was there a part of him, like her, who wanted her to be pregnant? Who wanted the choice to be taken away? She knew if she was pregnant Cristiano would marry her as he'd promised. He was a man who'd closed off emotions, yes, but he was also a man of honour.

Laurel tried to imagine what that life would look like: married to Cristiano, a baby in her arms, then a smiling toddler stumbling on chubby legs while they, the proud parents, looked on. It was a beautiful image, but one that was shrouded in the mists of impossibility. If Cristiano married her simply because of the baby, that code of honour that ran through him like a rod of steel would turn into resentment and bitterness because he'd be living a life he hadn't chosen.

Laurel took a deep breath as she glanced at her watch. Four minutes had passed. There could be no delaying it now. Reaching out slowly, as if it might bite her, she took the pregnancy test and flipped it over. She stared at the single pink line as her heart went into freefall. One line: not pregnant.

Even though she knew in her heart what the test was telling her, she scrambled for the directions and read them again to make sure. One line: not pregnant. It was irrefutable. And, really, she'd known all along. Her cycle was, in this case, depressingly regular.

She threw the test away and washed her hands at the

sink, staring hard at her reflection. So she wasn't pregnant. It was better this way. She knew it, felt it, even though part of her still railed against the unfairness of it all. A pregnancy wouldn't have helped anything. In fact, it most likely would have made things worse. So this was a good thing, she told herself as she dried her hands and then tidied her hair, determined to seem composed and even upbeat. In this moment she did not want Cristiano to see how he was crucifying her.

Taking another deep breath, Laurel opened the door. Cristiano stopped his pacing and turned to face her, his expression utterly fathomless. 'Well?' he asked when the silence stretched on for several seconds.

'I'm not.' Laurel spoke flatly, folding her arms across her body, needing to hold herself together.

Cristiano stared at her for a few moments, his gaze assessing, speculative. 'But, as you said before, it is not possible to know for certain at this stage?'

'No, but I'm quite sure, Cristiano, just as I was when you first mentioned the possibility. My period isn't due for another week.'

Something flashed across Cristiano's face too fast for her to discern what it was—disappointment, relief or something else entirely. 'Even so…'

'There's no point, trust me. If by some miracle or twist of chance I was pregnant, I would tell you. But I don't need to stay here until it's irrefutable, for heaven's sake.' *Unless you want me to stay…for my own sake. For ours.*

Neither of them said anything for endless moments, moments where Laurel felt the last, faint, frail thread of hope she'd still nourished fray and then snap. And, because she couldn't bear Cristiano to send her away, she spoke first.

'I suppose I should book my ticket.' She lifted her chin and forced a smile to her lips that felt like a crack in her skin. 'Pack my things. It's…' She swallowed. 'It's been fun,

Cristiano.' It had been so much more than that, but what else could she say? Cristiano did fun. He didn't do much more than that. And this entire affair had always been on his terms.

He stared at her for a long moment, his eyes hard, his expression still so unrelentingly inscrutable. 'Yes,' he said finally. 'It has.'

The next twenty-four hours seemed to go into hyper-speed. From the moment Laurel had walked out of their bedroom to the awful one when she left Capri, Cristiano felt as if everything was moving in a fast blur while he was stuck in slow motion.

His mind felt numb, frozen in the same gear it had been in when Laurel had walked out of the bathroom, her face wiped of expression, her eyes so terrifyingly blank. He used to be able to see everything in her eyes—every thought, every emotion, every hope. But standing there, with the silence yawning between them, he hadn't seen anything.

And then those awful words... *It's been fun.* Such a casual dismissal of everything they'd shared and experienced together. Yet how many times had he said it over the years? The words had tripped off his tongue with thoughtless ease. Sometimes he'd tossed them over his shoulder while strolling out of a room.

And now this.

That evening Cristiano found Laurel in their bedroom, packing a suitcase. Her face was pale and composed; she looked lovely, even peaceful. Perversely Cristiano wanted her to look heartbroken, or at least a little distressed.

She looked up when he entered, her hands stilling on the pile of folded clothes. 'I booked my ticket,' she said, her voice toneless.

Cristiano felt as if everything inside him was coiled so tightly he was going to snap. Fall apart into broken pieces like a clock too tightly wound. 'Have you?' he asked, his tone diffident. Almost.

'Yes; a morning flight from Naples to Rome tomorrow. And then on to Chicago.' She started packing again. 'I'll be home by tomorrow night.'

'Late.'

'Yes.' She resumed packing, her head bent. 'Late.'

Cristiano watched her pack for a few moments and then he realised how little she was actually putting into her one small suitcase. 'Wait,' he said, his voice coming out terse and demanding. 'What are you doing? Why are you not packing all your clothes?'

'I hardly need evening gowns in Canton Heights, Cristiano,' Laurel said without looking up.

An entirely unreasonable indignation rose up in him. 'They're yours. They belong to you. You should take them.'

'They'd require two or even three suitcases,' Laurel returned evenly. 'I don't want to pay the extra baggage allowance for clothes I'm never going to wear.'

'I'll pay it, then,' Cristiano insisted. It suddenly felt important that she take the clothes he'd bought for her, the gifts he'd given.

'And how would I manage to carry all those suitcases?' Laurel asked, a note of exasperation entering her voice. 'I'm taking the funicular to the ferry, and then a bus to the airport and then to the plane. I can't manage it.'

'I'll arrange private transport,' Cristiano said. It seemed simple to him, and for some ridiculous reason he really wanted her to take the clothes with her. 'A car from the villa that will take you all the way to Rome.'

Laurel gazed at him levelly for a moment. 'As eager as you may be to get me out of your life quickly, I'm fine with public transport.'

Cristiano stared at her, silently fuming, because of course he hadn't meant it that way. But he didn't even know what he had meant, or how to explain. So he stayed silent, and Laurel kept packing, and after a few more tense moments Cristiano turned on his heel and walked out of the room.

He didn't sleep that night, lying awake and gritty-eyed, staring at the ceiling as he went over the last two weeks and kept telling himself this was what he wanted. What he had to want.

Because what was the alternative, really? Their lives were so different. Laurel wasn't going to want to give up her job, or even that house she claimed to love so much. And Cristiano's life was in Italy, managing his hotels and making new business deals. This made sense. This was the only way. It had to be.

He didn't come out of the study when he heard her suitcase bumping down the stairs. Didn't trust himself to say goodbye in the cool, civil way he wanted to. He was being a coward, and he knew it, but the other option—of breaking down or begging her to stay—felt impossible. Unbearable. So he stayed still and listened as the suitcase bumped down each step and then the front door clicked softly shut.

The house suddenly felt deathly silent.

He buried himself in work for the next three days, trying not to think. He didn't sleep, and barely ate. On day four he finally dragged himself up to his father's bedroom, pausing in surprise on the threshold at seeing Elizabeth sitting next to him, smiling at something Lorenzo was saying, her head bent close to his.

The image was arresting in its poignant intimacy. The love was so visible between the two of them, it felt as if it shimmered in the air. Cristiano could hardly credit it, yet he knew it was true. Laurel had been right.

Elizabeth caught sight of him first, her expression freezing before she managed a cautious smile.

'Cristiano,' Lorenzo called, beckoning to him with one gnarled hand. 'Come in.'

'I don't want to disturb…'

'You aren't,' Lorenzo assured him. 'But you look terrible. You miss Laurel.' It was a statement, and one Cristiano chose to ignore.

'You seem well,' he said stiffly, although his father had been spending more and more time resting in bed.

'I feel well.' Lorenzo shot Elizabeth an adoring look. 'I feel very well.'

Cristiano gazed at the two of them, feeling flummoxed, weary, yet strangely cheered. Who was he to deny his father his happiness? Laurel had asked the same question and he'd dismissed it, because he had truly believed Elizabeth Forrester couldn't make his father happy. But, against all odds, it seemed she could.

He left them a short while later, drifting around the house like a ghost. There was no reason to stay here, of course, now that Elizabeth was proving to be such a capable nurse. He could return to Rome, to his penthouse, to his life. All of it felt empty.

'May I talk to you for a few minutes?'

Cristiano turned at the sound of Elizabeth's tense voice. 'Yes,' he answered, as tense as she was.

Elizabeth took a deep breath. 'I know you don't like me, Cristiano. I know you don't trust me. And,' she continued before he could protest against either statement, which he wasn't even sure he would have, 'I know I have not shown myself well in your eyes.' She grimaced. 'I've not shown myself well in my own eyes. I've made a lot of poor choices—choices borne out of fear, but that doesn't excuse them, I know.'

Cristiano felt compelled to say, 'Laurel told me something of your life.'

'Did she? Laurel has always been far more forgiving of me than I deserve. I know that.' She let out an unsteady breath. 'But I want to reassure you, Cristiano, that I love your father. I've always loved him. I know you didn't trust me ten years ago, and you had reason not to—good reason—but the only reason I took that money was because I'd known what it is to be poor and I never wanted to be it again.' She managed a rather wavering smile. 'It was wrong, and I accept that, but I was never going to leave him. I realise there's no reason for you to believe that, though. I don't deserve your trust in that or any matter.'

But Cristiano found he did believe her, much to his chagrin. 'I believe you loved him,' he said. 'And that you love him still. You wouldn't be here otherwise.' He paused. 'But are you really prepared to stay until the end, as difficult as that will be?'

She lifted her chin, reminding him of Laurel. 'Yes, I am, because that's what love does. I didn't come here thinking it would be easy, you know.' Her eyes flashed. 'I've had enough of easy.'

'Have you?' Cristiano asked, more curious than sceptical.

'Yes, I have. Love isn't easy. It's hard and messy and painful, but worth it. I believe that.' Her chin tilted up another notch and her gaze fastened on his, unrelenting in its perception. 'Maybe that's something you need to think about.'

Twenty-four hours later Cristiano stood in front of a small farmhouse of weathered white wood, with a view of rolling fields and a distant glint of the pond Laurel had once told him about. Cristiano let out a long, low breath as he surveyed the house with its bowed front porch and peeling paint that Laurel had thought of as home. Had been willing to risk everything for.

Slowly he mounted the steps; he could tell from the darkened windows and empty driveway that she wasn't home. It was six o'clock in the evening, twilight stealing slowly over the hills, the sound of crickets chirruping in the air.

Cristiano hadn't given a lot of thought to what he would do when he got here. He'd been focused on the how—the travel, the logistics—his mind buzzing and blank with the import of what came next.

And now she wasn't even here.

He peered in the windows, noting the mellow oak floorboards, the hand-made quilt thrown over the back of a squashy sofa, the many photographs on the walls. It was a well-loved home and, for a woman who had been dragged around the globe in search of the next boyfriend and protector, it must have felt like the ultimate sanctuary. No wonder Laurel had wanted to keep it.

But would she want to keep him?

He'd spent his whole life staying emotionally safe. Today he was going to risk it all.

The sound of a car had him turning. A beat-up truck pulled into the drive, and after a few seconds Laurel got out. She was wearing her nurse's scrubs, her hair held back in a ponytail, and she looked tired, lovely and so very, very welcome. Cristiano had to keep himself from catapulting himself off the porch and dragging her into his arms. There were things he had to say first. Things Laurel needed to hear.

She mounted the steps, fishing in her bag for her keys, still not seeing him. Not wanting to startle her, Cristiano said softly, 'Laurel.'

She stilled and then looked up, the blood draining from her face. She swayed slightly where she stood and Cristiano took a step forward.

'Laurel,' he said again, and this time he didn't hide how he felt. It came through in her name, the loveliest word in the world. Laurel's eyes widened and he knew she understood, or at least he hoped she understood.

'Cristiano.' Her voice was a breath. 'What are you doing here?' A wary look came into her eyes. 'I'm not pregnant. For sure.'

'That's not why I came.'

'Why, then?'

'Because I need to tell you that I love you.'

She blinked, looking dazed. 'You…?'

'Love you.' He'd agonised so much about saying it, three little words that cost so much, meant so much, yet suddenly seemed so surprisingly easy to say.

Cristiano felt buoyant and so, so light, as if a huge weight had just tumbled off him. A weight that had never really been there at all, except in the terrible void of his own fears. 'I love you,' he said again, just because he could. 'I was stupid not to realise it before, and even stupider not to say it. Stupid to let you walk away when you're the best thing in my life.' He laughed out loud, amazed at the words tumbling out of him. Amazed at how much he meant them.

'Cristiano…'

For one heart-stopping second he thought she was going to let him down. This was the risk he'd taken, and here was the danger, the awful, awful pay-off. But in the next second he realised it didn't matter. Well, it mattered; of course it mattered. His life was over without Laurel in it. But he would have said it all anyway, no matter what her response, because he needed to. Because he wanted to be a man who admitted his feelings. His love.

'I know I might be too late.' He spoke over her, his voice roughening. 'I know you might have changed your mind, or perhaps you didn't love me in the first place. I wouldn't blame you, considering how I've acted. How afraid I've been. But I'll still say it, because I want you to know. Because you deserve to know, after everything we've had together. After everything I put you through. I was so afraid, Laurel, of what love was. What it meant. How it could make you hurt. I was afraid, and I let that fear control me, but I won't any longer. I refuse to. I love you, Laurel Forrester, and that won't ever change.'

Tears sparkled in her eyes and she let out a trembling laugh. 'Good,' she said, and stepped into his arms. 'Because I love you too, and that won't change either.'

'Thank heaven.' He wrapped his arms around her, breathing her in, savouring the feel of her. 'Because we are done with all this drama, do you hear me? We love each other, we're getting married and we're not spending a single night apart ever again.'

'Back to giving orders, are you?' Laurel asked, tilting her face up to him as her mouth met his in a quick and breath-stealing kiss. 'Good thing I don't mind.'

Cristiano laughed and pulled her closer. 'Good thing,' he agreed in a murmur, and kissed her again.

EPILOGUE

Three Months Later

'YOU LOOK BEAUTIFUL.'

Laurel twitched at her veil as her mother sniffed and dabbed her eyes. 'The most beautiful bride that ever was.'

Laurel managed a tremulous smile. 'As long as Cristiano thinks so,' she said.

'Of course he will,' Elizabeth said. 'The man is mad about you.'

'As Lorenzo is about you.' Laurel met her mother's gaze in the mirror as they shared a sorrowful smile. The last three months had been filled with joy, as well as sadness. Lorenzo was holding his own, and he and Elizabeth were inseparable. But their days together were numbered, and they both knew it, making them all the more determined to seize love and happiness while they could.

While Elizabeth had remained with Lorenzo in Capri, Laurel had stayed for several weeks in Canton Heights to work out her notice, before moving to Rome to be with Cristiano. She'd informed him that she wasn't going to be a good trophy wife any more than she'd been a good mistress—she wanted to work and be active—and Cristiano wholeheartedly agreed. Already she'd joined several committees, including one led by Michel Durand, to help determine public policy on end-of-life care. After ten-and twelve-hour shifts in a hospital, this kind of work was different and invigorating.

But best of all was her life with Cristiano, the easy love they shared. The doubts and fears had fallen away for both of them, leaving nothing but love and joy, shining and pure.

A knock sounded on the door of Laurel's bedroom in Lorenzo's villa, where the wedding was to take place.

'Are you ready?' Ana, the wedding planner, called. 'Everyone is waiting.'

It was going to be a small wedding with a handful of friends from Rome and Capri in the villa's garden, overlooking the sparkling sea. Lorenzo wasn't able to travel and Laurel had never wanted a big ceremony of pomp and circumstance. She took a deep breath, gave her reflection one last, considering glance and turned to the door.

Elizabeth slipped her hand in hers for a quick squeeze before walking out. Laurel had chosen a simple dress as befit the occasion—summery and light, with *broderie anglaise* on the bodice and a gently swinging skirt. A circlet of flowers kept her veil in place and she held a small posy of violets.

Giving her mother a small, nervous smile, she headed downstairs.

The garden was bathed in sunshine, a trio of violins playing soft music as Laurel approached. Guests turned in their seats but she barely noticed, so conscious was she of Cristiano standing under an arbour twined with white roses. He looked magnificent in a navy blue suit, but it was the look on his face that stole Laurel's breath and reminded her that he already had her heart. Pure, shining love, the same as she felt.

The music swelled and, with a smile on her face and a song in her heart, and all the love she felt shining in her eyes, Laurel started down the aisle to meet her groom.

* * * * *

MILLS & BOON®

Coming next month

CLAIMING HIS NINE-MONTH CONSEQUENCE
Jennie Lucas

Ruby.

Pregnant.

Impossible. She couldn't be. They'd used protection.

He could still remember how he'd felt when he'd kissed her. When he'd heard her soft sigh of surrender. How she'd shuddered, crying out with pleasure in his arms. How he'd done the same.

And she'd been a virgin. He'd never been anyone's first lover. Ares had lost his virginity at eighteen, a relatively late age compared to his friends, but growing up as he had, he'd idealistically wanted to wait for love. And he had, until he'd fallen for a sexy French girl the summer after boarding school. It wasn't until summer ended that his father had gleefully revealed that Melice had actually been a prostitute, bought and paid for all the time. *I did it for your own good, boy. All that weak-minded yearning over love was getting on my nerves. Now you know what all women are after—money. You're welcome.*

Ares's bodyguard closed the car door behind him with a bang, causing him to jump.

"Sir? Are you there?"

Turning his attention back to his assistant on the phone, Ares said grimly, "Give me her phone number."

Two minutes later, as his driver pulled the sedan smoothly down the street, merging into Paris's evening traffic, Ares listened to the phone ring and ring. Why didn't Ruby answer?

When he'd left Star Valley, he'd thought he could forget her.

Instead, he'd endured four and a half months of painful celibacy, since his traitorous body didn't want any other woman. He couldn't forget the soft curves of Ruby's body, her sweet mouth like sin. She hadn't wanted his money. She'd been insulted by his offer. She'd told him never to call her again.

And now...

She was pregnant. With his baby.

He sat up straight as the phone was finally answered. "Hello?"

Continue reading
CLAIMING HIS NINE-MONTH CONSEQUENCE
Jennie Lucas

Available next month
www.millsandboon.co.uk

LET'S TALK
Romance

For exclusive extracts, competitions
and special offers, find us online:

f facebook.com/millsandboon

◉ @millsandboonuk

🐦 @millsandboon

Or get in touch on 0844 844 1351*

For all the latest titles coming soon, visit
millsandboon.co.uk/nextmonth